BEC McMASTER

STORM
of
DESIRE

LEGENDS OF THE STORM SERIES

Edited by: Hot Tree Editing
Print formatting by: Cover Me Darling and Athena Interior Book Design
Cover Art 2017 © Damonza.com

ALSO AVAILABLE BY BEC MCMASTER

LONDON STEAMPUNK SERIES
Kiss Of Steel
Heart Of Iron
My Lady Quicksilver
Forged By Desire
Of Silk And Steam
Novellas in same series:
Tarnished Knight
The Curious Case Of The Clockwork Menace

THE BLUE BLOOD CONSPIRACY SERIES
Mission: Improper
The Mech Who Loved Me
You Only Love Twice

DARK ARTS SERIES
Shadowbound
Hexbound
Soulbound

BURNED LANDS SERIES
Nobody's Hero
The Last True Hero
The Hero Within

LEGENDS OF THE STORM SERIES
Heart of Fire
Storm of Desire
Clash of Storms *(coming 2018)*

OTHER
The Many Lives Of Hadley Monroe

STORM OF DESIRE

BOOK TWO: LEGENDS OF THE STORM

The old eddas speak of *dreki*—fabled creatures that haunt the depths of Iceland's volcanoes and steal away fair maidens.

Haakon wants none of such myths. For years he's searched for the beast that stole his wife, desperate to slay the golden *dreki* and rescue his precious Árja. He has sacrificed everything to find her—including his honor—but now Haakon knows the truth. His entire marriage was a lie. The woman he knew as his wife was no victim, but the *dreki* herself. And when he finally tracks down the deceitful princess, there will be a reckoning of passion and glory....

She came to him on a storm...

Long ago, Árdís gave her heart to a mortal man, despite knowing it could only end in tragedy. When her clan summoned her home, she had no choice but to leave—or see her husband pitted against her vicious cousin, Sirius.

When Sirius insists upon a betrothal that will help him gain the *dreki* throne, she is forced to flee—straight into the arms of the now-ruthless dragon hunter she once called husband. But can Haakon ever forgive her deceit? And can she save him from a spurned *dreki* prince who would see them both dead?

GLOSSARY FOR
LEGENDS OF THE STORM

Álfar - Elves. Comprised of the *svartálfar* (black elves some commonly think are more dwarfish in nature, who work metals), *Dökkálfar* (dark elves that live within a hidden world within the earth) and the *Ljósálfar* (light elves who are fairer than the sun to look at, and live in *Álfheimr*). Some Icelanders say that to speak the word '*Álfar*' is to draw their attention, and so it's safer to call them *Huldufólk,* which technically, they are not.

Álfheimr - Land of the Light Elves.

Cycle - Sixty years or so. *Dreki* consider time in cycles. A *dreki* is not considered an adult until they are two cycles old, and they often live for twenty-five cycles.

Chaos-Bubble - a small side-world made purely of Chaos magic. Held within each volcano, this is the heart of the *dreki* court and guarded by magic. No human can enter a *dreki* court, unless they have a certain amount of magic within them, or have been rewarded with a *dreki* talisman, which grants them passage.

Clan - A group of *dreki* who share familial ties, and live together. The term is commonly used throughout Europe and the North Americas. Each clan rules a certain territory, the edges of which are formed by treaty with other clans.

Court - The official term for a clan or tribe of *dreki*. Also a place each clan refers to as home. Generally within a volcano.

Dreki - *Dreki* were created when the Great Goddess tore her soul to pieces, and imbued each piece into flesh within the Fire of the volcano, Hekla. *Dreki* therefore, are creatures created of Fire, Earth and Air, who also have an affinity for Tiamat's Chaos magic. Commonly mistaken for their lesser brethren—dragons—they have the ability to change forms if they desire. *Dreki* prefer to live within volcanoes, where they can be close to the elements of Earth and Fire. There are many *dreki* clans in the world. Many clans rule the West Coast of Canada, and the Americas. Another hotspot is along the East coast of Russia, and the string of islands that leads down through Asia. There are also a few scattered courts along the Mediterranean and throughout the East Coast of Africa.

Dragons - lesser children created by Tiamat, but borne from her flesh, not her soul. Monsters that hunger for *dreki* power, and emulate them by finding volcanoes to settle within. Lack the magic of the elements. It is considered an insult by the *dreki* to be called a dragon.

Great Goddess - Tiamat, Goddess of Chaos and Creation.

Huldufólk - "Hidden Folk". Those creatures from Scandinavian folklore.

Mate - To choose the one who will bear your children, and whom you will live out the end of your days with.

Plague of dreki - human term for a collective group of *dreki*. Insulting term to the *dreki*.

Sarratum Zamani - "Queen of Lightning"

Serpents - Created at the same time as dragons, sea serpents were hunted to extinction by ancient sailors.

Tiamat - Ancient Sumerian goddess who was killed by the Storm-God, Marduk, when she was in serpent form. The North Wind took her soul North, where it hibernated within the volcano, Hekla, for many eons, drawing power from the Earth and the Fire within. When Hekla exploded, she used the eruption to tear her soul to pieces, giving birth to the first of the *dreki* race, in one last act of Creation.

Tribe - African *dreki* term for 'clan'.

Trolls - creatures of myth in Iceland. Rarely seen, they have an affinity for the element of Earth.

Twin Flame - a *dreki* concept for the other half of one's soul. A soul-mate. *Dreki* consider their souls lacking, as they were created from pieces of Tiamat's soul, therefore to find the other half of their soul completes them. A rare occurrence, which goes beyond mating.

Wyrms - another name for dragons.

Zini Clan - Spirit of the Wind Clan, rules Iceland.

Zilittu Clan - Spirit of the Mist Clan, rules the north of Norway.

PROLOGUE

Norway, 1872

SHE CAME TO him on a spring storm, one wicked night.

Haakon Haraldsson strode across the mountainous countryside, slinging his bow over his shoulder. Night was falling, and there'd be no game in this brewing gale. Time to return home before he was caught out. The storm kissed the coastline to the east and blustered inland, bringing with it lashings of lightning. Thick, fat raindrops began to spatter down.

Perfect. Just perfect.

Haakon cursed, dragging the hood of his cloak over his head as he soldiered on. He'd spent most of the day out in the mountains, trying to linger as far from home as possible. At twenty, with his older sisters married off, his mother had turned her sights upon him, and he hadn't missed the insinuation when she'd invited her friend, Helga, and her daughter, Maria, to eat with them that night.

But it was one thing to avoid a mother's matrimonial intentions—quite another to freeze his balls off.

A jagged spear of lightning lit the world around him as he loped down the craggy mountainside. He thought he heard a roar, but perhaps it was only thunder, quick on the lightning's heels. Not far to go now. He could almost feel the heat of the fire in his mother's hearth, and smell the rich, gamey scent of the stew she'd been making. Something to warm him from the inside out in this wretched cold. Maria's attentions notwithstanding.

He was so caught up in imagining it that when he took a twist in the path, he almost plowed directly into a naked young woman.

A flash of golden skin seared his eyeballs.

And then somehow he managed not to brace his hands against a part of her anatomy she'd surely slap him for touching. A violent lurch to avoid slamming into her sent him sprawling, and his hands bit the gravel of the path as he tumbled head over heels into the soft leaf mulch.

Haakon froze, pushing himself off the loam and brushing off his hands. He slowly rolled over.

He was not imagining anything.

There was a naked woman.

A very wet, completely unclothed woman glaring down at him, gowned only in her hair. It clung in wet, serpentine streaks to her breasts, and though it appeared brown in that moment he had the feeling sunlight would paint it pure gold. His gaze followed the lengths of it, reaching her naval, and then—

He squeezed his eyes shut. He wasn't entirely innocent. There'd been kisses, and heated touches, and the press of a woman's mouth, but Viksholm was distant enough from civilization and his mother watchful enough that he'd not yet had a woman of his own.

Some stray thought tickled at his mind at the thought, but it wasn't working very swiftly in that moment. All he could picture was rosy nipples, and lips flushed pink, and curse him, but his cock was swelling in adamant need.

What the hell?

"Are you insane?" he demanded, trying to avoid looking at her as he pushed himself to his feet. "What are you doing out here?"

The woman scrambled away from him, crouching against a rock, one hand splayed over the granite and her expression feral.

Haakon stopped abruptly, and tried to make himself look less intimidating. *Think, you fool.* Any woman out here on a stormy night—wearing no clothes—was likely in some sort of danger.

Her long blonde hair tangled over her breasts, thankfully shielding them from view. She bared her teeth at him.

"I mean you no harm."

Swinging his sodden fur cloak off his shoulders, he wrapped it around her bare body, trying to ease her raking nails away from his face. She hissed at him, but subsided when he drew the cloak around her nakedness and held his hands up in surrender, as if to say, "*See?*"

And then she looked up, a distant flash of lightning illuminating her amber-colored eyes.

For Haakon, it was like an arrow to the chest. He felt breathless; lost. His entire destiny unfolded before him with a single glance and he knew, *knew* it revolved around this mysterious stranger.

Fate had clearly contrived to keep him chaste for her, because the very idea of knowing another woman would have felt wrong.

Hell. He felt as though the lightning must have hit *him*.

"Harm?" she whispered, in a voice that sounded like a velvet-wrapped purr. "You would not wish to have harm in your heart, or I'd kill you myself."

At any other time he might have snorted—he was a hunter, and a large man—but he was still feeling rattled.

He could barely look away from her, as he tried to loop the clasp on his cloak closed, so she would feel less naked. Every inch of her was perfect, though he was trying like hell not to stare. "Who are you?"

"A traveler."

"Do you have a name?"

She cocked her head on the side. "You may call me Árja."

Árja. It had the ringing tones of destiny written all over it.

"My name is Haakon."

Thunder rumbled, as if the gods themselves heard his name—and accepted it as a pledge.

The storm faded into the distance, the cold and the wetness evaporating from his awareness. She had a heart-shaped face, her wet hair clinging to a smooth throat, and those stormy eyes full of a thousand mysteries as she considered him.

"Are you hurt?" he whispered, suddenly aware his knuckles brushed each other just below her chin, where he held his cloak firmly around her.

The beautiful stranger eyed him as thoroughly as he'd done to her. The storm began to blow out. "No."

"What are you doing out here?"

"I was hunting these cows," Árja said, and tipped her chin up as if to defy him. "I'm hungry and there are many cows in this valley."

Cows? He shook his head. "If you poach one of my father's cows, he won't take kindly to it."

"These cows belong to him?"

"Most of them." Haakon cleared his throat. He couldn't quite place her accent. "Where are your clothes? Do you have a bow? Any weapons?"

She curled her fingers into claws and smiled a vicious little smile. "I am the weapon."

Maybe she'd hit her head. Or maybe she was mad.

His heart began to beat again, and suddenly he was freezing, and she was naked and probably even colder and—

"Come," Haakon whispered, swinging her up into his arms, where she eyed him with dark suspicion. Mad or not, she was his. And it was a freezing cold night, with both of them wet to the skin. "Let me take you to the healer to examine you, then I'll take you home. My mother has stew on the stove."

"I want cow."

"It's beef," he said dryly. "Beef stew."

And he couldn't let her out of his sight. Not now, when he'd only just found his future wife.

For him, this chance meeting meant his future was carved in stone.

It would take him many years before he discovered that for her, it was nothing more than a safe haven for a year or two... before she suddenly vanished as swiftly as she'd come, in the heart of another raging storm.

And the only clue to her disappearance was the flapping wings of a golden dragon.

CHAPTER ONE

Nine years later
Reykjavik, Iceland

THERE WERE MANY ways one could woo an estranged wife, and as Haakon Haraldsson nursed his ale at an inn in Reykjavik, he heard them all.

"...gift her with flowers," Bjorn argued. The boy had swollen into a giant of a man in the past two years, but he was still barely able to grow fluff on his chin. "It's a time-proven method to win a woman's heart."

The lady's more interested in emeralds, Haakon thought with a bitter smile. *All the more to add to her hoard of gold.*

But none of his men were paying attention to him.

Haakon's massive cousin, Tormund, snorted and shook his head. "Flowers? Sweep her off her feet and throw her over your shoulder. Make a woman of her."

Which would work perfectly if the lady in question couldn't breathe fire....

Bjorn snorted. "In my experience—"

"What little there be of it," Tormund said.

Bjorn slammed his tankard down and shoved to his feet. "There's damned near enough to make your toes curl. When was the last time you saw a woman naked?"

"Last night, as a matter of fact," Tormund said.

The two men stared at each other, their chests almost touching.

"Sit down, you bloody fools," Haakon's second-in-command, Gunnar, bellowed. "You break any of this furniture and I'll break your heads."

Gunnar shoved the pair of them apart, even as Haakon sank his head into his hands. What was he doing here?

Trying to get answers....

Tormund scraped at his beard. "Mind you, when I was chasing Gertrude, she did like flowers—"

Haakon faded out of the conversation. Loose timbers flapped against the inn's cladding as the storm outside began to drive through the town. He crossed to the window, peering through it. Light flashed in the distance. The heart of the storm hadn't arrived yet.

But when it came, it would descend on the town with driving force. There was a crackle of energy in the air, one he'd slowly learned to recognize.

This would be no ordinary storm.

Would it be her out there on the winds?

He'd spent months camped out in this hell-forsaken traders town, hoping to lure her out. Months showing the townsfolk the portrait he'd drawn of her face.

Yes, one or two of them had declared. *I've seen her. She comes to buy books every few months.*

She likes jewelry too, someone else had said. *I think she made Ivar a very happy jeweler.... Bought a pair of emerald earrings off him without even blushing at the price.*

That sounded like her.

Before his wife vanished in the middle of a storm, barely two years after they'd married, she'd been enamored of precious gems. Even the single wink of light on a set of rubies had caught her eye from across the room. He'd not thought anything of it at the time—except to think he'd like to buy her a set of her own one day—but in hindsight, there'd always been signs of the truth.

Seven years given over to hunting the dragon who took his wife. Seven years of lies....

His only purpose since her loss had been to hunt for any news of such a creature, until he'd finally gotten word earlier this year of a golden dragon in Iceland.

Well, he'd finally tracked down the golden *dreki*—as it preferred to call itself—only to hear the truth from its lips.

"You hunt the dreki who took your wife," Rurik had said. *"There is only one golden dreki beside myself. Her name is Árdís, and she is my younger sister. She resides in the dreki court below Hekla."*

"That dreki took my wife!"

"She did not steal your wife, you fool," Rurik had hissed. *"She was your wife."*

And in that moment, he'd no longer been able to deny the truth.

The storm rattled the shingles on the roof.

"Fucking cows," he muttered, staring into the skies and laughing humorlessly. *"I was hunting these cows."* He should have known the truth the moment he met her.

Why else would she have been naked in a storm?

Why else would she have been endlessly curious about the customs of his hearth and home, as if she'd never lived them before?

For a man who'd lived all his life among myth and legend, it had been remarkably easy to haul the wool over his eyes.

Anger brewed. Seven years spent believing his wife was either killed or kidnapped by a *dreki* who rode one of these storms, only to discover his wife *was* the actual *dreki*, had left him bitter and hollow.

It was time for a reckoning.

"Are you certain kidnapping your wife is the best way to go about this?" Tormund muttered, leaning against the wall beside him. "Bjorn might have a point about a dragon princess not appreciating being manhandled like that."

"*Dreki*," Haakon corrected absently. "They don't like to be called dragon."

Tormund gave him a strange look. "Either way, I would prefer to dine on the pig on the spit out back tonight. Not *be* the one roasting."

"Rurik said few *dreki* own the gift to actually breathe flame."

"Aye, and Rurik's her brother. Where do you think his loyalties lie?"

Haakon glanced toward the flicker of lightning through the window, before slinging back the rest of his ale. "He wouldn't have told me the truth about her if he intended me to die at her hand. He's... an admirable creature. He believes in debts of honor and fate."

He'd have never believed those words would come from his mouth before he set foot on these shores.

"Let us hope his sister believes in honor too."

Haakon's smile felt tight. "I wouldn't trust her sense of decency. She's already proven she has no compunctions with deceit, but I have means to counteract her powers, if it comes down to it."

The heavy weight of the gold cuff in his pocket seemed to warm.

Tormund stared at him. "I hope you know what you're doing. She was your wife—"

"She was a lying, conniving creature with a heart of ice," he corrected coldly.

"Still...." Tormund hesitated, but Haakon paid him little attention.

He'd spent months learning the difference between a regular storm and a *dreki* storm. This was it. She *had* to be here in Reykjavik somewhere. He was weary with waiting, but without magic he couldn't get into the *dreki* court beneath the volcano of Hekla, according to the exiled *dreki* prince, Rurik. He'd needed her to come for him, and he'd baited the trap appropriately. "Do you have any better ideas? Preferably ones without that flower nonsense?"

After all, he wasn't here to win his wife back, or to woo her, or whatever other nonsense the men were discussing.

He was here for answers.

Tormund winced. "Kidnapping it is then."

There were few things that gave Árdís pleasure these days, but the promise of an emerald necklace the likes of which she'd never seen before came close.

Gliding above the storm, she turned in slow barrel rolls, exulting in the wind beneath her wings. Reykjavik sprawled beneath her, the very sign of its humanity calling to her as she began her dive.

The storm lashed out as she pulled out of the dive and alighted upon a rocky crag overlooking the town. Lightning flashed as Árdís threw her wings out, a shimmer of power spilling through her. Heat washed through her veins. And then she was squatting on bare feet, her hands held aloft as she transformed to her mortal form.

Instantly fat raindrops splashed her bare skin. It always felt so strange to shift forms. The *dreki* was mighty and impervious, gilded by scales of gold that protected her from danger, but also from so much raw sensation. In her *dreki* form she heard each groan of the earth, and the whisper of winds through the skies in a way her mortal ear could not perceive, and yet to be human connected her to the world in ways she'd never been able to imagine before her first shift.

She'd felt hands on her skin in this form. Lips trailing down her neck. The weight of her husband pressing her down into their mattress as he made love to her for the first time.

And the utter destruction of a heart she'd broken herself.

To be human meant pain, suffering, and wretched emotion. But it also lured her with whispers of joy and freedom, and the sheer warmth one gained from other humans. Árdís had been born from fire, but she loved this mortal realm with a curious heart other *dreki* curled their lips at.

Picking up the leather bag she'd carried in her claws, she swiftly drew her gown on, lacing up the pale green wool dress over her chemise. Stockings and shoes followed, and then she looped around her throat the silver chain she always carried with her.

She could only ever wear it when she wore this form, and for a second her fingers fumbled on the plain silver ring *he'd* once given her. It dangled from the end of the chain, and warmed against her flesh as if it were finally home.

She'd taken it off over a dozen times, and even managed to bury it once, before she'd succumbed and dug it back out of the earth. The only reminder of a moment when she'd given in to the whim of her heart, it was past time she finally put it away, but.... Her fingertips grazed the silver ring. To put it away forever meant burying her heart entirely, and she wasn't certain she had it in her to do so.

A flash of icy gray eyes lit through her mind. A smile. The shape of his mouth as he leaned down to kiss her.... She refused to speak his name, but the memory of his face would not leave her alone, particularly at night, when her thoughts were unguarded.

He'd never smile at her like that again.

Árdís slid the ring inside her dress, and swiftly braided her hair. She'd made her choices long ago. She should never have married him. Never have given him her heart. She was a *dreki* princess and he a mortal man, and she'd known from the start it would only ever end in disaster.

But sometimes the head did not rule the heart.

Enough. Árdís turned toward the town, shedding her foolish regrets. It always hit her hard when she first shifted shape.

And she had emeralds to buy, and hopefully a certain *dreki* prince to thwart.

In the streets of Reykjavik, humans began to close the shutters on their windows, faces turned fearfully toward the storm that was rolling over the edges of town. With her no longer in the skies it would fade, but they didn't know that. Brightly colored roofs gleamed under the stormy skies as Árdís made her way unerringly toward the small jewelers she frequented.

Bells tinkled over the door as she entered.

The jeweler looked up at the sound of the bells, his hands scattering the fine beads he'd been trying to separate as he saw her. Árdís breathed in the stuffy fumes of pipe smoke and oil, her gaze flickering over the dull gleam of brass and gold in the display cases, and the faint wink of rubies. Too small to capture her interest, of course, but Hjálmarsson always kept his finest wares behind the counter, or in his safe.

"Good day, Master Hjálmarsson," she called. "I hear you have new emeralds?"

The jeweler set aside the small loupe he'd been peering through. His mustache quivered. "How do you always know? I've not breathed a word of it to anyone."

Because I can hear them whispering through the earth's crust, practically calling my name.

Every *dreki* was gifted with some natural affinity for one of the elements, and hers was Earth. Árdís smiled. "A lady cannot give up her sources, good sir. Please, may I see them?"

"Aye. I put them aside for you, as promised," the jeweler stammered, as he unlocked his glass counter and lifted a tray from within. She'd offered to pay him good coin for the privilege of seeing his finest wares first.

He stank of nervousness, enough to make her glance up from beneath her lashes. If he tried to swindle her, then he would be in for a rude shock.

Árdís's eyes narrowed, but then she saw what rested upon the red velvet nap upon the tray. An exquisite necklace of gold, with over a half dozen teardrop-shaped emeralds dripping from the collar. The smaller emeralds were the size of her thumbnail, but the one in the center... that one was almost a robin's egg, and surrounded by glittering diamond shards that winked in the light like the stars in the night sky.

It was beautiful.

Regal. Stunning.

A queen's necklace, the likes of which she'd never seen before.

This was the only thing that captured both her *dreki* and mortal hearts. Árdís had always felt torn between both worlds, but precious gemstones and gold were a dangerous addiction of both her selves.

"Bring the light closer," she whispered, her fingertips gliding over each polished stone in the set.

The jeweler obliged and the color of the gems warmed, as if there were a trapped spirit glowing within. Striations of green refracted off the counter as she turned the tray to and fro, painting her skin with faint oceanic ripples of color.

"Where did you get them?" They were nothing like his usual wares. Iceland was the last bastion of life in these arctic straits, and ships rarely carried fine goods north like these.

The jeweler hesitated, but the strange light within the emeralds, the one that called to her soul, captured Árdís.

"I was given them by a man several months ago. He told me...." The words continued, but Árdís had ceased to listen.

A faint imperfection in the main stone caught her eye, running through the emerald almost like a scar.

Or a streak of lightning.

Her breath caught. She had to have it. It had been *made* for her. "How much?"

A king's ransom to be expected, but if there was one thing *dreki* collected apart from fine gems, it was gold.

"I-It's a gift," Hjálmarsson stammered. "I was told it was to be a gift. I've already been paid."

Finally, his words caught her attention. "A gift?"

"For you."

Nobody knew her in this town, and humans would not recognize what walked among them. Which meant something of a supernatural nature had noticed her presence.

A fellow *dreki* perhaps.

And all those within the court knew she was betrothed to Sirius Blackfrost.

A flare of warning skittered down her spine, but she wasn't afraid. She was a *dreki* princess of the *Zini* clan, and both immortal and mortal crossed her at their peril.

"A gift." Hjálmarsson swallowed. "For a beautiful lady. He told me to say that."

"And does this mysterious man have a name?"

"He said if you want his name, then you'll have to meet him. He's residing at the Viking."

Curious. Árdís ran a fingernail along the gems, *reaching* for the light within. There was a strange echo upon the stones, a lingering presence, as if another *dreki* had touched them upon a time.

She wanted the necklace, and was almost curious enough to accept the invitation just to discover who thought to challenge her, but something stalled within her.

What was the point?

She'd given her heart once, and left it bleeding in Norway. And her mother, the queen, had recently decreed that her cousin, Sirius, would have her as a mate. No man had touched her since her husband, and she found she couldn't rouse the least bit of interest in the idea. It might be a way to insult Sirius, a challenge to his alleged authority over her, but something recoiled within her at the thought of a lover.

No.

Still... who was it? She ought to warn him that the Blackfrost was a dangerous enemy to have, and not likely to be impressed with another male seeking to steal his intended mate.

A male psychic scent infused the stones, one she almost thought she recognized. Pushing forward with her mind, she chased that presence and suddenly it fell into her mind. Hundreds of miles east of here a male *dreki* turned to look at her, catching the link on his end. Golden hair curled around his ears, and his eyes were the color of warm amber.

The same color as hers.

"Rurik?" she breathed, her heart expanding in her chest as the image of her brother's face obliterated the reality of the world around her. It was truly him. Her brother had been in exile for almost half a cycle, or thirty years as these humans translated time. She'd been but a kit when he vanished.

"Don't be too angry with me. It's time to pay your debt, Árdís."

She jerked her finger back, and the link was lost, leaving her heart pounding.

Debt.

What by all the gods did Rurik mean?

It wasn't the first time he'd contacted her of late. There'd been that brief whisper she'd woken to several months ago, almost a fragment of a dream. *"Árdís, what were you thinking?"*

She'd lain awake for long moments after that, uncertain whether to reach back. The *dreki* court beneath Hekla was watched by too many *dreki* minds, and she didn't dare contact the brother the court called the Traitor Prince.

But now?

She had this horrible feeling inside, as if the walls were closing in upon her. *Fate*, something whispered.

And whoever had given this jeweler the necklace knew her.

"I don't want them," she snapped, shoving the tray back across the counter, even as her lungs strained for air. "Good day, Master Hjálmarsson. I shall return when you have more goods."

She barely heard his stammering apologies as she escaped the jewelers. The crisp air was a shock to her skin, but she needed it. Her brother was involved in this. She didn't know what to think. He was miles to the east; to enter *Zini* territory meant provoking a war with her mother, the ruling queen of Iceland's *dreki* clan.

But what if he'd sent an emissary?

Could this be the hope her people needed? Could their prince be returning? She wanted so very badly to believe it.

Árdís wrapped her cloak tightly around her shoulders as she turned toward the edge of the city, the heavy jangle of the coin purse at her side mocking her. Wind whipped the cloak out of her fingers, and she looked up.

The storm was worsening.

Black skies had curled over the town while she was within the jewelers, the rolling edge of dark clouds looming like an enormous wave about to come crashing down. Jagged flashes of lightning slashed the sky in the distance. Once, twice, thrice. Her fingers curled around her arms. Three *dreki* on her heels, if she wasn't mistaken. Clearly her presence had been missed.

But who had her mother sent to fetch her back to court?

One of them would be Sirius, of a certainty. The very rage within that storm spoke of the Blackfrost and his power.

Árdís draped the hood of her cloak over her head, and turned into the nearest alleyway. She wasn't of a mood to return. Not just yet. All she needed was five minutes to circle the Viking Inn. It wasn't as though she intended to enter, but... maybe she could watch from a distance, and see if this truly was an emissary from her brother.

Surely that wouldn't be tempting fate?

Footsteps whispered behind her as she wended her way through the narrow streets toward the inn. Shutters slapped against the nearby windows of a house, carelessly untended.

A whisper of movement stirred behind her, and a large shadow drifted across hers. A big man following her none too stealthily—though he was clearly trying.

Árdís glanced sideways beneath her lashes, the weight of the gold burning a hole in her pocket. Someone thought to *rob* her? Well, they were in for the shock of their life. She bared her teeth, feeling her fingernails sharpen into claws. This was no helpless mark here.

"You might as well come out," she called. "I could smell you from three streets over."

Silence.

Árdís smiled as she turned toward the mouth of the alley behind her. "I should warn you—the cost of interfering with me might be your life. You'll find no easy prey here."

An enormous young man stepped out of the alley, holding a sack, of all things. His cheeks burned. "I thought *dreki* were bound by the old laws. You can't kill me."

"Why, you're just a boy," she said in some surprise.

And not alone.

Others melted out of the shadows. There was a net. A man crouched warily, as if prepared to pounce upon her. She laughed. Did they not realize what they dealt with? Surely, if the young man knew what she was, then they would know what she was capable of. The people of Iceland had long grown used to the lords of the skies.

"Begone, you fools. Whatever you're being paid, it isn't worth the cost of your lives. I cannot take a mortal life, not at a whim. But I can strike down any who dare assault me first." The wind whipped her skirts around her calves, and she bared her teeth in what *might* have passed for a smile. "And then, of course, the treaty specifically states I may not take a life. It doesn't say I cannot make you *wish* I had."

The three men glanced between each other warily.

"You do it," the large boy muttered to the one with the net, gesturing toward her, as though he needed someone else to make the first move.

The net-caster's knuckles tightened, his muscles bunching. So be it. She'd given them enough warning. Árdís moved before he could. She turned and kicked the youngest one in the stomach, earning a loud *whumph* from his throat as he staggered back into the nearest wall. The net fanned into the air above her, but she was already moving like the wind. Lightning flashed in the clouds above as she raked through the glistening ropes with her claws, parting the net like silk.

It fluttered to the ground on either side of her, little sparks of bright light rippling through the rope. *That* was interesting, and enough to distract her for a second.

Magic.

And not the elemental kind *dreki* used.

Someone grabbed her from behind, and the edge of a smelly hessian sack went over her head. Árdís drove her elbow back into the newcomer's sternum, and the harsh exhale of his breath sounded. Then she was whirling, spitting out the stink of the hessian sack as she ripped it free, and slamming her palm up into the boyish young man's jaw as he tried to grab her. Clearly he hadn't received her first warning with good grace.

She'd tried.

And then they had put a bag over her head.

Árdís puffed with indignation, shaking the hessian bag in her fist. "What were you thinking? You do realize I can transform into a creature that weighs seven tons?"

Imagine the shock on their faces if one of them ended up sitting on her neck, the hessian bag over her snout.

Groans littered the cobbled alley as two of the men curled into wretched shapes. Árdís looked into the eyes of the man who'd tried to throw a net over her.

"And *you*. I do not like nets," she hissed, letting a hint of the *dreki* show in her eyes. Her hand fisted in the hessian sack. "And I do not care to be treated like this morning's catch. You have a debt to me now, and I am angry enough to take my payment in blood."

His face paled, then he turned and fled, the soles of his boots slapping the cobbles in a satisfactory manner.

Árdís lowered the sack. That was better.

"Should have... gone with the flowers," said the larger man at her feet, rolling slowly onto his hands and knees. He looked familiar somehow. A large bearded giant with a neatly trimmed brown beard.

"Flowers?" she demanded, but he wasn't looking at her.

No, his gaze rested somewhere over her shoulder.

"Unfortunately, the net and the sack were just a distraction," said a voice husky with anger.

A voice that shivered down her spine.

A voice she *knew*.

Fate laughed in her ear, even as a hand locked around her wrist. Árdís spun, but the enormous man behind her blocked her blow. And then the second one. She caught a flash of icy eyes, and then her back slammed into the nearest wall, his hands pinning her wrists to the building as he crushed her there with his body.

Haakon.

For a second she couldn't breathe, but it wasn't from the impact. She'd thought she'd never see him again.

"Speaking of debts," Haakon said, his handsome face no longer that of the young man she'd once known, but carved from granite and fury. "I believe you owe me quite a large one. And I'm here to call it in."

CHAPTER TWO

"HAAKON," HIS WIFE breathed.

Shock flared in her amber eyes as she recognized him, and Haakon squeezed her wrists tightly to prevent her from escaping. He had her pinned to the nearest wall, but he'd seen the way she moved, and knew it was more likely surprise that momentarily stilled her, and not any sense of weakness.

He'd spent years praying for this moment.

And weeks obsessing over it, when he discovered the truth of her deception.

He'd practiced what he would say to her, until he was fairly certain he would keep his composure, but the second he laid hands upon her, every word he'd intended to state fled, along with his wits.

The storm was no longer solely in the skies, but within him. It lashed wildly within the cage of his ribs, and he could swear its lightning struck his charred heart, again and again, until he could barely breathe.

You lied to me.

You left me.

Was any of it ever real?

It was all he could do to choke the words down and stop the storm from erupting. And worse... he didn't know in that moment what he intended. Nothing was going right. In his head he'd planned this meticulously; a swift kidnapping, a cool interrogation, and then... then he'd walk away from her so she knew exactly how it felt.

But right now, all he could think of was the taste of her treacherous mouth and how long it had been since he'd kissed her.

"Did you miss me, wife?" he snarled, locking away those feelings.

"What are you doing here?"

"*What am I*—" He cursed, and then banked his rage, even as thunder grumbled in the skies. "Did you think I would forget you? Did you think I wouldn't *look for you*?"

"I—"

"You vanished," he rasped. "Without a word, without a single trace. And you dare think I wouldn't come after you?"

"Is that why you're here?" she whispered, her gaze darting over his face hungrily, as if she'd almost forgotten what he looked like. "For me?"

And he didn't know himself what the truth was.

Árja—no, Árdís—still looked the same, and she still smelled the same—wildflowers and green grass mixed with the aftereffects of a summer storm. He'd told himself he'd locked his heart away behind a wall of steel, but just the sight of her aroused feelings he'd thought long buried.

Pain, mostly.

Regret and bitterness, and worse, that whispering sense of desperation within him that promised if she'd just kiss him, just once, he could forget everything.

Forgive everything.

The skies opened up, a curtain of rain drenching them. Árdís's gaze lingered on a droplet of water that clung to his lips, and damn her, but his cock clenched, and he could almost taste her skin on his tongue. He knew every inch of her body, and the sounds she made when he kissed his way down her body. He knew the feel of the soft curve of her spine as she lay in his arms, her breath softening into sleep. The past flickered between them, ghostly images of a thousand memories he knew they both saw in that moment.

Lies. All of them silky, torturous lies designed to cripple him.

If he had any heart left, he thought it might have finally crushed him, but he was cold and empty inside. The storm of fury was all he had left, and even then she brought him to his knees with but one hot, silky-lashed look from those eyes.

Somehow he turned his head toward poor Bjorn and Tormund. "Leave us."

The pair of them vanished without argument.

"I am here for retribution," he said, his voice smoky and rough. That wouldn't do. He couldn't let her see how low she'd brought him. "I am here because I've spent the last seven years hunting for you. Killing dragons. Becoming little more than a mercenary. I have lost everything—my honor, my way of life—because of you. I won't ask you to repay that debt. But I will have answers from you, I swear."

Thunder rumbled. Slowly, he forced himself to unhand her, stepping back and curling his fists at his sides before he gave in to the temptation to brush the wet strand of hair from her lips.

He'd thought he was ready to bury this connection between them, but one glance into those amber eyes

34

revealed the truth: he could never escape what she'd done to him.

"Come."

"Why should I? You tried to kidnap me. Your man put a bag over my head. You could have gotten him killed!"

Tugging a bracelet of beaten gold from his pocket, he snapped it around her wrist. Light flickered as the ends fused together, and Árdís gasped.

"What are you doing? What is this?"

"The hessian bag was a distraction. And the cuff is a means to keep you confined until I am done with you."

"What have you done to me?"

"Insurance," he growled. "I made a little deal with a sorcerer I tracked down."

Árdís tried to pry apart the golden links. He could have told her there was no point in trying. Until he said the words to release the spell, the bracelet would hold her in her mortal form.

"I can't feel my magic," she hissed.

"And you won't be able to access it until I release you. You owe me a confrontation, Árdís. And I'm not going away until I've had it."

She shoved him backward into a wall, and he hit hard, surprised by her strength. Then she shook her hand, her amber eyes flashing with fury when she clearly encountered the spell work within the bracelet—a spell that would keep her confined to her mortal shape, unless he took it off her.

A thousand emotions danced over her face. He was prepared for rage, or fury. Prepared to fight her on this.

But what settled in her eyes was a flicker of fear. "And you *will* release me?"

A single hint of worry, and his guts twisted into knots. *Damn you, she's playing you for a fool.*

"Once we've spoken." He pushed away from the wall, and her body tensed, as if prepared to flee. The moment froze him, their gazes clashing.

Haakon slowly reached for her hand, moving with careful intent, so she'd have all the time in the world to shove him away if she wished it. "I promise."

Her shoulders slumped. Then she punched him in the chest with a balled fist. "You idiot! You should never make deals with such creatures. What did it cost you? Your soul?"

Far too late for that. Someone else had owned that from the moment he set eyes upon her.

"Not quite."

She glanced up at the skies, and lightning stabbed the town. Clearly the bracelet hadn't entirely muted her powers. "I swear to all the gods, Haakon, you should take this off me and let me go, right now."

"Or what?" He was beyond caring. "You'll tear my throat out?"

Her eyes flashed with heat. "You truly think the worst of me, don't you? Where are we going? And what do you want from me?"

"I have rooms in town."

"Rooms?"

"Don't fear, my lying little wife. I have no intention of touching you ever again. Once was enough, and I'd rather skin myself alive than taste such sweet poison again. All I want is answers."

"We don't have time for this," Árdís said, looking at the skies as Haakon dragged her toward the inn.

Haakon.

In the flesh.

The shock had cleared and she was able to think again.

All her secret hopes and dreams melded into one horrific nightmare—for though her heart soared at the mere sight of him, she could sense them plunging desperately toward a confrontation she'd given *everything* to avoid. There were *dreki* in town. She could feel the shiver of the storm over her skin, fueled by their power.

If Sirius caught sight of him....

If *her mother* heard word of this....

"I have all the time in the world."

"I'm not here alone. There are others, and they would not take kindly to you manhandling me," she cried, wrenching at his hold.

Haakon turned abruptly, and once against she was face-to-face with him. Or nose-to-chest, as it were. She'd forgotten how tall he was.

Or perhaps he'd changed over the years they'd been apart. He'd been a man just past the threshold of youth when they first met. Tall and lean, with shoulders twice as wide as his narrow hips, and hair that gleamed silver in the moonlight.

The promise of the man he'd mature into had more than been fulfilled.

Haakon was almost the same size as Sirius now, his shoulders heavily muscled beneath the strict black wool of his coat. The top button of his shirt was undone, despite the cool air, and a healthy swathe of tanned skin gleamed there. The bulky wool of his coat couldn't quite hide the strength in his forearms, or the firm grip of the hand locked around her wrist.

It thrilled her *dreki* heart, the one that secretly longed to surrender to this man, even as she noted the cold gleam in his eye.

Kissing him would be a mistake. She'd hurt him when she left him. She'd known she would. And she'd do it all over again, if only to protect him from the fate she'd bequeathed upon him the second she agreed to marry him.

Besides, she was starting to grow angry herself. She wanted this cuff off, and she wanted it off now.

"Others?" he demanded. "Well, they can have you when I'm done with you."

She tried to haul away from him, but it was like trying to move a mountain, despite her innate strength. Or maybe the cuff was sapping that too. "You don't know what you're facing. That storm hinted at three *dreki* on my heels. I intended to be back at court before they noticed I was missing, but now.... You're no match for *dreki* warriors, Haakon."

"Maybe I wasn't, once upon a time. But I'm not the man you once knew."

The sword at his hip and the easy way he carried himself hinted at that.

"They won't obey the treaty between human and *dreki*-kind if they think you've laid hands upon me," she warned.

His free hand rested on the hilt of the sword at his hip. "Then they're welcome to attempt to retake you."

Her teeth gnashed together. Stubborn, infuriating man! She'd almost forgotten how hard it was to change his mind once he'd set it upon something. "And your men? Are you so careless with their lives you would throw them away?"

Something flickered in the pale storminess of his eyes. "The men can find other lodgings. I'd prefer to keep this between the two of us anyway."

"All the better to interrogate me?"

He stared at her for a long second. "I just want answers. You're not getting free until I've got them, so you might as well concede now and spare yourself the indignity. The sooner I have what I want, the sooner you can return to your *dreki* cohort. We'll never have to see each other again."

Never? "You mean to let me go?"

His look held such utter contempt that all of her blood felt like it drained from her limbs, straight to her heart. "Why would I keep you? Once was enough."

Her heart stuttered to a halt, before kicking with furious intention.

Fine. She'd hurt him.

He wanted to hurt her back.

Árdís knew all about wounded pride.

And the lies one could tell oneself to protect a bruised heart.

"I'm sorry. I never meant—"

"Enough of this nonsense." His lip curled back off his teeth, and his temper flashed, igniting the steely gray of his eyes. Then he was moving, bending low and throwing her over his shoulder.

Árdís gasped as the world upended. "What are you doing?"

"What I should have done ten minutes ago," he growled, turning and making for the street and the inn across from it. "Don't think you're going to twist me around in circles with that wretchedly sharp tongue. Not this time. I am done playing your games. It's time you played mine."

Árdís's eyes narrowed. If he thought this was the end of it, he was sorely mistaken. "I've barely begun!"

Thank goodness there was no one in the street to see her. Árdís tried to clutch at the corner of the nearest building, but her fingers tore loose. Haakon strode like a man on a mission, as unstoppable as the tide.

Her heart was beating madly.

The inn door slammed open. Árdís caught a dizzying array of chairs and tables, and heard the screech of timber as a chair scraped back.

"Here, now," someone called. "What are you doing with the lady?"

"The *lady* is my wife," Haakon said. "And we are about to have a private discussion."

"He's kidnapping me!" Árdís yelled, slamming her fist on his backside. "You stupid, big oaf. Let me down."

"Your wife?" said the man's incredulous voice.

"Do you have a problem with that?" Haakon demanded.

Árdís caught a glimpse of the innkeeper, gaping at the pair of them as she pushed herself up, trying to right herself on Haakon's shoulder.

"Let him be," someone else said gruffly, and she saw a massive redheaded man nursing a tankard in the corner. Her heart skipped a beat as she recognized Gunnar, one of Haakon's oldest friends—and the one man who'd never truly approved of her. "The girl stole something that belonged to him, and now he intends to get it back."

"I did *not* steal anything—"

"Certain about that?" Haakon demanded, and Árdís craned her neck to glare at him.

His heart.

If they were being specific.

Or perhaps their wedding ring.

The innkeeper scrubbed at his jaw. "If she *is* your wife, then I'm of a mind to grant you your privacy. But I'd like to hear it from the lady's lips myself, if you don't mind."

Finally. A man who hadn't lost all sense.

Haakon lowered her against his chest, until her toes almost brushed the floor. "Certainly." His eyes gleamed. "Why not tell the good innkeeper the truth. Are you my wife, Árdís?"

Her mouth opened. Then shut. Curse him. She was *dreki*. She *could* lie, but the consequences might be catastrophic. Words were power, and when one was created from raw Chaos magic itself, to breathe a lie might reshape the air around her.

If she said *no, she wasn't his wife*, she could cost Haakon his life, if her magic chose to interpret her words in such a way.

One of the very first laws *dreki* owned was to speak no word that wasn't true, or pay the price of it.

"Come," he taunted, clearly fully aware of her limitations, though it was doubtful he knew the why of it. "Tell the man the truth. I know you've only a limited acquaintance with it, but surely all you have to do is say 'yes' or 'no.'"

So be it.

"I am his wife," she told the innkeeper, giving in to fate.

"And he means you no harm?" the good man asked.

Árdís glanced up from beneath her lashes at her husband. "He means me no harm. He's not that sort of man," she said softly, for there was nothing else in this world she was certain of except for the nature of the man she had married. "He just wishes to... talk. We've been estranged."

They stared at each other, and Haakon seemed almost surprised, though a new wariness lingered in his expression.

Anger she could handle, but not the hint of pain she saw there, as if he fought to guard himself against her.

There was no point fighting this any longer. She needed to remove herself from town before her brethren tracked her down, and the only way she was going to get out of here swiftly was by succumbing to Haakon's wishes. Árdís gathered a handful of her skirts and strode toward the stairs. "Well?" She threw over her shoulder. "Are you coming?"

A glance toward Gunnar, and then Haakon nodded abruptly, following on her heels.

"Don't think I suddenly trust you," he whispered, as they entered the darkened stairwell.

His enormous presence loomed behind her. Despite everything, a thrill ran down her spine.

"I owe you answers, and I will give you what I can," she replied, suddenly weary of it all. "And then I must leave, before the others find me. And you will take this cursed bracelet off me. Agreed?"

"Agreed. This way." Haakon directed her toward a door.

It wasn't until they were inside the room, and the door clicked shut behind them, that she suddenly felt the weight of consequence weigh upon her. It was clear he'd been staying in this room for a while. All his belongings were packed neatly, but the very air smelled of him. A hunting knife and oiled stone rested on the table in the corner as if he'd been sharpening the blade that morning, and the enormous fur-lined cloak on the bed bore his scent.

The bed.

Her gaze narrowed in upon the rumpled blankets.

If there was one place where she'd ever felt both vulnerable and strangely secure, it was there. He was the first lover she'd ever taken, and a part of her suspected he'd be the last. She'd never been able to hide her true heart when she was in his arms.

A hand softened in the small of her back and she realized she'd faltered.

"We haven't got all day," she said, turning around and allowing him past her. Her skin shivered where he'd touched her. "Speak your questions. I assume you wish to know why I vanished."

Haakon ignored her, lighting the small candle on the table. "You might as well sit."

It was either the bed or the chair, and to get the chair she would have to pass him. Árdís gingerly settled on the edge of the bed, summoning all her pride in an attempt to guard herself. "Please. I need to leave."

Haakon blew the match out, glancing up at her through the thin wreath of smoke left behind. For a second she could barely breathe for the sudden sense of longing that swept through her.

"Why?" he asked softly. "That's all I want to know."

"Why I left you?"

His eyes glittered like pure ice. "Why you married me."

CHAPTER THREE

"WHY I MARRIED you?" she repeated softly.

Haakon straddled the chair backwards, resting his muscled forearms along the back of it, and rocking back until the front two legs left the ground. His eyes narrowed as he waited for her to speak.

"It's a simple question."

It wasn't a simple question at all. She found her feet, pacing toward the window, as far away from the bed as possible.

"Because you asked me to." The window was grimy. Árdís dragged the hem of her sleeve up over her palm and wiped a small circle in it so she could see the street outside. Nothing moved out there.

Yet.

The heels of the chair hit the ground.

"Árdís," he growled.

She took a deep breath. She was *dreki*. She could spin words into pure life, careful truths woven together like a tapestry. She could do this in such a way that he'd never truly see the truth behind her words.

"Do you remember the summer we first met?"

Gruffness filled his voice. "Of course."

Árdís closed her eyes, conjuring the memories behind her lids. "I was travelling the world, drinking in all these new places, all these new sights, when I flew north one stormy night. The wind blew me off course, and I'd been flying all day, trying to get clear of the cities. When I landed, I only ever intended to stay long enough to hunt and feed, but you came barreling around the corner"—*into my life*—"and.... I'd never met a man before. Not up close. I'd watched them from afar, curious about their lives. And there you were, trying terribly hard not to look at me. Bundling me into your cloak and offering to take me into your home." Her lashes fluttered open. It was too painful to look back at that night, when their lives had slammed into each other, changing the course of both their destinies.

"I should have said no," she whispered. "I was curious. You were kind. And handsome. Sometimes *dreki* take mortal lovers, and the way you looked at me—" Árdís sucked in a sharp breath. "It was the first time I've ever felt like that before. It seemed a simple proposition. I would come home with you, and we would tumble into bed, and then I would vanish on the wings of another storm."

She could feel his eyes resting upon her, his gaze a molten hand that slowly caressed her spine.

Árdís rested her fingertips on the glass, her head bowing. *Breathe. Just breathe.* "But of course, you had other ideas. And your mother was there, greeting me with a hot bowl of stew and a kiss on the cheek. A welcome. It was the strangest night. People. Home. A family. It baffled me. I tried to kiss you when you showed me to my room for the night, but you shied away, and turned your cheek and all I could feel was the rasp of stubble beneath my lips. You cannot imagine my confusion when I found myself in a bed in the attic, all alone. *Dreki* males battled for my attention. They clamored to be the first in my bed. And I'd chosen you, only to be rebuffed. I spent all night staring at the ceiling, thwarted by your honor and determined to claim you."

A rough grunt escaped from him, but when she stole a glance, he was glaring determinedly at the floor.

"Originally I'd intended to leave the next morning, but the very idea you could find me wanting made me stubbornly determined to have you. None of the following days made any sense to me. You would bring me flowers, but merely smile at me every night as you shut the door in my face. You dragged me through the mountains, trying to teach me how to hunt with a bow and arrow, while I tried to lure you into swimming naked in mountain streams. You would barely kiss me. It was so maddening."

"I was there. I remember it all," he snapped. "What the hell does this have to do with marrying me?"

"If you'd just listen." Her fingers curled into a fist. "Do you think I wish to rouse these memories either?"

"I think you want to torture me."

"As you tortured me then?" Árdís crossed her arms over her chest and turned to face him. "I married you because you asked me to. Weeks went by. Months. You would kiss me. You would touch me. But it never went any further. And then you said if I wanted to be in your bed, I had to marry you, for it wasn't the sort of thing one did outside of marriage. I didn't know what it all meant. Not truly. Marriage is a word the *dreki* do not use. We take lovers when we wish them, until the storm between us is burned out and we wish to move on. We mate for the sake of producing children. And sometimes we find the other half of our soul, and we promise them forever. I thought this *marriage* meant you wished to claim me as a lover. And by this stage, I was madly in lust with you, and frustrated, and here you were, saying I could have you if we stood in your church and said these words.... I didn't realize it meant forever to you, until it was too late."

He looked like she'd hit him. "You didn't think to ask?"

Unease rippled through her. She rubbed the back of her neck. "I wasn't thinking at that stage, no."

"And you didn't want forever."

Her head bowed, and she rested her hip against the table. *It was never a matter of what I wanted.* "No. I-I couldn't. It wasn't—"

His sword belt had been leaning against the table, and as she knocked it the sword began to slide toward the floor. Árdís snatched at the hilt, trying to capture it before it clattered to the floor, but it was too late.

The chain around her throat slithered between her breasts as she leaned forward, and the ring slipped free of her bodice.

It hit the end of its length and dangled between them. Árdís snatched at it, but she wasn't quick enough.

Haakon froze.

Slowly his eyes lifted to hers, and her breath caught at the look in them. A single look, but it held a wealth of meaning in it—a thousand questions she didn't know how to answer, much less decipher.

"What the hell is that?" he asked hoarsely.

"It's nothing."

She tried to shove the blasted ring back inside her gown, but Haakon moved abruptly, his hand snaking out toward hers and locking around her wrist. She closed her fingers around the ring, but he wasn't done yet.

"Show me."

"It's nothing." Panic flared within her breast, and Árdís tore her wrist free, and darted beneath his arm.

She made it two steps before he snatched her up around the waist, tossing her down on the bed.

His knee drove onto the mattress beside her hip. The heat of his body momentarily overwhelmed her and Árdís fell back on one hand, the other clenched tightly around the ring, as her heart started racing. If he saw it, she was lost. His face was shockingly close to hers, afternoon sunlight staining the tips of his lashes blond. The scent of leather and steel invaded her nose. He loomed over her, his broad shoulders almost blocking out the light, and his knuckles pressing into the bed beside her other hip. Árdís found herself trapped. Caged in. And a sudden panic roused within her.

He couldn't see the ring. He'd never let her go if he thought there was any hope.

"Show me," he demanded.

"It's mine!"

"I can make you, but I'd prefer not to."

"To make me, you'll have to hurt me," she declared.

"Maybe not." His hand curled around her palm, his breath rasping through his chest. "Show me what you're hiding."

She wriggled beneath him, trying to escape, but his weight simply pinned her down, and Árdís finally slumped onto the mattress as his palm pushed down on her shoulder.

"The one thing you didn't count on is the fact that holding you contained is not the only thing this manacle does. *Clausðr. Binda í ér.*"

The words purred over his tongue, locking down on something deep inside her.

Golden light lit up previously invisible runes on the manacle's surface. They were neither Elder Futhark, Younger Futhark, or the Anglo-Saxon bastardization they called Futhorc. Recognition lanced through her. She'd seen this once. "Are you insane?" she hissed. "You bargained with the *svartálfar*?"

"There's no such thing." He was far too close to her now. Far too menacing. "I bought it from a sorcerer in Hólmavík. He promised me it would keep you in human form, and it would force you to obey me and speak the truth. The second I have what I want, I'll release you."

"You fool!" Árdís pulled at the bracelet, pain searing through her wrist as it tightened. She cried out and jerked her hand away.

Haakon's face sharpened, and he took her wrist. "What's it doing?"

The urge to speak burned over her tongue.

She couldn't continue to fight it.

Her *dreki* lashed within her, the runes branding deep into her soul. Waves of pain prickled over her skin, and Árdís bit her lip.

"Show me what you're hiding," he demanded again. "You owe me that."

The urge to open her hand drove up through her body like a fist. Árdís fought against the demand, but it bled through her veins until she felt like she was on fire. One finger pried open. Then another. Until finally her palm lay splayed, her wedding ring revealed in all its glory.

The magic finally let go of her, and Árdís panted, her entire body trembling. She didn't dare look at him. Instead she closed her eyes, feeling the roughened exhale of his breath on her décolletage.

"Your wedding ring," he breathed.

For a second it was all she could do not to reach up and touch him. Seven years vanished in the blink of an eye as Haakon's breath washed over her sensitive throat. Árdís's breasts swelled against her bodice, and she turned her face away, breathing hard. All she'd ever wanted was to fall into his arms. Suddenly she was clinging to the ring, as if it could grant her some sense of sanity in this passion-fueled moment. Every inch of her weak body screamed at her to touch him. Just one more kiss. One more taste.

One last touch....

Remember why you left him.

Do you want his death upon your hands?

"Get off me," she managed to whisper, pushing at his chest.

"What?" Tension radiated through his body.

"I said," she growled, looking up into his eyes, "get off me. I gave you what you wanted."

His large hand curved around hers and his eyes narrowed with tight focus, the hard line of his jaw firming. A thousand emotions danced through those icy gray eyes, and she felt them all, twisting her into knots inside. *Please don't.* She only had so much strength left within her.

Árdís didn't think he was going to obey, but then his expression settled into a hard mask, and he released her. "As you wish."

Haakon rose away from the bed as smoothly as a cat, turning toward the table in the corner. Árdís managed to take a quivering breath, but her dress still felt far too tight. What had almost happened? Cold fear made her lips tingle. She couldn't afford to give in to her lust and the temptation to touch him. There were *dreki* in this town, presumably hunting for her, and none of her reasons for leaving him had changed.

But it was too late.

He'd seen her greatest secret. He had to be wondering.

He poured himself a wine, his head bowed and his shoulders stiff. Árdís licked her lips, pushing herself to the edge of the bed. Haakon's temper had always matched hers, and they'd once had numerous shouting matches that ended exactly where she was sitting... but she was more wary of this cold quietness he now owned.

It felt like a leviathan swimming beneath the depths of a still sea.

A predator just waiting for her to relax before it swallowed her whole.

"Are you going to say something?" she whispered.

"Would you like to explain to me why you still have your wedding ring?" Still looking away from her, he lifted the goblet of wine to his lips.

"A keepsake," she admitted, for she couldn't entirely avoid the truth.

"A keepsake." His head bowed as he whispered the words, and his fingers trembled on the cup. "I want it back. That ring doesn't belong to you. It was my grandmother's."

The ring pressed into her flesh as she gripped it tightly. "And you *gave* it to me."

"I want it back," he snarled. "It was a gift, and you discarded it the second you threw me away."

I didn't— She bit down on the words and pushed to her feet. "No," she said, unable to conjure a single reason why she shouldn't give it back. Her *dreki* lashed within her.

"It belongs to me."

"Do you think I haven't tried to get rid of it?" she cried. "Do you think I haven't thrown it away a thousand times? I tried to give it up. But I couldn't. I couldn't. And I won't. It's mine."

"It has no worth to you," he said sharply, turning to look at her.

"That's got nothing to do with it!"

"Fine. What do you want for it?" He slammed the goblet down and snatched at his coin pouch, tearing at the strings. "I have gold. Killing dragons is rewarding work."

He didn't understand her.

"I don't want gold."

"Gemstones?" he snapped, throwing the purse aside. It clinked as it hit the floor, and gold coins rolled all over the floor. "Jewelry? A fucking crown?"

"I will *not* give it back! It's mine." *Bought and paid for in blood and tears.* She could see he still didn't understand. "I cannot," she pleaded, branding the metal into her flesh with the tightness of her grip. Her hand was no longer obeying her.

"It means nothing to you. Or you wouldn't have tried to throw it away."

He'd given it to her, along with his heart, and the *dreki* within her had claimed it. If she could no longer have his heart, then she would keep this. She *needed* to. The very idea of losing it scraped her soul raw, and made something violent shift within her.

"I *cannot* give it back. I swore an oath on this ring, and my *dreki* soul considers that binding."

"A shame you didn't consider our actual marriage binding."

She had nothing to say to that.

"If I could give it back," she whispered, "I would. I swear I would, Haakon. But my *dreki* demands it. And I will fight any man who tries to take it from me. Even you."

Haakon searched her eyes.

The sound of a sudden commotion caught her ear. Shouts downstairs, perhaps. And the crash of timber.

"I don't—"

She took two swift steps, and slammed her hand over his mouth, her head turning toward the door. "Be quiet."

Her heart slammed to a halt. Too late. She could sense the whisper of *dreki* magic calling to her. "They're here."

They'd found her.

"Go out the window," she said, turning toward the door. "I'll stall the *dreki* before they catch your scent."

A hand caught her wrist, and Árdís tumbled against his side. "Like hell," Haakon snapped, and then he reached for the hilt of the sword resting in its scabbard near the bed, and drew it with a steely rasp.

"They won't hurt me!" She grabbed a fistful of his shirt and shoved him against the wall. "But they'll kill *you*!"

He gaped at her, his arms splayed and the sword held loosely. Those eyes narrowed. "Didn't know you cared."

Careful now.... "Just because I consider our marriage to be over, doesn't mean I want to see you hurt. Or have your blood on my hands."

"You're choosing them?"

It had never been a choice. "Yes. I'm choosing them."

The tip of the sword lowered. Blue-gray eyes stared at her steadily, a question within them, one she didn't think she recognized. Árdís stepped back when she saw he wasn't going to fight.

"Those are my men down there," he said.

"And no *dreki* will break the treaty unless they're attacked first. If you go down there, your men will fight to the death to protect you. These are my people. My clan. They're only here for me. Once they have me, they'll leave peacefully."

"Taking you with them." His gaze searched hers again.

Árdís's breath caught

Another echoing crash drifted up the stairwell, one even Haakon heard.

"Go," she pleaded.

"What about the bracelet?"

She thrust her hand in front of him, and he took it in both of his. Then hesitated.

He didn't meet her eyes. No. His wretched gaze lifted to the ring still dangling between her breasts. Árdís shoved it down her bodice. "*Haakon.*"

They didn't have time for this.

"So be it," he said softly.

He spoke the words of release, and Árdís waited for the runes on the manacle to turn golden.

Nothing happened.

"Haakon?"

A frown drew his brows together. "That's what the sorcerer told me to say."

He tried again.

Again nothing. Árdís tugged on the manacle. It only hurt her wrist. Her heart pounded as horror filled her. "I cannot change forms," she whispered, looking up.

"I'll—"

"Get it off me!"

"I'm trying," he snapped, examining the links of the bracelet with his large hands. "I don't know why it's not working."

A loud crash echoed beneath them, in the inn. She froze, torn between her desire to rid herself of the cursed manacle, and her fear for his safety.

"*Where is she?*" a hard voice demanded, the words just loud enough for her to hear. "*Where is the princess?*"

"*Upstairs.*" A frightened bleat from the innkeeper. "*He took her upstairs to his rooms.*"

Fear won. Árdís pressed a hand to Haakon's chest, pushing him toward the window. "Go."

"But what about—"

"I'll find a way to remove it," she promised.

"But you cannot shift. You cannot defend yourself—"

Árdís scowled. "If you think I cannot defend myself in this form, then you're very much mistaken."

She pushed him toward the window.

Haakon resisted. "I have one more question I need you to answer."

"Damn you! *Anything.*" She glanced toward the door.

"Tell me there's nothing left between us."

Árdís's mouth opened.

The words locked in her throat.

"You can't say it," he whispered incredulously. "You can't deny it, can you? You say you've tried to throw my ring away, but you can't and you don't even know why. You say you choose *them*, but there's a part of you that wants me."

"I...."

"Yes?" Softly.

"I...."

His arctic eyes held hers for long seconds, and even as she watched she saw heat flare in them. Determination. Her heart kicked into her throat as he reached for her, moving like a striking snake. She knew what he wanted. She knew what he intended. And damn her soul, but she couldn't deny him.

A hand slid into her hair, dragging her into his arms. Árdís slammed against his chest, her hands crushed up between them.

His mouth crashed down over hers, claiming the kiss she'd spent years dreaming of. The hot lash of his tongue stroked against hers, their teeth clashing in his fury. One hand palmed her side, and she felt his fingers splay over her ribs, his thumb rasping below the under curve of her breast.

She didn't own the strength to fight him off. Not when a part of her so desperately needed this. She might as well deny the moon in the sky, or the tide itself. Passion swept through her, igniting every nerve in her body. Need. Árdís's fingers tangled in his hair, and she kissed him back, biting his lower lip.

She had to stop.

She knew it.

But his tongue danced over hers, slow and steady, and his hand began to slide up her body, arching over her breast. Árdís's knuckles curled in his shirt, drawing him closer. *Yes.* She pushed into his touch, and he captured her soft moan in his mouth. Seven years without a single kiss. She felt starved for his touch, her sex clenching as if it knew where this would end—

There was no time.

Árdís broke free from his mouth, shoving at his shoulder. "Stop."

Haakon captured her face in his hands, his expression implacable as he swooped down to capture her mouth once more.

"Stop!" She set both hands to his chest and shoved him with all her might.

He staggered back a step. Maybe two. His shoulders heaved, as if he'd run up a flight of stairs, and the look in his eyes—

"You still want me," he said breathlessly.

Somehow Árdís managed to straighten, pushing herself away from the wall and touching her kiss-stung lips. Somehow her shaky knees didn't betray her. "One last kiss, for old times' sake."

His expression closed over, fury flaring his nostrils. "Like hell." He took a step toward her. "I know you want me. This isn't over, Árdís. You can deny me all you want, but there's still something between us. And we both know it."

"That was a kiss goodbye!"

She darted beneath his outreached arm, and tugged the window up. "You promised."

Haakon stared at her. Footsteps hammered on the stairs, keeping time with her racing heartbeat. Her head turned in that direction, and then she looked back at him, desperation searing through her. "*Please.*"

Another long, drawn-out moment.

She didn't think he was going to go.

"I promised," he said softly, grabbing his sword belt off the bed and stepping one leg through the window. "And at least one of us knows what that word means."

Not forgiven. Never forgiven. It was a stab to the heart, but she simply shoved him through, flinching as voices broke out in the hallway outside the door.

"Search the rooms," a hard voice of command snapped.

Sirius.

Haakon paused there. His hand slid through her hair, and then she was kissing him once more, unable to resist, even as her heart broke into a thousand more pieces.

Haakon let her go, his fingers snagging in her hair. He teased the ends of one small strand of it between thumb and forefinger, and then slowly looked up.

"If you can forget me," he whispered, "then there is nothing more between us. I won't wait for you, Árdís. Not this time. I gave you everything, and you left me behind. You broke me, and you never once looked back."

Sirius would find her at any moment... but her hand captured his, her throat suddenly dry. "What are you saying?"

"My ship leaves in three days. I'm sailing home. Forever. Unless you give me a reason to stay."

Hope crested and broke within her chest. None of her reasons had changed. She loved him, and the only way to save his life was to make sure he never walked back into hers. She tried to memorize his face, knowing it would haunt her dreams for the rest of her life.

"There is no reason," she forced herself to say. "I cannot give you what you want. Only your freedom. We are done here. I'm sorry I didn't give you a chance to say goodbye. I'm sorry I dragged you through all these years. I should have released you properly."

His thumb stroked the fleshy pad of her palm. "Freedom? How am I ever free of you?"

"You could remarry. The name I gave you was false. The marriage isn't legally binding."

"Unlike others, when I give my word, I mean it." He gave her an odd look. "It seems your understanding of the word—and its customs—has improved over the years."

Árdís bit her lip. "Go. Go and... have children. Create a life for yourself and grow old."

His nostrils flared. "You don't mean that."

"I do. Find someone else...." *To marry.* The words caught on her tongue and stuck there, for it wasn't the truth of her heart and her *dreki* soul knew it. "Be happy," she said instead, for she could mean those words.

He stared into her eyes, and she thought he was going to argue further. A fist hammered on the door behind her. Árdís flinched.

"Three days," he said softly. "If you're not there by dawn when we sail, then I'll forget you. I swear I will."

And then Haakon vanished through the window, turning to stride along the gable.

Just as the door burst open behind her.

CHAPTER FOUR

YOU HAVE THE storm in your veins, and fire in your heart. You are a princess of the Zini court. You can face her.

Árdís took a deep breath, and slammed both hands flat against the golden doors leading from her private chambers into the royal wing, pushing them open. She'd dallied long enough, and her mother wouldn't be pleased to find her summons gone unanswered, but the events in Reykjavik had raised conflict in her heart.

She felt restless. Cagey.

A violent spirit gowned in gold silk.

It didn't help that the queen had called an audience before the entire court, and nobody seemed to know what it was about.

The rough-edged corridor Árdís stalked along looked like it had been carved straight out of basalt. The floor gleamed like a mirror, polished by the Chaos magic that had created the court. Located in the heart of the volcano Hekla, the court was a world outside of the natural one, a bubble in time and space created by Chaos magic, where the *dreki* of the *Zini* clan congregated.

Most of them had their own volcanoes and territories in the country. Her own was a small mountain in the south, where heat leaked from fumaroles, and she could lounge and listen to the hypnotic groan of the earth. But the court was where the clan gathered, and where those who had no territories of their own resided. It was enormous, a space that shouldn't have fit within the volcano—and didn't. Chaos bubbles existed in a side world of their own.

But despite the size, it was tradition that *dreki* would walk these halls in mortal form, and Árdís breathed a sigh of relief, for she didn't know how she'd explain the episode with the bracelet.

It had been all she could do to talk Sirius into allowing her to use the portal the servants used to travel back to Hekla, and even then his blue eyes had narrowed with suspicion.

Árdís strode toward the enormous throne room in the heart of the court, her golden skirts twitching about her ankles. *I'll forget you. I swear I will.* The words hammered in time to the sound of her racing heart.

Stop it, she told herself. *It's over. It's done.*

But the flicker of a rebellious flame smoldered in her heart.

She didn't know why she was so angry. For years she'd felt hollow and empty, but it was only now she realized the extent of it. Some sort of survival instinct must have dulled the edges of her pain. Her world had become a landscape of bleak shadows, one she navigated carefully, locking away her innermost hopes and dreams. And she hadn't even noticed. She'd played by the rules of her mother's court. She'd kept her head down, and tried to remain unnoticed by the more dangerous players at court. A slow, painful stifling, where Árdís became a marionette wielded by her mother's whims.

One glimpse of Haakon, and everything changed. Suddenly the world seemed full of color and life again. Dreams exploded to life in her chest. She could taste his kiss still. Her lips fairly burned with the memory of it.

And her heart ached with rage.

A shadow shifted out the corner of her eye as she reached the doors to the throne room.

A *dreki* in mortal form pushed away from the wall he'd been leaning against, his hair black, and his clear, almost colorless eyes locked upon her. "Princess."

Árdís stilled. "Roar."

Her illegitimate cousin prowled the court like a rabid dog seeking scraps. Of all her uncle Stellan's sons, Roar scared her the most. Magnus had been cruel, but disinterested in her; Sirius was frightening in his own unique way, but if she were honest, he'd never lifted a hand against her; and Andri, the youngest, was her favorite.

Somehow her brutal uncle had given birth to one son who knew what the words loyalty and honor meant.

Roar was not that one.

"I heard you led my brother quite a chase in Reykjavík." His smirk revealed how much he enjoyed the thought.

Sirius hadn't been quite as pleased. The second Haakon vanished, so had she, slipping through the window after him, and darting over the rooftops toward the docks, desperate to draw her *dreki* guards as far away from Haakon as possible.

"Sirius needed the exercise," she said, in the most casual tone she could muster. They expected a spoiled princess here, and so she gave them one.

The hallway was empty.

Every *dreki* in the court would be gathering in the throne room.

But if Roar thought, for one second, that she was *helpless....*

Árdís smiled, knowing what he saw when he looked at her. A gilded treasure he wasn't allowed to touch. It ate at him, but she could handle him. He wouldn't dare touch her, not with the threat of her mother's wrath looming over her.

Nobody crossed Queen Amadea if they valued their near-immortal lives.

He circled her slowly, taking her measure with insolent eyes. Árdís swallowed down the choke of rage, and turned her head to track him. His skin was as pale as the snow-capped mountains to the west. Thick black hair brushed against his collar. It always looked a little oily, as though he'd raked his fingers through it. Or perhaps that was just him.

"If you were mine," Roar whispered, his breath stirring across the back of her neck as he came around to her side, "I would keep you on a tighter leash."

She glanced sideways, beneath her lashes. "But I'm not yours. Am I?"

"Not yet."

"Not ever."

Roar angled his head and smiled as if he knew a secret she didn't.

Árdís swallowed. "You're going to make me late for my mother's announcement. If she asks, I'll tell her you waylaid me."

Roar clucked his tongue. "We wouldn't want that, would we?"

He knew what it was going to be. Árdís's eyes narrowed. The court had been on edge in the last month, ever since her cousin Andri returned with the news of Magnus's death. Stellan's eldest son had been sent to make a treaty with Rurik, but Rurik had killed him.

Or so they said.

A hand reached out, hovering just above her collarbone. A challenge. He wasn't touching her. He hadn't broken the rules. But she felt that touch as if he had, and he knew it.

"I swear to the gods that if you don't get out of my way...."

Roar's fingertips settled, just lightly, upon her skin.

"Get your hands off her," said a cold voice.

And Árdís sucked in a sharp breath of relief, despite the fact the *dreki* who appeared was little better.

At least he keeps his hands to himself.

Sirius melted out of the shadows, almost as if he wore a cape of pure darkness.

He towered over the pair of them, his shoulders broad, and his long brown hair tied back with a leather thong. A warrior, dressed from head to toe in strict black. Cool eyes the color of a glacial spring locked on the pair of them, but it was Roar he gave his attention to.

"Of course. *Brother*." Roar gave a smirk and held his hands up as he backed away. "I know what I'm not allowed to touch."

Sirius paused but an inch from his bastard brother. "And yet, you keep taking risks. Árdís is mine. See you remember that."

"For now." Another faint, mocking smile. Roar took a step back. "Let us see if you can keep her. She has a frightening tendency to bolt when least expected."

Sirius watched Roar stalk away, and the cold glitter of his eyes indicated a storm brewing between the pair of them. The very air seemed to chill with his temper, until it burned her lungs. Roar slipped through the doors into the throne room, and Sirius finally looked down at her.

"Sirius," she murmured, tipping her chin up. "As bleak and grim as usual. Killed anyone today?"

"Árdís," he replied, glancing around as he offered her his arm. "As frustratingly stubborn and painful as usual. And no, not yet, though the day's still young."

Neither of them looked in the direction Roar had vanished.

She could keep up this pretense.

But it seemed he was not going to allow her to do so.

"You should be careful not to be alone at the moment," he said, turning his attention toward her. "The bastard's starting to show his teeth."

"Perhaps he'd like to meet my claws?"

Sirius stared down at her. For a second she thought he was going to make some flippant remark. But his lips thinned. "Don't underestimate him. He's grown bold since Magnus died. He's always hungered for power and for father's attention, and without Magnus at my side, Roar sees a chance to take what he wants. And he wants *you*."

She'd spent most of the year avoiding Sirius. When they met, they traded careless barbs, but he didn't offer her warnings. This wasn't how the game was played. "You're the Blackfrost." Half of the court feared him. The other half dared not look his way. "Surely you—of all *dreki*—are not frightened of Roar?"

He'd never challenged his brother, but sometimes Árdís had seen even Magnus look at him in a speculative way.

She could rank every single *dreki* within the court on a scale of how dangerous they were. Except for Sirius. He didn't fight challenges. He didn't make idle threats. He bowed to his father's will. But the other males in the clan didn't challenge him either, and she'd seen unease in their eyes as they skirted around him.

That was almost an un-*dreki*-like action.

To be *dreki* meant one was arrogant to the bone. To be a male *dreki* only emphasized such a trait.

Sirius is a storm of ice and rage, she'd heard the servants whisper. *They say he single-handedly destroyed the German clans when they flew north to take what was ours. He turned their own storm against him. Ripped them from the skies.*

He'd earned the title of the Blackfrost years before she'd been birthed into this world.

"Frightened?" he mocked. "No. But wary. Roar knows he can't face me. Not one-on-one. If he makes a tilt at me, I know I won't see it coming. You should always watch an ambitious coward with both eyes, Árdís."

"Is that why you turned all snarly and overprotective?"

Hard eyes narrowed. "We're to be mated. Isn't that how I'm supposed to react?"

Ten years ago he'd tried to claim her, before she fled the court and fell into her husband's hands. It had been a power play, she suspected, for he'd never looked at her the way some of the other *dreki* did.

And he'd shown little interest in her since.

She snorted, resting her hand lightly on his arm as he turned them toward the throne room. "For a *dreki* male who's supposed to be mating with me, one could be forgiven for thinking otherwise. Or are the rumors true? They say you keep a cold bed."

Thick lashes obscured his eyes. "One could say the same for you."

Yes, but I have a reason. Her hand went to the ring around her throat. It was dangerous to wear it here, but some last hint of defiance within her had seen her slip the chain over her head before she left her rooms.

"And the entire court's been expecting you to set a date for the ceremony."

"The entire court?" he mused. "Or you?"

They paused before the enormous gold doors. Through them she could make out the hush of muted voices. Over a hundred *dreki* waited, her mother chief among them.

Anticipation stole her breath. She didn't know why she was so nervous. "If we both said we didn't wish to mate, then my mother might—"

"Find an alternative," he said softly. "Would you prefer Roar?"

She shook her head violently. "No. I'd prefer no one. I'll rescind my position before the court. If I step down as my mother's heir, then she'll have no choice but to name you. We wouldn't have to—"

"Árdís."

"We...." She saw his expression, and the words—and the hope within her breast—trailed off.

"Your mother's waiting," he said, "and she's not very happy about it. Something about insisting I should have made you fly back to Hekla."

"I wanted to take the portal," she replied, her teeth bared in what she hoped was a smile. The bracelet remained upon her wrist, despite her best efforts. "I had something to see to in the servants' quarters."

He shrugged. "Your head. But I do not think this the time to broach the subject of calling off our arrangement."

He isn't saying no.

They could discuss this another time.

Árdís took a deep breath. "Let us go greet Mother then, and find out what this is all about."

"You're late," the queen whispered the words to her on a thought-thread as Árdís paused before the dais. *"Sirius claimed he had to fetch you from the human town."*

Hundreds of whispers hushed as Árdís pasted a smile upon her face and knelt before the queen. At least the manacle didn't restrict her psychic abilities. *"I wasn't aware you were going to insist upon an audience. There was a necklace I wanted."*

Amadea reclined upon her golden throne, her hands curved over the ends of it. Golden waves tumbled down her back, and her face was as smooth and unmarked as Árdís's own. They could have been sisters. Perhaps even twins.

But the glittering green of her mother's eyes held a cruelty she could never match.

"Stellan," the queen murmured, turning her head toward her younger brother.

Árdís lifted her eyes as her uncle strode forward. Wearing the same unadorned black as his son, Stellan was the power behind the throne. With Amadea's magic, and his might, there was no hope in overthrowing them. As he stopped in the center of the dais, the crowd fell silent.

Árdís hastily moved to the right side of the queen.

"Bring forth the prisoner," Stellan boomed.

The line of warriors shifted, and a pair of them dragged someone between them, his knees scrabbling on the floor.

This was the part of court life she hated. Árdís steeled herself. Ever since her father—the rightful king—had been murdered, the court had begun to spiral into dark depths. Her mother and uncle were members of the *Zilittu* clan from Norway, and ruled not with her father's sense of law and fairness, but with the crushing might of fear.

Heads turned. People strained to see who it was. A woman cried out, clapping a hand to her mouth. "No!"

Then the two warriors—Balder and Ylve—threw a *dreki* down before the dais.

No, not a *dreki*. A *drekling*. Árdís felt ill. Children could be born between *dreki* and humans, and though the child might bear some of its *dreki* parent's powers, the further the bloodline bred, the weaker the blood became. It had become tradition for mortal mothers to make the treacherous trek up the slopes of Hekla and leave their unnatural children upon the doorstep to the court, a tradition started by her father who welcomed all. The court was filled with *dreklings*—those with *dreki* blood who were unable to shift forms and soar through the skies. The queen saw some use for them, but Stellan did not.

"Show them the mark," Stellan insisted.

The pair of warriors tore the man's shirt down his arms, baring his back. He kicked and fought, but one of them simply captured him by the throat, and hauled him upright, so everyone in the court could see the tattoo on his back.

A crown encircling a scrolling R.

"For the true prince!" the *drekling* yelled, his eyes rolling with fear. Ylve turned and slammed a fist into his gut, and he went down on his knees, choking with pain.

Árdís's fingernails bit into her palms. This didn't happen often. Both the queen and Stellan dealt with such matters swiftly and harshly. But sometimes they decided they needed an object lesson.

Stellan stared down at the man on the floor. "This *drekling* has been found guilty of attempting to break into the prisons and rescue a prisoner—"

"He's your s—"

A hand slammed the *drekling's* face into the floor, and a gag was produced, cutting sharply into his lips.

Another warrior brought a brazier to the dais. The hiss of burning coals made Árdís flinch. There was a hot iron burning white-hot in the center of the coals.

"Such an act—as well as the tattoo—can only prove where Marek's loyalty lies. And it is not with this court," Stellan said, drawing the end of the brand from the coals. He advanced, taking the steps down from the dais slowly.

Marek's screams were muffled by the edge of the gag as Ylve and Balder flipped him onto his back.

"He is declared a traitor, and will earn a traitor's death. The bonfire is being prepared."

Árdís turned her face away as the hiss of burning flesh and muffled screams echoed. Heels drummed on the floor. The stink filled her nostrils. It was too much. She had turned away, pressing her hands to her lips, when Malin—her *drekling* handmaid—suddenly appeared, offering her a scented handkerchief.

Árdís curled it in her fist, her eyes meeting the haunted brown depths of her handmaid's. She didn't press the handkerchief to her face, shame flooding through her. She could barely bear the stink and the sound of it. What a jest. Marek was the one feeling the *T* burn right into the middle of his forehead.

"Take him away and prepare him for the execution tomorrow night," Stellan said, discarding the brand back in the coals.

Marek moaned through a raw throat, as if he simply had no voice left to scream. Or perhaps he'd passed out, there at the end. She hoped.

Árdís turned as the guards dragged him away. Malin's hand squeezed hers. But Árdís's gaze locked on her uncle, and she hated him in that moment, more than she'd ever hated anyone in her life.

But she did not dare speak.

None of them did. Not even Sirius, whose head turned toward her, their eyes locking for one long moment in which she wondered if he even cared.

Silence.

The entire court was rocked with silence.

The only sound was the dying screams that grew weaker the further the poor *drekling* was dragged from the throne room.

"Does anyone else wish to throw their allegiance to the Traitor Prince?" Stellan asked softly.

Nobody moved.

"We didn't think so," the queen mused, sliding to her feet with graceful elegance. She paused at her brother's side.

"It has been over a month since Magnus, our prince, our hope, was taken from us by the traitor, Rurik," the queen called. "I have heard the unrest at court, and the whispers. As much as Magnus would have wished for us to grieve for him...."

An absolute jest. Magnus had been a monster, and half the court knew it.

"...it is past time we set aside our mourning and looked to the future. To the shining light within our midst." Amadea held her hand out, a sidelong glance shifting to Árdís. "My dear sweet daughter."

Shock slammed through her. She wasn't prepared for this. Marek's punishment had thrown her off-balance.

It was rare she was required to mount the dais. Árdís hesitated a fraction too long, and saw the faint lines around her mother's mouth tighten.

"Get up here," Amadea hissed in her mind.

Gathering her skirts, she somehow made it to her mother's side, sliding her hand into the *dreki* queen's. Over a hundred faces stared back at her, and not a single one of them smiled. The *dreki* warriors who served her mother and Stellan simply stared, and the others looked at her with hollow eyes.

The fate of the *drekling* had broken them.

"And the greatest of us all, the Blackfrost."

Sirius's head turned just as sharply.

Their eyes met for a second before Árdís looked away. He pushed away from the wall, moving with slow, careful steps, his face devoid of all emotion.

Did he support his father in this?

Had he known what was coming?

"It is the dearest hope of myself and my brother to join our two bloodlines and present a unified court." Amadea drew their hands together, and Árdís found her palm resting upon Sirius's.

What was going on here? She hadn't protested the betrothal too hard, knowing whichever way she looked, her back was in a corner. With both of her brothers fleeing the court, she was the only heir, but she'd never hold such a position without a strong male behind her—the way Stellan backed the queen.

But it had been over a year.

Neither the queen nor her uncle Stellan had pushed this, beyond the odd mutter, and Sirius never breathed a word about the betrothal.

It had loomed over her, and yet protected her from the attentions of other *dreki*. Both threat and savior. Her heart began to pound as she realized what her mother intended.

"Let us bring in the equinox with a celebration." Amadea's voice rang through the enormous cavern.

"Tomorrow night, I shall watch as my beloved daughter takes the Blackfrost as a mate, and I can officially announce him as my heir."

Árdís's breath sucked through her. *Tomorrow night?*

She didn't realize she'd flinched until Sirius's fingers laced through hers, forcing their hands together.

"Don't," he whispered on a thought-thread.

Cheers rang out among her mother's warriors, and hands clapped together. The rest of the hall was silent. Some of her father's remaining coterie of *dreki* exchanged glances. The *drekling* didn't move. It all seemed so distant. Árdís's world was narrowing in around her, caging her within their false cheer. The laces on her dress seemed to pull tighter. She couldn't breathe.

"If you'll excuse me," Árdís said, unable to stay there a second longer. Gathering her skirts, she fled the dais.

"You selfish little bitch." Skirts stalked after her, a menacing swish that told her she couldn't flee. "Do you think this is a game? Do you think you can defy me like that in front of the entire court, and I shall merely turn the other cheek?"

Árdís spun around, her heart beating wildly behind the cage of her ribs as the queen stalked toward her. "How could you do that? Right after.... You could have warned me."

The queen's smile was thin. "You've had a year to grow used to the idea."

"He's not my choice!"

"Do you think your father was *my* choice?"

Movement flashed. Her ears rang as the slap drove her sideways. Árdís caught herself on the wall, and looked up.

Defiance was unwise. Her mother was dangerous, and had long proved she held no sense of loyalty toward her own children.

But Haakon's kiss blazed across her mouth, and Árdís's *dreki* writhed within her, as if it had woken from a long slumber to find the world burning around it.

Or perhaps the kiss had woken *her*.

The heart of her. The *real* her.

How much of herself could she bury? How much of her soul could she cage, before it was too late? No *dreki* should ever have its wings clipped.

No *dreki* should live in fear, the way the court did.

Deep inside her lurked a secret fury that boiled up, as if someone had set a match to oil. She rounded on her mother, and it no longer mattered if this was dangerous or unwise, or could possibly get her killed.

A line had been crossed.

A decision made.

"I will *not* do this," she whispered hoarsely. "You ask too much of me—"

Amadea lashed out, and Árdís went to her knees as a whip of burning Chaos magic lashed around her throat. It choked the breath out of her, searing through her nerves. She screamed, pain obliterating every thought, on and on, until she didn't think she could bear it any longer, and the noose finally vanished.

When she came to, she was on her hands and knees on the floor. Spit dribbled from her lips. Snot bubbled from her nose. She was surprised her head was still attached, for it had felt as though the lash burned right through her spinal cord, but when her palm wrapped around her throat there was not a single mark there.

"I wasn't aware I was asking."

Árdís panted, her rage burned to ash in her throat. How could she ever fight that? How could she ever escape? She smelled again the stink of burning flesh.

She might have little recourse against her mother's powers, but she would not crawl on the floor and beg for forgiveness. Wiping her face with her sleeve, Árdís looked up.

It took her long seconds to gather her weight beneath her, mocked by shaky knees. Árdís's palms scraped the wall, and she hauled herself to her feet, every inch the *dreki* princess as she stared her mother in the eye.

"Be very careful," Amadea said. "Both of your brothers defied me. I will *not* have another traitor who shares my own blood. I will *not*."

Don't be unwise, screamed her sense of self-preservation.

She will kill you.

Or worse.

Árdís forced herself to bow her head, but her fists curled at her side, so tightly her knuckles ached.

"This court is full of rebellious hearts," Amadea warned, and her red skirts swished into the field of Árdís's vision. "Some say your brother is still the rightful heir, despite your father's murder—"

"He didn't do it. I know Rurik would never have—"

A cruel hand caught her chin, forcing her to look up. Fingers dug into the flesh of her jaw.

"You were a kit, Árdís. You know nothing. Do you think Rurik looked back once he left this court?" Amadea's eyes glittered. "I know you think he loved you—I know you think Marduk loved you—but did they ever offer to take you with them? Or did they leave you behind, like the refuse sailors throw overboard their ships? Vanishing without a single goodbye...."

Her heart absorbed the blow. They loved her. Her father had loved her, before someone in this wretched court ripped his heart out.

But that didn't negate the fact she was alone here, with not a single ally.

Or that they had left her behind, knowing what their mother was like.

Claws dug into her skin, and Amadea's glittering green eyes became the center of her vision. "I will crush this rebellion if it is the last thing I do. I will not allow your father's lawless *dreki* fanatics to bring mutiny to my court. Word swims of Rurik's power and might following Magnus's death, and each whisper is melding together to become a roar that shakes the foundations of this court."

"That's why you did that?" A public punishment to whip the court into line, and a mating ceremony to offer a future.

"We *need* to look strong in the face of these rumors. We need Sirius named as heir. If there is one thing that can counter the might of their golden prince, then it is the Blackfrost. And you will do your duty to protect this family, this court. You will mate with him, Árdís, so I can name him heir and weld this fractured court together again. I will not allow your selfishness to ruin us."

Amadea held her there for another brutal second, seeming satisfied with what she saw in Árdís's eyes.

Then she let her go and strode away, leaving Árdís gasping behind her.

CHAPTER
FIVE

ÁRDIS SLIPPED THROUGH the portal that led to her chambers, her ears still ringing.

The world around her remained silent. Someone had cleaned her rooms, and the silk spread on her bed gleamed. She barely saw it.

She was alone.

She'd been beaten down, the queen showing her just how easily it was to cut Árdís's rage out from under her. She'd seen the price of failure. Would they do that to her?

No.

A spark of hidden defiance beat within her chest like wings.

You will do your duty....

The words swam through her, like careless hands that tore through her will power, shredding it.

I'm sailing home. Forever. Unless you give me a reason to stay....

Haakon didn't know how much those words destroyed her. She couldn't go to him. She'd get him killed.

She'd get them both killed. She'd *seen* what they did to those who thwarted them. If she mated with Sirius—

I cannot.

Silence finally reigned in her head. The press of all her conflicted emotions thickened in her throat. The *dreki* within seemed to hold its breath.

"I cannot stay," she whispered, so softly she could barely hear the words herself, but they filled her from within, smoothing out all of the wretched hollows within her. Flooding her with certainty, with rage, with a sudden decisive intention.

The words seemed to break some sort of spell.

Suddenly, it was all so clear.

If she died, then was it not worth it, for the merest taste of freedom? She couldn't go on living like this, and it had taken both Haakon's reappearance in her life, and the scene in the throne room to make her realize that.

The cage walls seemed to shatter around her, and suddenly she felt like she could take on the world.

Árdís broke into action, stripping her shimmering dress down her body, and tearing open her trunks. She dug through them, discarding silks and velvets, hunting for her fighting leathers, for something warm. She couldn't wear the leathers when she left court—if anyone saw her they'd wonder what she was about—so she dressed herself swiftly in a green wool dress that wouldn't draw any eyes, nor rouse any suspicions. Spare clothing went into the pack she carried when she flew, so she'd have something to wear when she landed.

Once she got this bracelet off.

What else did she need?

A sword. Marduk's sword. The one he'd left for her when she helped him escape, knowing that her brother's defiance had caught the eye of their uncle.

Didn't even say goodbye.... Árdís bared her teeth. She hadn't been ready. She'd been afraid, drawing the cage door shut herself. No more. She was done with hiding her hopes and dreams. Done with bowing to her mother's whims.

She couldn't stay here. She couldn't mate with Sirius, knowing her husband was out there somewhere. And she couldn't throw herself into Haakon's arms with her mother's threats whispering in her ears.

She'd never forgive herself if her actions led to Haakon's death.

But perhaps there was a middle path. A chance for freedom from Sirius, and a means to live her life alone.

There was one place she could flee to, where her mother would not dare follow.

She turned to gather the sword, when the portal opened and a hooded figure appeared.

Malin paused, her brown eyes widening when she saw the pack. Then she swiftly closed the portal that led to the court behind her.

"You're leaving?"

"I can't.... I—" Árdís's shoulders slumped. "I cannot go through with this. I cannot mate with him."

Malin hurried toward her. "You saw what she did to Marek! If you're captured—"

"Then it is worth it, for the few minutes of freedom." She captured Malin's hands. "You don't understand."

"I know the Blackfrost is not of your choice." Malin shuddered. "He wouldn't be mine either. But he's not as cruel as his father or his brothers. And he's the only one who can protect you. It would be a reasonable alliance for you."

"I'm already married," she blurted.

Malin sucked in a sharp breath. "*What?*"

Malin's mother had been human. She'd lived among her mother's family for fifteen years, before power began to whisper through her veins. Unable to shift, she could still light a fire with a snap of her fingers, and so she'd come to court, to find her father and learn to control her elemental magic.

She knew what marriage meant.

Árdís withdrew the chain from her dress. The ring dangled on the end of it, spinning in swift circles. Slowly, she poured the ring into her palm. "When I fled court the first time, there was a man." She closed her eyes. "I loved him. With all my heart. I thought I'd found a place for myself, until my mother sent her nephews to hunt me down. I had to leave him. I didn't dare let my mother know."

Her fingers curled over the ring.

"I thought I could forget him. I thought I could survive the loss of him, as long as I knew he lived. But he's found me. And I cannot go through with this mating bond." Her eyes turned warm. "I cannot do this, Malin. My *dreki* won't allow it."

Malin let out a slow sigh. "Oh, Princess."

"Come with me," she whispered, holding her handmaid's hands. Malin had been her only friend at court. Her mother watched so carefully she did not dare walk among the other *drekling*, or venture into the lower halls, where those *dreki* who'd been her father's faithful warriors tended to reside.

Malin shook her head. "I cannot. My father is here. My younger sister. I have nowhere else to go."

"You could join me. I'm sure my—"

Malin slammed a hand over her mouth. "Don't you dare. If I know nothing of your plans, then I cannot share them."

They stared at each other, and Malin slowly lowered her hand. "I already know too much."

"They'll question you," Árdís said, her mind racing.

"Which is why you need to make it clear I wasn't part of this plan."

A ruthless proposition, but a wise one. She nodded. "Help me pack."

It was easier with Malin by her side. Nobody would think anything of seeing her walking the halls. The *drekling* handmaid slipped back into the court, and returned with a flask of water and food to eat.

"How are you going to sneak out?" Malin whispered. "They'll see you in the skies."

"Unfortunately not." She showed Malin the manacle and explained her sudden deficiencies. "I'm going to try and free Andri from the dungeons. If he's in any condition to fly, then he can help me. If not, I'll use the Reykjavik portal." She slung the pack over her shoulders.

"Good luck." Malin hugged her. "I hope you find your husband, and live a happy life with him."

Árdís's smile waned.

"If I run to him, then they will follow. And they will find him. I dare not stay with him."

Malin took a deep breath and stepped back, presenting Árdís with the ropes. "Please don't put me in the trunk. I don't like the dark."

"You are my only friend," she said, kissing the *drekling* woman's cheek. "I will never forget you. I will never—"

She slammed a psychic assault through Malin's mind, knocking her unconscious in an instant. Malin slumped into her arms, but she'd wake within the hour. Árdís set to work, making sure she tied Malin's hands and feet tightly before gagging her, and leaving her in the middle of the bed.

Time to leave.

There was one *dreki* who could help her, and demand not a thing from her. One *dreki* whose territory the others would not dare enter. She'd be safe there. She'd have her freedom, even if she dared not have her heart.

Rurik had spoken of debts.

Well, now he owed her one himself. If he'd kept his mouth shut, then she'd never be in this predicament.

She was finally going to see her brother again, after all these years.

But first, she needed to track down a certain husband of hers and get this bloody manacle off her wrist so she could fly.

In for a penny, in for a pound...

If she was going to betray her mother, then she might as well do some good while she was at it.

With the manacle still locked around her wrist, Árdís had little choice but to make her way to the lower levels of the court, using the passages the servant *drekling* used. There was a portal down here, available for those *drekling* like Malin, who couldn't manage the shift to *dreki* form. One step through, and she'd be within walking distance to Reykjavik. Nobody from the higher echelons of the court would see her go—she'd be surprised if any of them even knew the portal existed—and the servants dared not rouse the wrath of the queen.

Her heart hammered even as her boots slapped lightly against the rough, rock-hewn steps that tunneled down into the mountain. Haakon's bracelet made her vulnerable, but she couldn't remove it, so she might as well use it.

Nobody would expect her to flee in human form.

And nobody would expect her to break prisoners out of the dungeon while she was at it.

She kept smelling the stink of burning flesh. Tomorrow night, they would burn the *drekling*, Marek, on a bonfire for the sheer audacity in backing his prince. Árdís's heart beat fiercely. She didn't have time for this side excursion, but she knew she'd never be able to look herself in the mirror if she didn't *try* to do something to save him. And then there was Andri, her favorite cousin, who had been involved in Magnus's death. While she didn't *think* Stellan would kill him for his betrayal, there was a small part of her that wasn't entirely certain.

Her footsteps slowed as she reached the dungeons. There were only two prisoners at the moment and so she hoped the guard detail was light.

Her luck held. A swift glance around the corner of the hallway revealed a single *dreki* guard slumped in a chair as he picked at his fingernails.

Now or never. Her breath caught. If she was captured here, before she could even escape the court....

You can do this.

Summoning every inch of hauteur, Árdís dipped her gloved hand into the leather pouch at her belt and withdrew a small glass vial. She'd been thinking of how to disarm the guard for the last hour, but Malin had been the one to provide her with the means. All she had to do was get close enough. Árdís strode out into the hallway as if she owned every right to be there.

The guard noticed her instantly. A trickle of sweat dripped down her spine as she approached and he eased to his feet, one hand resting on the hilt of his sword. His gaze flickered behind her, and then back.

"Are you going to apprehend me?" she mocked.

He blinked at her.

"The sword," she said. "Do you intend to draw it upon me?"

"No." He ripped his hand off the hilt.

"*No?*"

"Princess." A faint begrudging nod.

Árdís stopped directly in front of him, arching a brow. He stared at her for a moment, then realized she intended for him to step out of the way.

"May I ask—"

"Am I not allowed to visit my cousin?" she demanded. Her mother had insisted she stay away from Andri, but what guard would know that? She vaguely recognized him as one of her mother's lickspittles. There were more than a few *dreki* who'd joined the court only in recent years, outcast from their own clans, but welcomed by the queen.

"The queen's orders, princess." His gaze turned flinty. "Nobody may enter without her permission."

"Do you *think* I am here without her blessing?" Árdís laced her tone with pure petulant incredulity. She stepped right up to him, her gloved hand curling around her prize. "I'm her daughter. Her own blood. How dare you question my boundaries."

"I was told—"

"To turn away the court heir?" she sneered.

"No, but—"

"What is your name?" Árdís raked him with an arrogant glare. "I will be sure to mention it to her the next time I see her."

His lips thinned. "Claus, your highness."

"Now get out of my way so I might visit my cousin."

Claus's eyes slowly narrowed. "If her highness would allow me the opportunity to speak... then she would know her cousin is not held within the dungeons. Perhaps the queen failed to mention this when she granted you permission to visit?"

Sweet goddess. Árdís's bravado faltered for a single moment. "Andri's not in the dungeons?"

"He's been contained elsewhere."

What was she going to do? Rescuing her cousin was out of the question. Suspicion already gleamed in Claus's eyes, though he most likely thought her merely up to some mischief. She could hardly demand to know where Andri was.

But she *could* still save Marek.

So be it.

Árdís sighed a little petulantly. "A shame, really."

Then she threw the contents of the small vial in her hand into Claus's face.

The blood of a leviathan. Rare and extremely dangerous to *dreki*. She didn't have time to wonder how Malin had gotten her hands on it. He screamed and clapped a hand to his face, as if burned by acid, and Árdís spun past him and slammed the hilt of her dagger into the base of his skull.

Claus slumped to the floor, and Árdís glanced around, panting hard. Her heartbeat pounded in her ears.

Nothing moved.

The door to the dungeons was locked, but she found the key on the ring at Claus's belt. By the time she'd opened it, he was starting to stir. *Dreki* males were incredibly difficult to injure. Grabbing him under the armpits, she hauled him through into the hallway beyond, and shut the door.

Whipping her leather belt loose from her waist, she bound his hands behind him, then opened one of the empty cells and hauled him inside.

Claus wheezed as she dropped him in the moldy straw. "P-princess?"

Árdís slammed the cell door shut and locked it, before she dared breathe easy. Nobody would hear him calling for help. The dungeons had been designed to stifle all noise. But who knew when the next guard rotation was planned?

Time to find Marek. All she had to do was follow her nose.

He was in the third cell down the hallway.

"Marek?" she called softly.

No answer, but she could hear someone shifting inside.

Árdís unlocked the door, and Marek scrambled to his feet, his hands bound to the wall as he squinted at her.

"Princess?" His brown eyes widened in shock.

"Hush." She hurried to his side, rifling through the keys for one small enough to fit the lock on his steel manacles. They hadn't even bothered with spell work, as if assured a mere *drekling* could not escape.

"What are you doing?" He slumped against his chains again, as if she presented no threat to him, and he no longer had to maintain any pretense at good health. The brand in the middle of his forehead looked angry and swollen, and he'd been beaten good and proper, by the way he held himself so stiffly.

She finally found the right key, and freed him from the manacles. "I'm getting you out of here."

"You're... *what?*" Marek rubbed at his wrists, but the first step he took ended in a limp. He stopped short, firelight gleaming in his eyes. "I can barely walk. If they catch you—"

"They're not going to catch me," she replied, with false bravado, as she slipped beneath his shoulder. "We're using the servant's portal."

"You're coming with me? Why are you doing this?"

Árdís flinched. Perhaps she'd played her part too well over the years. "Because I can no longer stand to watch my mother torment her people." Their eyes met. "You're not the only one who remembers what it was like when my father ruled this court. I'm not brave. I'm not strong enough to defy her—not openly. But perhaps there is another who can."

"The prince," he whispered, and hope flared to life in his eyes.

"Prince Rurik," she agreed, "but we need to hurry if we're going to have a chance to flee to his side."

They took a step and Marek's weight sagged against her.

"I'm sorry. Someone hit me in the shin with an iron bar." He was trying not to limp as they staggered out into the hallway, but it was clear he wouldn't be moving fast.

Árdís bit her lip. "I doubt anyone will see us."

She hoped.

Claus slammed against his cell door as they passed it, and Árdís stifled a small scream. Dust shivered around the doorframe. She hadn't counted on that. *Dreki* males were difficult to contain at the best of times, what with their inhuman strength and magic.

So she locked the main door to the dungeons behind them, just in case he did get free. Marek stared. "The cell won't hold him for long."

"I know. This way," Árdís said, and backtracked to the servant's passages, where it was dark and *dreki* would be few and far between. She found the bag and sword she'd left down here, and then paused by the healer's storeroom to steal a makeshift crutch for Marek and some healing balm for his burn.

"Thank you," he breathed, looking at her as if he'd never seen her before.

They could risk a little light here. Whispering in old Norse under her breath, she released the small spell Malin had taught her, and the emerald the girl had given her began to glow as she reached the darkest bowels of the catacombs. Purebred *dreki* like she had no need of spell craft when they could channel pure Fire, but those like Malin made do with spells. She'd never before had to consider what it would be like to live like the *drekling*.

Shunned by the purebreds. Considered *less*.

Made to serve the *dreki* and the court, or be ostracized forever.

Or worse, killed to keep the bloodlines pure.

Marek's fear ate away at her as they scuttled down the dark stairs. If they were captured, he'd be granted a particularly gruesome death, while she might escape such a sentence.

Almost there. The passage delivered her into the first of several wide cellars. Hurrying past barrels of wine and hanging slabs of dried meat, she ducked through another small passage, and found herself in the dark. Marek hopped along behind her, painstakingly slow. Her pulse hammered. The walls were rough-hewn here, as if carved by a pickaxe and not magic. The portal hummed somewhere ahead of her, but it felt like miles with Marek's hobbling gait. She couldn't resist slipping ahead, trying to scout for danger.

A shift of leather on stone alerted her to the fact she wasn't alone as she entered the next cellar. Árdís muted the light with a whisper.

"Don't move," she told Marek on a thought-thread. *"I can hear someone."*

Instantly she was plunged into darkness.

She wasn't alone, however. She could sense someone moving through the oppressive dark with whisper-silent feet. Her heart leapt into her throat, and she pressed her back to the wall, barely daring to breathe.

Fingers clicked.

Light suddenly burst into being as one by one the torches on the wall burst into flame.

"Who's there?" Árdís whispered, putting her hand to the hilt of her sword and blinking.

A mocking drawl lit through the cellar. "Well, if it isn't my sweet betrothed. Wherever can you be going, Árdís? Especially with a sword that doesn't belong to you, and a pack full of clothes."

Sirius dissolved from the shadows.

CHAPTER SIX

ÁRDIS'S HAND WENT instantly to the hilt of the sword. "Creeping around in the dark again, Sirius? It suits you."

He ignored her, and made a small gesture with his hand. The fire in the muted lantern in his hand flared higher, highlighting the stark planes of his face. A villain like him should have showed some outward sign of his black heart, but the face the lamplight lovingly caressed was blessed by the gods.

"Creeping around in the dark *doesn't* suit you," he said, in that rough-velvet voice. "People might notice."

"What?" she scoffed, turning her entire body to face him so she'd have room to move. "That I was using the back tunnels? Perhaps it's the quickest way to the jousting rooms. I do have a sparring appointment with Master Innick most days, even after that debacle in the throne room. And the main cavern is awash with your father's louts. I was trying to avoid them."

"Avoid them? Or me?"

"Why differentiate?"

He smiled faintly. There had never been any love lost between the pair of them, and they both knew it.

Sirius set the lantern down, his long hair streaming down his back. He'd bound some of it back with a leather thong. "You're running away."

"Why ever would I do such a thing?" She mustered all of the haughtiness she could, and turned away from him. "What I am is late. Master Innick might be waiting for me. I'll leave you to your musty cellars."

A hand grasped her forearm. "You're lying."

Árdís found herself turned and shoved back against the wall. A gasp escaped her. She'd never been manhandled in her life—unless one counted the time her husband tried to kidnap her.

"Princess?" Marek.

"Don't show yourself," she sent back, surprised at the strength of his telepathy. *"He doesn't know you're here. Yet."*

Sirius glanced around, and then looked down at her. A new fear began to lick through her as she realized how little space existed between them. He didn't know Marek was there, but even if he did, what did it matter? It wouldn't take the Blackfrost long to dispatch an injured *drekling*. Nobody else would hear her scream, nobody would know to come looking for her.... He could do anything he desired, and though she'd fight, she knew she couldn't overwhelm him. Sirius had been training for battle since birth, and his sheer size dwarfed her, even if she *could* access her elemental magic. Curse Haakon for weakening her so.

The knife at the small of her back felt like it grew hot. She'd have to take him by surprise.

And make it hurt.

"I swear, if you think to touch me," she hissed, "then I'll do my best to geld you."

It took a second to get the knife, and another to drive it forward, angled down toward his groin. Sirius's eyes flared wide, then he caught her wrist and twisted. The knife scored flesh; she smelled the hot coppery scent of it. And then he brought his other hand down in a sharp chop.

Pain echoed up her arm, but she didn't dare let go of the weapon. It was her only hope. She'd never get the sword free in time, and with her back to the corner, she'd be hampered by both walls. Not enough room to swing it.

His shoulder drove into her chest, and Árdís slammed against the wall, the breath in her chest escaping as though her lungs were a set of fireplace bellows someone had compressed. Strong thumbs drove into the tendon in her hand, and she caught a flash of Sirius's face up close, the meager light turning his irises to hot lumps of coal.

Tiamat's breath, it hurt.

She twisted her head, trying to find some space, but he had her pinned. The pressure on her fingers increased, and Árdís felt him take the knife from her. *No.*

But there was nothing she could do about it.

Sirius tossed the knife behind him with a clatter, and held his hands up, showing her his empty palms. "I don't intend to hurt you," he said in that deep voice.

Árdís's breath caught. She wiped her mouth, and pushed herself upright. In what world did he think she'd believe him? Her gaze flickered to the knife.

"You'd know if I were lying," he told her. "The same way I knew you were. *Dreki* cannot lie, Princess. Our very words are power, made to shape the world. You should be more careful with them."

"What part of *'I was trying to geld you'* sounded like a lie?"

He grunted, and she saw him shift his weight onto his right leg. Blood trickled down his left thigh. "That, at least, was the truth. You came remarkably closer than anyone else."

"A shame I missed. You might have had to forgo the pleasures of our bonding night. Oh, but it seems you'll have to somehow convince me to agree to the mating bond first, and let me assure you these words are the truth: I would rather rot in Helheim than *ever* mate with you."

"No offense, Princess," he growled, "but I'm as eager to mate with you as you are to mate with me."

What?

"You expect me to believe that?" She was one of the paths to being named heir of the *Zini* court. The other was to confront her elder brother, Rurik, and battle him for the right. Many *dreki* had tried the second route in the past thirty years, and none had returned.

Magnus included, it seemed.

Her eyes narrowed. "You're your father's son, Sirius. What's the motto of the *Zilittu* clan again? To take and to hold? My mother's about to name you her heir, and I won't believe you're going to allow someone else the chance to use me to get to that throne. Roar would see this move and swoop in before either of us could blink. So what are you really doing here?"

"Let me assure you of this truth: I don't want to mate with you. I don't even like you very much."

Árdís's heart kicked a little faster. There were ways to twist words—to sculpt them so carefully one had to really follow the twist to see what a *dreki* was truly saying. But *I don't want to mate with you* left no margin for mistakes.

There has to be a twist.

"You don't want to be named heir?" she questioned suspiciously. Whether he liked her or not, Sirius wanted the line of succession to be very clear in everyone's mind.

Sirius rubbed at his knuckles, and when he looked up at her, his blue eyes were searing. "I didn't say that."

There was the twist.

If he didn't want to marry her, and yet he wanted to plant himself in the line of succession....

Árdís scrambled away from him, looking longingly at her sword across the chamber. All it would take would be one *dreki* princess with her throat cut. The *dreki* whispered through her veins, alarmed by her fear, but the blasted manacle locked her away from the other half of her nature.

Sirius knelt, picking up the knife he'd taken off her. Despite the handsome cast of his features, his expression was cold. "I told you I wasn't going to hurt you."

"If I recall correctly, the exact words were, 'I don't *intend* to hurt you.' There's a world of difference in that sentence."

He looked up and held the knife out to her, hilt first. "I don't want to hurt you. I'm not here to hurt you. I just want you to listen to me."

Árdís stared at the knife. "Mating or murder. They're the only two ways I can see you getting what you want."

"There's another way."

Another way? She couldn't— And then she realized what he meant. "Exile."

"It seems we're of a mind." Sirius unfolded himself slowly, and reached for her hand with exquisite gentleness. He folded her fingers around the hilt, his expression beseeching. "We both saw what happened in that throne room. Let's pretend I'm correct and you're not really heading for your training session with Master Innick. Let's pretend I know what that ring you wear on your chain represents, and that I saw the look on both you and your mortal lover's faces when I chased you from the inn...."

93

She pressed a hand to her leather bodice. Few *dreki* moved among mortals. Even fewer paid attention to their customs. "You saw him?"

"I could smell him all over you. And now you're leaving, and that suits both of us," he said. "Go to him. I don't care."

She still couldn't quite fathom it. "You wanted to mate with me eleven years ago. You made that quite clear."

It was one of the reasons she'd first fled the court, yearning for something more. And she'd found it for nearly three glorious years, until her mother finally tracked her down.

A slight sideways sweep of his lashes. "*Dreki* change."

"Give me one good reason to believe you." She stepped closer to him, putting the tip of the knife to his unprotected breast. Sirius glared at her, but he didn't back away, and Árdís tipped her chin up stubbornly. "Because I never promised not to hurt *you*. And I find it quite difficult to believe you suddenly changed your mind about wanting to mate with me. I'm not stupid enough to think 'I don't like you' is a strong enough reason."

"You don't want to mate with *me*."

"I don't have any good reason to do so," she hissed. "I despise you and mating with you earns me nothing but a bond we'd both hate. My motives aren't opaque."

He looked away.

Árdís pressed forward, the tip of the knife finding resistance. Blood welled on his shirt. "You're hiding something."

"You're hiding many things—"

"And I'm not leaving until you tell me what you're hiding. I don't trust you not to immediately turn me over to my mother, or to set my uncle's pack of *dreki* dregs upon me. Maybe you don't want to get your hands dirty, but you're content to let them do it for you." She looked into his eyes, determined to call his bluff. "So I'm not leaving until I hear the truth, even if I *do* have to mate with you as a consequence."

Stalemate.

The pair of them glared at each other, until Sirius's gaze dropped to the collar of her gown. She didn't know what he intended as he reached for her, but he tugged the silver chain around her throat free, his fist curling around her marriage ring. "Who is he?"

"If you think I'm going to give you a name, then you're out of your mind. And he's gone from my life."

Sirius slowly opened his fist and examined the plain ring. "And yet your heart still belongs to him. Or you wouldn't be wearing this."

"It's none of your business." She jerked it from his hand and stuffed it back within her bodice. Then she shoved him back against the wall and put the blade directly against his throat. "Enough games, tell me what you're hiding."

"The same thing you are," he spat.

Árdís froze.

"You're married?"

It was impossible.

Sirius traveled occasionally, but there'd been no hint of a human in his life, and he'd never bothered to correct his father's vehement intention to grind all humans beneath his heel.

"Not married."

"Mated."

"Not mated." The fury showed in his eyes.

And suddenly she knew.

There was one *very*, very good reason he wouldn't wish to bind himself to her. Árdís backed away, lowering the knife. "You found her, didn't you? The other half of your soul; your twin flame."

Her people called it *kataru libbu*, a bastardized version of Sumerian that at its most basic meant an alliance of the heart, and yet was so much more.

Soul mate. The missing piece. Forever.

One that was undeniably yours, and likewise.

Her heart felt like it clenched into a tight little ball. She'd loved and she'd married, but she'd also hoped to find something more between her and Haakon.

Yet, it was *dreki* males who first knew.

And without that instinct, Árdís had never been entirely certain.

"Who is she?" she whispered, jealous of him all of a sudden.

Sirius pushed away from the wall, looming over her. "It doesn't matter. She's nobody. And nothing will ever come of it. But just as you would prefer to keep his name to yourself, so would I."

"Ylve?"

"Sweet goddess, no! Who would ever lie with that bitch?"

Whoever it was, she had to have arrived in the court beneath Hekla sometime in the last ten years for him to change his mind about acceding to his father's wishes and taking Árdís as a mate.

Sirius captured her jaw. "I can almost see you thinking. Her identity is none of your concern. Just know she's my reason to want to avoid this mating. Is it a good enough reason to trust me?"

"Good enough. Because if you betray me, I'll tell your father everything you just said. Whoever she is, she's clearly unsuitable or you would have pursued her openly."

"The second you do so, you condemn her to death," he growled fiercely.

"Good. Maybe it will help whittle the ranks of your father's followers."

His grip tightened unconsciously. "She's not... she's not someone my father would care for. And I want power. I cannot have both."

Which left only those who had been born in Árdís's father's court. *Her* people. Those she'd fought so hard for, until her mother finally found the one thing guaranteed to drive her away.

"You want to tell my father?" He laughed bitterly. "Then go ahead, Árdís. How will you feel when the blood on your hands is that of someone who loves *you*?"

It struck her deeply.

"I won't say a word." Backing away, she held the knife between them. "I'm going. You get your wish and so do I. Allow me enough time to get as far away as I can before you rouse the alert."

"Judging from the presence of the *drekling* in the next cellar, I think the alert shouldn't be too far away," he said softly. "Just how *did* you get past Claus?"

Árdís froze. "What *drekling*?"

He sighed. "I can smell the brand on him, Árdís. And you've both been making enough noise to make it easy to track you. You're playing a dangerous game."

"You're not going to stop Marek from escaping?"

"Father will be furious." Sirius's lashes obscured his eyes as he glanced down, fingering his dagger. "And I might be able to smell him, but it appears I didn't see a thing."

Árdís released her held breath. "Why?"

A faint malicious smile kicked at the edges of his mouth. "*Because* father will be furious. And I don't particularly enjoy seeing *drekling* burned alive. Just don't get caught. Stellan would like nothing more than to bring you to heel, and he'll most likely insist I do the honor."

"I didn't know you cared."

"I don't." The Blackfrost gave her a dark look. "But if I'm forced to do his bidding, then my mate will never, ever allow me near her."

Who could it be?

For a second she felt an odd sense of kinship with him. Both of them were forced to play a role they despised. But she was taking her chance to escape it.

"All you have to do is defy your father, just once," she whispered. "Then you could have it all. You're strong enough to challenge him. And if you don't like what they're doing to the court—"

"Oh, Árdís." A humorless smile stretched over his mouth. "If only we could all be so naive. My father has never been the threat." Sirius reached out with his hand, curling his fingers to snuff the flame of the torches. "Go. Before I think myself a fool for letting you escape. Before your enemies rise to tear you down. Go. And don't come back."

She didn't hesitate any longer.

Árdís hurried back to Marek's side, and together they fled.

CHAPTER
SEVEN

GULLS PINWHEELED OVERHEAD, squabbling among themselves for scraps. Haakon watched as his men loaded the ship, helping to haul some of the heavier items aboard. The waters of Reykjavik harbor gleamed like the flat plane of a mirror, and ships bobbed in the water here and there. Rising over the town in the distance, snow-capped mountains taunted him.

Somewhere out there lay Hekla, several days ride to the east.

It wasn't as though he expected to see a *dreki* in the skies, but some part of him hoped.

No matter what she'd told him.

But the sun was setting, and the ship was loaded. His men laughed as they slapped each other's backs and headed down the gangplank for one last night in Reykjavik.

Twelve hours, and he would leave these shores forever.

"Have you made up your mind yet?" Gunnar asked.

Haakon startled, and tore his gaze from the skies. "We sail with the dawn tide."

"Aye, but are you coming with us?"

A knot of uncertainty lodged in his gut. Haakon dragged his fur-lined gloves off, his breath fogging the cool night air. "I don't know yet."

"Bloody hell," Gunnar muttered. "There's nothing here for you anymore."

"My head knows that," he replied, tucking the gloves behind his belt. "But my heart is not yet ready to accept it. She's here, Gunnar. A part of me doesn't want to leave. Not until.... Not until I'm certain there's no hope remaining."

And she'd kissed him, even as she'd told him to go and raise children with another woman. He could still taste that kiss on his mouth. The decision tore him in two. He'd meant to confront her and demand answers, but every answer she'd given him had only roused more questions.

"I thought she told you there was no future between you."

"Aye." He hadn't mentioned everything to the men, just granting them a curt shake of the head before he sank himself into a night of drinking. Gunnar knew more than most, but not everything. Only Tormund held that honor. "And then she kissed me. If we hadn't been so rudely interrupted...."

"She's no good for you. You know the truth. She told you to go with her own lips. And yet here you are, twisting yourself into knots again." Gunnar scowled. "I wish you'd never laid eyes upon that—"

"Careful." She might be deceitful, but she was still his wife.

Gunnar sighed, slapping a hand on his shoulder as they turned back to the inn for one last night. "Bloody cursed *dreki*. Life was simpler when we just had to kill them."

Inside the inn, the men were settling in with tankards. Haakon found one shoved into his hand and sipped at the warm beer. He hadn't the heart for it tonight. But Tormund and Bjorn saw him angling across the inn toward the stairs and cut him off before he could vanish.

"Have a drink with us!" Tormund said, forcing him onto one of the benches, a heavy hand upon his shoulder.

"I want a clear head tomorrow." There was nothing worse than sailing on a gutful of bad beer.

Bjorn scowled, but Tormund grinned at him through his beard. "Bjorn and I have a bet. I don't think you're going to be on that ship when it sails."

"He'd be a fool if he wasn't," Bjorn muttered.

Tormund ruffled the boy's hair. "You're young. You've not yet known the lure of a woman who's captured your heart. It's a siren song, boy, and once a man hears it, he's more than willing to throw himself overboard for the slimmest chance he'll taste heaven before he drowns."

"I told her I was leaving," Haakon said sharply, swilling a mouthful of beer. "I meant it."

Tormund marched his fingers across the table idly. "Aye. You meant it. I could see that when she left. I could also see what a man looks like when he's got his hopes up."

"That wasn't what you said," Bjorn added. "You didn't use the word hope at all."

"I didn't want to blister my cousin's poor innocent ears," Tormund shot back.

Haakon rubbed at his eyebrow. "Tormund—"

"She kissed you, aye?"

"She told me to go find another woman and beget children."

"That's not fair," Bjorn broke in. "You can't influence him."

"Didn't hear that rule." Tormund shoved his empty tankard toward Bjorn. "Go fill this for me. And get another one for Haakon."

"Fill it yourself."

Tormund lifted his brows, and Bjorn straightened to his full height, growling under his breath as he stomped off.

Tormund rested his elbows on the table and leaned forward. "You're a bloody fool if you get on that ship. I know what the rest of them think—that it's been a long seven years hunting for a bloody ghost. They're weary for home. They don't want to see you hurting anymore. But I know the truth. You'll carry that woman in your heart to the grave. I saw it in your face the second she stormed into your life all those years ago. She might have told you to go marry and breed fat, happy children, but then why is she wearing your fucking ring still? Something made her leave you. Something drove her away. And I don't think she's told you the full truth of that yet."

Haakon's gaze sharpened on his cousin's face. "She was wearing the manacle. She couldn't lie to me."

"Aye, but did you ask the right fucking questions?"

His breath arrested. Jesus. "You're not helping."

Tormund shot him a grin. "I've got twenty Danish kroner riding on this. I don't intend to help."

Haakon drained his tankard. Nothing Tormund said was a revelation. The same arguments had been ringing in his ears for days.

But she would have to meet him halfway.

He wasn't going to waste the next seven years of his life hoping she'd give him the time of day. "It's her choice," he said, slamming the tankard down. "Not mine. Not this time."

"And if she does come to you before you leave?"

Haakon swallowed the flash of hope that seared his insides. "Then I don't know what I'm going to do."

"I do." Gunnar snorted, leaning on his shoulder as he slung his leg over the bench Haakon was sitting on. "You'll stay. Despite all argument to the contrary. Despite good common fucking sense."

Tormund hesitated. "Just don't—"

"Do anything foolish," Haakon promised. "I'm not going to storm the *dreki* court singlehandedly."

"Wasn't what you were saying a month ago," Gunnar grumbled, slinking down onto the seat on the other side of him.

Some of the men had had to restrain him. "I wasn't in the right frame of mind a month ago."

After all, he'd just discovered that the wife he'd feared dead, or worse, had been the *dreki*. It wasn't his finest hour.

"You have less than twelve hours." Tormund drummed his fingers on the table.

"Thank you. I hadn't noticed."

"Might as well get some sleep. It's going to be a long sail home," Gunnar grunted.

"She'll come," Tormund disagreed, shaking his head. "I'll put money on it."

Gunnar reached out and offered his hand. "Fifty kroner."

"Done." Tormund grinned, clasping hands with him.

"Do you mind not betting on my future," Haakon muttered. "Where the hell is Bjorn with the beer?"

"Thought you wanted a clear head?" Gunnar asked.

He'd changed his mind.

"I told you, I'm not the one making the decision. It's been three days. I told her I was leaving. She knows I'm sailing with the dawn. If there's some part of her that still holds a place for me in her heart, then she has one last chance to admit it. I'll wait for her until morning."

"And if she's not here?"

He dragged his gaze toward the window, sighting the harbor. "Then I'll set sail with the rest of you. And never return."

Árdís had never resented her mortal form more than she did in that moment.

Rain poured from the skies in a steady curtain, as she hauled the donkey Marek sat upon, up the steep slope. At first she'd been grateful, for it would make it harder for anything in the skies to see her, and few *dreki* would be flying on a night like this, but after almost six hours of being wet and miserable, she was starting to wish for clear skies. And the donkey—stabled near the servant's portal for their use—might have been trained to accept the scent of *drekling*, but it clearly didn't like her.

How long would it take for her to be missed from court? The portal had cut her journey by days, but the press of time still weighed upon her.

It was doubtful anyone would miss them. Not until dark when the guard's rotation changed, according to Marek. That should give them at least a full day's head start.

But what was a full day on foot, compared to a single hour in the skies for most *dreki?*

They wouldn't be looking for her on the ground, true, but it still made her feel entirely too vulnerable.

The blasted bracelet around her wrist made shape-shifting impossible, and it was becoming very easy to hate it.

"I swear to all the gods, Haakon, if I ever get this off...." The threat died as she slipped on the slope and almost fell flat on her face. Árdís grazed her palms as she slammed onto a boulder, and lay there, gasping hard.

"Princess?" Marek called.

How on earth did mortals manage to live their entire lives in this form?

It would be easier to just return to court and accept her fate....

What difference did it make if she was bound to mate Sirius tomorrow night, or at some indeterminate date in the future? She'd made it clear she would not invite him into her bed, and if Sirius had found his twin flame, then he wasn't going to insist.

Haakon would vanish on the winds of a tide in a matter of days, and he'd be safe forever.

But Marek would be slaughtered.

And her mother would never allow her out of her sight again.

No.

"I'm fine," she called, as Marek tried to dismount.

She couldn't accept the mating bond with Sirius without at least attempting to break free of her mother's chains. Rurik had done it. Marduk had done it. It was time she threw them off herself.

No matter what it costs you?

Cursing under her breath, she forced herself back to her feet. She'd deal with other *dreki* when they became a problem. She was made of sterner stuff than this. She wouldn't melt.

She was, however, freezing. And her back ached from the heavy oiled pack she carried. She was fairly certain she'd be moaning about her feet too, if she could feel them.

"Quit your whining," she muttered, trying to haul the sealskin hood up over her forehead. A single trickle of water slithered down her neck and between her cleavage, which was a sudden shock to her dry body.

Nothing important was ever gained without a little discomfort.

And Marek had suffered worse.

She slogged through acres of mud, gritting her teeth and trying to hide as much of herself beneath the oiled sealskin she wore as possible. Reykjavik had to be nearby. It all looked different on the ground, but surely they were close.

"How far?" she called.

"Three miles, perhaps."

They had to move faster.

For the day was swiftly giving over to night, which meant her head start would soon vanish as her mother started to wonder where she was.

And Haakon had promised to sail with the dawn tide.

"You wished to see me?" Sirius called as he strode through the enormous golden doors that marked the *dreki* throne room. The room stood empty now, apart from his father, aunt, bastard brother and a handful of guards, but Amadea preferred to make her demands from a position of power.

The summons had come almost half an hour ago, and he'd stalled as long as he could.

His father scowled down from the dais, his hand resting lightly on his sister's shoulder. Queen Amadea regarded Sirius with glittering eyes, but she lifted a hand to rest her fingers on her brother's and said nothing.

The two of them had shared a womb, but the alliance between his father and aunt always made Sirius a little uncomfortable. It wasn't a sexual relationship as some of the court whispered, but Stellan would kill—or die—for his sister. And if forced to make a choice between the queen and one of his sons, Sirius knew which way his father's choice would fall.

One good reason to stay in the queen's graces. Stellan was dangerous, but Amadea was a snake.

"You're late."

"I was busy," he replied. "I only just received your message. What's wrong?"

"Busy doing what?" Stellan demanded.

Sirius began to remove his gloves, his lips thinning. "I was seeing my brother, if you must know. Andri's starting to wake from his healing sleep, though it's barely begun to mend his torn flesh. I wanted to be there when he did, to find out exactly what happened when he and Magnus confronted Rurik."

Because a part of him didn't quite believe his father and aunt's version of events.

"Perhaps it's a good thing to have the vision of Andri's torment so fresh in your mind," Stellan seethed. "It should warn you not to fail me in this quest."

"I never fail." No matter what the cost. "And what quest?"

His heart beat an unruly pulse in his chest, but that was too dangerous and his father's threat lingered. He'd seen the bruises on his brother's ribs, and face. Seen the broken jaw, and the blackened eye. Someone had beaten his little brother half to death, and he knew it hadn't been his cousin, Prince Rurik.

Had Stellan enjoyed it? Or had he given the task to Roar? A side glance showed his bastard brother watching proceedings with a faint tilt of amusement on his lips.

"It seems you already have," Amadea said, her rings glittering as she stared him down. "Árdís is missing."

He'd spent all night practicing his look of shock. One hand went to the hilt of his sword. "What do you mean, she's missing?"

"There's no sign of her within Hekla," Amadea replied, leaning forward. "Her cloak and boots are gone, along with her riding leathers. Her brother's sword isn't in the chest where she thinks she hides it. And nobody has seen any sign of her."

Sirius bowed his head. "You shouldn't be surprised. She made it quite clear she would refuse the mating bond."

A fist thumped against the throne. "It doesn't matter what she intended," Stellan snarled. "If you were truly my heir, then you'd not have given her a choice. This is a disaster! The entire court hangs on a hinge, and I can almost hear them whispering rebellion in the halls. Árdís was our key to controlling this rebellion."

"I am many things, Father," Sirius said coldly, glaring up at the man who'd sired him. "But I am *not* the type of man to force a woman where she does not wish to go."

"No," Stellan sneered. "You never did have the balls for it. It's a pity I didn't send *you* to challenge Rurik. Your brother, Magnus, was the better *dreki* all along. He wouldn't have hesitated to do what was necessary with Árdís."

"If one considers a lack of conscience a boon," he snapped, "then yes, Magnus was better." It was one thing to wonder if his father wished he had died in Magnus's place, quite another to hear it spoken. "We are *dreki*. Is there no honor among us?"

"You're starting to sound like the king," Amadea said.

"And we all know what happened to your mate," Sirius replied, his voice falling into a quiet sort of maliciousness. "Is that a threat?"

"It's a warning," Amadea whispered. "Don't push me, Sirius. Not right now."

They glared at each other.

Then Stellan gestured for a pair of his warriors to shut the doors. "You have a loose tongue. That can be dangerous."

"Everything is dangerous right now. We are outsiders in a court that plots against us," Amadea hissed, and for a moment she looked very much like her daughter—if Árdís had ever been the type for pure malice. "Regardless of your feelings in the matter, we need my daughter back and mated."

"No matter what I must do?" Sirius asked coldly, the *no* on the tip of his tongue.

"If my brother is so hesitant to do what needs to be done, then why not give another a chance?" Roar called, making his presence known.

"You're not my brother," Sirius said in a whisper-soft voice.

Just a by-blow by some forgotten woman who'd left the boy on his father's doorstep. Roar was one of the few half-breeds who could actually shift, which made him *dreki*. His illegitimacy had never bothered Sirius—but the hunger in his eyes did. If there was anyone who shared Magnus's innate sense of cruelty, it was Roar. But even Magnus had despised him.

The other *dreki* smirked. "You're right. I'm starting to wonder if there's any of Father's blood in you at all?"

"Enough," the queen cried, slamming her palms on the arms of the throne. "Enough," she repeated, and somehow managed to hiss the word, despite the lack of appropriate consonants.

Shoving to her feet, she glared at both of them. "I will have my daughter back, or I will have the heads of everyone in this throne room."

Silence fell across the room.

Sirius slowly bowed his head under her fierce regard and felt the others doing the same. Sometimes he had to wonder at the queen's hold on sanity. What he didn't wonder about was whether she could do it.

They called Amadea the witch-queen, and her powers were fierce enough to rattle the stars. No *dreki* at this court could match them.

She, alone, had the gift of Chaos magic that had been bequeathed to her by the ancient goddess, Tiamat.

"Find her, Sirius," Amadea told him. "Or suffer my wrath."

Perhaps he shouldn't have called Árdís naive. For if so, then he suffered the same fate.

He should have known Amadea would never let her daughter go free.

"I will do my best, but we all know Árdís is cunning. Where would she go?" Sirius asked, lifting his head to meet her gaze. Perhaps he could make an "attempt," and when it failed, he could succumb to the queen's viciousness and bear the punishment. Surely his father wouldn't allow another of his sons to die. "If I'm going to find the princess, then I shall need some place to start."

"I'm glad you've come to your senses," the queen rasped, sinking back onto her throne.

"So am I," Stellan murmured to him, as he strode to the front of the dais. "Bring the girl forward."

A startled scream broke the silence of the cavernous throne room, and Sirius whipped toward the sound, his heart sinking into his stomach.

Lor, one of his father's most brutal guards, dragged a young woman forward, a fist in her curly brown hair. A young woman with skin like cream and a heart-shaped face that haunted his dreams. A young woman whose scent of wild grass and sunshine wrapped around his heart, taunting him at every step he took in this accursed court. She'd been shielded from view by Stellan's *dreki*.

Malin.

No.

It took every ounce of will Sirius owned not to simply rip the bastard's throat out, but he knew if he took half a step toward her it would be an almost fatal mistake. She was his. But declaring for her would earn them both little more than a brutal, torturous death, and he didn't miss the sudden sharpening of Roar's eyes as Sirius stiffened.

If he wasn't trapped so poorly in this dilemma, Sirius might almost have laughed at the hand fate had dealt him—Árdís had not missed the mark by much. Malin was so beyond unsuitable, his father would rather kill him than see him mate her.

And Malin….

Stellan would do far worse to her.

It was the only thing reining his impulses in.

"Let me go!" Malin cried, beating at Lor's thigh with her fist.

"If there's anyone who will know the princess's plans, it will be her maid." Stellan's cold blue eyes locked on the young *dreki* woman. "And she'll speak them before I'm through with her."

Sirius stepped between them, trying to contain the sudden fierce surge of the *dreki* within. "She's a nothing. A nobody. Why would she know anything about Árdís's intentions?" He tried to laugh. "She's not even a full-blooded *dreki*. She's lucky Árdís even glanced at her, let alone took her as a handmaid."

"They're cunning, these half-breeds." Stellan never took his eyes off the girl. "Scuttling around court in the shadows, listening to whispers.... I see them everywhere. We should never have accepted these bastard *drekling* scraps into the court. If the princess confided in anyone, her maid will know about it."

"Someone needed to do the drudge work," the queen mused. "We've been over this."

Stellan shot his sister a sharp glance, but subsided.

"I don't know anything!" Malin cried desperately. "The last I saw of her highness was when I walked into her rooms to bring her supper. The next thing I remember is waking up on her bed, with my hands and ankles tied. I swear! I didn't even see who hit me. I didn't realize she was missing until Lor—Lord Lor—found me."

"You lie," Stellan said.

"I swear on my *dreki* blood, I do not, my prince."

It was the worst thing she could have said.

Stellan moved to draw his knife, and before he even knew what was happening, Sirius had his hand on his father's hilt, forcing it back into its sheath.

"Let *me*," he gasped, as his father's shocked eyes turned to him. He'd crossed the distance between them in an instant, and it had not been a conscious decision. Control hung by a thread. "Let me do the questioning. Árdís is my betrothed, after all. You want me to be hard? Then let me do this. Let me regain your trust. I'll take Malin to the dungeon and make sure I know every little secret the bitch has ever known. This is my future we're talking about. If anyone's riding after Árdís, it's going to be *me*."

"Why not make it a hunt?" Roar mocked behind him. "Whoever brings her back first gets the princess's hand in marriage. I think dear Sirius has already proven he can't keep a mate in hand."

He wanted to gut his illegitimate half brother in that moment. But instead he held his father's gaze, willing Stellan to give Malin to him.

The only other alternative was to kill every other *dreki* in the room, and as much as the *dreki* within him surged to the surface, he didn't like his chances in handling over six full-grown *dreki* warriors.

Not enough to risk *her*.

Stellan withdrew his hand from the knife, allowing Sirius to take a slow breath.

"Do as you will with her then," Stellan commanded. "The girl's yours. But I think Roar has a good point. If you were more careful, the princess would not have had a chance to run. And you've disappointed me enough today." Stellan turned to survey the room. "Let it be known, whichever of my sons brings back the princess Árdís will take the prize; her hand as a mate."

Roar smirked as he clasped hands with one of the guards, and another clapped him on the back.

Sirius ignored them, and strode to Malin's side. Sweet Tiamat, Mother of Chaos. That had been far too close for comfort. As she tried to scramble away from him, he snatched her up, his hand curling around her upper arm as he jerked her against him. The *dreki* within him stopped pressing at the inside of his skin, determined to get out. It could scent her, and the smell eased its protective urges a mere fraction. Enough to breathe again, anyway. His other hand locked around the back of her neck, and he shoved her toward the enormous gold doors.

It was the first time he'd ever laid hands upon her.

He did not dare allow the act to fall in front of his father or the others, but he allowed his thumb to caress the side of her neck gently, just once, as they left the throne room. The second they were through the doors, she twisted in his grip like a weasel, raking her nails down his arm sharply enough to draw blood.

Sirius grabbed her by both wrists, forcing her back against the wall with her hands pinned above her head. "Be still, damn you."

Every inch of her soft body melded to his. His gaze dropped, unerringly, to her mouth.

Malin spat in his face. "I'll tell you nothing."

"Yes, you will."

Her life depended upon it. He wiped the spittle from his face with his sleeve, his hands softening on her wrists.

"Careful, brother," Roar mocked, as he passed by, two of Stellan's warriors at his heels. "She might begin to think she has actual claws. You're weak enough to be wounded by them."

"Anytime you want to challenge me, let me know."

Roar merely smiled, walking backward with his arms spread. "But only the weaker of the two warriors challenges the other. And I'm not entirely certain I should simper at your feet. Besides, why bother? I'm off to win the princess. Have fun in the dungeons with the half-breed. Perhaps you can challenge me when I return with Árdís."

Curse Fate. She had to be laughing at him. Allowing Árdís to leave had caused more of an uproar than he'd planned. He couldn't allow this to spiral out of control any further.

He needed the princess back.

Only she could speak up for Malin's protection and escape unscathed.

"Come with me," he snarled, dragging Malin toward the cellars, though he didn't intend to mark a single hair on her head. He couldn't.

What a catastrophe this was turning out to be.

CHAPTER
EIGHT

DAWN TIPPED THE horizon.

Haakon leaned on the rail of the ship, watching the harbor. The wind had picked up since yesterday, and the ship rocked slowly beneath his feet.

"Well?" Gunnar asked.

Haakon breathed out a sigh. The skies were clear. Not a sign of her on the horizon.

There wouldn't be, you fool. She might not have managed to get the manacle off.

His heart skipped a beat. No. He'd made enough excuses. She'd promised him she'd find a way to free herself. She'd told him to go. Shutting down everything he felt, he straightened and tipped his head toward Gunnar. "The lady has made her decision. Push off."

Time to go home.

Men bellowed as they hauled in the ropes. A curse caught his ear. Sails unfurled with a sharp flap, and then began to bloom. The ship rocked.

Home.

He longed to see his mother again. It had been over a year since he'd docked near Viksholm. His nieces and nephews would be growing. It would be good to see them again.

And then what?

Haakon shied away from the question as he curled a coil of rope into a circle around his elbow and palm. He caught Tormund looking at him, and turned away, handing the rope over to Finn.

"Pay up." Perhaps it was the wind that sent Gunnar's words whispering across the deck into his ears.

"We've not left harbor yet," Tormund replied.

Hope, you cruel, capricious bitch. Haakon locked everything down inside him. He didn't dare set his eyes on the harbor as the ship began to move. He couldn't. Instead, he threw himself into labor, helping to set the sails.

"Ho!" A bellow went up. "Haakon!"

Tormund.

His head snapped around, and he saw his enormous cousin pointing toward the docks. Haakon's stomach dropped through his feet.

"She's there!"

He strode to the railing, leaning out over it.

A figure ran along the docks, coming to a halt at the end of it as she stared across the water at him. Her cloak flapped in the breeze, her braid gleaming. But it was unmistakably her, and she looked like she was panting.

She came back.

He felt breathless with the shock of it.

"Impeccable timing," Gunnar muttered, looking like he'd seen Ragnarök on the horizon.

Haakon didn't care. He strode along the side of the ship, running his palm along the rail. Árdís kept pace with him, and he saw her lips move, though the words were torn from him in the wind.

She came back.

He could barely breathe.

"Well, what are you waiting for?" Tormund demanded, slapping him on the shoulder. He turned his head and bellowed, "Turn the bloody ship around."

Haakon scraped a hand through his hair as he strode down the gangplank. He was leaving. Today. Without her. And then she simply swept back into his life, as if she hadn't finished toying with him.

"What the hell are you doing here?" he demanded.

She hadn't run into his arms.

He hadn't dared hope.

But it filled him now, a whisper of everything he'd ever dreamed of.

Árdís opened her mouth, as if to say something, and then shook her head. "You said you would stay for three days."

The words took him by surprise. He felt breathless, slightly buoyant. "You came back?"

Instantly she seemed to realize where his thoughts had turned. A flicker of guilt swept over her face. "No. I'm sorry. I need help."

His heart fell.

Of course. The faint swell of hope broke like a tide within him, scraping the shoals of his heart raw. She threw him the merest scrap and a part of him leapt upon it like a starving beggar.

Well, he would not be that man anymore.

"Help?" His gaze raked her from head to toe, noting the mud on her cloak and the bedraggled hem of her skirts. "I'm done playing your games, Árdís. I want to go home."

"I'm not here to play games."

"No?"   The very thought of being her puppet infuriated him, and he forced himself to harden his heart, despite the plea in her voice. Turning, he lifted one arm, gesturing toward the ship, and the rail full of interested sailors. "Then what do you want? Somehow I doubt it's to give my ring back."

"Will you just listen to me?" she demanded.

"You have five minutes. Convince me why I should help you."

"Because you're the bloody reason I'm in so much trouble!" she snarled.

He blinked.

"Remember this?" She shook the bracelet at him. "I cannot fly. I cannot shift shape, and I cannot touch my magic."

"You said you'd remove it somehow."

"Well, I cannot."

A knot formed somewhere in his gut. "I never meant to trap you like this."

"And yet, you did."

"So you want me to remove it?"

"Yes!"

And then she'd be free to soar out of his life forever.

Haakon captured her hand, trying to ignore the sensation of her smooth skin in his. He looked down, into her heart-shaped face. It didn't matter how angry he was with her, in that moment, all he could see was what they'd had together. Tormund was right. He would love her forever. There would be no other woman for him.

But he could not force her to stay.

Swallowing hard, he never took his eyes from hers as he murmured the words of release, "*Er þér sjálfrátt fararleyfi....*"

Light sparked against his fingers. His heart twisted in his chest. Árdís licked her lips, as if to say something, but then heat flared and both of them jerked their hands apart as the links of the bracelet began to stretch, and then snapped back together and fused as tightly as ever before.

It hadn't worked.

Árdís tried to pull at it. "Why is it not working?"

Haakon stared. It had almost broken apart, but something stopped the spell from releasing her at the end. "They were the exact words he told me to speak."

"And you didn't think perhaps he was lying? You didn't think he might find it amusing to trap a *dreki* princess into her mortal form?"

"I wasn't... I wasn't in the best frame of mind at the time."

She looked up.

"It was barely a week after I'd discovered the truth. I was angry"—*furious*—"and I wanted to get the truth from you." He closed his eyes for a moment, hating the depths to which he'd stooped because of her. "I'm sorry. I truly am."

Árdís pressed a hand to her forehead, and turned to stare sightlessly at the docks. Haakon reached for her.

And then stopped.

A man hobbled his way toward them, leaning heavily on his crutch. Árdís's stare locked upon him, and her resolve seemed to firm. "I need to know where to find the sorcerer who gave this to you is. Perhaps I can get him to remove it."

That would take her days. "Can you not ask one of your *dreki* friends to take you there?" He looked to the north. "There's bad weather on its way."

"I know. And no." She drew her cloak tightly around her, as if she felt the chill coming. "I cannot ask another *dreki* for help."

"Why?" The tone of her voice gave her away.

Árdís glanced up from beneath her lashes, and he saw there the ghost of the woman he'd once known. The one who looked to him for reassurance once upon a time. "Because I'm fleeing the court."

A gull screamed as they stared at each other.

"Fleeing the court," he repeated softly.

Despite his anger, he couldn't help starting to think now. Three *dreki* had been "sent" to find her the other day. And none of Árdís's actions had been that of a woman who wanted to return with them.

"Are you in trouble? Nobody's going to hurt you, are they?" His voice thickened.

"No, they won't hurt me." She tucked a loose strand of hair behind her ear. "I'm a princess, and the last of my mother's direct descendants." Bitterness soured her voice. "If they hurt me, then they cannot get what they want from me."

"Which is?"

"My mother wants me to mate with Sirius, one of the males at court. The mating ceremony is set for tonight."

The years fell away, a stew of jealousy simmering within him. He had no right. "He's the one who came for you the other day."

"Yes."

"And you don't wish to mate with him?" After all, she'd told him to find another woman. What did he expect? That she would never replace him?

"No, I don't! This is my mother's doing. I just.... All of my life I've obeyed her rules. I won't do it, not this time."

Running away. Again. The same as she'd done when she swept into his life and tore it apart.

"Where are you heading then?"

She looked out across the harbor, tendrils of blonde hair brushing across her pale forehead. "I have only one place to go, where my mother and her court won't come for me. They won't risk facing Rurik, and he would take me in. I know it. I could be free to make my own choices in life."

The implications made his mouth tighten. "His lair is days away from here."

"I know."

"You cannot fly."

"I know." She looked up then. "I'd hoped...."

"That I would remove the manacle. And then you'd be on your way." Curse her. Curse her for giving him a moment of hope, and then dashing it across the cobbles.

Turning to stare out toward the sea, he raked a hand through his hair. The knot in his gut was back. He'd been torturing himself for far too long. He wanted to go home. He wanted to see his family again, and hold his nieces and nephews in his arms. To taste his mother's cooking, and sweep out the dust in his home—the one that held such memories for him.

Or perhaps burn it.

But he was the one who'd put that fucking manacle upon her. She could have been by her brother's side by now. Safe. Free to chase whatever sort of life she sought.

One without him in it.

Árdís cleared her throat. "I was actually hoping... for a little more help than that."

He looked at her incredulously.

"You want me to take you there?"

"Just as far as the svartálfar. It would be a few days' journey. That's all. I know it's out of your way, but I don't have a great many options at this point in time. If I could fly...."

But she couldn't.

Because of him.

He'd made so many mistakes in the past year, consumed by his quest for revenge upon the dragon he'd thought had stolen her. He was still making those mistakes, driven by hurt and pain. The gaping hollowness within him yawned.

"I know I ask for too much," she whispered. "But you don't understand. This is not just me asking for help." Árdís glanced toward the stranger who'd almost made it to their side. "Marek is one of the court. They sentenced him to death. If you won't help me, then perhaps.... Would you consider helping him?"

The stranger looked like he'd been beaten within an inch of his life, and a bandage covered most of his forehead. Haakon recognized fever when he saw it in a man's eyes, but he also saw the sort of look a man gave when he worshipped a woman.

One of the court? Was that *all* he was to Árdís?

Every muscle in his body locked tight. She couldn't be asking this of him. Could she?

"Who is he?"

"A servant," she replied, without a hint of anything more in her voice. "He is loyal to my brother and will pay the price for it, if I do not help him escape."

Relief. Sweet relief. For whatever this Marek felt for her, it was clearly unreturned. But how easily had jealousy stirred?

"This will only end in tragedy," he said, half to himself. A reminder, to steel his nerves.

"It doesn't have to," Árdís murmured.

He'd be better off cutting her from his life.

He'd gotten what he wanted; not answers, not truly, but a chance to stare into her deceitful eyes and tell her how he felt.

It wasn't anywhere near enough to slake his pain.

But....

"You still want me."

For a second he'd believed, truly believed, there was something left between them. And maybe that was another question he needed to answer, before he could bury her in his heart.

Perhaps Tormund had the right of it when he'd suggested Haakon had asked the wrong questions.

She'd married him because she hadn't truly understood what he'd meant when he asked for her hand, but why had she left him?

"We'll destroy each other," he said, though it was more a recitation of facts. "And I don't know how much of myself I have left."

He hadn't realized, until her face fell, how much hope there'd been in her expression. "I see."

No, you don't, he wanted to scream.

He'd dragged himself out of the depths of a never-ending tankard of ale. He'd burned for one purpose only in the last seven years: to find his wife and rescue her. To save her. To hold her in his arms one more time.

The truth of her deception had shattered him like a cheap vase, and he felt as though he might have glued the pieces together again, but the fracture lines still showed. All it would take would be one more blow and he'd fragment into a million pieces.

And this time, there would be no more putting himself back together.

"If you won't help me," she said, as she turned away. "Then I shall find someone who will."

Like hell. His hand locked around her wrist, and he belatedly realized he'd taken three sharp steps. "Who?"

Árdís froze and looked back. But the spark of defiance in her eyes told him she knew exactly how to play him. "It's none of your business. Sail home, Haakon. Live a wonderful life. I'm no longer your concern."

Heartless dreki princess. But the muscles in his gut clenched as a shiver of need trembled through her eyes, and she looked away. He was afraid some part of him would always twist in knots when he saw her, as if his very soul yearned to let her wrap him around her little finger once again. His only consolation was the fact it seemed he wasn't the only one so tempted.

Haakon looked down, his thumb stroking the smooth skin of her inner wrist, and brushing against the cursed manacle. He couldn't, with any good intentions, allow her to remain shackled like this. No matter how much he didn't dare trust her.

"I will help you," he said, his gaze flickering to the stranger. "And your friend."

"And what will it cost me?"

"I owe you a debt for binding your magic like this. It wasn't my intent, but my honor"—*or what remains of it*—"insists I stay at your side until I can help you remove the manacle. I will help you, Árdís." His resolve began to form. "I will escort you to the sorcerer, where we can remove that shackle. Then you'll be free to fly to your brother's side. I owe you nothing else. And then it ends, you and I."

"Ends?"

"Yes. Ends. In exchange I want only one thing."

Árdís's breath caught again. "What?"

"My grandmother's ring," he told her.

Instantly her hand went to the valley between her breasts, where his ring no doubt hung. This time she looked troubled, and all for a fucking *ring*. "It's mine."

Haakon reached out, his fingertip caressing the silver chain around her throat. "Silver's never truly been your color. You always preferred gold, to match your mercenary heart."

Árdís snatched at the chain as he began to withdraw its length from her dress, her fist curled around the damning ring at the end of it. "What would you know of my heart?"

His face closed over. "You're right. I wouldn't know a damned thing, except to wonder if you even owned one. Regardless, the ring is not yours. It is, however, my price."

"I don't know if I...."

"It's just a ring, Árdís. My ring. I gave it to you with the intention of seeing you wear it for the rest of your life; however, that's not to be. Leaving it with you indicates there's something left between us. And that's not true, is it?"

He practically dared her to deny the truth.

She didn't.

Yet nor did she offer him an answer to that question.

"I need an end to this," he said roughly. "I cannot go on with even a shred of hope left. I told you that you'd ruined me. Perhaps that's a lie. I ruined myself. I've done things"—he thought of Rurik's mate Freyja, whom he'd used as bait in order to trap the mighty *dreki*, without a care for her feelings—"that I would never have done. I don't even think I like who I've become. But I cannot move on, not until I know this marriage is truly buried. And if you give me back that ring, then I know there's nothing left for us."

The wind blew Árdís's braid behind her, and she stared through his chest, as if trying to find some sort of answer herself.

Turmoil filled her amber eyes as she slowly lifted them. "If you help me remove this shackle, then I will do my best to hand the ring to you."

Done. It was done.

He nodded shortly. "I'll go tell the men our plans, and then we'll board."

"Board?" She shook her head. "We cannot go by ship."

"Why not?"

"Because they're *dreki*," she insisted. "They'll be looking for me in the air. The second they realize I'm not flying, they'll start searching elsewhere. They'll search all the ships leaving the country. On land we can hide, but on a ship we'll be too vulnerable. There's nowhere to run, and I cannot hide for they will feel my presence if they come close enough."

He considered the ride north. It was more days than he'd hoped to spend with her. "We're just as vulnerable on the ground."

"But unexpected," she stressed. "The last time I fled, I went to the continent. There's no reason for us to head north. There's nothing there—except your sorcerer. We have to be unpredictable if we're to escape unwanted attention."

"Surely they'll expect you to flee toward your brother."

"But not from this direction. I just have to make it onto the lands Rurik has claimed. If they broach his territory, it's an act of war, and he's powerful."

Far too many days of riding ahead of them, with her at his side. "What about your friend?"

"My name is Marek," the servant's eyes glittered watchfully, "and I will help protect the princess."

He'd be lucky if he could even fall at an enemy's feet if they attacked, judging by the look of him. Haakon assessed him. "You won't make it more than a day's ride north."

"I can," Marek said fiercely, "and I will."

"He's unwell," Haakon said, turning the question over to Árdís. "The ride will either kill him, or he'll slow us down. He needs rest and a healer."

"Marek, he's right. You have a fever." Árdís pressed her hands to her temples. "They won't sense him if they board the ship and he's hiding. He's a *drekling*, not a *dreki*. His lack of magic is a boon in this circumstance." She looked up. "Could he sail with your men?"

Gunnar watched him from the ship, as if wondering what they were talking about, and a thought occurred. "He can rest in the passenger cabin. I'll send the ship north, to meet us in a cove near where the sorcerer dwells. If anyone sees it leaving Reykjavik, their search will turn up nothing. Then you can hand me the ring, I'll board the ship, and you can fly east. The subterfuge might work."

Árdís bit her lip thoughtfully, and he was struck by how familiar an expression it was.

Haakon shook himself. He could *not* allow himself to fall for her charms.

"It might work," she whispered.

He nodded abruptly. "Stay out of sight while I unload the horses."

She obediently tugged up her hood.

"Oh, and Árdís?"

"Yes?" She looked up warily.

"The second you have your wings back, I leave with the ring. Until then, I'm your guard. Nothing else."

"Agreed," she said softly.

It was the only way he could protect himself from the inevitable heartbreak, for it seemed she wasn't the only one skirting the truth.

His heart still belonged to her.

A part of it always would.

But he didn't dare let her know.

Malin hit the stone floor of the cell and rolled, turning to face the prince.

Sirius loomed in the middle of the cell door, his broad shoulders almost filling the frame. There was no way past him. No way through him. And the implacable expression on Sirius's face told her she wasn't going to be able to distract him.

No, he was just like his father. Stellan and the Queen sneered at those like she who were born with impure blood, and couldn't manage the transition to full *dreki* form. Malin knew the *dreki* was within her—she could feel it whisper through her veins at the sudden implications of danger, and sometimes she almost imagined she could make flame wield to her whim—but it wasn't enough for those who preferred purebloods.

Like the prince before her.

If not for the old laws the Loremaster insisted had to be maintained, Malin knew she'd have been outcast from the clan, or worse, *made to vanish.*

She had the terrible suspicion she was going to discover where it was certain *dreki* vanished *to*. She found her feet, her knees bruised. There was no way in Hel she was going to greet her death on her knees. Not for him. Nor for his bastard of a father.

"Do you need any help, my lord?" one of the guards asked, peering around Sirius with a leering quality to his gaze.

"I can handle this," Sirius said coldly.

"Are you certain—"

"Certain." He slammed the door in the guard's face and turned toward her. "Let me make one thing very clear. Your life is mine, right now—"

"Then take it," she declared, lifting her chin and meeting his eyes. "For I won't betray my princess, even if I had any idea of where she'd gone. Though I don't blame her for leaving. What sane woman would ever mate with *you*?"

If anything, his alpine blue eyes narrowed to slits. He glided toward her, the menace radiating off him and sucking the heat from the air. All *dreki* had some power over the elements, though their abilities varied. Sirius was pure frost, brought to life in *dreki* form. A demon of ice, who cared for nothing and no one. Malin trembled, but she wouldn't step back.

She would *not* cower.

Even as her breath began to fog in the suddenly frigid cell.

"If you don't tell me what you know, then you're condemning Árdís to death—or something worse," he said, his hand coming up to grip her throat.

"Why should you care? And what's worse than being sentenced to a life as *your* mate?"

He held her there, but the grip was not harsh. No. She almost thought he flinched. Once again his thumb made that odd stroking gesture it had in the throne room. Malin gasped as the prince's face lowered toward her, so she could hear his whisper. "I'm trying to help you survive this," he hissed under his breath. "Why are you making this so difficult?"

"Why should I not make this difficult?" She grabbed a fistful of his shirt, trying to gain her balance. "You call me a 'nobody' but I'm a woman with my own hopes and dreams, and I'll be damned if I'll go down without a fight."

The entire court looked at her as if she were filth. Only Árdís had never pitied her for the lack of the ability to shift, and to fly. Only Árdís had ever treated her as if she were an equal.

"I will never, ever," she snarled, "reveal a single one of Árdís's secrets."

Sirius glared at her, and it was only then she felt some trace of heat radiating off him. Her fist clenched in his shirt, and her knuckles brushed against his chest. His skin was warm against her fingers, and his thighs crushed her skirts. It left her feeling remarkably off-balance, in more ways than one.

"You care for her," he said, sounding surprised.

"She's my princess, my hope." Malin shivered, for the way he was looking at her was not at all the way he usually did, as if she were some insect to be crushed beneath his boot. "She's the only true heir left in this rotten court, and when her people rise, they'll crush you and the cursed blight of your family from existence."

Dark lashes fluttered down to hide his eyes, and his mouth softened. "Careful sweetheart," he murmured. "You're starting to talk about rebellion, and if my father catches a glimpse of it, he'll crush every bone in your body to discover the truth."

"What little is left of me," she whispered, finally feeling the nerves bubble up within her, "once you're done with me."

The Blackfrost was not the sort of *dreki* one denied. Sirius lurked in the shadows, as his father's personal assassin. Or so it was said.

"I'm not going to hurt you."

That hand softened, and slid around to cup the back of her neck. Suddenly Malin was clinging to him in truth, to avoid falling flat on her backside.

Her heart started beating a little faster.

None of this was going the way she'd expected.

"No? You heard what your father said. And if he thought you were harboring a traitor, he'd string you up beside me. Why should you care?" she breathed.

Sirius glanced behind him, and she knew he could sense the heartbeat pulsing beyond the door. *Dreki* ears were sharp, but their words were barely a whisper. Even so, he leaned closer, breathing in her ear. "Because you don't have to tell me Árdís's secrets. I know she left last night, using the southern cellars that lead to the servant's portal. I know she's going after her mortal husband. I was there. I let her go."

Malin staggered back as he released her.

Splayed against the cell wall, she stared at him. He'd let the princess go? "You're lying."

"You know I'm not."

A silky whisper.

He knew too much about the princess's plans... Or had Stellan's spies seen the princess leave, and Sirius was using that information to trick her? No. *Dreki* couldn't lie, which meant he had to be telling the truth.

"Why?" Malin whispered.

Sirius glanced again at the door, and she gained the impression she wasn't the only one keeping secrets. Again he loomed closer, resting one hand flat against the cell wall beside her face. Her body tightened as he leaned closer, but it was only to brush his lips against her ear. "Because I did not wish to mate with her, nor her with me. It seemed the only way to avoid the situation. But I think it wise if we both keep our voices down. My father wouldn't appreciate knowing I allowed Árdís to leave. If you cannot trust me, then trust that. You hold this secret over my head."

Malin could barely breathe. She turned her face to the side, and her lips almost brushed against his stubble. None of this made any sense, and her heart pounded as she sought to work her way through it all.

Could she trust him?

The *Blackfrost*?

"I just need to know where she's going," he said. "That's all. And I shall take you with me. If you help me, then I shall set you free."

"You're going to bring her back," she blurted.

His lips thinned, as he drew back fractionally, just enough to look into her eyes. "I like this little more than you do, however, I'm running out of cards to play. This has not gone as expected. I need the princess back, and I'll mate her if forced to do so. Or would you prefer that Roar finds her first? Neither of us want him named as heir."

He had a point.

He also had to be playing some sort of game. But what? He'd given her his secret, after all, one that could see *him* torn apart by his brethren if they knew he'd had a hand in Árdís's disappearance.

If she couldn't entirely be certain she could trust him, then at least she had something to hold over his head. And she needed to help Árdís. The princess couldn't escape an entire hunting party of *dreki* males intent on claiming her for Roar. The stakes had changed.

"There's only one place for the princess to flee to," Malin said, her heart trembling at the choice she was making. "Only one place she's safe from those who might follow."

The prince's pale blue eyes raced. His face suddenly paled.

"Rurik."

"Yes," Malin breathed, feeling like a traitor in her bones. "She's going to find her brother, Rurik."

CHAPTER NINE

THE FIRST PROBLEM occurred before they'd even mounted.

Árdís captured the reins of Gunnar's chestnut and tried to swing her foot into the stirrup, but the mare was having none of it. She snorted and sidled to the side, her eyes rolling. Árdís was knocked off balance, and the mare nearly bolted.

Haakon caught the bridle with a grimace.

"It's the smell," Gunnar said, and spat on the docks as he folded his arms across his enormous barrel chest. "Hela knows the girl isn't human."

Out of all of his men's horses, Hela was the calmest. Usually. Haakon ground his teeth together.

"Fine. You can ride Snorri," Haakon snapped, tugging the fat little baggage pony they had forward. Snorri dug his heels in and extended his neck as far as it would go in protest, until he was practically dragging him across the cobbles. "We can reassemble the bags."

"I am not riding that thing," Árdís said, echoing Gunnar's stance. "It looks like a carpetbag with legs. And it

135

hates me. Look at it glaring at me with those beady little eyes. I don't trust it not to dump me in the mud. Or bite me."

"Then bite him back. You seem to have a fondness for such a thing," Haakon said, through his teeth. "Snorri is bred for this terrain. And we're running out of choices. Unless you'd prefer to walk?"

"Then you ride him," Árdís said, crossing to Sleipnir's side. "And I will ride your mighty steed, who seems to like me better."

Sleipnir snorted, his eyes rolling toward her, but he was an ex-cavalry mount. He'd been trained to ride right into gunfire and not flinch. Or directly at a dragon, come to think of it. And while he might not precisely like the idea of Árdís sitting on his back, he was clearly not about to suffer a fit of vapors like the rest of the horses.

That wouldn't be at all manly, and the stallion had a reputation to protect.

Haakon's eyes narrowed. *Traitor.* He already wanted to tear his hair out. "Gunnar, you might as well remove Hela's tack. Take her with you. She's going to be useless."

"I don't think I like the idea of you riding off alone with her," Gunnar muttered.

"Yes, but a pair of riders is going to attract less attention than a handful of dragon hunters. None of us look like farmers or merchants," Tormund said quickly, slapping Gunnar on the shoulder. His fingers locked there, as if to restrain the man. "This isn't going to end in a fight, if Haakon uses his wits. He knows what he's doing. And one or more riders at his side isn't going to be able to drive a *dreki* away. We'd need the entire company and the ballista for that, and we might as well burn a massive beacon and drag it along behind us."

Haakon ground his teeth together and glared at his cousin. *I don't have a fucking clue what I'm doing.*

Tormund flashed a quick smile. Then waggled his eyebrows up and down.

Curse him. This wasn't going to go the way Tormund expected.

The next few days stretched in front of him.

Alone. With Árdís.

And the nights....

Pure bloody torture.

And now she insisted she wasn't going to ride the baggage pony?

Tethering the reluctant pony to Sleipnir, he shifted his saddlebags, relocating some of the straps. This was not a major problem. He could work out a solution. His willpower wasn't going to fail at the thought of having her in his arms.

"So you *are* going to ride the carpetbag?" Árdís looked brightened by the prospect.

If Sleipnir could handle this, then so could he. It was just a few days in close proximity to her.

She was the one who'd be getting a sore backside.

"No," Haakon snapped, swinging up into the saddle and adjusting his seat as the stallion danced. His sword and crossbow were going to be a problem, but he could manage. "You're going to board the ship while I ride out of Reykjavik alone, just in case anyone is watching. I'll meet you five miles north of the town, where Tormund can row you ashore. Then you can ride behind me."

He nudged Sleipnir forward, nodding at Tormund. "Make a fuss out of taking her aboard. Make sure she's seen, so if anyone comes offering gold around, they'll happily say she boarded a ship. I'll see you in a couple of hours."

"See?" Tormund said, offering Árdís his arm. "Your husband is a strategic man. You'll be safe with him."

Haakon met her eyes as he reined Sleipnir in a tight circle.

Who was going to protect him from her?

It swiftly became clear Árdís had few allies aboard the ship.

Marek had vanished inside Haakon's cabin, and sought the bed, proving Haakon's assessment of his condition correct. Most of the men ignored her, a few gave her curious looks, but Gunnar outright scowled.

"Stay there," he snapped, pointing to what he called the bow of the ship. "And don't move. Don't speak. Don't get in the way."

Then he turned and strode away.

"Have I done something to offend you?" she called.

Gunnar paused in mid-step. "Did you not hear me?"

"I think the not speaking rule is a trifle overwhelming." And she had her pride, after all. She was *dreki*.

He turned on her. "I've spent the last seven years at Haakon's side, hunting for you. He never gave up hope, until last month when your brother told him the truth of your deception. He went mad. Tore apart his room, shattered furniture like it was made from sticks. We had to chain him up for days, so he wouldn't mount an armed assault on your *dreki* court by himself. You did that to him. Men *died* because of your lies. I've lost good friends to dragons' teeth because you decided to toy with Haakon's heart on a fucking whim."

She was taken aback. "It wasn't a whim," she said softly.

"That's enough, Gunnar."

Tormund. The only one who seemed to be on her side. The bearded giant stepped between them, twitching a brow at Gunnar. "And it's not entirely true. Bjorn, Gunnar, and I are here for Haakon, but the others like the scent of gold. Dragon gold. Those men that died knew the risks when they signed on, and they chose to attack a dangerous beast because of their greed. Lay what you want at her feet, Gunnar. But not that."

Gunnar's face turned red. He didn't appear to be breathing. Without another word he turned around and stomped away, bristling with anger.

"Thank you." Árdís eyed the large man. She remembered his face. "You're Haakon's cousin. You were there, at the...."

"Wedding?" He cocked a brow. "Can't say it, Princess?"

She turned to stare out at the waves primly. "It's just a word."

"Aye." He leaned on the rail at her side and grinned at her. A handsome man who towered over all the others, his beard was several shades darker than his long hair. Brown eyes twinkled at her. "I was there at the wedding. I'm surprised you remember me. The pair of you barely took your eyes off each other. You danced all night in Haakon's arms, and you smiled at him like you'd just discovered an entire hoard of precious gems nobody had seen for centuries. Brunhild was certain you'd give her grandchildren a mere nine months later. It's the only time I've ever refused to accept a bet."

Children. Always children. Her hands tightened on the rail. "You don't seem to despise me like the others do."

"Gunnar's only mad because he owes me fifty kroner."

She'd felt the truth vibrating in Gunnar's words. "No. He hates me for what I've done to Haakon. But you don't."

"That's because I'm smarter than Gunnar." Tormund made a muffled grunting sound, and scratched his beard. "My mother said there's always a reason for the choices people make. I told you. I remember that wedding. You were so in love with Haakon you could barely see anyone else. Your choice to leave him makes no sense to me." He turned his head to look at her, and she realized she wasn't fooling this man at all. "If Haakon could see straight right now, he might realize that. You loved him. And then you left him. And I don't think you've told anyone the reason why. And there is a reason. I'll wager you fifty kroner—no, I'll wager you a handful of emeralds—that something else drove you from his side."

"You don't have a handful of emeralds."

"No, but you do." His smile widened. "And I'm not going to lose this wager, am I, Princess?"

The rowboat rocked as Tormund heaved against the oars, salty spray splashing over Árdís's lips. She watched the ship grow smaller, feeling a little nervous. Every delay narrowed her chances of escaping.

Claus would have been found by now.

Her rooms would have been searched, and Malin discovered.

No doubt her mother had sent her *dreki* guards into the sky. Árdís had seen no sign of wings on the horizon, but she had no doubt they were out there. Somewhere.

"Nearly there," Tormund promised, as they began to crest the breakers closer to shore. "I'll keep an eye on your servant for you."

"Thank you."

She turned to face the bay. A solitary figure waited on the beach, the fur-lined cloak on his shoulders flapping around his calves. Cliffs lined the bay, and in the distance snow-capped mountains gleamed.

For a second she let her gaze rove over him, and she didn't bother to hide the feelings inside her when she did.

Haakon.

Once upon a time, he'd been all she'd ever wanted.

And it hadn't simply been lust, though that was tangled in the mix of emotions inside her. No. There was so much more. And she'd never even realized it until the night of their wedding, when he'd finally made love to her, and they'd lain in each other's arms, spent and panting.

Being in his arms felt like home in a way the court had never been. She *belonged* there. Nothing could touch her when Haakon was there. No one could ever hurt her. All she'd ever felt was happiness.

Until her mother's shadow began to brush against the edges of her little world.

Árdís sighed as Haakon made his way down the beach toward them. She was no longer welcome in his arms.

He strode into the foamy surf, helping to haul the boat in closer. The sharp cut of his cheekbones looked particularly foreboding, and his eyes glittered with ice as he looked at them. "You're late."

"The winds weren't in our favor," Tormund called. "And you're welcome."

It took her a second to compose herself, when Haakon turned that hot-eyed stare upon her. It always did. But Árdís had spent years playing her court-appointed role. He wouldn't see the longing in her eyes. Or the vulnerability in her heart.

She'd make sure of it.

"Ready?" He held the boat steady and gestured to the foot of water surrounding them with his other hand.

Árdís clambered to her feet, swaying as the waves rocked the boat. In the past, he'd have never demanded this. He'd have carried her, so she wouldn't get her boots wet.

But that man was long buried beneath this imposing half-stranger.

And she'd be damned if she'd give him the pleasure of seeing her falter.

Grabbing a fistful of her skirts, she tried to plant her boot on the edge of the boat. Haakon offered her a hand to help her, at least, but as she shifted her weight forward the boat suddenly rocked and she found herself thrown forward with a squeal.

Hard arms locked around her, and Árdís slammed against Haakon's chest as he caught her.

A soft curse broke from him as her breasts pressed against his face. Her arms locked around the back of his heavily muscled neck automatically, and for a second, she inhaled the scent of warm, clean male.

Her male.

Oh, gods. She nearly groaned. She'd never been good with temptation, and this was only a reminder of what a strain on her willpower these next few days would be. She could feel the silk of his hair against her hands and wanted to curl her fingers through it.

"Sorry," Tormund called, sounding anything but.

"Son of a bitch," Haakon muttered. He shot a glare over his shoulder, and Árdís suddenly realized it hadn't been a wave that sent her falling, but one clearly unrepentant matchmaker.

Haakon growled under his breath and swung an arm under her thighs. He hauled her up into his arms, and Árdís grabbed at him inelegantly as he juggled her.

It seemed he'd changed his mind about making her walk through the water.

"Ride safe, Princess," Tormund called. "And remember our bet."

"What bet?" Haakon's gaze cut to hers.

Árdís's cheeks burned, as he started to carry her toward the beach, striding through the skim of waves. "Nothing."

Behind her, Tormund merely laughed as he began to haul the boat back out to sea.

The second challenge came later that night, when they stopped to set up camp. They'd covered only a handful of miles with all the subterfuge with the ship, before Haakon insisted upon pulling off the road and finding a secluded place to sleep.

He'd barely spoken to her all day.

Despite what Tormund had told her on the ship, there was no sign of the man who'd married her. Nor the one she'd met again in Reykjavik. Haakon wasn't mad with fury, nor boiling with frustration. He was cold. Closed off.

A part of her wanted to break through those walls that locked him away. Ever since Tormund had spoken of their wedding, she'd been unable to think of anything else.

"There's only one bedroll," Árdís pointed out as she finished building the fire.

Haakon continued to roll the bedroll out, his movements quick and sure. She'd always liked that about him—he was constantly moving, constantly doing some chore. The only time he'd ever been still had been those moments when she'd managed to talk him into lingering in bed, or those rainy mornings when he was trapped in the house they'd shared and they would talk or read together.

"Are we sharing that too?" she dared to ask.

Haakon's hands paused, and then swiftly resumed the task as if it had never happened. But she noticed.

"No."

"Then how are...?"

"You're taking the bedroll. I'll keep watch."

He was making good on his promise not to touch her.

It was sensible.

It was... frustrating.

"You need sleep too," she pointed out.

"I'll wake you when it's my turn."

Then he turned and tugged his bow from the pile of baggage. "Stay here and don't leave the fire. I'll be back."

He vanished long enough to return with a rabbit for dinner, and then roasted it in silence once he'd finished skinning it. The quiet between them was beginning to irritate her.

"Are you not going to speak to me?" Not touching her was one thing, but he would barely look at her.

"I'm speaking." Using an old rag, Haakon cleaned the blood from his knife.

"Yes. You've mastered the art of the terse reply. It's going to feel like the longest journey I've ever been on, if you insist upon continuing in this vein."

There. There was a hint of emotion tensing his shoulders. Haakon stabbed the knife down into the log he was sitting upon.

His eyes flashed. "What do we have to speak about?"

"You're not curious? About why I fled?"

"I thought it was to avoid a mating ceremony," he said curtly, oh-so-curtly.

Fat sizzled as he turned the rabbit on the spit.

She couldn't reach him. It ached through her, and her hands fell uselessly into her lap. A foolish sort of pain, for she shouldn't even be pushing at him like this. If he was going to remain walled-off, then perhaps that was for the best?

But a part of her still remembered the stirring arguments they'd always had. He'd always challenged her to think in other ways—pushed at her to be more than a spoiled princess who had *dreki* males falling at her feet. This quiet, contained Haakon was a stranger. She wanted the one who growled back at her. The one who got that certain look on his face when the argument intensified, and they were no longer merely arguing over something, but yelling just for the sake of it.

She wanted the one who kissed her when the tide finally turned, his mouth crashing down upon hers. His hands wrenching up her skirts as their bodies tumbled to the bed....

It was both a secret joy and a misery to be so close to him after all these years, and yet so far.

"When you left me" —he broke the silence— "where did you go?"

Árdís looked up slowly, her pulse beating thickly in her throat. It took her a moment to reorient herself. Haakon carved a slice of meat off the rabbit, passing it to her. He looked utterly disinterested in her answer, but at the last moment, their eyes met and she saw heat simmering there, before his gaze returned to the rabbit.

Not entirely impregnable then.

It gave her hope. She knew how to stir this man and breach his defenses.

145

Árdís chewed thoughtfully. Did she dare? The tension between them was becoming almost unbearable, and it felt like there was only one safe way to defuse it.

"I returned to court. I had no choice, not truly. My mother was furious with me for vanishing for three years without a trace. I've been there ever since. She barely takes her eyes off me. And you? Tormund said you were dragon hunters."

"I'm surprised he didn't tell you more than that," Haakon muttered.

"He did." She watched his face carefully. She'd been doing that all day, trying to map the differences. There was a faint scar above his lips. Another slashing through his blond brow. He'd turned from a handsome young hunter who'd left flowers on her doorstep and promised his mother he'd have her home by nightfall, to a hard battle-scarred warrior who looked like he'd throw her over his shoulder if given half a chance. Dangerous to rouse.

She wanted to rouse him.

Árdís moved a little closer, shifting along the log. "He said they call you Dragonsbane now. Haakon Dragonsbane."

Haakon's lips tightened. "They're fools."

"No, I like it. It's a worthy name. You've killed three dragons. There are few men who could claim such a thing."

"Hell, Árdís. I didn't do it for the bloody accolades—"

"I know." This was not going the way she'd hoped. "He told me you went mad when I left. You drank too much. You didn't eat enough. And you insisted upon rescuing me. You gave yourself over to hunting dragons and searching for word of me. Tormund had to ride along with you to keep you safe."

"Tormund rode along because he thought it would be a grand fucking adventure," Haakon snapped, "and he wanted to hear his name sung in the ballads they'd sing."

"There are ballads sung about you?"

"No. There are no ballads." A vein throbbed in his jaw. Firelight gilded the sharp slash of his cheekbone, as he turned to look at her. "If I'd known he'd dribble such foolishness into your ears when you boarded that ship, I wouldn't have bloody put you upon it. What did he do? Tell you everything that's happened in the last seven years?"

"Not everything." She twitched her skirts.

He hadn't, for example, answered the question of whether Haakon had ever had another woman in his bed.

"You want to know the answer to that, Princess, then you're going to have to ask him yourself."

"Bloody meddling fool." Haakon yanked his knife out of the log, and swung the rabbit off the fire.

"He did, however, bet me a golden crown and a fistful of emeralds that we're going to fall into bed together by the end of this journey."

Haakon froze.

His stormy eyes found her, but they didn't linger on her face. A swift glance dipped lower, stroking over her lips, her hands, her breasts. Then away. "I swear to the gods, I'm going to kill him."

A thrill lit through her. This was one way to fight his coldness. Árdís straightened, letting her cloak fall away from her shoulders.

"You didn't ask," she whispered.

"Ask what?" He tore a joint from the rabbit with impatient hands, and set it on a tin plate to cool for her.

"Whether I accepted his bet."

Haakon stilled. "Árdís. Are you *trying* to torture me?"

A flush of heat went through her, like the glide of heated honey across her skin. "I wouldn't consider it torture."

His eyes darkened. He'd finished separating the cooked rabbit onto a pair of plates, and licked his fingers and thumb. Slowly. "No? What would you call it then?"

Árdís bit her lip. She suddenly wanted to lick those fingers herself. "I would call it... an opening gambit."

Haakon straightened to his full height. The leather of his body armor flexed as he stiffened. "An opening gambit."

It was hard to gauge whether she was making any headway. If he were a castle, he might as well have just drawn up the drawbridge. But the soft way he repeated the words.... And the way he crossed his arms over his chest, while staring down at her, didn't feel like he'd slammed the cannons into the breach. Wary, yes. Defensive, yes.

But he was also listening.

Intrigued.

"Making amends, perhaps."

A muscle in his jaw ticked. "And how would you begin to make amends?"

"I could kiss it better," she whispered. "I could kiss it all better."

The heat of his gaze had weight now. Firelight caressed him from head to toe. He shifted and she could make out the faint, hard shape pressing insistently against his leather trousers.

She liked them much better than the wool he used to wear. They did terribly tempting things to his strong thighs and firm backside.

The heat flickered. And died. "And just like that, the pain goes away, does it?"

One step forward.

One step back.

"What did I promise you on the docks?"

"That you were my guard," she said, "and nothing else."

She thought he was going to finish the conversation there, but he merely circled the fire, watching her the entire time. She'd seen *dreki* stalk their prey like that before, and her sex suddenly clenched in response.

How odd. She'd never thought of herself as prey before.

And she certainly hadn't expected to like it.

"So you're pushing at me to get a response?"

"I don't know," she cried, curling her fingers into fists. "We fight. We argue. We—"

"*Fuck?*"

The word slammed through her, leaving her breathless. "That's the way it's always been with you. I keep waiting for you to explode. I hurt you, but you're not angry enough. I don't know...." *How to respond to this.* She shrugged helplessly.

"Maybe I'm not the same man I used to be. And maybe our lack of communication was the problem, hmm?"

It unsettled her.

"Or not?" He cocked his head on an angle.

Árdís stared down at her lap, knowing he sought answers she couldn't give. "I liked arguing with you. And the aftermath."

"Aftermath?" His voice softened with a hint of a laugh. "That's one way to put it. Carnal warfare is another."

Her nipples pressed roughly against the linen of her chemise. The rough edge of his laugh held a hint of anger, and that always stirred her blood. She felt at ease now, for she knew how to deal with this.

149

"I wouldn't call it anything as civilized as that," she whispered, remembering times when he'd pinned her to their bed, their mouths clashing in a heated mix of teeth and tongues even as he jerked her skirts up. She'd leave little imprints of her teeth across his shoulder and throat, relieved to unleash the *dreki* within her, even if she couldn't tell him. Carnal warfare implied that at least one of them—if not both—had held any control over what happened in their bed.

He knelt in front of her, setting both hands on the log on either side of her hips as he leaned tauntingly close to her. "What do you think is going to happen here?"

"If I'm being perfectly honest—"

"Please do so."

"Then I'm not entirely certain I'm thinking right now, at all." She searched his eyes, holding perfectly still. His mouth was so close to hers, that a simple push forward would meld their lips together. *One inch.* But she couldn't read his intentions at all. Frustration churned through her. She wanted those hands on her skin, not beside her. "I know we said there would be nothing more between us until I got this bracelet off. But...."

"You want me," he whispered, his eyelids growing heavy as his gaze dropped to her mouth.

Árdís's heart pounded even as she watched the slow flush of red creep up his throat. She didn't dare move in case she broke the spell. But her fingernails were curling into her palms again. *Touch me. Please.*

She closed her eyes, unable to bear the look in his. "I thought we'd already established that in Reykjavik. I want you. I most likely always will. Nothing has changed."

If anything, the pain of unfulfilled lust only twisted the knot tighter inside her.

His breath stirred the sensitive skin of her throat. Árdís sucked in a sharp breath, her lashes fluttering. She wanted to take his hand and cup it between her legs, where it ached the fiercest. To push against him, and take what she needed.

Soft lips ghosted over her jaw. Árdís tipped her head back to grant him full access, her breasts feeling heavy and flushed. She sank her teeth into her lower lip.

"Does it ache, *Árja*?"

"Yes."

The answer came out softer and breathier than she'd expected.

One hand reached out, brushing a lock of her hair behind her shoulder. Árdís's breasts lifted as she breathed in. She wanted, very badly, to feel that touch on her skin.

She reached for him, but he captured her wrist.

"Good." The sensual languidness slid from him like a cloak, his eyes shuttering down firm and hard. Then he pushed to his feet and stepped away from her.

The course of lust slammed to a halt within her.

She was slower to react, her lips parted, and heat crawling all over her skin. She curled a hand around her throat. "You're playing a game with me?"

He picked up his plate, cool and implacable. "It's not very enjoyable, is it?"

Árdís slammed to her feet, gaping at him. "But I'm not—"

"Eat your dinner," Haakon insisted, flinging his fur cloak around his shoulders and stalking to the edge of the circle of firelight. "Then get some sleep. I'll wake you when it's your turn to keep watch."

"How am I supposed to go to sleep after that?" she demanded. He hadn't even touched her, and she felt ready to melt.

The ghost of a smile played over his hard mouth. "That's not my problem."

Árdís's eyes narrowed.

You, dear husband, just started a war.

CHAPTER TEN

THE NEXT MORNING, fog lay across the land like a thick blanket. Haakon swiftly secured everything to the back of Snorri, and then went to wake his wife.

Árdís's hands were tucked up under her chin, and her golden hair streamed across the blankets. Thick golden lashes fluttered against her cheeks, along with the faint splash of freckles. The sight of her so vulnerable felt like a mule kick to the chest. She slept as though she had absolutely no doubt in her mind that he'd protect her.

He wanted to.

And that was the rub, wasn't it? Despite all the years between them, despite everything, a part of him would open his arms to her if she gave him a single hint she'd run into them and stay there forever.

But last night had been about scratching an itch, nothing more. He knew if he'd given in to her, they'd have ended up in bed. Perhaps they'd stay there for the next couple of nights. But the second she got her bracelet off, she'd fly away, and he'd be the one trying to pull himself back together again.

"You didn't ask... whether I accepted his bet."

The innocent look didn't become her.

At all.

Leaning down, he curled his hand around her shoulder. "Árdís?"

Her lashes fluttered, revealing the slow dawning of awareness in her amber eyes when she saw him. A smile softened her mouth, and she brushed her cheek against his hand like a cat, stretching in a yawn before she suddenly stiffened.

He became the recipient of a hot-eyed look that felt like her hand curled directly around his cock. She wasn't the only one who remembered the way they'd solved arguments in the past, and his cock recognized that expression as if it had been trained to rouse at the sight of it.

"You," she said, sitting up, the blankets sloughing around her waist. "Is it morning? Did you sleep at all?"

"Me," he agreed, straightening away from her before he could do something foolish. "I dozed here and there. Time to get on the road again."

"You should have woken me."

Haakon shrugged. "You were snoring. I didn't want to disturb you."

"I do not snore."

"It wasn't Snorri. Sounded like him, but he was wide awake too."

"Ha." She rolled her eyes.

Árdís dressed with stiff-legged enthusiasm, grumbling her way through a mouthful of bread and cheese as he stowed the bedroll on Snorri. She'd never taken to mornings well. Always preferred to drag him back into bed with her, where she'd nestle her face against his shoulder and soften back into sleep, or slide a playful hand down his abdomen. Haakon tugged the leather straps into place stiffly. As much as he kept trying to pretend they were strangers, he was sharply reminded of how much she *hadn't* changed. It was difficult to put the truth together. What had been real? What had not been? And could he trust that anything had been real, when he had no idea, which was which?

"Ready?"

Árdís eyed Sleipnir with as much enthusiasm as she would have shown if asked to stick her hand in a bucket full of mice. "I guess."

Haakon mounted and reached down to haul her up behind him. She settled there gingerly, and his first guess had been correct. She was new to this body, and hence to its aches and pains.

"We'll go slowly," he promised her.

Árdís wrapped her arms around his waist. "I'm dreaming of a hot spring right now. I want to soak in it for hours."

Maybe they'd find one. He nodded brusquely, his anger subdued and diminished. He could handle her games, and her argumentative nature. Even her teasing offers. But he was not immune to her pain.

The ride north stretched into hours. Árdís dozed against his back, and Haakon kept his eyes on the sky. Despite the ploy he'd played last night, they seemed to have settled into somewhat of a truce today.

Tormund's words kept tormenting him.

But did you ask the right fucking questions...?

He still hadn't discovered what had driven her away. He'd been too consumed by pride, by anger, to think his way through her careful answers in Reykjavik.

He needed to start thinking, if he was going to discover the truth.

"This Sirius," he forced himself to say, after lunch. "Your mate."

"He's not my mate. We were only betrothed, and that was the queen's idea, not mine." Árdís's arms tightened around him. "What of him?"

"Has he ever kissed you?" he asked bluntly.

Árdís stiffened against his back. "What?"

"It's a simple question."

"I thought you didn't care."

"I don't." Even to his own ears, his voice was so rough it had to be a lie. It had been easy to play games with her last night. But it hurt when those games skirted dangerously close to the truth.

"And if he *has* kissed me?"

Haakon forced himself to shrug. At least she couldn't see his face.

"Once," she admitted.

Nothing else.

There were a thousand different sorts of kisses. A gentle caress to the back of her hand. A soft brush of lips against hers. But Haakon's mind forced him right to the other end of the scale. The one he knew so well.

Lips capturing hers, his tongue stabbing insistently into her mouth. And who said the kiss had to be upon her sweet, lying mouth? He could almost taste the musk of her body, his gut curdling with an odd mix of jealousy and lust.

He wanted to fill the air with curses. Mostly at himself.

"Lost for words?" He could hear the flicker of triumph in her voice. "What's wrong, husband? Does the thought of another man kissing me bother you?"

"No." The blatant lie sounded like rough gravel on his tongue. "I was wondering what you consider a kiss."

"What do *you* consider a kiss?"

"A chaste press of his lips to yours."

Árdís laughed, a smoky sound that reminded him of another time. "It wasn't chaste, if that is what you're asking. But it was on my lips, and it never went further." She sighed. "Sirius kissed me long before you came into my life."

A tension he hadn't known he was holding relaxed within him.

"And what of you? No other woman?"

He ought to say yes. He wanted to spike her wheels, destroy some of her equilibrium, the way she'd done to him. Instead, all he could summon was a shrug. "Would it matter?"

Árdís fell silent.

Her hands were laced around his middle, and yet he could almost feel the tension in them, as if she didn't want to touch him in that moment. The press of her breasts against his back didn't come; she hadn't drawn breath, but it was a quiet sort of shock. No swift intake. No gasp. It seemed as though she'd swallowed that brief spurt of pain and was trying to manage it, somewhere deep within her.

He'd wanted it to hurt her.

He'd wanted her to feel some part of the pain he'd felt.

And yet, all it left him with was a bad taste in his mouth, and the sense he wasn't cut out for cruelty.

"No," he added curtly. "There has never been another woman for me."

And there probably never would be.

He heard the gentle exhale of her breath, and squeezed his eyes shut for a brief second. Despite her studied nonchalance, this was affecting her too.

"You were gone for seven years," he added, in a roughened voice, "but it never felt as though you were dead. I was so certain you weren't. I would have felt it somehow. And there are tales of *dreki* seducing mortal women, or stealing them away. It was the only thing I could focus upon; that you'd been stolen from me, and all I had to do was find you and rescue you, and...."

Then she'd be back in his arms where she belonged, and this hideous nightmare would be over.

There was always a happy ending to the tales his mother told him as a child.

But not this time.

Perhaps that was why this hurt so much. It was one thing to lose her to a *dreki* or death. The pain hurt, but the memories he had of her—of *them*—had been pure and untainted, his love for her the one thing that sustained him through those dark days. He'd been able to put one foot in front of the other *for her*. Not once had he given up, pushing his body out of bed each morning in his quest to find her, taking grievous injuries and fighting on, because he'd known she was out there somewhere, and when he found her....

When he found her, he could wrap her in his arms and never let her go again. They would be together, and somehow he'd forget the dark days, the pain, the torment. He would remember what it felt like to be loved, to be happy.

He would be the man he'd once been, without so much weight on his heart.

Discovering the truth had torn him apart.

He'd have sold his soul to the devil for her.

He'd have offered *his life*, in order to protect her.

He'd have burned the world to ashes for her, or fetched the moon from the fucking sky.

But she'd walked away and hadn't looked back.

Had she ever truly loved him?

"Haakon?" Árdís rocked against him, and her arms tightened around his waist. "What's wrong?"

"They're not particularly pleasant memories. I don't want to think about the last seven years. I don't want to speak about it."

He could practically hear her thinking.

And that was dangerous.

"And you?" He studied the landscape, seeing none of it. Just because this Sirius hadn't kissed her since she met him, didn't mean there hadn't been others.

"No," she whispered.

"You were betrothed."

"Not by choice. Ten or so years ago, Sirius made it quite clear he intended to pursue me as a mate. He's ambitious, and knew mating with me strengthened any claim he might make to becoming my mother's heir. I hated him. He's the threat hanging over the court, keeping us in line. The Blackfrost.

"But... It's all a little confusing now. The night I escaped, he caught me in the cellars as I was leaving. He wanted me to leave, to forestall the mating ceremony my mother insisted upon. It seems he's found his twin flame, and no longer desires to own me."

"Twin flame?"

"The other half of his *dreki* soul," she said, and he heard the quiet yearning in her voice. "Our true mates. It's a *dreki* myth that when the goddess, Tiamat, created us, she gave us a piece of her soul. It both strengthens us and weakens us, for we all feel the yearning within us, a hollow ache, as if we're not whole. Not complete. Humans are. They have their full soul. But we do not. And the only thing that can complete us is the one mate who can fulfill us."

"And there's a twin flame out there for all of you?" he asked carefully. So carefully. "For you?"

Árdís rested against his back, as if she'd leaned her cheek there. "I don't know. That's half the problem, you see. The males always know first. It's an instinct I lack. I suspect I shall never know."

And she longed for it.

He heard it in her voice.

"So...." He stared straight ahead. "Seven years without a man in your bed. I suppose last night starts to make sense."

"When you left me wet and aching in my bedroll alone?"

Despite everything, his mind locked on the words "wet" and "aching" and stayed there. Because she hadn't been the only one whose bed was empty for those seven years.

"It's your fault," she said, leaning against him, and her hands sliding down his hips, pausing to rest innocently at the tops of his thighs. "You've ruined me for all other men."

"Árdís." Damn her.

"What?" She shifted, her breasts brushing against his back. "You started this last night. Does it *ache*, Haakon?"

A growl echoed in his throat. He wanted to tumble her down to the ground and drive himself into her.

Those fingers stroked up and down his thigh, so lightly he barely felt it. Heat flushed through him, his cock hardening. Which was a damned dangerous thing for a man on a horse. Haakon caught her hand and squeezed in warning.

Árdís laughed and withdrew her devilish hands. "Two can play that game, I'll have you know."

"Not on horseback."

"Oh?" She brushed her lips against his ear. "Are you setting some rules?"

"Would you listen if I did?" He half turned his head, wanting to meet those damned lips.

"Maybe," she teased mercilessly, then held her hands up. "Not on horseback. Everywhere else is fair game."

He groaned. The second they dismounted for the night, she was going to renew her assault. And the only person he had to blame for that was himself.

He'd practically thrown the gauntlet down between them.

"Haakon!" A sudden tug came on his sleeve.

"What?" He reined Sleipnir in tightly.

Árdís pointed over his shoulder, and he looked up. Massive white clouds boiled on the horizon.

"A *dreki* storm?"

"Worse. A *dreki*. I can see him flying in the skies. He's flying back and forth, as if he's looking for something."

He couldn't see a damned thing.

Sleipnir nosed at the reins as if he wanted to continue.

"We cannot take this road," Árdís whispered.

"I thought you said they'd be looking for you in the skies? Wearing scales?"

"They will be," she snapped. "But they're not stupid. And they have better eyesight than an eagle. If they see a strange pair of travelers riding this road, they might overlook it. There have been enough farmers and riders to make us unusual, but not extraordinary. But they also might not. And while I can drag the hood of my cloak up, if they catch even the slightest glimpse of me...."

His hands tightened on the reins. "Dúrnir's village is along this road."

"And so is the *dreki*."

"We need to go north," he said. "Gunnar's given us a week at most, and we need to get to Hólmavík and confront my sorcerer before then."

The problem was the roads. The center of Iceland was one large inhospitable mess to traverse, which meant the best way to travel was a circular path around the coast. Practically the only way. That meant they couldn't diverge. It would add days to the journey, and with few roads there was more chance they'd be seen, but they had no choice.

Árdís's hands tightened on his hips. "He's looping toward the coast. If we cut across country—"

"Do you have any idea what the terrain is like?"

"No, not at all. It's not as though I fly regularly. Or have spent decades in these skies. Why, I spend all my time lounging around at court, or counting the coins in my collection of gold and jewels—impressively collected over the years, might I add. Sometimes, when that grows wearisome, I venture into the world of mortal men to find some particular fool to seduce."

He turned in the saddle and stared at her. Árdís stared back, one eyebrow rising in a challenging manner.

"It's not difficult to find one," she added, unnecessarily. "A fool, that is."

He was not going to answer that.

"It's different on horseback. Put one foot wrong, and we're walking to the coast."

"These beasts are frustratingly delicate."

"Would you prefer to walk?"

One ear flickered back, but Sleipnir largely ignored them.

"We're staying on the roads," Haakon said, straightening up and taking the reins once more. "He's heading toward the coast. There haven't been a great deal of other riders to hide among, but we can avoid the *dreki* if we keep our eyes open."

"You cannot even see them until they're on top of you."

Haakon ground his teeth together and nudged Sleipnir into a trot that should silence her for at least a minute. "Then perhaps you ought to stop arguing, and start keeping an eye out."

CHAPTER
ELEVEN

"IT DOESN'T FEEL very fair of me to take the bed again," Árdís protested, as Haakon rolled out the bedroll that night.

"Are you offering to take the watch and doze in my cloak?" he muttered.

His wife looked at the fire, and the cloak he'd been wearing. Dark shadows dwelled under her eyes. She took a crippled step toward the cloak, and then slowly dragged it over her shoulders. "I can sleep here tonight," she said, moving with slow, careful steps as she aimed for the boulder he'd been planning to rest his back against.

His eyes narrowed. Every time they'd dismounted today, she'd hobbled. He knew she wasn't used to the saddle, especially perched so precariously behind him, but she hadn't breathed a word of protest. Instead, she'd merely rested her forehead against his back, and held onto his waist, growing quieter with every mile.

Quiet was not a natural state of Árdís's.

Her silence infected him too, leaving him lost in the thought that she'd never taken another man to bed. *Dreki* males had thrown themselves at her feet, but she'd never been tempted.

"You've ruined me for all other men."

It had been said laughingly, but there'd been a hint of truth there too.

He didn't know what to think. Rage had been smoldering within him ever since Rurik told him the truth. All he'd wanted to do for the past month or two was smash things, and demand answers.

What he hadn't expected was for those answers to raise more questions.

Árdís might have revealed a hint of her reasoning, but he was fairly certain she hadn't told him everything. He could practically see the iceberg floating in front of him, barely the tip revealed. There was a depth of secrets between them that he didn't like.

He'd always been a careful man. A hunter who followed the near-invisible tracks of his quarry. And anger had blinded him, for there were signs here that something wasn't quite as it seemed.

"Take the bed," he said, tugging the blankets open for her. "I'm used to hard travel. You're not."

"No." She tried to drag his heavy cloak around her shoulders, and he fought the urge to help her. "I'm not even that tired."

"Árdís, stop being bloody stubborn."

"I will as soon as you do," she snapped back. "I'm not weak. I can handle this body. And you barely slept last night."

Starting toward her, he stopped when she tried to hobble around the fire to avoid him.

"Lie down," he said. "You need the rest more than I do. You have several more days in the saddle ahead of you."

The look on her face said it all.

"I'm fine," she insisted, but it lacked her earlier adamancy. "You've been taking all of the watches, and doing most of the work. It's your turn to sleep. I'm not just some pampered princess."

It wasn't as though he'd forgotten how stubborn she was, but the years apart had dulled the frustration. Árdís could give a mule lessons in obstinacy. Years ago he'd argued against her, their wills clashing in a storm of passion, but he was a different man now. Not a young man who'd never left his village, his days sorted into a routine of monotony, but a man who'd challenged the seas, and the storms, and the beasts themselves. A man who no longer simply met each challenge headlong, but one who sidestepped it, outthought it.

He stared at her.

She stared back.

Haakon's eyes narrowed with slow determination. "Fine."

The second she relaxed he made a sudden grab for her, and swung her up over his shoulder. One hand clamped firmly on her backside, he turned and strode toward the bedroll.

She was tired. She was sore. She was stubborn.

There was more than one way to deal with this.

Árdís yelped, kicking him in the gut. "Put me down, you big oaf!"

He stroked his hand over her bottom, and she sucked in a startled breath. Haakon smiled to himself. Revenge against her earlier entreaties on the horse. "You're not going to win this argument, so you might as well simply concede."

"*Concede?*"

"Yes, concede." He dumped her down onto the bedroll, one of his knees trapping her skirts to the ground, as he followed her. "You have heard of the word, have you not?"

Árdís lay flat on her back, staring up at him with her mouth agape. Haakon pinned her there, hands on her wrists, and just like that they were seven years into the past. This could have been any night during their marriage. Argument ringing in his ears, even as blood raged through his erection. He wanted inside her. Now.

Old habits died hard. If this was seven years ago, then he would have simply fused his mouth to hers and kissed her. Dragged her skirts up, as he settled between her hips.

He did not.

Amber eyes narrowed in glorious fury. "While I have heard of the word, I have simply chosen to strike it from my vocabulary."

"You would."

"Dreki do not concede. We fight until the bitter end."

Haakon lowered himself, until their faces were barely an inch apart. Some part of him was enjoying this. "You're not going to win this fight."

"You sound so certain." Her voice roughened.

His thumbs stroked against the inside of her wrists. "Should I not be?"

Uncertainty sat like a foreign object on her expression. For all her bravado, she seemed to hesitate, and that gave him pause. Árdís had been a virgin before their marriage, but her manner had always been unabashedly sexual. She'd pursued him with such fervor it had been all he could do to deny his base instincts as he courted her.

But here, now, he saw a hint of vulnerability in her eyes he'd never seen before.

She cleared her throat, and the faint flickering smile that stole over her lips was nothing more than an act, he was certain of it. "Do you mean to share the bedroll then?"

Haakon's lashes lowered. "No." There were limits to what he could tolerate.

"Then this is a game?"

It felt like something was lodged in his throat. Flirting with her last night had been a test, one that opened Pandora's Box, for she'd had no compunctions in returning the favor today. Yet, the look in her eyes spoke to him as she searched his gaze, trying to work out his intentions.

It said; *please touch me.*

And yet, it also said; *please don't hurt me.*

He'd been so lost in his own anger that he hadn't noticed until now that perhaps he wasn't the only one hurting. The realization left him slightly breathless, and changed the aim of this encounter.

Haakon pushed to his knees, giving her some space. "Roll over."

An arched eyebrow met this request.

"Just roll over," he said gruffly, grabbing her by the hips and turning her.

"What are you up to?" She pressed her hands flat to the bedroll, and craned her neck so she could see what he was doing.

He paused, resting on his knuckles above her. The pose was incredibly tempting. He'd taken her like this, many a time.

But this was not about sex.

Nor was it about revenge.

This was about discovering what was real.

"Here," he muttered, dragging her skirts up her legs. Mud flecked her stockings.

"What are you *doing*?"

168

"If I don't rub out some of the stiffness, you're barely going to be able to walk tomorrow, let alone sit on a horse."

He found the top of her woolen stockings and began to work them down her legs, trying not to think too hard about what his hands were doing. Árdís froze.

"It's not like I haven't seen it all before," he reminded her, hauling his pack closer and tugging open the tin of liniment he kept for the horses. Dabbing his fingers into the strong-scented mix, he warmed it between his palms, before setting them on her calves.

"Yes, but...." She made a choking sound deep in her throat as he skated the flats of his palms up the back of her legs, pausing just above her knees. "*Oh.*"

Soft breathy gasps proved to be torture. She'd sound like that as he fucked his way into her, her head thrown back, and.... *No.*

He needed to focus.

Árdís groaned, pressing her cheek into the bedroll. "If I'd known this was what you intended, I wouldn't have argued."

"You can't help yourself."

She laughed, and that too was pure torture. He loved the sound of her laughter.

Haakon twitched her skirts higher. The simple fact of the matter was that her calves were not the part of her that was aching. Running his palms over the backs of her knees, he quested higher, each movement a little slower, as if those hands asked a question.

Árdís's entire body *melted* beneath his touch.

He pushed into the soft muscle at the back of her thighs with his thumbs. Árdís moaned, her fingers curling into the blankets. If there'd been even a hint of sexual pleasure in the sound, he might have been unable to resist, but the sound was pure surrender. Begging of a different kind.

"Sweet goddess," she breathed, turning pliant and helpless beneath him. "You don't know how good that feels."

Haakon kneaded tender muscles, rolling his knuckles across her bottom as he teased out every ache and pain. Then clasping one thigh in both hands and stroking his thumbs and fingers up her soft skin. Árdís lay undone beneath him, making soft helpless noises.

Fuck.

His thumbs skated up the inside of her thighs and she flinched, as if it hurt there the most. Warm molten skin shivered beneath his palms, and he pictured his thumbs sliding up, up, into the shadowy depths of her inner thighs. She'd be wet there. And her legs would part, just another inch or two, if he dared do it.

But this wasn't the first time he'd denied his own pleasure when it came to getting what he wanted from her.

Haakon slowly dragged his fingertips down her bare thighs, before he bowed his head, and stopped touching her.

Breathing hard, he rested over her on all fours, his knuckles pressing into the blankets on either side of her skirts. Firelight glimmered on the bare skin of her legs. He wanted to grab her by the hips and drag her up onto her hands and knees.

Or bury his face between her thighs, and lick his way up.

The thought wrapped velvet hands around his cock, a flush of heat spreading through his balls. Seven years without the touch of a woman. Seven years without *her* touch.

He was only a man.

"Why are you stopping?" she whispered.

Because I'm about to lose my mind.

Or all sense of control.

Somehow he reared up onto his knees, and climbed to his feet. "Because we're done here."

Even he heard the gruff tone of his voice.

Árdís rolled over onto her bottom, her skirts rucked around her thighs as she stared up at him. Firelight picked out the golden streaks through her hair, and flickered in her amber eyes. Her lips were flushed and full. Slightly parted. The press of her nipples against her dress drew his eye, but he forced himself to look away, wiping his hands clean on an old rag. Trying to think of something else—anything else—other than the feel of her skin beneath his palms.

"Thank you," Árdís said very softly.

"You're welcome," he muttered, dragging his cloak around him, and discreetly rearranging his cock.

"Where are you going?" Árdís demanded, rolling onto her side.

He'd never wanted to touch anything in his life more than he wanted to touch her in that moment.

"For a walk," he said, and turned into the darkness of the night, staggering blindly as his eyesight adjusted.

And hopefully a cool swim.

There had to be some water fresh off the glacier around here somewhere.

"Get some sleep," he called.

This time she didn't deny him.

It seemed there was more than one way to win an argument.

CHAPTER TWELVE

"ARE YOU CORRUPTING my warhorse?"

Árdís drew her closed fist into her chest guiltily, though she kept stroking the silky muzzle of the beast with her other hand. "Absolutely not."

They'd stopped for lunch, and so Haakon could rearrange most of the bags, and allow the sweat on Sleipnir's back to dry. Sleipnir made sloppy crunching noises as he made short work of the wizened apple she'd been feeding him. Snorri had demurred, still not quite trusting her. He practically had a seizure every time she glanced his way.

There'd been no signs of any *dreki* in the skies this morning, but she couldn't help feeling on edge.

Both thanks to the *dreki* hunting them, and a certain husband who'd left her pleasantly boneless on the bedroll last night.

Árdís closed her eyes momentarily. Climbing back onto Sleipnir this morning had made it clear not all of her aches were gone, but it hadn't been painful, the way she'd been expecting.

Last night had been a thoughtful gesture, nothing more. She didn't deserve it.

It reminded her of when he'd been courting her. *Dreki* males had battled for her attention, delivering gaudy rings and necklaces dripping with jewels at her feet, but only Haakon had ever truly cared for her feelings. At court she'd been a prize to be won. Haakon made her feel as though nothing could ever hurt her, when he was at her side. There'd never been jewels, or gold, or anything a *dreki* princess expected to find. Instead, there had been wildflowers waiting for her on her pillow when she woke, or berries he'd gone out of his way to find for her once he realized how much she enjoyed them. A thousand thoughtful little gestures that made her heart ache so badly, now that she knew she couldn't have him.

"Sleipnir's a foul-tempered brute." Haakon looked faintly disapproving as he came to her side, glaring as though his horse had betrayed him. "And he bites like a bastard when he thinks your back is turned."

Someone was in a bad mood this afternoon, and she had a good idea why.

"He wouldn't dare," Árdís cooed, capturing the enormous bay's face in both hands and pressing her lips to his nose.

The horse's nostrils flared out as she stared into those velvety brown eyes, letting it see the *dreki* in hers. Sleipnir gave a nervous snort that sprayed snot and chunks of apple slobber all over her.

"We have an understanding," Árdís said, but she looked at the mess down the front of her dress and curled her lip up. Ugh.

Haakon dragged a rag out of his pocket and caught Sleipnir's bridle. "That's what you get for coddling him."

"For a vicious warhorse," she retorted, taking the rag and brushing herself down, "he practically rolls over and shows me his belly when I pat him."

If only his owner would do the same.

But it felt as though he'd spent all night thinking of what a mistake it had been to massage her. And now she was paying the price for it. The second she broached his walls, he began bricking them back up again.

Haakon slung his saddle blanket over the bay's broad back, settling it high on his withers. The stark line of her husband's profile made her shoulders slump a little when she saw his expression soften as he rubbed his knuckles over Sleipnir's flank. There was genuine affection there.

He'd looked at her like that once.

"How far can we get today?" Árdís demanded, trying to force down her confusing feelings. She'd made her sacrifice seven years ago, knowing full well what it would cost her. "These beasts move so slowly."

"Maybe fifteen miles, if we're lucky. Sleipnir isn't used to carrying two people." He patted Sleipnir's glossy neck, muttering in the horse's ear. "How does that apple taste now, you traitor? She's talking about you, you know?"

Fifteen miles. She felt the frustration of it all the way to her bones. "I could cover that in ten minutes," she muttered. "Or less."

"I thought the point was subterfuge," he said, easing the saddle into place, and cinching it tightly.

"Or hiding in small nooks and crannies whenever something flaps in the wind?"

"If we make it to nightfall without any more sightings, I'll start to rest easy." He looked at Sleipnir. "Breathe out, you big bastard."

"He doesn't like it when you speak to him like that." Árdís watched the horse's ears flicker back and forth, and stepped closer to rub her hand over his velvety muzzle, his whiskers prickling her.

"He'll like it even less if I slide right off the other side when I try to mount." Haakon grunted under his breath, and dragged the girth tighter. "If we move too fast, we'll draw attention."

"And here I thought you just wanted to spend more time with me." She glanced at him from beneath her lashes.

Haakon paused, swiftly buckling the girth into place. His attention shifted toward her, his pale eyes narrowing in upon her with a tight focus that made her catch her breath.

It felt as though the world around them vanished.

"I want my grandmother's ring back," he finally said.

"And that's all you want?"

His pupils dilated, and he took a jerky step toward her, before stopping. "No, that's not all I want. But it's all I'm going to get, so what is the point in pretending otherwise?"

Árdís folded her arms over her chest, even as her sex clenched tight with need. Being with him for so many nights began to seem an agony of its own. Seeing his cold, closed-off face counterbalanced against the heat in his eyes had given her nothing but a restless sleep ever since they'd set off. "We don't have to be at odds. Last night—"

"Last night was a mistake, Árdís. I shouldn't have touched you like that." Haakon clenched his eyes shut, leaning against the saddle.

"I didn't mind."

"Why?" His lips pressed firmly together, stark, angry color flooding through his cheeks. "So we can pretend there's anything left between us? Why bother, *Princess*? It's only a lie."

She felt sick to her stomach, hating the way his tongue caressed the word princess, as if to mock her.

"I want you safe," he said, turning to his saddlebags and the assorted weaponry he carried. "I want you to see your brother again. Then I owe you nothing else but a goodbye."

Árdís captured Sleipnir's muzzle between her hands again, trying to swallow down the choking fist of hurt in her throat. She'd broken the part of him she loved the best—the part that looked at her as if she'd set the very moon in the skies, the part that promised her forever and made her believe it.

And she couldn't even tell him why.

Somehow she forced herself to smile, though she didn't dare let Haakon see her eyes. They felt far too warm, and she blinked to clear them. "Let us be going then. The sooner we arrive, the sooner you can be rid of me."

She simply didn't have the strength of will to continue the conversation. Turning around, she began helping Haakon to load up both horses, though Snorri, predictably, refused to allow her anywhere near him.

It wasn't until Haakon had mounted and reached down to offer her his hand that she realized perhaps her subterfuge hadn't gone unnoticed.

"I didn't mean it like that, Árdís," he murmured, helping her to swing up behind him. "I just meant, can there be anything left between us when all is said and done? *Is* there anything left?"

Somehow she wrapped her cold arms around him. "No."

There was a moment where he might have said something else, but instead the words died on his lips.

Árdís looked up, into the hard line of his profile. Though he was in her arms, it felt as though the distance between them had never been greater. And she wanted to change that distance. She wanted to obliterate it. To tell him how she truly felt.

But that would only cost him his life. She couldn't be selfish.

It was better this way.

"Perhaps we should be going?" she said instead.

"Two *dreki*," Árdís pointed out, though even *he* could see faint hints of the second one.

Haakon cursed, watching the skies from the overhang of a vast shelf of rock. They'd taken shelter beneath it the second Árdís noticed the *dreki*. "Why isn't it bloody raining? It rains nine days out of ten here. I had to clean mold off my riding leathers last week. But the second you decide to flee the royal court, we receive a blast of sunny, clear days."

"It was raining the night I fled. I had to crawl up hills slick with mud. I, at least, am not cursing the sunlight."

"What are they looking for? Do you think they know you're on the ground?"

"I doubt it. What *dreki* in her right mind would *choose* to flee in mortal form?"

"Then what are they looking for?" He squeezed his leather gloves in his hands. "They've been doing sweeps all morning."

"Perhaps they think I'm trying to hide in some crevice? There are mountains, fissures, and glaciers all over the island."

"I've seen your brother, Rurik, in *dreki* form. He gleams like a gold twenty-crown coin. It's not precisely the best color to blend in with the rocks, and he said you're the exact same color."

She hesitated.

"What?"

"It's nothing."

"Árdís."

"I've rarely left court," she snapped, more than a little defensively. "I have a small mountain and territory I call home, but my mother insists I spend most of my time close to her wing. Perhaps they think I *would* be foolish enough to hide on a gray mountainside."

"Then they don't know you well enough." She'd never been a fool.

The answer seemed to mollify her, despite the lingering tension between them. Haakon scrubbed a hand through his hair. They couldn't travel at night. Not only was it dangerous, but they'd never see the *dreki* coming.

"There's one place we could go where they won't fly over," Árdís said.

He looked at her sharply, alerted by her tone.

"You're not going to like it."

"It's off-road, isn't it?"

Árdís nodded.

If they had to hide like this every two minutes, then they'd never get to the coast. He breathed out his frustration. "Why won't they go there?" Not much scared *dreki*.

Árdís shuddered a little. "Because it's the territory of He Who Should Not Be Woken."

He Who—? He looked at her sharply. "Is this some sort of *dreki* legend?"

"No. It's my great-grandfather, Fáfnir."

"I've heard stories about Fáfnir. He's a myth."

"I assure you he's not. He's a grumpy, spiteful old *dreki* who's not very fond of the rest of us. Fáfnir was once the king of the *dreki* court," she said. "He helped forge the treaty between *dreki* and mankind in this country, until his grandson—my father—overthrew him. He's near the end of his existence now, and spends most of his time in a hibernation state, deep in the heart of his volcano, listening to the rumblings of the earth. Some rumors state he's almost turning to stone himself, but no *dreki* wants to find out the truth for himself. Just in case they wake him.

"If we skirt the edges of Fáfnir's territory, then we can ride north with no one the wiser. By the time we leave his territory, we should be clear of the sweeps they're making, and can rejoin the road."

"And what makes you think your great-grandfather will allow you in his lands?" From what he'd seen of Rurik, most *dreki* were frightfully territorial.

"He probably won't even know I'm there. My resonance is smaller when I'm in this form."

"Resonance?"

She shrugged. "It's... got to do with *dreki* magic. In our natural forms, we're more focused on the earth and the elements. We exist in a state closer to the magical and the spiritual, and hence we exude stronger magical emissions. In this mortal body, the echo I cast is smaller." She held up her wrist, producing the manacle. "And I daresay I'm emitting virtually nothing at this moment. I feel blind to the world around me."

Haakon stared north, along the gravel road. Then he turned and glanced to the east, and the spine of snow-capped mountains that existed here. A single pyramid of stones shaped like an old woman marked the trail into Fáfnir's territory. The locals called them *kerlingar*.

"Trust me," she whispered. "Please. I don't want to be caught any more than you do."

Haakon sighed, and turned Sleipnir east. "Let us hope your great-grandfather doesn't wake."

Thunder rumbled.

Árdís scrambled up the slope at Haakon's side, tugging the hood of her cloak over her head. "You *had* to question the lack of rain, didn't you?" she yelled.

They'd dismounted to give the horses a rest, especially on the shale-coated side of the mountain path they traveled.

"Curse the gods," he muttered under his breath. "It doesn't feel like a *dreki* storm."

"It's not. It's the cold northern wind meeting the warmer air from down south. Or perhaps Thor took exception to your tone."

Haakon slicked his wet hair back off his face and led Sleipnir forward. Rain washed runnels in the dirt track. "We need to take shelter."

Árdís scrambled along behind him. He had to grant her this; she had a will of pure iron when she set her mind to something. Every step she took was stiff with the ache of sitting in an unfamiliar saddle, but she'd barely complained.

He helped her crest the top of the slope. Sleipnir bounded over the stone lip in their path, and then hauled up short at the end of the reins. Árdís bent over at the waist, sucking in breath. The hems of her skirts were a sodden mess.

Haakon turned and surveyed the valley. The storm wasn't going away anytime soon, and she was wet through and exhausted. The horses needed a rest too.

"There!" He pointed along the valley to where a black mouth gaped in the side of the mountain. "We'll take shelter there."

The cave afforded them some shelter from the weather, though it wasn't deep enough for more. Haakon unsaddled the horses, moving brusquely as he rubbed them down and settled their nosebags over their faces.

Árdís's teeth chattered by the time he returned to her side. She'd unrolled the bedroll, but hadn't moved beyond that. Strands of her hair hung in a bedraggled braid. She looked wet, sore, and hungry. His lips pressed together. "Sit."

"I'm wet."

Cold could kill a man faster than a gut wound, in these lands. "We both need to get out of these clothes and dry off. I'll get the fire started."

His store of kindling was small. He'd need to keep an eye out tomorrow. But he set a small fire, and turned to find her unmoving. "What's wrong?"

"Can you...?" She turned around, presenting him with her back as she dragged her damp hair forward over one shoulder.

Haakon stared at the row of buttons tracing her spine. Hunched over and shivering, she didn't precisely present the picture of a woman determined to torment him, but you never knew what she had in mind.

Still, she was wet and cold, and judging from the long periods of blessed silence in the last hour, probably miserable.

"Truce," he muttered. "Just for tonight?"

"Are you trying to say you find my drowned look irresistible?"

He smiled a little at that.

"Utterly. If I gave you some soap, you could simply walk outside." They'd both bathed in a frigid river that morning, one at a time, but it had been swiftly done, out of necessity.

She sighed. "I don't think I even have the energy for that, let alone seducing you."

Moving to her side, Haakon wiped his hands, then began to undo each small button with shriveled fingers. She'd managed the task herself this morning, with some small help, but the wet wool of her dress constricted her tonight.

"I like rain better when I'm in my *dreki* form. I forgot how cold it is to wear skin rather than scales. I miss my volcano."

He helped her strip her dress down her arms, then paused and encircled them with his hands. She was freezing. Haakon rubbed briskly, and she tilted her head forward in surrender, her eyes half shut. A soft purring sound echoed in her throat. Pleasure. Only, not of the erotic kind. If he didn't hurry, then he was going to have a sleeping *dreki* princess in his arms.

"Here," he muttered, kneeling at her feet and tugging her sopping gown down over her hips.

Lightning flashed behind her, highlighting the wet press of her chemise to her body. Every single curve was seared into his retinas as the world plunged back into darkness. He could even make out the darker circle of her nipples.

Haakon released a slow breath. So it was going to be torture tonight, no matter whether she was the instigator— or his own frustrated imagination.

Gathering her up in his arms, he carried her to the bedroll and laid her down, Árdís blinked at him sleepily as he drew the blankets up over her.

"Are you hungry?" he asked.

"Not really."

"Then sleep." He needed to eat, otherwise he'd be feeling it tomorrow. Finding some dried strips of beef in his pack, he chewed them mechanically as Árdís shifted in the bedroll.

Gods, he was tired. He'd barely snatched a few hours last night.

"Haakon?" A plaintive question.

"Yes?"

"I know you're going to think this is some trick, but would you consider joining me? Please," she whispered, shivering despite the blankets. "I'm cold, and that fire is pathetic."

Scrubbing at his face, he sighed. Fending her off when she wanted to fuck him was bad enough, but the idea of falling asleep beside her did something far worse to him.

"I promise I will keep my hands to myself."

It wasn't her hands that were the problem.

"Move over," he murmured, stripping his boots off, and then his wet clothes. Laying them by the fire, he turned back to the bedroll.

Heat warmed the blankets from her body as he lay down behind her. But she'd not been lying. Her skin was cold to the touch, and her chemise damp.

"You're not wearing anything," she blurted.

"I know. Everything's wet." He shifted a little to tuck the blanket between her bottom and his burgeoning erection. She fit against the curve of his body as perfectly as she ever had. There was an inch between them, and a fold of blanket. It wasn't enough.

Árdís lay still for long seconds. "I thought we had a truce. This isn't fair."

"I'm not trying to tempt you."

"You don't have to," she muttered under her breath.

He smiled a little at that, and shifted. The press of her chemise against his chest made him flinch momentarily. It wasn't a good idea to stay in wet clothes.

It was a terrible idea for her to be without them.

Could *dreki* even fall ill?

"At the risk of having my intentions mistaken," he muttered, "I think you should remove your chemise. If you fall ill from the cold, it's going to be a difficult trip."

Árdís groaned. "You're making this very difficult to behave."

Wriggling against him, she began slipping the hem of the chemise up her body. His world narrowed to focus on every hint of contact between them.

Inch by inch, she dragged the wet linen up between them. His cock, which had been mildly interested before, but hampered in its enthusiasm by the cold, surged to rampant attention. *Sweet merciless Hela.* Haakon rubbed at the bridge of his nose, squeezing his eyes shut. It mattered little. Every whisper of movement gave his imagination far too much to work with.

"There," she whispered, and threw the wet chemise toward the rest of their clothes.

Árdís lay back down with careful precision, maintaining the space between them. The blankets shifted up, revealing enough space along his back to allow a small draft in. His ass hung out.

The bedroll had only been made for one person.

Silently cursing her, he wrapped an arm around her middle and hauled her back that precious inch. Árdís yelped, then relaxed the second she realized what he was doing. A single fold of blanket kept the caress chaste. The chilled skin of her back against his chest made him flinch, but neither of them would get much sleep if she spent all night shivering. He managed to tuck the blankets around the both of them, and then draped his arm over her waist.

The storm raged outside. Sleipnir whickered.

Haakon nuzzled his face into the curve of Árdís's nape and breathed in the scent of her hair. Too late, he realized how dangerous this was. Denying his lust was one thing, but he hadn't realized how much his soul hungered to simply have her in his arms. To feel her fingers stroke lightly over the hairs on his forearm, a simple habitual move she probably wasn't even aware of doing.

He could almost forget the last seven years.

This. This was real.

And it made his heart ache fiercely, for the sheer want of it.

"Thank you," Árdís whispered. "You're so much warmer."

"My foolish mortal body is good for something, it seems."

There was a long moment of silence.

She had to break it. "As I recall, it was good for a lot of things."

Haakon groaned, burying his face in her hair. "I swear to the gods...."

"You swear to the gods quite often, it seems. That's new."

He'd begun this quest thinking of revenge. He'd pictured how he'd repay her a thousand times. Kissing her, and then denying her anything more. Making her beg for sweet mercy. Or walking away after he coolly told her she meant nothing to him anymore.

Somehow, it didn't seem as though he held the upper hand here.

Árdís was right. He was a fool.

"Just go to sleep," he growled, and shut his eyes, though the throbbing ache between his legs told him it would be a long time before he got any peace himself.

CHAPTER THIRTEEN

SUNLIGHT WASHED DOWN over her as Árdís strode along the grassy mountain slope, searching for her husband. The basket in her hands swung, and she wore a smile. It seemed she was never without one these days. Two months married, and her happiness settled over her like a warm cloak.

This world was so far removed from the one she'd known. She couldn't remember feeling this way in over half a cycle, since her father died and her brother fled. She'd still had Marduk at her side, but life had become different, wariness staining the court. She hadn't realized how empty her life had become once Marduk vanished as well, until she met Haakon.

Home.

It felt like she'd found a home. And there were people here who loved her, and drew her into their lives as if she belonged. Every time she saw Haakon, her heart seemed to expand in her chest, until it felt like it grew three sizes. She could chase forever in his arms, and never regret a thing.

Everything felt right.

Or almost everything.

Her *dreki* shivered within her. It had been weeks since she'd last shifted shape and flown. She missed it dreadfully, but there were always eyes upon her at the moment, and Haakon hadn't been hunting in over a month. He'd been too busy with the harvest, and then the cows were birthing, and now some of the goats had escaped and—

It was never-ending. But it pleased her, this simple life.

And if she had to sacrifice something, then perhaps it was worth it.

Her smile slipped. If she were being honest, it was no small sacrifice. It was the one thing that jarred her perfect life, but how could she expect Haakon to react if he knew what she was?

"Hiya, hiya!"

Her heart swelled. She knew that voice, and hurried over the rise, sighting her husband below. Stripped of his shirt, with sweat gleaming on his bare chest, Haakon was trying to capture the last goat. Sunlight flirted over his tanned skin as he made a lunge and brought the beast down. Muscles flexed as he knelt on its flank, binding its feet together swiftly as he panted. The others were lashed in their wicker pen, bleating when they saw her.

Some creatures couldn't be fooled. They smelled the truth on her skin. She kept telling him animals had never liked her, and he'd finally banned her from the milking shed after the cow kept kicking the bucket of milk over every time she went near it.

"I should have known you had something to do with this," he growled as he straightened and brushed his hands off. His hair was growing longer, the sides shaved, and a top knot of silky blond drawn back off his face with a strip of leather. He tried to maintain his fierce expression, but laughed when she rolled her eyes.

"I didn't go anywhere near them." The stupid creatures panicked within their wicker yard.

"Stay right where you are," he said. "I've spent half the morning hunting them down."

Haakon was forced to come to her, his long strides eating up the ground. Árdís bit her lip, exploring every inch of him with unabashed interest. Lean hard muscle gleamed with sweat, the ridge of his rippled abdominals sinking into the edge of his trousers. By the time he reached her that familiar twinkle was in his eyes, and he simply grabbed her by the back of the neck and jerked her against his chest.

Yes, please. Árdís moaned as their mouths met. The basket with his lunch pressed between them, and Haakon growled, tugging it from her fingers and setting it aside without breaking the kiss. Both hands tore through her hair, and she bit his lower lip as the tension between them began to shift.

She kissed him hungrily, her legs lifting to wrap around his waist. The playfulness evaporated, and Haakon's hands began to map her body, slow, gentle strokes down her sides that tormented her. Then they stilled on her waist.

"*Árja*—" He groaned as she captured his words on her lips.

A tongue lashed against her own, and a shiver ran through him. He set her down, and pushed her away, his lips breaking from hers at the last moment. "I thought you were here to bring me lunch. Not *be* lunch."

"Can't I do both?"

He cupped his hands behind his head, as if to remove temptation, his pectorals tensing as he looked at her with faint amusement. "You are going to be the death of me, woman."

A shiver of trepidation went through her, and she pressed her hand over his mouth. "Please don't ever say that again."

Haakon bit her palm, missing the shiver that ran through her. He winked, then turned and made his way back to the last goat, bending to throw it over his shoulders. It bleated as he wrapped his hands around both sets of its bound legs. "Come on. As much as I'd like to oblige you, there's a storm coming. We'll eat back at the house."

A storm. Her eyes shifted to the horizon swiftly. How had she not noticed?

Thick white thunderheads brewed, growing darker with every second.

"Are you coming?" Haakon called.

The storm rolled closer. Boiling thunderheads darkened the skies. Árdís looked up, feeling something unnatural on the horizon. Pressure pushed inside her head, as if something was trying to force its way inside.

"Aye, little dreki, the storm is coming," something whispered, running its mental fingers all through her memories.

Árdís blinked. The storm vanished, though she could hear it in the distance, and Haakon was swept away. There was only darkness now.

Where was he?

"Haakon?" No matter where she looked, he was gone. "Haakon!"

"You dare walk my dreams?" said that voice.

"I'm not in your dreams."

A husky chuckle shivered over her skin. *"No, but you're in my lands. There is a price to pay for those who trespass."*

The pressure started to push harder. Árdís cried out, grinding her hands against her forehead to try and ease it.

"Árja? Wake up," said a low, sharp voice in her ear. "Wake up!"

Árdís came awake with a gasp, feeling a hand curl over her shoulder. Her ears popped as the pressure vanished. For a moment she didn't quite know where she was, still feeling the warmth of sunlight on her skin.... No. Not sunlight. The heat of a male body against hers.

She was in a cave that smelt strongly of horse, curled snugly in blankets that still held the warmth of her husband. She'd been dreaming, but not about everything, it seemed. Some of it had been real.

"What is it?" she whispered, holding the blankets to cover herself as lightning flickered outside the cave.

Haakon knelt by the bedroll, clad in his leather trousers and nothing else. The sight of his bare chest seared its way into her memory, but her heart was rabbiting in her chest. Unease spilled through her.

"There's something moving out there in the night."

"*Dreki?*" she breathed.

"I don't know."

She pressed the heel of her palm to her temples. "I think I was dreaming. I think something was *in* my dreams."

Some *dreki* could do that, if they willed, and though she still had the gift of her psychic shields, perhaps they'd weakened with her exhaustion.

Haakon's fingertips brushed her cheek, "You're not hurt, are you?"

She felt light-headed, after all that pressure, and simply shook her head. The concern in his eyes felt like a lance through the heart. She pressed a quick kiss to his fingers in response.

"Get dressed." He moved toward her saddlebags, and tossed them toward her. "I'll see if I can catch another glimpse of it."

Árdís dressed swiftly, dragging on a shirt and tunic and the leather trousers she wore for sparring practice instead of a gown, just in case they needed to run. The horses were still loaded with the gear, their girths loose. Árdís joined Haakon at the cave mouth.

Mud streamed down the side of the mountain, slick in the rain. It had lessened to a drizzle, but the slope looked treacherous. Nothing moved. Nothing she could see anyway, but Árdís settled down patiently, resting her hand on Haakon's thigh.

"I cannot see anything," she breathed.

"Maybe it knows we're watching?"

Silence.

"I can definitely feel something out there." Her senses were muted, but an itch prickled down the back of her spine, and her *dreki* was on edge. "A pity," she said with a soft sigh. "I was hoping to wake in your arms. I'd finally gotten you naked."

His eyes cut to hers, dark in the night. "Feeling better, I see?"

"Our truce only lasts until the sun rises."

"Fair warning. I'll be on my guard." His lips kicked up.

Clearly, his ill temper of the day had been dulled by sleep. Árdís stroked his thigh with her thumb. He'd been pushing himself for two days, snatching a few hours of sleep curled up in his cloak. He should have taken her offer of the bedroll the night before.

A flicker of movement shifted in the corner of her eye. Árdís leaned forward, her grip on his thigh tightening.

"What is it? Is it He Who Should Not Be Woken?"

She held her breath. A shape shifted. It was big, whatever it was, but it blended into the countryside well. Too well. Another rock shifted behind it, and Árdís nostrils quivered. She could just make out a faint hint of basalt and rotten flesh on the breeze.

Damn it.

"Trolls."

"Trolls?" he said incredulously.

Thunder grumbled in the distance.

"What? You can believe in dragons and *dreki*, and wyrms and kraken, but you don't think trolls actually exist?"

"I just—" He seemed taken aback. "I've never seen...."

"Well, no. I doubt you would have. They cannot walk under the sun, and they prefer isolated places, rather than those close to mankind. Humans rarely see them, though if a farmer goes missing, or a traveler vanishes on the road, one assumes.... There used to be more of them, but the rise of the church in this land has driven them away. They don't like church bells for some reason."

"What do we do?"

"They're moving slowly, trying to take us unaware, but they can run fast when they want to." She bit her lip. "*Dreki* and trolls do not go well together. My people call them Destroyers of the Storm-sun, and they are afraid of lightning, thanks to us."

"So they'll leave us alone?"

"They eat men," she muttered, casting him a look. "And if there are enough of them, they may attempt to attack us, if they see me in my mortal form."

Haakon peered out of the cave. "I think I've seen at least three shapes moving."

"Then we should perhaps consider leaving ourselves." The rain had lessened, though the sun was still hours away.

"We don't want to find ourselves trapped in here, and our swords will do nothing but break on their skins."

"How do you kill them?"

"You don't," she said, heading for the horses. "Fire might drive them away, but I doubt anything will burn right now. I could strike them with lightning, if I wasn't wearing this cursed manacle, but unless you can make the sun rise swiftly, we don't have a lot of options. Are you coming?"

"Damn it," he muttered, following her. "I'd just dried out too."

It was a slow chase, with Haakon and Árdís slipping and sliding down the mountain with the horses. The rain was merely a fine mist now, but Árdís squealed as her feet went out from under her and she landed on her backside.

Haakon grabbed her before she could vanish off the side of the mountain, his fingers probably hurting her, he was squeezing her so tightly. He helped her to her feet, heart racing. "Be careful."

"Sorry. I wasn't looking where I was walking. They're getting closer," she whispered. "I think they're starting to gather their courage to attack."

Haakon cursed under his breath. "Down there," he said, pointing to a valley filled with a low-lying miasma of steam. "I can see mud bubbling, and smell the sulfur. If we can pick our way through the mud pools, then they can't rush us."

"That's your brilliant idea? They can't come at us, but what if we trap ourselves? We can't run either."

"Running out of options," he said sharply. "As you've pointed out, I can't make the sun rise."

Árdís hissed under her breath. "Curse this stupid damned bracelet. I hate feeling so helpless."

"Welcome to the mortal world," he snapped, guilt stirring through him. "Not all of us can fly our way to safety, or strike our enemies with lightning."

Árdís glared at him, and his blood rushed through his veins. "I cannot help being what I am."

"And neither can I!"

He pushed her forward, hovering close enough to grab her if she fell again. She was *dreki*, and he only a man. The difference between them wasn't insurmountable, but then she'd left him and he still didn't know why.

Árdís marched with stiff steps, her spine straight.

Damn it. Haakon raked a hand through his damp hair. She wasn't the only one who felt trapped or helpless. What sort of man was he if he couldn't save her? His gut knotted up tight. "I'm sorry I snapped at you. I don't like feeling like I can't protect you."

It was worse since she'd vanished.

And now to have her back within arm's reach, but in danger?

The very thought churned within him.

"Apology accepted." Another couple of stiff-legged steps. Her shoulders slumped, and her voice softened. "If it is any consolation, I know exactly how you feel. I would do anything to save you from harm."

It wasn't as if she could kick his pride any harder. "You don't have to protect me, Princess."

Árdís glanced at him, and for the first time he felt like all her defenses were lowered. There was something in her eyes—pain, sadness, even perhaps a hint of longing—that made him catch his breath. He felt like he was on the verge of discovering her deepest, darkest secrets. Her soul.

Then her gaze shuttered. "What sort of *dreki* would I be if I didn't protect you? I dragged you into this mess. I will get you out of it, no matter what I must do."

"Árdís—"

She shook her head. "Not now. We both need to focus. We're here, and while I could survive a mud bath, I daresay it would melt the flesh from your bones."

They'd reached the bottom of the valley. Steam rose off the ground, creeping from open vents. Haakon took the lead, picking a path between the patches of bubbling mud. Behind them a loud deliberate grunting suddenly echoed through the canyon, and all the hairs on the back of his neck lifted.

"You watch your feet," Árdís called. "I'll keep an eye behind us. They've paused at the edge for now."

The scent of sulfur made his nose curl. Every sense felt stronger and more focused. He could barely see, but the mud gleamed a different color to solid ground. Despite the rain, the underground heat seemed to have baked the moisture out of the clay where the track meandered between mud pools.

"Oh, no," Árdís whispered, when they were almost all the way across the field of mud pools.

Oh, no? He looked behind him sharply.

"There's a reason those trolls haven't followed us." She turned in slow circles. "He's here somewhere. I can smell him."

No questioning who she meant.

He Who Should Not Be Woken.

"How the hell can you smell anything?" A bubble of mud popped with a splat nearby. "Apart from sulfur, I mean? Perhaps we should move a little quicker?"

Snorri gave a nervous whicker, dancing on his toes and straining at the lead that tied him to Sleipnir's saddle. The whites of his eyes showed.

"I can't see him." Árdís pressed a hand to her head. "But I can feel him." She winced. "Damn it. He's in my head."

"Where is he?"

"I don't know." Her teeth ground together. "It's all I can do to push him out. But he's aware of us."

The terrain ahead was far too treacherous, but there were trolls behind them, and a *dreki* who even other *dreki* feared somewhere nearby. Not a lot of options. Haakon picked out a path through the bubbling mud pools with his eyes. "There," he said, pointing to the ridge in front of them. "Hurry. I'd prefer not to make his acquaintance."

Moving forward, he picked his way between mud pools and made it to the base of the cliff.

The horses began to snort, and Haakon reeled in Sleipnir's reins, holding them in a fist just beneath the stallion's muzzle. Sleipnir's ears flickered, and he made a muffled *whumpf* sound, his nostrils flaring in a snort.

"Nothing to be frightened of," Haakon murmured, stroking the stallion's soft muzzle.

"They can smell him too."

A curious thought occurred. "The same way all the animals on my farm knew what you were?" Well before he did, it seemed.

Árdís nodded, her eyes searching the landscape as she grabbed Snorri's reins and added her weight to the reluctant little beast's head.

If the horses bolted, they'd drown in a pool of hot mud, or break a leg. Damn it. Haakon used his shoulder to push the flighty stallion onto the narrow path along the side of the cliff. If Sleipnir behaved, Snorri might too.

"Are you all right?" he called back, pausing by a particularly craggy cliff. Steam made it difficult to see properly. "Can you handle Snorri?"

"Suddenly he's my best friend," she shot back. "Better the *dreki* you know, it seems."

An enormous golden eye blinked open, right beside him.

Haakon swore as Sleipnir shied away. He was suddenly battling both a terrified stallion and trying to draw his sword at the same time, even as his balls clenched tightly. *Fuck.*

Not a mountain. Not a cliff.

But a *dreki* blending into the slope as if its rough-hewn body was partly made of stone.

Haakon jerked back, lifting his sword as he shoved Sleipnir behind him. Gravel scattered under his boots. "Árdís?"

"No!" she cried, snatching at his hand and forcing it to lower. "You cannot challenge him!"

Probably correct. The mountainside shivered and shifted, enormous bat-like wings heaving as the *dreki's* head lifted from its front paws. The ground shook beneath his feet, and it was all he could do to remain standing. The heat drained from his face as the *dreki* turned its head and hissed at them.

Sleipnir screamed, and reared up on his hind legs.

"Down!" Somehow he hauled the horse's head low. "Come on, boy. Easy. *Easy.*"

A chuckling rumble shivered through the air. "You've brought me a worthy dinner, little man."

Sleipnir slammed into him, and Haakon went down flat on his back in the middle of the narrow track as the stallion galloped past him, bucking and kicking. Árdís screamed and then Snorri was following, narrowly missing Haakon's hand, but delivering a fierce kick to his ribs.

He flipped onto his hands, watching them race up the cliff path. They reached the crest.

Which made two of them.

"What the bloody hell is that thing?" he gasped, trying to catch his breath. The blow had winded him.

It was four times the size of Rurik. He doubted its wings could even lift it into the air anymore, and a swift glance showed calcified stretches of granite and gravel along its wing-spars. His sword lay on the ground, but was there any point in grabbing it?

How could you kill a mountain?

How could you pierce a hide made of solid stone scales?

"A pity," growled the *dreki*, in a voice like thunder. Its head turned toward Haakon, and a long tongue slithered over its lips. "Now you must pay my tithe for disturbing my rest."

Árdís leapt between them, her arms outspread. "You cannot eat him," she cried. "Remember the treaty! You swore an oath, great lord. He's human."

"He's in my territory."

"But he hasn't raised a hand against you!"

A long slow blink of its translucent eyelid. Haakon's heart slammed to a halt as it bared its teeth at her. He'd never reach her in time. He'd never be able to—

Fáfnir's nostrils flared as he sniffed at Árdís. Her shirt blew back in the gust. "*You.*" This time, the rumble sounded like a volcano erupting. "You smell like treachery."

Árdís went to her knees, and pressed her face to the ground. "I am his daughter," she admitted. "Blood of his blood. But I am also your great-granddaughter. Blood of *your* blood."

Fáfnir's lip curled back off his teeth as they gnashed together.

"*Do not move*," she ground out, and Haakon realized she meant him.

He knelt on one knee, frozen.

It was the first time in his life he'd felt truly helpless. There was nothing he could do to protect her. Their odds of surviving this relied on Árdís's wits.

Árdís suddenly cried out, digging her fingers into the mud as if some sudden pain pressed down upon her. Fáfnir's eyes gleamed as he flipped her onto her back with his nose, baring her belly.

"You stink of dwarven magic," he hissed.

"It's the bracelet," Árdís gasped. "It traps my *dreki* magic within me, so I must wear this form. I do not wear it by choice."

"It keeps me out of your head."

Árdís's mouth twisted in a rictus of pain. "Then ask me what you want to know!"

"What are you doing here? Why have you disturbed me?"

"I fled from court," she cried, curling her fingers into claws as if to fight the pressure. "My mother wishes me to mate with a *dreki* not of my choice. We were forced to cross your lands to escape them."

"And this one?"

Haakon stifled a yelp as the enormous head swung toward him. Hot wet breath gusted over his face as he stared into a nostril the size of a boulder. He didn't dare wipe his face dry. *Mother of fucking kraken.* Every instinct screamed at him to run—or attack—but he didn't dare.

"He's my husband," Árdís gasped. "We are married."

"Your mate."

"N-no." She crawled to her feet, one hand held out beseechingly. "Not my mate."

"Your scent is all over him. You are mated."

"Marriage is like mating, in the human world," she said, trying to explain. "But your souls do not combine. You are not one. You merely choose to live together. And we have shared blankets, hence why he smells of me."

"I'm not talking of his odor, you foolish kit."

Árdís grew very still. "What do you mean?"

Fáfnir withdrew to look at her again. "You are linked somehow, but there is a chasm between where your souls touch. If he is yours, then why is there a chasm?"

Yes, why?

He slowly gained his feet, but all of his attention was locked upon her.

Árdís hesitated. "I am *dreki*, and he is mortal. We have been estranged, but..." She took a quick breath. "Haakon is trying to help me remove this cursed bracelet."

A discontented rumble sounded, as if Fáfnir sensed her skirting the truth.

Haakon quite agreed. Anger suddenly flared, hot like a coal in his belly. "She vanished in the middle of the night. I thought she was taken by a *dreki*," he said softly, "only to discover she *was* the *dreki*. If we have been estranged, it's because she left me, great lord."

Árdís paled.

"You left your mate?" Fáfnir sounded surprised. "Ah, that explains this chasm. Two halves that do not touch, and perhaps never will."

"Will you grant us passage, great lord?" Árdís blurted, with an intensity that made Haakon look at her sharply.

She was hiding something.

Fáfnir's eyes narrowed, and a wicked gleam shone there. "There is a cost involved for trespassing."

"What do you want?" Árdís asked carefully. "Our horses are long gone. You cannot eat them. And we have little of value upon us."

"Then that is a problem for you. Give me something precious. Or one of you must stay, until the other fetches a prize to tempt me."

Árdís trembled as she reached up to the back of her neck. What was she doing? Her face had gone deathly pale.

She unlocked the simple chain around her throat, and poured the ring and chain into her hand, holding it out flat.

"No!" He stepped toward her, but drew up short as that enormous head swiveled in his direction. He looked past the enormous *dreki*. "Árdís, *no*."

Not her ring.

He didn't know why, but until she gave that ring back—or cast it aside—he felt like there was some hope between them.

"We don't have anything else," she whispered.

"This is barely silver." Fáfnir looked disgusted. "Do you mean to insult me?"

Árdís released a slow breath. "You're right. It *is* only silver. But it's also the most precious thing in the world to me. If I had gold or gems upon me, I would give them to you without hesitation, before I offered this."

Haakon's gut twisted. What was she saying?

Fáfnir eased back down into a crouch. Rain began to patter down. "You are speaking the truth. I do not understand."

Árdís swallowed, and offered him the ring. Her hand shook. "My husband gave this to me. It is a sign of our commitment to each other."

Fáfnir looked like he was enjoying her pain. "This is indeed a gift. I will accept it."

Haakon stared at her. *Don't do it.*

"I'm sorry," she whispered, as she fought to place the ring in the curl of the *dreki's* great claws.

"I have gold in my saddlebags," he snapped. "I can fetch it for you, in exchange for the ring."

The *dreki's* claws closed around the ring, and it vanished from sight. "Keep your gold, mortal man. You have nothing to tempt me with."

"Then what would tempt you?" he demanded, stepping right up to the *dreki's* face.

"Careful," the *dreki* snarled. "Or I'll ask for your heart."

You already have it.

"Haakon, no!" Árdís grabbed his wrist. "We'll leave, great lord. Please don't take offense. He doesn't know what he's saying."

"I—"

"*He wants to hurt me*," she hissed. "Because of my father. This is revenge, nothing else. Don't make it worse."

Rain dripped down his lips and chin. He glared into the *dreki's* eyes. "What *would* tempt you?"

"A black diamond. A king's crown. The Holy Grail. The heart of a kraken." Fáfnir smirked. "Your soul."

"For a silver ring?" Haakon demanded incredulously.

The *dreki* rested its head on its claws. "What is the price you would pay for it, mortal man? What is it worth to you?"

Everything.

"*Don't*," Árdís warned, her eyes wide as she shook her head at him. "Please, don't agree to anything he says. You don't know what you're doing. It's just a ring."

Haakon's nostrils flared.

It was not just a ring.

"Now begone, peasants." Fáfnir's eyes blinked slowly in the night. "Before I change my mind... and take both your hearts."

CHAPTER FOURTEEN

THE DOOR ON the shepherd's hut banged shut as the wind tore it from Haakon's fingers. Dust covered the floor, and there was a cold emptiness to the hut that hinted it had been long abandoned. Little wonder. It was right on the edge of Fáfnir's territory. He'd probably eaten any sheep that dared stray close enough.

Haakon tossed his bags and bedroll on the ground with a carelessness he'd never displayed before. He peered through the windows, frustrated at the renewing of the storm.

"Damn it," he muttered, locking the door. "We're so close. But we'll get nowhere today." The horses were both exhausted, the conditions were worsening, and both he and Árdís had ridden through most of the night.

Árdís turned in slow circles, surveying their surroundings. They'd left Fáfnir's territory an hour ago, and they'd barely spoken a word.

Perhaps she could sense his anger and frustration.

Or perhaps she was exhausted. Dark circles shadowed her eyes, and she looked hollow, as if handing over the ring had drained her more than he'd have expected.

For a moment, a conflicting twist of sympathy curled through him.

You're imagining it. She didn't struggle to hand over the ring at all. She practically threw it at the ancient dreki.

"Tomorrow we should arrive at Dúrnir's. You'll have the bracelet off, and you'll be free to leave," Haakon said. There was a fire already laid out, thank goodness, and it flared to light with the swift strike of one of his matches. "You should get some rest while you can."

Árdís flinched. "What are you saying?"

He flipped the bedroll open, grateful for the oiled sealskin that kept it all dry, and rolled it out, while flames licked hungrily at the small pile of wood in the grate. "I'll give you a couple of hours sleep before we need to rejoin the road. Hopefully the rain will have died down by then."

"You're angry with me."

He paused, leaning forward on his knuckles. It wasn't as if the ring meant anything anymore, but... he'd still had hope. "You gave it away, like it didn't even matter."

"I'm sorry," she whispered. "I know it was your grandmother's. I know I promised you I'd give it back to you—"

"I don't want the fucking ring back, Árdís." He shoved to his feet, his temper spilling through him. He'd been holding on to it for days, and today had only pushed him further over the edge. "I want it on your finger, where it damned well belongs."

She ignored that.

"I had no choice," she cried. "What would you have had me do? He wasn't going to allow us to leave without it."

"I had gold!"

"He didn't want gold!" Her face lit with beautiful fury. "He didn't even truly want the ring. He wanted to repay my father for overthrowing him, and I was the only option he had of restoring his pride."

Haakon drew up shortly.

"He was trying to get in my head, damn it." She turned and took three sharp steps, her fingers curling into claws. "Searching for a way to get at me. And there you were, just desperate to give him an excuse to hurt you! I had to get you out of there before you gave him any sign you might challenge him."

"So it's my fault?" He stepped in her path.

"No!" She raked her fingers through her hair. "What do you want me to say? Why does it even matter? I made a choice between the ring and you, and I chose *you*. Do you think it didn't hurt me to give it away?" One hand splayed over her chest, pressing the fabric tight across her breasts, as if she felt for it.

Those glorious breasts.

He refused to look down.

No, she was not going to tempt her way out of this one.

"I don't know," he shouted back. "I don't know if you give a damn about me, or my ring, or any of this. I don't know why you left me. I don't know what you—"

"I told you—"

"You've told me nothing," he snapped.

Her eyes turned wide with hurt. "Why are you yelling?"

"Because I missed you so fucking much it hurt to breathe." It came out choked. "You left me; you gave my ring away; you push me and pull me, and tear me in two. Do you even care? Do I even mean anything to you?"

"Of course you do." Her mouth worked. "I loved you. I-I...."

Loved.

Like an arrow straight to the chest. "Do you even know what that word means?"

Árdís glared at him. "I'm not going to continue to argue, if you're not going to listen to a word I say." She began to strip her wet cloak off, and draped it over the chair. No, tossed it. The movement made the wet wool of her tunic press tightly against her breasts. "Or denigrate me for it."

Oh, yes. He wasn't the only one feeling the bite of anger. And seeing her like this stirred his blood in ways only she ever could.

"You're just saying that because you're losing the argument."

Her glare was a potent thing, but then her expression suddenly shifted. Turned devious. Árdís bit her lip. "Was I?"

"Don't you dare," he warned, as she took a step toward him.

"Why not? You're thinking about it. I'm thinking about it."

He refused to step back, every muscle in his body locking tight as she stopped in front of him, those catlike eyes tilting as she glanced up at him from beneath her wretchedly long lashes.

Árdís placed both hands on his chest, flexing her palms against him. Her fingers curled in the open collar of his shirt, as if threatening to tear it open.

He wanted her to.

His cock flexed. Damn his flagging self-control. His sense of preservation was shaky, but he knew if he gave in—*just once*—then he'd never be able to get her out of his mind.

Are you ever going to be able to get her out of your mind anyway?

"Do it," she dared him. "Kiss me. You know you want to. You know that's what's truly gotten your back up."

Of all the damned ways she could torture him....

"It won't change a thing," he warned.

Her fingers flexed on the heavy muscle of his chest. "No. It won't. But it will make both of us feel better. This doesn't have to be complicated."

"When the bloody hell is it *not* complicated?"

He breathed heavily through his nostrils, and glanced down.

A mistake.

Her breasts heaved with the force of her breath, smooth globes that thrust forth from her bodice. The neckline was modest, but at this great height, he could see straight down it. And wet wool clung to her figure, making his fingers itch.

Her voice softened. "Punish me, Haakon. You know you want to."

Jesus. He met her eyes.

"No," he said, and enjoyed the sensation.

Shock flared there, as if she simply couldn't believe he was denying his base self.

One thumb caressed her waist. He couldn't help himself. Acting on instinct, his hand slid over the curve of her hip, calluses snagging in the wet wool.

"Your mouth is saying no," she said, "but everything else is saying yes. Make up your mind."

"I'm not going to punish you," he said softly.

It was never about punishment.

But perhaps a little sweet torture....

It all came together in his mind. Why the hell was he arguing?

He began to strip his coat off. Árdís pushed away from him, a scalded sound in her throat.

"Well, I cannot continue like this!" she hissed at him, her eyes turning molten as the pupils shifted, becoming cat-slits as her *dreki* roused beneath her skin. "With you looking at me with eyes that want to eat me alive. Or your arms wrapped around me last night, driving me insane with want, before you simply walk away. I know you want me. I can feel it every time you look at me. And I want *you*. Just one last time."

One last time. Haakon tossed his coat aside.

She'd thought his "no" was a denial.

He began to roll up his sleeves. Just a change of plans. There was one way he could take what they both wanted, and emerge unscathed.

"Strip," he said, the word loaded with heat.

The word fell into the quiet of the room.

"What?" Her eyes blinked in surprise.

"You heard me. Take it all off." A ghost of a smile curled over his mouth. "But do it slowly."

Árdís looked him in the eye, and then her hands went to the buttons on her tunic. It buttoned up the front. She got halfway down and then her fingers paused. They fell away. "No."

Heat flared between them. She'd realized what he was about.

"If you want my clothes off, then you may remove them yourself," she said, defying him.

Despite his intentions, he felt a flare of heat. *Stubborn* dreki *princess*.

Haakon kept a good few inches between them. He reached for the lowest undone button. And did it back up, not looking away from her.

Árdís sucked in a sharp breath. Haakon's thumbs stroked up her rib cage. Tugged the next button closed.

A shiver slid through her.

"Is this plan working out the way you thought it would?" he murmured, and slipped the next button shut. And the next. All the time, he stole small touches of her, the rasp of his fingers darting over her pointed nipple before she captured his wrist.

"It... worked better in my head."

Haakon stepped back. "Then take it off. Do as you're told."

"Fine."

She began again, bending to strip her leather trousers down her legs. "What are you proposing?" The thought had her breathless, as she returned to the buttons on her tunic.

"I thought you were the one setting the terms." His hands itched to touch her as each inch of skin was revealed. Button by button, the mysterious curves of her body were revealed. "One night, wasn't it?"

One last night to see if there was anything left between them at all.

Firelight gilded her hair and skin as she gave a determined little wriggle, and the tunic slid all the way down her legs, pooling around her ankles. His mouth went dry; his cock hard.

His best intentions fled.

"One night, Haakon," she agreed, starting to slide the straps of her chemise over her shoulders.

Haakon's eyes locked on her, and suddenly heated with an intensity she hadn't expected. "Leave it on."

She didn't know who reached for who, but suddenly he was in front of her, and she reached up to kiss him, but he turned his head at the last moment, his lips skating over her jaw instead.

She knew how to drive him wild, but as she slid her hand down his abdomen, he caught her wrist, shaking his head.

"No."

For a second she thought he was denying her, but he simply turned her around, pressing both of her hands against the wall, and holding them there for a long moment, as if to show her what he wanted.

That hard body molded around hers, the press of his erection butting against her bottom. Árdís sucked in a sharp breath, anticipation shivering through her. Her body knew every inch of him. Welcomed the glide of his hands down her sides, where they rested on her hips with firm intention.

So many years since she felt his touch. Too many years.

It wasn't just his body that had changed. There was a thrill of dominance in his voice that ignited within her like brandy poured on pure flame.

"If we do this," Haakon rasped, his breath whispering over the sensitive skin of her ear, "then you will not be in control. Not this time, Princess."

She thought she understood. He was trying to protect himself. To hold himself back.

Challenge lit through her. One kiss, and she'd have him. She knew it. She'd always known it. But that seemed too easy. He demanded her surrender, and some part of her wanted to give it.

A means to say sorry.

Árdís bent her head forward, resting her forehead against the wall. "One night. Do what you want with me."

Soft lips skimmed the sensitive skin at her nape. "Don't tempt me."

A fist curled in the hem of her chemise, dragging it up until her thigh was bared. Her mouth went dry, and she must have moved, for his other hand was suddenly in her hair, pinning her there.

"No," he breathed. "I didn't give you permission."

She found herself splayed against the wall, her full breasts aching and her palms pressed flat. Árdís turned her head to the side, her cheek flush against the timbers. She didn't know why she liked it so much, but her breath came in sharp ragged pants, and she wanted so desperately to spread her legs. To invite his touch.

"Oh, gods." She couldn't move. Could do nothing but submit. "*Haakon.*"

"What's wrong, Árja?"

A mocking little whisper, as if he knew all too well what afflicted her.

Lips traced her hairline, his body pressed firmly against hers. "You know I'm a patient man," he murmured, his tongue tracing the shell of her ear and his breath hot. "I've spent *days* imagining what I'd do to you when I finally got my hands upon you."

"A bit presumptuous, wasn't it?" she teased.

A tongue darted out and stroked the lobe of her ear, and then he suckled it into his mouth.

It wasn't as though his mouth was between her legs, but her thighs clenched, arousal making her wet and needy.

A callused hand curved down over her breast, kneading it. Árdís's hips ground back against him, her breath coming with a short hitch.

"I don't know," he murmured, his stubble grazing her jaw as his straining erection pushed against her bottom. "You tell me."

Teeth nipped at her throat, and then his thumb was tracing slow torturous circles around her nipple. He pinched her there, rolling it between thumb and forefinger until she could barely see. Barely breathe.

Sweet goddess. Her mind went blank, and her spine arched. More. She wanted more.

An insistent knee pressed between her thighs. Finally. She cried out as the slick feel of his leather-clad thigh pressed against her.

"Beg me." His hips gave a teasing thrust against her, his palm sliding down between her body and the wall to cup her between the thighs, fingers rough against her naked skin. "Do you want this, Árdís? Do you *need* this?"

Sinking her teeth into her lower lip, she moaned, her hips flexing as she sought to drive his hand lower. Those fingers were a merciless tease.

"*Beg*," he repeated, slipping two fingers between her folds, parting her, but not quite giving her what she wanted.

Defiance flashed within her. She shook her head, feeling his palm come around to capture her mouth, as if to hold a scream within her.

"You're so bloody stubborn," he snarled.

Likewise.

Sinking her teeth into his hand, she felt him laugh against her back, the rumble of it rocking through his chest. "You always did have to challenge me," he whispered, and she could feel his anger turning, becoming somewhat more playful. "Curse you, Árja. But there are two ways to play this game."

Soft lips brushed against the sensitive area beneath her ear, even as his fingers changed direction. His index lashed up in a light flick, exactly where she wanted it. Her fingers curled into little claws as he wreaked havoc upon her. *Oh, gods.* Slow, torturous circles. Just enough pressure. She was dying a slow death, shifting against him, silently begging for more.

"Do you like that?" His hot erotic whisper burned in her ear. All the trappings of civilization had vanished from his demeanor, leaving her with a husband who intended to claim her.

The pressure intensified, as if he could feel the edge building within her, threatening to burn her to ashes on the inside.

Árdís whimpered, his palm wet with her muted breath. *More. Oh, gods, more.* Her hips rocked against him.

A shiver of violence and pleasure threatened to overwhelm her. A storm of his own making. Árdís cried out, her entire body tensing as he worked his fingers within her, delving and spreading the slickness there in small teasing circles. She wanted more. She wanted him to push her over the edge. But he always drew away, just as the knot within her wrenched tighter. Teasing her. Destroying her. Working her body as astutely as a puppet master flexing her strings.

He hadn't forgotten a damned thing about what she liked.

Master of storms.

The hand slid from her mouth, and then he fumbled between them.

Árdís gasped. "What are you—?"

The blunt head of his erection pressed between her thighs. Árdís stopped breathing. And he didn't move.

What was he waiting for?

A desperate shiver worked its way through her.

"*Please.*"

The word stole from her treacherous lips.

A pause, the blunt head of his cock holding at the edge of her opening. She almost thought he hadn't heard her, but a faint hiss of breath escaped him, and then he thrust inside her.

All the way.

Árdís's breasts pressed flush against the wall, her cheek imprinting in the rough timber. She was trapped here. Held at his mercy. The angle meant he couldn't get as deep as he wanted to. She felt his frustration as he bit her earlobe, a harsh growl echoing in his throat even as his hips rocked against her. He held himself there, as if soaking in the sensation of her body around him. A soft groan escaped him.

There. Not as restrained as he'd have liked.

Árdís bit her lip wickedly, and tightened every muscle around him in a slow curl.

"*Fuck.*" He slammed one hand against the wall beside her head, pushing inside her as if he couldn't get deep enough.

"Two can play these games," she whispered, and squeezed again, taking herself right back to that edge.

One arm slid beneath her breasts, and he hauled her back against him, his cock slipping from inside her.

"No." She caught his arm, but he simply drove her down onto her knees, and then she was on all fours on his bedroll, and his hands were settling on her hips again.

"I don't want you getting splinters. Are you ready for me?"

Lightning flashed outside the hut, highlighting the interior for one brief second. This was exactly what she'd wanted; Haakon undone.

"Yes."

His hips slammed into hers, driving her forward onto her forearms as he buried himself to the hilt. She screamed as the storm finally washed over her, sweeping her along in its wake. She couldn't breathe. Could barely see. Waves of pleasure broke within her.

Again and again, as Haakon fucked his way inside her.

Harder. Deeper. The intensity of it forced her teeth into her lip again, to trap a cry. Árdís curled her fingers into the blanket, holding on for dear life. Every single time he took her to bed, it had felt like a clash of passion between them, burning so fast and furious that they left marks on each other's skin, but she couldn't touch him here. Sweet goddess, but every slow withdrawal left her panting, begging, and every hard invasion only seemed to twist the tension within her tighter. Haakon's hands dug into the flesh of her hips, pinning her exactly where he wanted her. She was completely, utterly at his mercy, her breath turning to rough pants. Every thrust of his cock only spread the slickness between her thighs, as if to prove how much she wanted him.

It wasn't enough.

She wanted to touch him, wanted the connection. Somehow she reached back, her hand covering his. "*Haakon.*"

Fingers slid over her thigh, pushing her knees wider, as if he fought to get right to the heart of her.

His hand curved up her throat, drawing her upright until her breasts were splayed obscenely, and her spine bent. Her back met his chest, as he gave short, hard little thrusts.

"Árdís, oh gods, you torture me so."

She bit her lip, reaching up to twist her hand through his hair. "Come for me."

A hand speared down her soft belly, slicing unmercifully through her curls, and pressing exactly where she liked it.

"You first."

A second wave of pleasure overwhelmed her. Árdís lost herself in the wake of it, feeling his body jerk as his own pleasure overtook him. Teeth sank into the muscle of her shoulder, and Haakon grunted softly as he came.

I've missed this.

I've missed you.

She fell forward onto her hands again as he gasped and ground himself within her one last time.

The pair of them collapsed onto the bedroll, Haakon melting over her. His chest heaved, and his weight forced her into the blankets. Not unpleasantly. Árdís shuddered as her body kept clenching, little shivers of aftershock lighting along her nerves.

He withdrew in a wet gush of seed, and fell beside her, dragging her back into his arms. Árdís's hips ached, but she drew her knees together and curled her arm over his, pressing a kiss to the smattering of blond hairs along his arm.

If she'd hadn't been exhausted before, she was now.

A soft laugh shuddered through her. "I finally concede. You've destroyed me."

He rolled her onto her back, leaning over her. Panting. She'd quite forgotten the storm outside, but lightning flashed again, highlighting the stark ridges of his face. In that moment, he wasn't hiding anything, and she saw it painted across his face in a mixture of raw pain, hope, and something else.

Longing.

Árdís sucked in a sharp breath, her fingertips pressing gently against the stubble on his cheeks. She was grateful the world fell into darkness again, for her eyes were flushed with sudden heat.

"Best get some rest."

"Why?" she whispered.

His hand slid between the skin of her breasts, and she sensed him leaning closer, as he bent to kiss her throat ever so gently. "Because tonight is our last night together. And I plan on taking advantage of every single moment of it."

The fire crackled in the grate, and the smell of roasting meat made her mouth water. Árdís dragged her boots on, her body a mess of heated bruises and bite marks.

She pressed a hand to her chest, feeling the ache of the loss of the ring still. It felt like something was missing. A piece of her, perhaps.

But... she'd somehow been able to hand it over.

She'd been physically incapable of throwing it away for years. Haakon had demanded its return and she couldn't even give it to *him*.

The heat of blood draining from her face made her lips tingle. *You are mated.* She felt like that bell was ringing in her ears again.

You are linked somehow, but there is a chasm between where your souls touch.

I'm not talking of his odor, you foolish kit....

What did he mean?

Could it be? Had she somehow imprinted upon Haakon? Started forming a mating bond with him years ago, but never finished it?

The stormy afternoon slipped by in a burst of lovemaking and sleep, the questions haunting her. Haakon had left at some stage, and only returned hours later, shaking the water from his oiled cloak as he slicked back his hair and delivered dinner.

"Dare I ask where you found a goat?" She settled beside him at the grate, tucking herself against his side and resting her head on his chest, as he turned the makeshift spit.

"It was tethered out in the middle of a rocky plain."

"A tithe for Fáfnir." Some of the villagers in Iceland had arrangements with the local *dreki*, to keep their livestock safe. "He's not going to be happy."

"Good."

He offered her a joint, and Árdís picked at the meat hungrily with her blunt teeth. She hadn't been eating enough since she'd been trapped in this mortal form. While her energy requirements weren't as significant as the *dreki's*, she still needed to consume more than she had been.

Her stomach grumbled as she licked at her fingers. Haakon sliced another piece of goat for her, and offered it to her on the flat of his blade, their eyes meeting. Árdís leaned forward to take it from the blade, her teeth closing carefully around the meat.

"Are you trying to tempt me again?"

"Is it working?"

The faintest of smiles curled the corner of his mouth up. "Always. Despite my best intentions, despite the past." His eyes filled with sudden shadows. "Despite the future."

His face shuttered.

The past. The future. All of it knotted into one tangled web she didn't think she could ever undo.

"I never wanted to hurt you."

The words were raw, stripped from her soul. In them, she could hear the quivering loss of all those years, all those moments when she'd been alone and hollow, and wished she could reach for him, just once.

It was only in his arms that she'd ever felt whole. Or safe.

And he stopped talking.

Stopped breathing, in fact.

But he was listening, as if he sensed the sudden shift in the air between them.

And suddenly it all seemed to want to spill from her. Every last damning word. Every dark secret. Árdís curled her fingers into her palms. She didn't dare. This was only the lingering aftereffect of passion. He'd brought her undone in so many more ways than merely the physical.

"Let's not think of the future tonight. Or the past." Árdís leaned up to kiss his cheek, before easing back onto her bottom. "Please."

He'd refused to kiss her on the mouth, and she didn't dare push for it.

One night. Those were the terms she'd set herself.

And if it hurt, then it was her own damned fault.

Haakon sat stiffly, as if he *knew* she'd been on the verge of confessing, and had chosen cowardice instead. But he looked away, staring into the flames, his fingers toying idly with the fabric covering his knee. "As you wish."

Just like that, the moment was gone.

"You've lost weight," he muttered.

"It happens."

Such inconsequential words. Safe, *nothing* words.

Árdís ate swiftly, ignoring the long, slow looks he gave her, as he fed her more and more of the delicious meat. Eating it from his knife and hand felt somehow intimate. As if he needed to provide for her. Protect her.

"Why didn't you tell me you were hungry?" A faint frown crossed his brow. "You always had an appetite, but it didn't seem as strong back in Viksholm."

"It was, but I hunted," she admitted. "When you were working the fields, or away. I managed to keep the worst of the hunger at bay, and your mother always fed me."

Because she wanted me to be fit and strong enough to bear your children.

Suddenly, her appetite vanished.

Árdís wiped her fingers clean on the rag Haakon handed to her. She was recognized as an adult in the *dreki* world, but she'd never felt the press of the mating urge before. And it wasn't as though she'd hoped. Birthing a *drekling* would have been catastrophic for both her and the child, but sometimes when his mother had spoken of grandchildren, she'd felt this peculiar twisting deep inside. She was seventy years old, and few *dreki* females had ever felt the mating urge so young.

Haakon would have been an old man before she'd ever have delivered him a child. If they were bonded, he'd age as she would, but they weren't. Even time seemed to weigh against them.

"What's wrong?" he asked, clearly seeing it on her face.

"Nothing," she said sharply, and pushed to her feet. All of a sudden she couldn't handle this idle conversation. This nothingness. Guilt weighed so heavily upon her. "I need some fresh air. Perhaps dinner disagreed with me."

Stumbling out into the darkness, she paused at the edge of the river they were camped by. She would have stolen his future from him—the joy of having a family—if she'd stayed with him. Within a handful of years, his mother's gentle good wishes would have become a little sharper.

And she couldn't have borne seeing the eventual disappointment in his eyes.

She'd never felt lonelier in her entire life.

The door to the hut creaked as Haakon followed her. The rain had slackened into a fine mist, and she turned her face to the sky so he'd hopefully think the tears in her eyes were just that. Rain.

"You're upset."

"No, I'm not," she whispered.

"I swear you would say the sky was green, if I said it was blue." He made a growling sound deep in his throat as he joined her. "Do me the courtesy of presuming I know you."

"Do you?"

"Yes," he said shortly. "I do."

Cool wind blew past both of them. She had no words. Everything she wanted to say caught within her throat. And if she let a single word out, she was frightened more would follow. A spill of emotion she couldn't contain. Being in his arms had broken down her defenses too far.

"Here." Haakon slipped the enormous wolf fur cloak from his shoulders. He draped it around hers, and Árdís couldn't help snuggling into the heated folds.

She could scent him in the fur, and turned her nose into the collar to breathe it in, like a guilty thief.

She wanted to press her face there, to drink in the heat left from his body. To cling to something she'd thought long lost.

"Something's gotten into you tonight." Slowly, his hands drew the cloak closed, and he pushed the pin through it to hold it in place. His knuckles rested there, holding the cloak. "I didn't hurt you, did I? I wasn't gentle, but I tried...."

"Of course not."

Her head reached almost to his chin.

If she lifted up onto her toes, and he bent his face down, their lips might meet. She wanted that kiss so badly.

The night seemed so quiet around them. They were alone out here, miles from anywhere. And the gathering darkness seemed to wrap around them like some sort of conspiratorial cocoon, tempting her to whisper her secret confidences.

"It's not...."

He waited.

"I...."

Soft hands cupped her face, slowly lifting her eyes to his. Haakon stroked her cheeks with both thumbs. "I was angry before, because I thought you were throwing everything away. No. I thought you were throwing *me* away. I didn't understand."

"It's just a ring," she said swiftly.

It's not the ring, you fool. It was never the ring.

She'd finally figured out what she'd been holding on to so tightly. She'd never dared give in to her feelings for him, so she'd somehow transferred that to the ring. If it belonged to her, then there was a part of him with her at all times. But now it was gone, and then he would vanish too, and she'd be left with nothing.

It hurt. It hurt so badly.

Árdís slowly looked up, feeling the truth unfurl within her, like a flower blooming. She'd never stopped loving him.

She never would.

"I would have ruined you," she blurted, "if I'd stayed."

Haakon's eyes, dark in the night, sharpened intently.

"Did you think leaving hurt me any less?"

No. She'd made an utter mess of it all. Pressing her hands to his to hold them there, she shook her head.

"I'm so sorry. For everything." The words tore free from her. "I should never have married you. I knew that. I always knew that. And I'm sorry I didn't have the strength of will to walk away before things grew too far. It was too late by the time I realized what was happening. I didn't want to hurt you. I couldn't see any way not to."

"You could have told me."

"*What?*" Her voice sharpened. "That you had married a *dreki* princess who could never give you children? That she would never grow old, while you did." *If* he'd grown old. *If* he'd escaped the vengeance of her mother. "I brought you into a world you didn't belong in, and I did it carelessly. I didn't think of the consequences."

I didn't want to think.

For you were everything.

Somehow she was still cold, even within the cloak. Árdís tore away from him and wrapped her arms around her waist, but he wasn't going to allow that. Arms wrapped around her, drawing her back into a warm embrace. Árdís finally let the tears slip down her face, crying silently as he held her.

"You couldn't give me children?" he asked hoarsely.

She slumped against him. "It's rare that a *dreki* female goes into heat so young."

"But not impossible?"

She didn't want to give either of them any false hope. "Not impossible, no. But such children would never be welcomed in my world. They'd feel the call of their fellow *dreki*, a siren song on the winds, but they'd never be accepted."

"Árja." He turned her in his arms.

He'd wanted to give her children. But she'd always smiled and shrugged, and changed the conversation when he brought it up. He'd thought it was because she was young, and they were so newly married, and she'd never dared enlighten him.

"It wouldn't have mattered, if I'd had you. And if it had happened, then I would have taken that as a blessing. If not, I would have loved you anyway."

She pressed her closed fists against his chest.

"You would have been enough—"

"*Please don't.*" She buried her face against his chest, her shoulders shaking with her sobs. "I just wanted you to know." Her voice held the desolation of all those lost years. "That I never meant to hurt you. I never meant any of it. But we could never be together and it broke my heart to leave you."

A hand stirred through her hair, clasping her against him, and that only made it harder.

She didn't deserve his forgiveness.

"We only have tonight," she whispered hoarsely, lifting her tearstained face to his. "I don't want to waste a single second of it on tears."

Clasping his cheek, she pressed her mouth to his, begging for his kiss.

And this time he gave it to her, burning away all the sadness as he lifted her up into his arms, her legs around his hips, and strode back inside the hut.

CHAPTER FIFTEEN

ONE MORE DAY. Árdís curled her arms around Haakon as they rode north, feeling quiet and subdued. She was beginning to hate the silences that fell between them, as if neither of them dared break it.

One more day and she'd be free of the cursed manacle. One more day and he'd be on his ship, sailing away from her forever. Safe. No longer plagued by the machinations of *dreki*.

And she only felt utterly hollow at the thought.

What if she was right? What if she *had* somehow begun to mate with him? She couldn't feel any link herself, especially not with the manacle on, but what if this was it?

Don't be selfish. She squeezed her eyes shut. Haakon deserved a long and happy life, even if it cut her heart out of her chest to see him walk away from her.

Just when she thought she couldn't stand it anymore, a *dreki's* bugle suddenly cut through the air.

Árdís looked up, and Haakon stiffened as if he felt the tension radiate through her. This was not quite what she'd had in mind when she'd wanted an end to the oppressive silence.

"What is it?" he asked.

"Shh."

"Did you hear something?"

If she narrowed her eyes, she could just make out the bat-like wings of something passing through the sun. It flickered, and then vanished into a bank of clouds. Dread shivered through her, all of the hairs on the back of her neck lifting.

Too late.

"I think we've been spotted," she said, hunting for it through the clouds. A feeling of horror twisted deep inside her abdomen.

Haakon reined Sleipnir in, and the enormous bay snorted. "A *dreki?*"

"At least one." Hopefully, just a scout. "How far is it to this *svartálfar*'s village?"

"At least five miles."

"We could make it." Maybe.

Haakon's neck twisted as he surveyed the area. "Wasn't it you who said you could cover that much ground in minutes?"

"Run," she pleaded. "If we find a town—or a village even—then we have a chance. *Dreki* are bound by the oath Fáfnir swore at the Althing. We cannot harm humans, not unless they attack us first, or we risk breaking that oath."

"Bloody hell, Árdís, that was over a thousand years ago!"

He booted Sleipnir into a canter.

"It was barely sixteen cycles, as we measure time," she retorted, grabbing hold of his waist. "It wasn't that long ago to the *dreki*. And while my mother doesn't care to play by all the rules, she cannot afford to break that one, or she risks the censure of all the *dreki* in Iceland. They'll have to change into their mortal forms if they enter the village, and we might be able to lose them."

Haakon muttered something under his breath that even her sharp ears couldn't catch. Then he began to rein the horses in.

A cry of pure delight rang out, sending a chill down Árdís's spine.

That cry said: *Yes, run. Give me a good hunt.*

And then a second one answered it.

"There are two of them." She raked her gaze through the skies as hope died. Maybe they could outrun one, but not two *dreki*. She caught a flash of shadow moving slightly behind the clouds, as if to surprise them with its presence. "No, three! Haakon!"

"We're not going to run, Árdís. We'll never make it in time, and that's what they want. I just needed to find defensible ground. Here," he said, hauling Sleipnir to a halt. "We make a stand here."

A pile of rocks loomed, looking like the sort trolls might hide beneath. They guarded the top of a small hill, which would give them some shelter, though when the predator was in the skies, she doubted the good it would do. Haakon offered her a hand down, before he swung from the saddle, tethering both horses.

Above them, the three *dreki* began to circle like vultures.

"You're not the only one with a few tricks up their sleeves," Haakon said coolly.

"Oh, you have some mysterious weapon that can bring down a full-grown *dreki*?"

"As a matter of fact...."

Haakon hauled a large leather-wrapped bundle from the back of the horse and tore the buckled straps open. A strange crossbow-like shape emerged, and Haakon snapped the limbs open, sliding several metal pieces into place.

"You're not seriously thinking you can bring one of them down with an arrow?" Árdís saw the answer on his face. "It wouldn't even penetrate their hide!"

"Not an arrow." He unwrapped the other side of the leather roll and revealed exactly what he intended. "I told you. I hunt dragons for a living now."

A strange mix of horror and respect filled her as he slid the grappling hook into place, and attached a wheel with a thin steel rope wound around it. Three sharp prongs gleamed with lethal intensity at the end of the hook, but they were designed to attach under the edge of armor-plated scales, not to penetrate them. Haakon's hands moved with brutal intensity as he fit it altogether, snapping pieces into place and locking in metal pegs that were clearly designed for the purpose.

A device built to foul a *dreki's* greatest weapon; its ability to fly.

"Brought my first dragon down with this in Norway," he said.

"No! There are two of them, and I cannot help you." She'd never felt more hopeless. Her fingers found the edge of the manacle, but all she managed to do was bruise the skin at her wrist. "If I could just get this damned thing off!"

"We've tried."

"Use your sword," she hissed, her gaze cutting to the skies again, before she realized he'd frozen. *What is he*—? "Not that like that, you fool! I don't want you to cut my hand off! We have to break the bracelet. The only way we can fight is if I'm free to use my magic."

Haakon took her by the wrist. "Árdís, just trust me, will you?"

"It's not you I don't trust."

This was her worst nightmare come to life. They'd kill Haakon, and it would be all her fault for getting him mixed up in this life.

One of the *dreki* screamed out a challenge, cutting through the clouds as it began to spiral downward in a taunting curve.

Roar. The heat drained from her face. Correction. *He* was her worst nightmare.

"You're going to get yourself killed!" She turned on him, her finger stabbing toward the sky. "That mottled-gray overgrown bat is my illegitimate cousin, Roar." Her tone turned pleading. "Sirius has just enough honor left within him to make bargaining with him reasonable. And some of the others *might* not kill you just for the joy of it. But Roar is every single one of my uncle's worst instincts bred into *dreki* flesh. *Please.* Please, just run. I'll give myself up to give you time to get away. But please don't do this."

A muscle in his jaw jumped. "I'm not leaving you behind. Not again."

"Don't be a hero! I don't want to see you hurt."

"Then what makes you think I want to see you in the hands of a man you're terrified of?" he bellowed.

"I'm not frightened for my own sake," she declared. "He won't hurt *me*. He wouldn't dare."

Haakon's eyes hardened, as if he saw the hopelessness in her eyes. "Breathe, Árdís."

And then he captured the back of her head, and dragged her up onto her toes. Their mouths met, his lips claiming hers in a scalding kiss that quite stole her wits.

Then it was over, and Árdís swayed as her heels touched the ground again.

"I don't know how that's going to help me breathe," she murmured, touching her swollen lips with a startled hand.

The flat look her husband gave her was one she knew all too well. Of all his traits, that hardheaded, pure sense of stubbornness drove her mad. She might as well argue with the tide when Haakon wore that expression. "The decision is made. I'm not going anywhere, and that is final. For heaven's sake, Árja, I need time to prepare. Stop arguing with me and help!"

She swallowed down the lump of fear in her throat. "What do you want me to do?"

He showed her, and they set about anchoring the end of the grappling hook's chain to a boulder. Haakon moved with frightening precision, but Árdís couldn't take her eyes off the skies as the *dreki* overhead drifted lower in slow circles.

She grit her teeth at the sheer mockery inherent in the gesture. Roar was taking his time, as if to taunt her.

"You know them better than I do," Haakon said. "Tell me their weaknesses. Tell me how to play this."

"Aim for Roar," she told him. "You need to take him out of this fight if you're to have any chance."

"And the others?"

One was the murky green shades of swamp slime; the other a vibrant red with a scar of gray across his grizzled shoulder. "Ylve and Balder. Ylve's mine. She's the more vicious, and I know how to fight her. We need them on the ground, and in mortal form."

"Easier said than done."

She shook her head, hurrying toward the slim, leather-wrapped bundle on the back of Snorri. "We just need to make the air above us unsafe. Then they'll have to land, if they want a chance at me."

The chestnut shied away, but Árdís grabbed his bridle and glared into his beady little eyes. "Not now, you fat carpetbag. If you're good, then I won't let the bad *dreki* eat you."

She withdrew her sword with a steely rasp, and then let him go.

"They won't seek to wait us out?"

"They're *dreki*, Haakon." She stepped to the middle of the opening into the rocky tor, and glared up at Roar. "To wait us out indicates they consider the pair of us a threat. Arrogance will be their downfall."

"A specific trait of the species, it seems."

"I heard that."

A faint chuckle sounded. Then it died. "What are you doing?"

"Are you ready?" she demanded, waving her sword to get the *dreki's* attention. "And what do you think I'm doing? I am playing bait. You just focus on your shot. If you miss, then we're doomed."

"I'm not going to miss," he growled.

"Now, who's being arrogant?"

"I swear to the gods—"

"Roar!" she yelled. "You ugly, overbred bat!"

Roar screeched.

A shiver ran down her spine, but she could feel something else rising up within her. An answering roar of fury within her that made her blink. She'd never felt her *dreki* bare its teeth like that before.

"I think you got his attention," Haakon muttered, and she could hear him winding something behind her.

She shot him a ferocious grin, then returned her attention to her half-cousin. "You overgrown lizard! Your mother was a dragon! Why don't you come down here and fight me?"

Roar banked, his eyes narrowing to thin slits. She could sense him trying to communicate psychically with her, and refused the link. Letting that vile creature connect with her mind would be like diving naked into one of the stagnant pools that dotted the landscape.

"Here he comes," she warned, taking a steady step back.

"Got him in my sights. I need him as close as you can get him."

Roar began to dive toward them, his wings tucking flat against his sides. Árdís's breath caught. If Haakon missed the shot, then she had little doubt she'd be plucked in those ferocious claws and dragged kicking and screaming into the skies. Her hand firmed on the hilt of her sword. If so, then she was going to do her best to shove her blade right between Roar's teeth....

"Get ready to get out of the way," Haakon warned.

Árdís's knees flexed. Then she hesitated. She didn't want to make a move until Haakon was ready. If Roar dodged and the shot missed—

"*Árja!*"

The gray *dreki* banked at the last second, his claws coming up to pluck her from the ground.

"Now!" she screamed, and dove out of the way.

A crack sounded, and something flew past her ear. Roar hissed in fury as he saw her hit the ground and roll. Árdís's shoulder ached, and she landed against the base of one of the boulders, her view of Roar obliterated. All she could see was the metal rope grow taut, and a sudden scream of rage.

"Got him!" Haakon bellowed, leaping over the cable as it snapped taut. He dragged her to her feet, and shoved her head low as the rope suddenly cut toward them.

It shot over their heads, as Roar veered to the side, flapping madly. Haakon pressed her back to a boulder, his face intensely focused as he watched the *dreki* battling to

233

free itself. The other two *dreki* veered out of their dives, flapping a hasty retreat, as if the attack flustered them.

The shot had flown true. The grappling hook had hooked into Roar's flank, the cable twisted hopelessly over his body and wing. The more he tried to free himself, the more he tangled himself up. Roar threw himself against the weight of the rope, but it was holding, and though the enormous boulder shifted and slid a fraction, it was too heavy for the *dreki* to move.

He was going down.

She was surprised by how much she enjoyed the sight. Árdís jumped into the air, punching her fist toward her cousin. "We did it."

"The only way he's going to free himself is to change forms," Haakon said, with grim satisfaction. "He'll have to face me as a man."

As if the *dreki* heard him, Roar landed with a faint whump, hissing in their general direction.

"Be careful. He can control the elements," she warned. The other two *dreki* landed beside Roar, sniffing cautiously. "That's the three of them on the ground."

Dreki warriors carried travel bags with them. Ylve shimmered with a golden light, her spread wings shrinking into arms. The glow subsided, and the woman looked up, her teeth bared fiercely as she found mortal form. She picked up her bag, and yanked her clothes on before withdrawing her sword.

"She's mine," Árdís said.

Balder made the shift to mortal flesh, helping untangle Roar. Her cousin looked furious when he changed shape. The three of them were dark blurs in the mist.

Árdís planted herself between the two enormous stones, holding her sword with both hands, the tip pointed toward the ground. She had the higher ground here, and her position between the boulders meant Ylve could only come at her from one direction.

The enormous *dreki* warrior bared her teeth, her braids swinging. Ylve was *Zilittu*, an outsider from her mother's clan who'd followed the siblings across the sea. An enormous scar bisected her cheek, and she had several holes in her ears where she normally wore her gold hoops.

Not today.

"I'm going to enjoy this, Princess."

"Likewise," Árdís replied, shifting lightly on her feet. Thank the goddess she'd worn breeches and a tunic today. She'd needed the extra padding for the saddle, but the skirts would have hampered her now.

Ylve sprang at her, trying to take her by surprise so Árdís's advantage with the higher ground didn't matter as much. Steel rang as the pair of swords met. The first blow jarred up her arm, but it also served to slam sense into her.

She'd spent years in the training halls with Master Innick, drilling relentlessly under the brutal *dreki* warlord who'd once served her father. A *dreki* princess didn't need to know how to duel, but Árdís had always felt more than just a little unsafe in her mother's court.

And when one had to rely on the males around them for protection, it left one remarkably vulnerable.

Árdís beat back the first assault with a swift flurry of precise blows. Ylve's eyes widened, and the older *dreki* stepped back to assess the situation for a second. It was clear she hadn't expected to find a worthy foe here.

"Come out and play, Princess," Ylve taunted, gesturing to the wide-open space.

"Thanks, but I like it here."

Ylve couldn't flank her with the enormous stones standing sentinel on either side of her.

A clash of swords behind her broke her concentration. Haakon.

"Are you all right?" she yelled, not daring to take her eyes off the female in front of her.

A startled scream of rage returned, and someone grunted.

"I do this for a living," Haakon bellowed.

Ylve was slightly taller than her, and broader through the shoulders. She sparred on a daily basis, and had years of experience beyond Árdís's.

"Your mother wants you alive," Ylve said, and then smiled. "She didn't say it had to be in one piece."

"I dare you to harm a single hair on my head," Árdís taunted. "You might be her lapdog, but I'm her daughter and she has plans for me. Do you remember what happened when Ion broke Marduk's arm?"

Ylve darted forward, blade held low. Árdís disengaged with a prompt sidestep, but Ylve was inside her guard now.

A fist became the center of her vision and Árdís's head snapped back as it landed, her ears ringing and the inside of her head vibrating. She barely had time to swing her sword up before the whip of Ylve's blade clashed against it.

This wasn't sparring.

Nor was it practice.

She deflected the next blow, but the jar of it ached up her right arm. Ylve lashed out, sinking her boot into Árdís's midriff, and she staggered back, tripping on a rock. The second she hit the ground she rolled backward over her shoulder, coming up onto one knee, with her fingertips on the shale. Ylve strode forward, lifting her blade, but Árdís's eyes narrowed. Fine. They weren't sparring. It was clear the other woman planned to fight dirty.

Launching forward, she drove her shoulder into Ylve's midriff, sending the other woman crashing back into a boulder. Árdís dug her knuckles in under the woman's ribs, and then darted to the side, her sword scraping along Ylve's and slicing down the woman's forearm as she gained some space.

"First blood," Árdís said, breathing hard. Her shoulder ached.

A flicker of black entered the field of her vision. Balder, slinking in from the side. Ylve had forced her back within the ring of standing stones, most likely precisely for this very reason.

"Árdís, watch out!" Haakon called.

One sword against two. Árdís immediately backed her way between two of the enormous standing stones so they could only come at her one at a time. "Focus on your own fight," she yelled. Haakon couldn't afford to be distracted.

Wise advice.

She ought to take it herself.

Swords swung at her, and she moved like lightning, breathing hard as she avoided each blow. Her only saving grace was that they couldn't afford to hurt her. They were trying to hem her in, and disarm her. Árdís's head rang again as the hilt of Balder's sword slammed into her cheekbone. Her world narrowed down to a moment of pain as she staggered, and doubt whispered through her heart.

Haakon.

She was fighting now in desperation.

A knee drove into her thigh, and Árdís's vision exploded into white. It felt like she'd been stabbed. Ylve caught her by the shoulder, and drove the same knee up into her abdomen.

Árdís crumpled over the blow, her breath choking her as her lungs seized up. Her vision narrowed to a pinpoint, a rushing sound echoing through her ears. She saw Balder turn away from her to face some new threat, but she couldn't see what was happening.

"I'm enjoying every second of this, Princess." Ylve's whisper somehow broke through the ringing echo in her ears, as the female's fist clenched in Árdís's braid. "Every. Second."

The *dreki* drove her to her knees, pinning her there. Without her magic or her sword, she was helpless to resist. Árdís forced herself to breathe through the ache, until she could almost focus again.

"Don't hurt her."

A pair of boots came into her field of vision.

Ylve forced her to look up as Roar sauntered into view, clad in strict black leather. She bared her teeth. What was happening? Where was Haakon? She could hear someone grunting, and the hard slam of a fist burying itself in someone's flesh, but she didn't know who was who.

"Did you say something about me being an overgrown bat?" he taunted, his pale gaze caressing her face with an intensity that sickened her. "I swear, Árdís, you should be nicer to the *dreki* who's going to mate with you."

"I'd rather cut off my own wings," she shot back, "than mate with you."

His smile softened, and he took a menacing step toward her, his hand sliding behind her head, as he drew a knife from the sheath at his hip. "Perhaps I'll do it for you, so you can never, *ever* run away from me."

"Get your hands off her!" Haakon yelled, and a flurry of movement blurred in the corner of her vision.

"Haakon!" Árdís screamed, straining against Ylve's hold.

"Is that his name? Thank you, Árdís. I always like to add their names to my list when I kill them." Roar traced the tip of his blade down her cheek, but something came over her. Something she'd never felt before.

You will not have me, roared the *dreki* of her soul, and something surged within her. Something wild and chaotic, and utterly overwhelming, pressing at her skin from the inside as it fought to escape.

"But first, the man," Roar said, flipping the short ugly dagger in his fingers. "Pin him down, Balder."

Haakon.

A flush of terror flooded through her. Her lips felt numb. Time slowed as Roar turned and started toward her fallen husband. Balder had a foot planted on Haakon's throat, and her husband's arms were outflung, blood smearing the fingers she could see.

It was everything she'd ever feared.

Pain vanished. The world went away. Only the knife in Roar's hand remained, and the blood on her husband's twitching fingers.

All she could hear was that ringing in her ears again, but this time it felt like it was coming from somewhere deep inside her, like someone had struck a bell.

Or not a ringing.

It was her soul screaming "*No.*"

Heat filled her eyes as the *dreki* rose within her, choking her with rage. Árdís screamed. The manacle kept it chained within her, but it was forcing its way through her pores, shredding her soul in half....

The world turned green as Árdís surrendered.

She tore free from her own skin, exploding into a spirit form of pure green light, her wings flapping madly and her maw opening. The weight of her fleshly body fell away.

She was a spirit of pure vengeance and fury, a firestorm of passion and rage.

Raw Chaos magic turned the air into a miniature aurora borealis around her as Árdís rose above them all on wings of pure light.

From this height, she could see Haakon groaning as he rolled onto his side, and Balder gaped up at her. Relief flooded through her, but she could also see the blood on Haakon's nose and his flanks. Directly below her, her own body stood swaying, and Árdís blinked to see herself from the outside.

What had she done?

What was this?

"Roar!" Ylve cried a warning, and it rippled through the air on sound waves Árdís could almost see.

Roar's eyes widened with surprise as Árdís dove toward him. *"He's mine!"* she yelled.

The air rushed past her as she opened her gaping maw.

Roar screamed, hands flung up to protect himself.

She barely had weight or form. She was merely a churning mass of pure Chaos, the magic fighting to tear free of the spirit form she'd bound it in. Somehow her teeth closed over his shoulder. She could feel them sinking into his flesh as he cried out, batting at her, his hands sweeping straight through the rest of her.

Rage obliterated any thought she had. She was might and power and pure vengeance. She was immense and weightless and formless.

She was Death.

She flung Roar to and fro, her teeth ripping at his mortal flesh. Driving her claws through his unprotected belly, she tore him open.

Something hissed through the air behind her, and Árdís turned gleaming eyes upon Ylve as the bitch ran at her mortal body with her sword in hand.

A single pounce and she was ripping her way through Ylve, tearing the *dreki's* spirit free of her mortal body. Ylve collapsed, her body thrashing and jerking as Árdís's claws curled through her spirit form. Ylve's spirit opened its mouth to silently scream, but then she was fading, her form evaporating from between Árdís's claws like smoke.

A heavy weight began to suck her back down again.

She could feel her body dragging at her, lured by the proximity of her spirit. And though the rage still burned within her, she didn't know how to maintain her form, or keep herself burning through the Chaos magic that twined around her.

The world went black.

Árdís came back to herself, her body swaying, something hot and wet dripping from her nose as she slumped to her knees.

All three *dreki* lay on the ground around her. Balder kicked his heels in the shale as he drove himself back against one of the rocks, the whites of his eyes gleaming. There was blood all over Roar's chest, and he made a wet sucking sound deep in his lungs as he scrambled to escape her.

Ylve stared sightlessly at the sky. When *dreki* died, their spirits turned into pure Chaos and streamed across the skies like the northern auroras, but nothing of her spirit remained. Árdís had torn it clean from her body.

It was only so much meat, left behind.

"Sweet... goddess," Roar gasped, trying to stuff his entrails back inside him.

The steely rasp of a sword leaving its scabbard caught her attention. A hand locked around her arm, and then

Haakon was there, limping a little. He'd wiped his bloodied nose, but it smeared his teeth.

Árdís flung her arms around him, her racing heart finally settling as she felt the press of his hard body against hers. Relief flooded through her. The *dreki* settled, no longer fighting to push free of her skin. "You're alive."

She'd never been so grateful in her life.

He squeezed her ribs, and then drew away when she flinched.

"What happened?" he demanded. "There was this enormous glowing green dragon in the air—"

"*Dreki*," she corrected fiercely. "And that was me."

"Are you all right?" He rubbed a hand down her arm, his eyes serious.

"Are you?"

He pressed his fingers to his temples. "I was doing fine until they hit me with something. It felt like an invisible punch." He winced.

"A psychic attack." And she wasn't able to shield him.

She could barely shield herself.

Haakon's fist clenched around the hilt of his sword as he stepped past her.

"No," she said sharply, catching his hand and forcing him to lower the sword.

"They won't stop hunting you," he said, turning and giving her a look that almost made her shy away from him.

"If they have any sense they will," she said, partly for the benefit of Roar and Balder. She squeezed Haakon's wrist. "But if you kill a *dreki*, then my mother will call a blood debt down upon your head. They'll never stop hunting you. Never. And they'll make sure your death is particularly bloody."

He opened his mouth, but she shook her head sharply.

Her ears were starting to ring.

"Please, Haakon."

His gaze narrowed in on the blood dripping from her nose, and he gave a short jerk of his head. Árdís sighed in relief as the sword returned to its scabbard.

She had little doubts this husband of hers—a man she barely seemed to know anymore—could cut a *dreki* down.

But thankfully, there was enough of *her* Haakon left inside this brute warrior to listen to her.

"Perhaps you should see to your bastard prince," she suggested, meeting Balder's eyes. "He looks like he might need some help breathing."

Then she reached for Haakon's arm, tucking hers through the crook of his elbow as a lady might.

He shot her another look, clearly feeling the way she leaned upon him. Árdís didn't dare let her knees shake. The second she betrayed any sign of weakness to the *dreki*, they'd attack. And she could lose him before she ever got the chance to love him again.

Forcing herself to put one foot after the other, she let him guide her toward the gravel path. The horses had scattered, and she couldn't see them. Couldn't smell them. Her vision was starting to thin, little white spots dancing through the center of it as they left the *dreki* far behind.

"What was that?" Haakon demanded, hauling her up the slope.

"I don't know," she whispered, or thought she did. "Don't let them see me fall."

"Are you all right?" he asked again.

"No."

His grip on her arm softened. "A little further, Árja. We're nearly there. You can do this."

Blood still dripped from her nose, and she could barely see. Somehow they made it to the top of the hill, and then she was staggering over the crest of it. The world existed in a thousand different planes in front of her, crystalline lines running through everything. "Get me out of here."

Her knees gave way, and the last she knew, Haakon swept her up into his arms.

CHAPTER SIXTEEN

HAAKON RESTED HIS wrists on his knees by the fire as he waited for Árdís to wake.

The night sky loomed above them, and he'd managed to put several miles between them and the *dreki* warriors who'd been hunting them down. He didn't think they'd be coming after them, especially at night, but he didn't dare rest. Not until Árdís awoke.

If she woke.

Árdís had done something, and it had terrified the other *dreki*. He'd thought her magic compromised with the cuff on her wrist, but an enormous flaming *dreki* of pure green light—like the colors streaking across the horizon right now—had burst from her skin and driven the others away.

And then she'd collapsed.

Slowly he focused on polishing his sword, on the rasp of the whetstone gliding down the oiled edge of the blade. Today felt like he'd stepped into a new world, one where nothing he knew seemed secure.

"He's mine!"

The words kept echoing through his head. He'd seen the anguish upon her face, and the knife coming toward him, and though he couldn't help himself, he knew he was the reason she'd managed to touch this new magic.

Setting the sword aside, he crossed toward her, checking her color. Her nose had stopped bleeding, but he didn't like the heat of her skin, or the sweat at her temples. It was a brisk night, and though she was wrapped tenderly in his furs, she shouldn't have been this warm to the touch.

Árdís murmured feverishly as he cupped his hand over her forehead. "Don't go," she whispered, and her eyes blinked open, though they stared right through him. "Don't go. Please don't leave me."

"Árja." He brushed the back of his fingers down the smooth slope of her cheek. "Árja, you're dreaming. You're safe. I'm here. I'm not going anywhere."

The two smallest fingers on her right hand curled around his pinkie. Árdís burrowed her face against his thigh and settled back into sleep.

It was a pose they'd assumed so many times in the past. His throat felt dry. He'd been struggling to understand who his wife truly was, but the hardest part was comprehending that the Árja he knew was still there. Along with a powerful *dreki* princess who faced battles he couldn't even imagine.

She was both a stranger—and the one person in this world he knew intimately.

And she'd loved him.

He finally believed what she'd been telling him last night.

Settling the curve of his spine against a boulder, he stretched his legs out in front of him, and ran a hand through her unbound hair. Árdís curled a hand over his thigh and settled against him, her entire body softening into sleep as if she felt safe there at his side.

Haakon tucked her hair gently behind her ear. Despite all of his best intentions, it was clear he wasn't going to be able to walk away from this unscathed.

But maybe he didn't have to walk away.

She wanted him.

But something was keeping her from his side, and despite her declaration last night, he didn't think it was merely the inability to give him children, or both their worlds colliding.

"What are you thinking?" came a silky whisper from her lips.

Her eyelashes fluttered, but she merely pressed her face into his thigh, as if she wasn't yet ready to stop touching him.

"Árja." His fingers stilled on her temples. "How are you feeling?"

"Sleepy." She yawned. "I feel like an enormous *dreki* just battle-slammed me. Everything hurts. But I'll be fine by morning."

"Are you hungry?"

The feral look in her expression didn't vanish, but she nodded. "Starving."

Crossing to the pot he'd swung over the fire, he stirred the soup he'd made. Game was scarce this far north and so late at night, but he'd packed dried strips of beef, and enough root vegetables to provide some nourishment. She'd devoured most of the goat by herself last night. He'd have to hunt soon if he wanted to continue to feed them.

"You can fight," he murmured, as he ladled the broth into a small tin cup.

"My father put a sword in my hand before you even drew your first breath," she said. "It's tradition for *dreki* to duel with swords. We're such large, powerful creatures that the destruction we create when we battle each other can be catastrophic. My grandfather insisted blood debts and arguments be settled with the sword instead. I needed to learn how to protect myself from any challenges."

He'd known she was older than he, but to hear it so blithely stated.... He knelt at her side, staring down into the broth. "You never picked up a sword when you were with me."

"I never had to." Árdís hauled herself onto her elbows, but her hands shook, he noticed. Not quite recovered then. "I enjoy the physical side of dueling, but if I didn't have to...." She shrugged. "And I knew you were there to protect me, if anything should go wrong. It was nice not to have to be on my guard all the time."

It wasn't the first time she'd hinted she didn't feel safe in her world.

"What was that?" he murmured, tilting the cup of broth to her lips, and cupping the back of her head to help her. She drank almost all of it, not even wincing at the bland flavor.

"What?"

"What happened today? The green *dreki* of light that erupted from your body."

"Chaos magic," she said, pausing to take a breath.

Which explained precisely nothing. "How did you use it with the manacle on?"

"I don't know. Chaos magic is.... It's not like any other magic in the world." She looked troubled. "It doesn't obey the normal rules. It was what Tiamat used to shape the world."

"It scared them away."

"As it should," she said, and pushed the cup of broth away. "No more." She tried to sit up, and he helped her as best he could. "I scared myself."

"Why?"

"The great goddess, Tiamat, created the *dreki* out of both Chaos magic and elemental magic. We're all able to access the elemental side of our power, but... Chaos magic is wild. Unpredictable. Some *dreki* can use it to create Chaos bubbles—a world outside our own—but what I did today"—she stared at her hands as if she saw something else there—"I was no longer inside my body. My spirit melded with Chaos magic, and I was able to affect the physical world with my spirit body."

"I've never seen anything like it. One moment you were there, and the next this enormous being of pure light erupted from your flesh, like an aurora given shape and form." His voice softened. "It was beautiful."

You *are beautiful.*

He'd always thought her the most stunning woman he'd ever seen, but this creature was powerful and exotic in a way he'd never been able to imagine. It was like holding pure flame cupped in his hands, and wondering if it would burn him.

She shivered. "I can name three living *dreki* who are able to wield it like that and survive. My mother is one of them."

Her mother.

It wasn't the first time she'd mentioned the *dreki* queen, but she never spoke of the queen with any warmth or affection. No. There was fear there.

He needed to understand what was going on. Something didn't feel right here.

"So she's passed the gift onto you?"

"I do not think she would see it that way," Árdís whispered, staring into the flames.

"As a gift?"

"Only my mother can wield Chaos magic," she whispered, grinding the heels of her palms into her eyes. "It's how she holds power, and why none dare challenge her. She doesn't have to challenge other *dreki*, for they all know she can rip the spirit directly from their bodies without ever touching them."

"But surely she wouldn't think you would challenge her."

"You don't understand," Árdís cried. "I shouldn't have been able to do that. But now I have... I'm a threat to her, Haakon. My mother will have felt Chaos warp the land, and if she doesn't, then Roar will tell her. And yes, she will know that given time, I could master the magic only she commands. Of course she'll see it as a threat."

"She's your mother—"

"Giving birth to Rurik, Marduk, and me meant she'd fulfilled the contract she owed my father." Árdís shook her head. "I know when you think of the word 'mother' you see your own. And I understand why, because Brunhild is the kindest, sweetest woman I know—"

"When she's not harassing you for babies." The words were out of his mouth before he could stop them. He couldn't forget what she'd said last night about being unable to give him children.

Árdís paused. "If that is the worst thing your mother can do, then you know nothing about horrible mothers."

"And your mother doesn't want grandchildren?" He couldn't fathom it.

"Not if they're not purebred. A *drekling* child would be slaughtered before it could draw breath." Her fist pressed against her chest, as if she missed the ring. Her voice dropped to a whisper. "It would be an insult to my bloodlines to birth a half-breed. She'd probably kill me too."

He froze, feeling the words wrap around him like ice.

She'd said it might be difficult for her to go into heat and give him children.

But had she been frightened, too?

"I'm not strong. I cannot fight her, not like my brothers can." Árdís's fingers curled in his sleeve. "I wasn't born to be a warrior. I only wanted...."

"*What?*"

"To be safe," she whispered hoarsely. "To be free."

His arms tightened. He had the feeling he knew exactly what she could not say. She'd been abroad in the world. And she'd found him. Suddenly her curiosity about his life when they first met made so much sense. She'd lingered there, beyond when she'd known she should. She'd stayed in his arms, when she'd never intended to do so.

She'd married him.

And then she'd suddenly left him, without a word. Without a goodbye.

He felt breathless.

"Why did you leave me?" He captured her face in both hands. "Why? If it tears you apart so much?"

Tears glimmered in her eyes. "You stupid fool, have you not guessed?"

She kissed him suddenly, with a storm of passion. Straddling his hips, she pushed herself into his lap, her fists curling in his hair.

It was everything he wanted. But it wasn't enough. He wrapped his fist around her braid, and drew back. "I want to hear it from your lips."

"Haakon." She moaned and rocked against him. *"This changes everything."*

He paused. He'd heard those words in his head, as clearly as if she'd spoken them out loud. "What does it change?"

Árdís's eyes shone like glittering diamonds as her tears obscured the topaz depths. "Because she would have *killed you*. My mother would have killed you, if she came for me and found me in your arms. She would have salted the very earth your village stood upon, until nothing remained, not even the memory of your family, or its name. I had to leave. I had to leave and I had to make sure you would never, ever come after me."

She was right.

It changed everything.

Haakon paced in front of the fire, glancing at her now and then. Árdís sat wrapped in his cloak, watching him with an expression he'd never seen on her before: defeat.

"Tell me," he said hoarsely. "Tell me everything."

"I shouldn't have said it. You caught me at a weak moment."

Yes, you damned well should have.

But it wasn't her he was angry at.

"*Please*. I need to know the truth, Árja."

"Ten years ago," she whispered, looking down into her curled hands. "I fled the *dreki* court. I'd finally reached my majority, and it's expected that a... a *dreki* female will begin to consider certain alliances. Sirius wanted to mate with me, but he wasn't the only one. And, I don't know what came over me. My mother is powerful. She murdered my father—or arranged for him to be murdered, and then she blamed my elder brother for his death, so she could claim my father's throne in Rurik's stead. She drove my younger brother, Marduk, away from court, when he became another rallying point for those still loyal to my father. It was just me, and I was alone and on the verge of adulthood, and I felt trapped." She looked up suddenly. "I wanted to see the world. I wanted to know what my purpose in it was. And I wanted freedom. Choices. A life away from my mother and all the pressure to mate. And so I fled.

"I spent weeks on the Continent. All these places, all these cities, all these people.... I was too frightened to enter the cities, for it was so new to me. So I watched, and when I couldn't meld with the mortal world I flew north, and there was this land, this beautiful land full of glaciers and rivers and forests. So alien to my homeland, and yet so familiar. And I was hungry and curious, and that was where I met you."

"I remember," he said softly. He hadn't known she was so young, or so inexperienced. She'd never been like the women he knew—she'd always been arrogant, and demanding, and capricious—and yet he could see the uncertainty in her eyes now.

"You were the first man I'd ever kissed," she admitted. "And you were kind, and fascinating, and... I made up my mind I wanted to lie with you. I wanted you to be my first, my *choice*, but you had these ideas about marriage. In the *dreki* world, sometimes we mate for breeding purposes, and sometimes simply for the joy in taking a lover. But it is rare that two *dreki* promise each other forever, for we live such long lives." She looked away. "It was only afterward I realized that for you, marriage meant forever. And I could not give you forever."

She bowed her head.

Haakon couldn't breathe.

"I never wanted to hurt you," she whispered. "I loved you. But I am *dreki* and you mortal, and I could hear the passing thunder of wings on the horizon as my mother's *dreki* hunted for me. I could hear them coming closer. Every day for that last year, I would watch the horizon. I knew lingering there meant offering you a death sentence, but I couldn't bring myself to leave. Just one more day in your arms, one more week..." She closed her eyes. "It was my younger cousin, Andri, who found me, thank all the gods. Of all the *dreki*, he's always been my ally, and he warned me the queen knew where I was. Sirius was coming for me, he said. I didn't dare linger."

He didn't know what to say. "That last afternoon, you came to me."

And we made love.

She'd been frantic with need, dragging him into the barn, where she pushed him onto the straw and had her way with him. Once. Twice. Three times. She'd told him she loved him, but that hadn't been all she'd been saying. He realized it now.

"I was saying goodbye," Árdís whispered. "And then it started raining. A *dreki* storm on the horizon. I knew I didn't have much time. I had to flee before they came looking for me and found you."

"So you let me believe you'd been stolen away by a *dreki*?" he rasped, feeling the weight of all those years of guilt and grief. "I heard you scream. I saw it—*you*—fly away. Do you know what that felt like?"

"It was the only way I could be certain you wouldn't follow me!" she cried desperately. "I wanted you to grieve for me. I wanted you to be free to live another life, to be free to marry again." The words sounded as though they were ripped from her. "And I hated that thought, but I didn't want you to be unhappy. You always wanted children. You wanted a wife, a home, and I could not give you that. So I tried to make it clear I was gone from your life. I never dreamed you'd not stop looking for me."

"You were my wife," he said hoarsely. "I could never stop looking for you. Not when a chance you lived might exist."

Tears flooded down her face. "I never wanted to hurt you."

But you did. He stared at her with clenched fists.

"Do you think it has been easy for me? To live such a life with you, and then to throw it all away out of fear? To bury myself in my mother's court and live a half-life, *knowing* what it could have been? I should never have left court the first time, for then I wouldn't understand what I have been missing." A breath tore through her. "And here I am again, dragging you back into my life. Putting you at risk. I shouldn't have asked you to help me. It's selfish."

"That was my decision to make."

"You don't understand. It's worse now, because I've dared to flee again. If she gets her hands on you—"

"I'm aware of the risks," he snapped. "And it's my choice whether I take it. I would risk my very life for you—"

"Well, I won't!"

"Not even for a chance of happiness?" He stepped closer. "You don't know that she will capture us. You don't know she cannot be defeated." He went to his knees in front of her.

"No!" Árdís shook her head desperately. "No. I won't allow it. I can't lose you. Not like that. I can face forever, knowing you lived a long and happy life. I could bear it, if only—"

His mouth met hers, capturing the words, even as he claimed her face between his hands.

Seven years he'd thought her gone. The loss had nearly broken him.

But for Árdís, it had been a sacrifice she'd made, knowing he lived. A loss she could bear, as long as he drew breath out there somewhere.

It didn't mean those seven years apart ached any less for her, but he finally understood what had driven her to such lengths. This had never been about not loving him. This had never been a *dreki* princess spurning her mortal lover.

She'd loved him enough to sacrifice her happiness for him.

And while it had hurt him just as much, she'd considered that pain a worthwhile sacrifice in exchange for his life.

Haakon drew back from the heated kiss and pressed his lips to her forehead gently. He lifted his head, studying her heart-shaped face, with her burning *dreki* eyes. And he suddenly understood her.

She'd lost two brothers and a father she adored. She'd been born into a brutal court, and when she'd finally fled, trying to spread her wings and discover who she was, her mother had threatened to break her world down around her. Árdís's every moment of existence had been that of a young *dreki* princess, trying to survive a hostile world without a single ally at her side.

The only choice she'd ever made of her own desires, had been him.

Árdís made a small choking sound in her throat. "I *loved* you," she whispered, as if she did not dare bring such an emotion into the present.

Haakon's fingertips flexed on her jaw, as the words went through him like a spear.

Their mouths clashed together, hot and furious. *I loved you.* The words rang in his ears. Righting something inside him. All he'd ever wanted to know was if it had been real.

He had her in his arms, and a part of him shook badly, never wanting to let her go. But there were a pair of palms against his chest. An insistent pushing, even as her tongue flicked over his.

They broke apart, both of them breathing hard. And he saw the doubt in her eyes, as she tried to open her mouth, to say the words that were clearly trapped there. Haakon pressed a finger to his lips. He didn't need her to say them. He could see it, shining wetly there. Árdís wanted him. She had loved him. Perhaps still did, even if she refused to admit it to herself.

But.

I can face forever, knowing you lived a long and happy life. I could bear it, if only....

He closed his eyes, needing the moment to control himself, before he could look at her again.

Nothing had changed. Not in her mind.

Only in his.

"One last night," he whispered, and felt the tension dissolve as she shuddered. This was the only way he could have her.

Haakon slowly lowered his face to hers, kissing her ever so slowly, as if to savor the moment.

If only....

But all they had was this.

For now.

CHAPTER SEVENTEEN

DAWN LIGHT BROKE over the small village as they crested the rise the next morning.

Haakon's arms curled around Árdís, as she swayed in the saddle in front of him. She was still weak enough he didn't want her pitching off the back of Sleipnir before he could grab her. Occasionally her head would loll back against his chest, and he'd hear her breathing soften. He took an almost guilty pleasure in holding her while she slept, pressing his face to her hair to breathe in the scent of her.

From the start he'd been holding her at bay, still mired in pain, but yesterday had changed everything.

He'd wanted to hurt her when he traveled to Reykjavik, because she'd hurt him.

He'd wanted to lock his heart away, and not let her in ever again, but it was clear she'd never truly left.

She'd fled from him to save his life. She'd loved him.

And today, when they finally got her bracelet off, she'd leave him again. To save his life.

He didn't want to let her go.

But that was not his choice to make.

"We made camp barely a mile away," Árdís muttered, waking with a sleepy yawn. "We could have been here last night."

"You needed the rest."

And I wanted one last night with you.

If he let himself, he'd want every single one of them.

He let Sleipnir pick his way down the slope, and they wended their way along the faint track through the grass he guessed the locals called a road.

There were few locals around. Haakon found a small boy, and gestured for him to feed the horses and mind them while he and Árdís saw to their business.

"This way," Haakon muttered, taking Árdís by the hand, feeling dread twist his insides. She deserved to be free of the manacle, but he couldn't help feeling like he was losing her all over again.

"We're nearly there," Árdís said breathlessly. "I can scarce believe it. A matter of moments and I will be free of this cursed manacle. Your debt to me is paid. And mine.... You know the truth now. I cannot give you back the ring, but I hope.... I hope the truth is enough."

He didn't know if she realized how her hand pressed restlessly against the empty space between her breasts, searching for her missing ring, even as she said the words.

"You will be free to go," she continued. "To live your life without guilt, and to live the life I'd hoped you would have."

His heart rebelled. *Is there no life where we could be together?*

But he swallowed his pride, and forced himself to ask, "And you?"

"I don't know. I haven't thought about my future, beyond these next few days. I'll be safe with Rurik." She colored. "It frustrates me to know I've still been living the life my mother planned for me."

"What sort of life would you desire, if it were your choice?"

Their eyes met.

You, said her expression.

"I would live a life knowing you were safe," Árdís whispered. "That's all I want."

It was all she would allow.

He ground his teeth together. Nothing had changed. There was no point arguing with her.

There are other ways, something whispered inside him. He couldn't force her to face her fears.

All he could do was encourage her.

"This way," he said, leading her to a small house at the end of the street that looked little more than a door cut into the side of a grassed hill.

Rapping his knuckles sharply against the door, he waited. Runes had been carved into the timber at some point, and a goat bleated at him from the top of the grassed roof. The tiny village was barely more than a collection of houses atop a windswept knoll.

"Do you think he's at home?"

"He's at home." Haakon hammered on the door.

"All right, all right. I heard you the first time," someone grumbled from within, and the sound of the door being unlocked echoed.

The door jerked open, and a small man blinked up at them. He stood barely four and a half feet tall, with glittering golden eyes that seemed somewhat unnatural. The breadth of his shoulders, however, was wide, and his barrel chest showed a great deal of power. Tormund had challenged Dúrnir to an arm wrestle the last time they'd been here, and Dúrnir had won.

"You," the *svartálfar* said flatly, blinking up at the pair of them. His eyes suddenly widened when he caught a glimpse of Árdís.

The door came flying back at them, but Haakon shoved his boot in the gap before it could slam shut.

"Dúrnir, is that any way to treat paying customers?"

Dúrnir staggered backward as Haakon pushed through the door, gesturing Árdís inside.

"I don't want your custom!" Dúrnir snapped, bracing himself against a small round table. He stared at Árdís as one would a snake. "Especially from her kind."

"Relax, little man," she drawled. "I've already had breakfast."

Dúrnir paled.

Haakon gave his wife a long, steady look.

"What?" she asked, her nostrils flaring. "This entire place stinks of bad magic. And the only reason I'm in this predicament is because this evil creature tricked you."

"I thought it was my fault for being stupid enough to dabble with magic?"

"You're not entirely forgiven," she said, with a sniff.

"You see what you've done," he said to the dwarf. "My wife isn't impressed with the efforts I've gone to in order to win her back."

"You *married* a *dreki*?" The words exploded out of Dúrnir, and he turned toward the kitchen. "Odin's balls. These humans and their insane ideas."

Haakon tugged a small leather pouch from his belt, and followed Dúrnir, ducking beneath the arch of the doorway. Everything in this place was undersized, which made him feel like a giant in a house full of antiques. One wrong step and he'd obliterate something. A dead chicken hung over the sink, its blood filling the small copper washbasin. A burning stick of sage clouded the room, and

261

the smoke settled near the ceiling, which meant his head was directly in the haze. Haakon waved a hand, his eyes stinging.

He dropped the pouch on the table, letting it give a satisfying clink. "I have another task for you."

"I don't want it."

"That's too bad." He reached for Árdís's hand, lifting it up to reveal the shackle. "There's a slight problem with the bracelet."

Dúrnir poured himself a drink of something that smelled vile. He drained half the cup, before setting the silver goblet back down with a clink, and placing both hands flat on the table. "You wanted something that could contain a *dreki* in her mortal flesh. It appears to be working perfectly."

"The words of release don't work."

Dúrnir shrugged, and settled into a chair, kicking his boots up on the table. "Not my problem."

"I can make it your problem," Árdís muttered.

Dúrnir eyed her warily. "No magic. No fangs." He forced a smile and waggled his fingers. "I wouldn't be making threats if I were you."

Árdís rested her hands on the table and leaned over it to glare at him. "I'm not entirely powerless."

A flash of Chaos green rolled through her eyes.

Dúrnir yelped, and the chair toppled over as he twisted. He landed with a loud bang, disappearing behind the table.

Haakon circled the table, grabbing the little man's hand and hauling him to his feet. "Are we done with the posturing?" He frowned. "You two don't even know each other. What's with this mortal enemies pact?"

"I told you." Árdís's eyes narrowed. "Long ago, the *svartálfar* and the *dreki* went to war for this country."

He didn't have to ask who'd won.

"Long ago?"

"Two thousand years or so," she replied dismissively.

Haakon had been in the middle of brushing dirt off his hands, but he paused. "You mean to tell me you hate him because of a war that happened millennia before any of us even walked this land?"

"We remember."

"And so do we," Dúrnir shot back. "Never trust a *dreki*, with their arrogant and vicious natures."

"Never trust the *svartálfar*," Árdís retorted. "With their wretched magic, and lying tongues. I told you this was a trick. He probably laughed himself silly the second you left this house."

Haakon very, very badly needed a drink. Pinching the bridge of his nose, he considered the problem. "Can you remove the manacle?"

"Give me one good reason why I should," Dúrnir said.

Haakon opened his mouth, but Árdís beat him to it. "Because I have an entire court of *dreki* hunting for me. If you do not help us remove this manacle, then I shall sit here and wait for them. I'll even open the door and welcome them inside, and tell them you trapped a *dreki* princess into mortal flesh."

Dúrnir paled.

"You'll be compensated," Haakon said quickly, hefting the weight of his purse. "The sooner you work your magic, the sooner I haul her over my shoulder and take her out of here."

"A very tempting offer." Dúrnir's eyes narrowed. "As much as I would like to say we have a deal, there is one slight problem. There's nothing *wrong* with the manacle. I cannot remove it, *dreki*. Only the one who placed it upon you can."

The pair of them looked at each other.

"We're tried that," Haakon said. "Numerous times."

"The manacle's magic is will-based," the dwarf said, with a smirk. "So if your barbaric Norseman here cannot remove it, then it's got naught to do with trickery. It's because he truly does not wish to do so. Not deep in his heart, where the magic lies."

"I *want* to remove it," Haakon growled.

"Do you? You said she was your wife. You said you were trying to win her back." Dúrnir slapped both palms on the table and leaned forward. "I think someone's not being entirely honest with himself."

Haakon straightened, taken aback. "I...."

"You cannot break the bracelet," Dúrnir said. "I cannot remove it. The only way you're getting it off her is if you truly wish her to be free of it, deep in your heart."

They didn't speak all the way back to the horses.

Haakon paid the young boy for minding them, then led her down the narrow track to the beach. Smooth oval pebbles gave way to black sand, and the seas were particularly choppy this afternoon. Though the sun was out, it barely warmed her skin. The wind was too cold.

Árdís kept trying to work out what to say. She'd been so certain she'd walk out of the *svartálfar's* house and be able to take to the skies. She hadn't even considered defeat.

Or was it truly a loss, after all?

Árdís realized she was toying with the bracelet. This would have been goodbye, if they'd succeeded. And she didn't want to say goodbye. Not truly.

Haakon kicked at a pebble, wending both hands through the back of his hair and clasping them there. The movement pulled the drape of his coat tight, and it rode up, revealing his shirt underneath. Sleipnir nosed at his lax reins, but stood obediently.

"I didn't know," Haakon finally said. "I swear I had no idea I was sabotaging you."

She stared out at the sea, strands of her hair whipping across her face. "I believe you."

His startled gaze cut to hers.

Árdís reached up, her fingertips grazing his cheek and the rough stubble that lined his jaw. "It's all right, Haakon."

"No, it's damned well not." The muscle in his jaw flexed, and he cupped her hand there, closing his eyes briefly as he turned into the touch. His voice roughened. "I'm endangering you by keeping you trapped in this form. You could have been safely in your brother's lands by now. You would have nothing to fear. Your mother couldn't drag you back."

It was what she'd set out to do at the start of this escape, but there was one thing missing in this scenario.

Her heart skipped a beat. A part of her held no regret. "And you'd be gone."

Something dark moved in his eyes.

"I thought that was what you wanted." His voice roughened.

The pad of her thumb brushed, just lightly, against the soft stubble on his cheek. Longing filled her. She opened her mouth to speak. To tell him how she felt. Doubt brewed in her heart, an uneasy storm that stole the words from her lips.

I love you. I will always love you.

But she would be the death of him.

"Damn you," he whispered. "What do you want?"

"What do you mean?"

"What do you want in life? Us? Me? If you could have anything in your life, without repercussions, what would it be?"

Nobody had ever asked her that before. "I don't want to be selfish—"

"You're not being selfish." Haakon captured her face between his hands, his arctic blue eyes seeming to see right through her. "It isn't wrong to take what you desire out of life, Árja."

She licked her lips, hearing her mother spit the word again and again. "I...."

"I think that word came from someone else. I think whoever told you that you were selfish wanted to force you to follow the path they'd set out in life for you. And the one time you fought free, the one time you took what you wanted, you were punished for it. Am I correct?"

Árdís clenched her eyes shut, but the truth reverberated through her like she was a struck drum. She could have fled the court with Marduk all those years ago. But she'd been scared to break free, frightened to take what she wanted... and laced with enough guilt to make her question her every move.

"If your mother wasn't involved, then what would you choose for yourself? Me?" Haakon's voice shivered roughly over her skin. "Would you still deny me?"

"No." She didn't even have to think.

"You're stronger than you think you are. I *saw* the look on your cousin's face when you unleashed your power upon him. You could burn the world to ashes with your magic."

But so can she. Her fingernails snagged in his damp shirt. She wanted so very badly to believe him. She wanted to claim what was hers.

But if she wasn't strong enough—if she couldn't defeat her mother—then she would lose him.

Forever.

He saw all of it in her eyes as she looked up at him, his own softening. And a look of ragged fury came over him. Desperation.

Haakon's head lowered toward hers, and her breath hitched. He'd stolen kisses in the past few days, but he'd been so careful with them, as if he did not dare allow her to know how deeply he wanted her. He'd been holding back. Hot, wet kisses designed to inflame her, but distant somehow. Hands all over her, stroking her body to the edge, each move designed to give her pleasure, but nothing more.

This was different, in almost every way.

A fierce, hungry kiss, unlike all the others they'd shared since they'd met again in Reykjavik. She could remember meltingly slow kisses, kisses that lingered all over her skin when they'd shared a bed as husband and wife, but they seemed a distant memory. It felt as though there were not enough moments left between them now, and she could feel the same urgency echoing through his tightly strung body.

A kiss, before time caught up to them again.

A kiss, before she remembered the weight of everything that lay against them.

A kiss to stay the darkness in her heart when she faced such an uncertain future.

She clung to him, her hands curling around his wrists. And a desperate thrill lit through her veins as his tongue touched hers. Árdís melted against him, letting him know in so many silent ways how much she'd longed for this.

Touch me. Please.

Promise me forever, even if we both know it's a lie.

"It's not a lie," Haakon whispered, against her mouth, and she drew back with a startled jerk, mentally checking her psychic shields.

They were firmly in place. But the moment had jolted her, sending her tumbling into a stormy sea of hope that her greatest wish was coming true, and fear it was not. That it was simply a joke Fáfnir had been playing upon her.

They separated, both breathing hard. Haakon studied her face, her eyes, her swollen lips. "I will wait for you," he whispered, as if he saw her indecision. "No matter how long it takes, Árja. I will wait for you to make your choice."

This man. She didn't deserve this man.

Árdís pressed her forehead against his chest, and he wrapped his arms around her as if he knew how much she needed him to hold her. Not even the frigid air blowing in off the sea could touch her. All she could feel was the heat lingering in his skin.

"What do we do now?" she whispered.

He'd tried once more to remove the manacle the second they were out of the svartálfar's house, and had failed again.

"I said I would get you safely to your brother and I meant it. I'll signal the men. We'll sail for Akureyri. From there, it's another day or so to your brother's lands." His hand stroked up and down her spine, pausing to cup her nape. "You'll be safe there, Árja. Finally free of your mother and her machinations."

A tremor ran through her. "We're not there yet."

"Not yet," he replied grimly. "But do not doubt me."

Árdís swallowed. There was something to be said for his stubborn, infuriating nature.

Nothing could vanquish it, when Haakon set his mind to something.

The signal fire on the beach was dying down as Haakon leaned on the rail of the ship and stared across the sea. It winked on the edge of the horizon, before blinking once and vanishing in a snuff of light.

"Well?" Tormund asked, joining him at the rail as the ship splashed through massive breakers.

He couldn't see Árdís anywhere on the deck. He'd spent the last hour shouting orders and hauling rope, and she wasn't in her cabin where she was meant to be. Or in Marek's cabin, where she'd headed when they boarded.

"Well," he repeated, knowing exactly what his cousin wanted.

Tormund grinned at him. "Forgive me if I'm mistaken, but wasn't your wife supposed to be free of her bracelet, and flapping her way through the skies right now?"

"It's a long story."

"Not that I mind the detour. I mean, this is the most enjoyment I've had in years. I've made eighty kroner off Gunnar in the last week alone." He reached out and touched Haakon's throat. "And I think I'm about to make another twenty off Bjorn. Is that a bite mark on your neck?"

Haakon growled, and slapped his cousin's hand away. "Leave it alone."

He didn't want the men discussing his wife and his bedroom habits.

"On one condition. I want the full story. She's still here, we're heading for Akureyri, there's a bite mark on your neck, but you look like you've just buried your dog. Things don't add up, my friend."

He stared out at the waves, the splash of salt water wetting his face. "She left me because she thinks her mother is going to kill me."

Tormund's eyebrows shot up. "Somewhat shorter than I imagined, but intriguing. Go on."

He scraped a hand over the back of his neck. "And her mother is hunting her now...." He let the words flow out of him, feeling his shoulders soften as Tormund listened.

It felt somewhat akin to lancing a wound.

"Well," his cousin finally said, when Haakon had run out of words. "That makes my brother's mother-in-law sound like a saint. Can you kill her?"

His head turned sharply. "What?"

"The *dreki* queen is just another monster, my friend. And *you* hunt dragons." Tormund held both hands out, and then cupped them together. "The solution seems simple."

"Have you been drinking? She's locked away in a court full of *dreki*."

"Then lure her out."

"With what?" He saw Tormund's expression shift. "No. *No*. I am not going to put Árdís in danger."

"The same way she's afraid to put you in danger by letting herself love you?

Son of a— He'd never thought of it that way before. "It's not the same," he said weakly.

Tormund scratched his jaw. "Do you love her?"

"Of course."

"Then you're a fool if you don't fight for her."

Haakon leaned on the rail and saw nothing. "Me fighting for her was never the problem. It's whether she'll fight for *me*."

"Perhaps you need to give her a reason to fight. And then let her do so, regardless of the risk."

He looked at his cousin sharply. "Is our love not reason enough?"

"Loving you was never the problem. I knew that the moment I saw her look at you when we tried to kidnap her in Reykjavik. She looked at you as if you put the moon in the skies—or no, as if you *were* the moon, but she knew she could never touch you." Tormund peered upwards. "I mean, look at her."

Haakon craned his head back, his gut dropping as he saw her in the crow's nest. "What the hell is she doing?" He swore, and then strode along the deck, but Tormund captured his arm.

"Leave her be. She spent most of the previous trip up there too. I think it makes her feel as though she's flying."

Flying.

His stomach felt like it plummeted. His first instinct had been to get her safely down, but as he watched her lean into the wind, her red skirts fluttering behind her like wings as she laughed, he realized she was exactly where she needed to be.

"She's a *dreki* princess, Haakon. And you're still thinking of her as Árja, the woman you married, but she was never truly that woman. She buried her true nature, and there's only so long she can live that life. This was never going to end with you throwing her over your shoulder and sailing back to Viksholm. The life you knew is gone. If you want her, truly want her, then you might have to accept a different Árja. A different life. One filled with volcanoes, and treasure, and a host of *dreki* males who would see you a threat. Enemies you cannot even conceive of." His voice softened. "I think she knows exactly what she's dragged you into. She's frightened you can't accept her world. She's terrified you'll be killed. And her reasons for such an assumption are legitimate reasons. If you want her to fight for you, Haakon, then you need to convince her you want the *dreki* princess, and not just the dream the pair of you conjured. You need to convince her you're man enough to handle *her* world. And survive it."

Everything Tormund said was the truth.

She wasn't just Árja, the wife he'd promised to protect until his dying breath. Saving her had been the only thing that kept him going for the last seven hellish years, but Árdís didn't need saving. Not the way he'd been thinking of. She'd fled her mother's court, saved Marek from certain death, and managed to tear her cousin Roar to pieces when provoked. If it came down to it, he was more vulnerable than she.

Nor was she merely a *dreki* princess, tied to her court and her people, but determined to live her own life.

She was both the woman he loved, and the princess who wanted him to see her. To understand her. A woman taking her first brave steps into a new world where she finally had choices, and throwing off the shackles of her mother's domineering shadow.

If he wanted Árdís to fight for him, then he had to let her do so.

If he wanted her to choose him, then he had to confront his own stifling urges.

Keeping her in his life was not his decision to make. He'd known that, but he'd only been halfway to the truth.

She needed a warrior, one who wasn't afraid to stand *at her side*, instead of in front of her, using his body as her shield. Her mother had planted so many doubts in her head. He couldn't continue to contribute to them.

To save her, he had to set her free. To let her become what she was always meant to become.

He had to get that manacle off her. She was born to soar the skies, and his own contrary nature was keeping her locked away on the earth.

But how could he release her when he wasn't even consciously aware of keeping her contained?

It was his innate fear of losing her that held her captive.

Fear. It all came back to fear. Árdís's fear to reach for what she wanted. His fear of letting her go, knowing she might be too afraid to choose him.

Running away from her mother was only half a solution. If they didn't deal with the queen, then perhaps she'd never truly be able to spread her wings. Rurik's territory would merely be another cage, albeit larger than the one she'd inhabited.

And he wanted her to live this new life she craved so badly, even if she did not choose him.

His gaze began to focus, and he realized he was staring at his cousin. Through him.

"It's a lovely face and all," Tormund said, "but I know I'm not what's held you speechless for the last minute or so. What are you planning?"

"You're right." About everything.

"You can say that a little louder if you want to," Tormund said promptly.

"I cannot mount an assault on the *dreki* court," he said thoughtfully. Slowly. Plans began to stir through his mind. "And I cannot fight the queen's magic, or her *dreki* pawns. I have nothing but a sword, a ballista, and my own body. Árdís can wield her mother's magic, but she can't fight alone. We need each other, if we're to have any chance of defeating her mother."

Tormund blinked. "You're going to let her fight her mother?"

"If she will." He turned toward the passenger cabin. "That doesn't mean I'm merely going to stand back and watch. Árdís is better equipped for this fight than I ever will be, but she needs me to stand at her side. I hunt monsters. I kill dragons. Magic or not, the *dreki* queen is merely another monster. She's not invincible. There has to be some way to defeat her."

"I'm liking the sound of this," Tormund said.

You would. It made him pause though. People would die if he threw himself into a war with the *dreki* queen. "I need allies. But this is not your fight."

"Remember that little discussion we had about choices? Count me in." Tormund's heavy step fell in behind him. "This sounds like a legendary quest, and while Haakon Dragonsbane has a certain ring to it, Tormund Sigurdsson is missing a little something."

"Certainly not humility," Haakon said, with a tight hawkish smile that faded as he rested his hand on Tormund's shoulder. "There's no one else I'd rather have at my side. Make sure you don't get yourself killed. Dead legends can't reap the rewards. Think of all the hearts you might break."

"I don't intend to die." A flash of white teeth. "I have good solid Danish kroner to spend, and Árdís owes me a fistful of emeralds. And a crown."

Haakon rapped on the door to the passenger cabin, where Marek was still recovering.

"You think the *drekling* can help?"

"I think the *drekling* knows more about the queen's court than any of us, including my wife. Her mother guarded her fiercely, whereas Marek was part of the brewing revolution. He knows who wants to throw off the queen's yoke. And he might know some of the queen's weaknesses."

"Clever," Tormund said, rubbing his hands together, as Marek opened the door.

CHAPTER EIGHTEEN

"WHAT ARE YOU doing?" Malin demanded as Sirius strode to the edge of a sharp jutting cliff. She was tired and sore, and so far there'd been no sign of Árdís. They'd spent a day in Reykjavik, trying to track the princess down after a young man said he'd seen her get on a ship. Sirius had left Malin in an inn while he scoured the countryside on wings. He'd picked up the trail outside of town, and came back for her, and they'd ridden across half the countryside in circles, while Malin stubbornly kept her mouth shut.

"Why is she moving so slowly?" He'd sounded utterly perplexed.

"There's a man with her. Just one."

And: *"What in Tiamat's name is she thinking to venture into Fáfnir's territory?"*

He'd finally given the horses to a farmer, with coin and instructions to hold them for him, and led her up here to the top of the cliff.

She had a bad feeling about his intentions.

"I'm changing form. I'm done with this slow meander, and this body." Sirius paused, his black cloak fluttering around his heels. "We'll hunt her from the air. We know where she went, but we can't follow her. Not in mortal form."

Malin glanced up, to the flapping shapes on the horizon that were not birds. Roar and his fellow hunters had all wheeled toward the volcanoes that graced the interior of Iceland, presuming, perhaps, that the princess would have sought allies. But they'd been circling back around all morning.

Unsuccessful. She smiled on the inside.

Sirius held his hand out toward her and growled. "Do you want them to find her first?"

"No." Malin's good humor faded and she eyed his hand. "I've never flown before."

Something shifted in his expression. "Never?"

"Did I forget to mention the one time I finally changed shape and managed to flap my ways into the skies?" she snapped. "No? Oh, that is right. It never happened."

"Ah." Faint amusement crinkled the edges of his eyes. "I get to be your first, then."

A flush of heat went through her. Surely he hadn't meant that the way it sounded...?

"I can stay here," she protested. "You'll be unencumbered without me."

"I swore I'd deliver you to Rurik," he replied. "And that's what I intend to do. You're not safe here."

"I shouldn't think you'd be so concerned."

Dropping a bag at his feet, he swung the cloak off his shoulders. "I keep my promises."

"A sense of honor, my lord?" A startled laugh burst from her. *From you?*

Sirius's eyes narrowed, and his fingers went to the buttons on his shirt.

What is he—? Malin stared at him for a second, but when he began to slip the shirt from his broad shoulders, she suddenly comprehended. Sirius paused, as if aware of her eyes, and gave her a very smoky look.

"I don't mind if you watch me strip," he said, "but something tells me you'd rather chew rocks."

Malin turned around so abruptly her skirts swished. "You stole the words right out of my mouth."

Except she could hear the rustle of fabric, and even though she wasn't looking, some infernal part of her mind insisted upon filling in the details she was missing.

Gods. What was wrong with her?

A shimmer of power washed over her, like molten honey dripping down her skin. She heard the rasp of his breath, loud in the quiet, and knew he'd made the change. Every inch of her skin prickled, and she looked down, feeling something shift inside her in response to his magic.

But then it died.

Malin looked around.

The enormous *dreki* twisted its sinuous neck, eyeing her with eyes the color of gray ice. Malin's breath came a little quicker. Regardless of what she felt for the Blackfrost, his *dreki* form was pure perfection. Every black scale gleamed, and the lash of his tail was like a whip. Where his brother Magnus has been the size of a brutish conqueror, Sirius was sleek and agile. An arrow of death that mastered the winds he rode.

Sirius lowered his wing, inviting her toward him. Her breath caught in a strangled mix of fear and temptation.

What she wouldn't give to fly just once....

The brush of his mind caressed her own, and Malin threw up fierce barriers against his psychic touch. She might be unable to shift, but her psychic protections were strong.

There was no way she was going to allow him inside her mental shields.

The *dreki* bared its teeth at her, and her gaze darted to the side but there was nowhere to run.

A growl caught her attention.

They stared at each other, and again she felt his mind brush against hers.

"No," she said sharply, and very loudly.

If anything, it almost looked like he sighed.

Then he picked up a fist-sized stone in his enormous left claw and deliberately released it over the edge of the cliff.

Malin blinked. "You're going to drop me off the side?"

The *dreki* shook its head vehemently.

"Oh." *You're not going to drop me.*

He stared at her patiently.

"It's not that." Once again she glanced over the edge, and then closed her eyes when the ground fell away sharply. "I'm... I'm afraid of heights."

There was... a certain silence she could almost interpret.

"Yes, I'm a *dreki* and I'm afraid of heights. It's not that amusing. If you fall off this cliff, then you can fly away safely. If I fall off this cliff, then I'll become a bloody splat on the ground below. It tends to play on a girl's mind."

Wings flapped, and Malin's eyes slammed open just as the *dreki* filled her entire view. The downdraft of his thrust almost flattened her against the rock, and she screamed and curled herself into a small ball.

The expected pluck of his claws didn't come.

Malin lowered her arms.

The enormous *dreki* sunk its chest toward the ground, in some strange almost bowing maneuver. Then he paused and glanced up at her, a soft *whumpf* sound echoing in his chest.

"You want me to sit on your back?" she blurted.

Dreki were lords of the storm. They didn't carry people around like pack mules. The best she'd hoped for was for him to curl his claws around her and haul her into the air, but that would be painful and precarious.

One gray eye blinked.

Oh.

Malin stared at his sleek scales. What would it be like to fly? For a moment she could almost forget her fears, for the only thing more powerful was the yearning for the air. For years she'd watched *dreki* take to the skies, and stared longingly after them. Sometimes she stood outside Hekla when the storms raged, and let the wind whip her hair around her face as she closed her eyes and imagined what it would be like.

Her fingertips glanced his scales. They felt like polished gemstones to the touch, though the heat beneath his skin was hotter than she'd expected.

The enormous *dreki* prince curled his wing around her, and Malin froze as it curled her against his side. Then she realized he was dipping the finger joint of his wing low enough for her to use his shoulder to climb up.

Her mouth went dry.

He nudged her.

"Yes, well," she said sharply, squeezing her eyes shut. "I am *trying.*"

The ripple of muscle shifted beneath her hands, sharp-edged scales rasping her palms. Malin blinked. It was easier if she thought only of him, and not of what he intended. Her gown constricted around her ribs as her lungs expanded. Malin stroked his scales, blanking everything out of her mind except the feel of him. He felt almost like an enormous cat, sinuous with muscle and covered in diamond-hard armor.

Somehow she put the tip of her boot on the spine of his wing. It shifted beneath her foot, and then she was gasping, clinging to his side like a nervous rider hanging precariously of the side of a horse. Malin scrambled for purchase as he shoved her higher, and then there was nothing she could do except swing her leg over the curve of his shoulders, or fall face-first over the other side.

Before she knew it, she was sitting astride him, her dress hitched up around her calves and her heart hammering in her chest.

Sweet goddess. She was mounted upon a *dreki* prince with a notorious reputation.

One who glanced at her as if to assure himself she was fully seated, before spreading his wings.

Malin cried out, her knees digging into him. "Not yet!"

The *dreki* beneath her froze.

Wind curled through her hair. Malin looked up at the rosy skies above them. By all the gods, this was amazing. And the heat of his skin warmed her right through her stockings.

She had the sudden horrific thought she was straddling what was technically a naked *dreki*.

You have the Blackfrost between your thighs.

You are not *going to think of that.*

But a burst of nervous laughter tore from her, and Sirius bared his teeth as if to question *what the hell* was wrong with her, and she had no answer to that. Or at least, none she could share with him.

The laughter subsided, and she suddenly felt ill. This was going to happen.

"I have a confession to make." *Traitor*, whispered her heart. But she was so damned confused. And he... he hadn't hurt her. Perhaps he truly did want to rescue Árdís. "I didn't tell you earlier, because... well, I didn't really want to help you. And I didn't trust you."

Muscle shifted beneath the plated scales, and she grabbed hold of the heavier ones that ridged his neck as he glanced at her.

Now was probably not the time to irritate him. Malin swallowed. "I wouldn't have told you this if you'd simply hauled me into the air. But there's something you should know about the princess. She's not going to be able to change into *dreki* form. That's why she's moving so slowly. Someone put a magical bracelet upon her, and trapped her in her mortal form. So Roar and the others... they're looking in the wrong place. If you want to find her, then we need to continue north. She's clearly heading in that direction for a reason. And she won't have gone as far as you think."

He considered her for a long moment.

"Well, what-are-you-waiting-for?" All of the words fell out of her mouth in one unbroken stream. She was not ready for this, but then she didn't know if she ever would be.

And the wind was calling her name, lifting strands of hair off her back.

"Please," Malin blurted. "Just do it. Before I lose my nerve."

Once again she felt him brush against her mind as he hopped toward the edge of the ledge.

Malin's fingers and thighs tightened around him. Oh, sweet goddess. The world vanished beneath his shoulders as he paused right on the edge, and her throat closed over in pure fear.

"Be at ease, Malin," Sirius whispered in her mind, and she realized she'd somehow let him in during her panic.

"And focus on enjoying the wind rushing past your ears, rather than the ground beneath your feet. I won't let you fall. I won't ever let you fall."

The *dreki* prince exploded into the skies.

"Haakon Dragonsbane?"

The first thing he noticed was the chill creeping along his arms. *Cold?* He'd fallen asleep in an oven, with Árdís curled up in his arms—

Arms that were now empty.

Haakon reached out blindly, turning his head to try and find her. The imprint where she'd lain held no heat, and the hollow of the blankets revealed only the ghostly shell of her body.

He had a split-second moment of horror. A realization, *she's gone, again....*

"Árdís?"

There was no sign of her in the cabin. The ship lurched.

"Haakon."

Árdís. Her voice sounded very scared, and far away.

He slung his legs out of bed, slipping into his trousers and grabbing his sword. The ship rocked as if a storm lashed it and the door to the cabin banged as it hit the doorjamb.

Staggering through the door, he found himself in a nightmare. Enormous waves crashed and rolled. The skies were black, though lightning flickered all around the ship. No sign of any of the men. Water sprayed over him as a wave smashed against the port side.

"Árdís?" he bellowed, staggering forward to grab hold of the mast. He needed to find rope and tie himself to the mast. But there was none lying around.

"Haakon!" A soft cry.

He saw a small figure in a white nightgown near the bow of the ship. What was she doing out in this weather? Fear twisted him in tight knots. He'd not said a thing to her about sitting in the crow's nest, but this was far more dangerous. Where the hell was Tormund? Gunnar?

Another wave slammed the ship. No time for rope.

That slim figure staggered against the railing.

Haakon fought his way forward, casting the sword aside. He wouldn't need it. Spray wet his cheeks and face, until his hair dripped.

Árdís slipped away from him, her skirts rustling around her legs and her bare feet leaving little imprints on the deck that glowed with green fire.

"Árja!" He was losing her.

"Please save me!" she cried, turning and reaching toward him imploringly.

A monstrous wave curled up over the top of her. Lightning flashed. His scream tore the air. "*No!*"

Her eyes widened in horror as she turned and saw it coming. Gray waters engulfed her, sweeping her over the side of the rail. He saw a flash of her white nightgown, and those frightened eyes locking on him as she reached for him—

Then she was gone.

Haakon slammed against the rail, leaning over it to search for her in the violent churn of the seas. "Árja? *Árja!*"

A head bobbed, hair shielding her face as she lashed out, fighting to stay afloat.

Thank all the gods. He tried to climb the rail, preparing to dive in after her.

"Haakon?" a voice called in the distance. *"Haakon! What the fuck are you doing?"*

"Please save me," Árdís cried, her arm reaching for him through the pounding surf. "Haakon! You're my only hope."

A hand snatched at his arm, and a body slammed against his. She was going under, her blonde head vanishing for a moment. Haakon strained against the unseen grip, fighting to climb the rail. "I can't lose her. Let me go, damn you!"

"Haakon?" Árdís's voice. Behind him.

He paused.

Árdís?

"Don't let go of him," she cried.

"Trying not to." Tormund. A grunt. *"He's as strong as an ox."*

The storm lashed against the side of the boat.

The blonde woman surfaced again, her eyes glowing green, and a shiver ran down his spine as she smiled at him. It wasn't Árdís. Now he could see her face properly, he could make out minute differences. She could have been Árdís's twin, if his wife had ever looked at anyone with that sort of malevolence.

Mocking laughter filled his ears. Haakon froze. What the hell was going on? He could still feel the spray of water against his face, and taste the salt on his lips.

Raising her hand, the woman clenched her fist.

His lungs arrested, as if a fist wrapped around his heart and squeezed. Agony seared through him, and he felt his knees hit the deck.

He couldn't breathe.

"Haakon!" Someone screamed, and a soft hand pressed against his chest, letting his airways open up. He could feel heat pouring through him from that touch, and a golden tingle of lightning in his veins. "Stay with me."

Always.

"A pity," the strange woman whispered, directly in his mind. *"It would have been a kind death."*

Then the squeezing sensation vanished, and Haakon surged awake with a gasp. He felt like he'd run thirty miles. In heavy chainmail. He was on his back on the deck, with a handful of faces looming over him. The only one that mattered was Árdís. Green light glowed around her, but she looked frightened.

"What the hell was that?" Tormund demanded.

There was something wet in his throat. Haakon convulsed, turning onto the side as he coughed. Árdís's hands held him there, her hand rubbing his back as he vomited a small amount of blood.

"Haakon." Her voice came out anguished. "Damn her!"

The ship rocked beneath them. His throat felt raw as he sucked in air. Sweet, precious air. Other sensations began to intrude. Every inch of him was wet. He felt cold from the tip of his toes to the top of his head. The only warmth came from where Árdís rocked him in her arms. She pressed her cheek to his, and somehow he managed to grab her hand.

"You'd better explain yourself, *dreki*," Gunnar growled.

"That was my mother." Her fingers tightened unconsciously on his arms. "She was in his dreams. Trying to lure him to his death." A sob caught on her breath. "That bitch. That bitch."

"I thought it was you," he rasped. "I thought you went overboard."

Árdís's face was far too pale. "He's freezing. I need something to warm him up. Tea. Or soup. And we need to get him back to the cabin."

"I'm fine."

"You are *not fine*," she suddenly screamed, and all of the men fell silent.

Tormund helped her to her feet, tucking her under one massive arm. "Aye, lass. He'll live. I've seen him take worse."

A storm of tears suddenly rolled over her. Árdís never cried. His stomach dropped. Haakon tried to sit up, and Bjorn helped him. "Árja...."

"I'm fine," she whispered, pushing away from Tormund.

Who opened his mouth to say something. Haakon shook his head sharply. Now was not the time.

She dashed the tears from her face, shaking violently. Every move she made was stiff with a growing rage. Tears gleamed in her eyes, but there was a fierceness there he barely recognized, and her pupils were cat-slit, as though the *dreki* rose to the surface. "What did she say to you? Did she say anything?"

"She said it would have been a kind death."

Árdís bared her teeth, as Tormund and the others reached down to help him to his feet. "That vindictive bitch. I swear to all the gods I will show her what an unkind death means."

Finally ready to fight.

But for the first time, he had a true idea of just how powerful the *dreki* queen was.

CHAPTER
NINETEEN

ÁRDIS PACED THE small cabin they shared, and if she'd been in *dreki* form, he would have sworn her tail lashed behind her.

He was practically swaddled in enough blankets to warm an army, and the tea warmed him from the inside. Every inch of him ached with tiredness, but a part of him didn't dare fall asleep again. He wanted to drag his wife into bed and hold her in his arms, but she was having none of that.

Rage burned within her.

The clouds outside weren't quite a storm, but winds whipped them into large gusts, and though she wore the manacle, some part of her power must have been leeching through. If he wasn't so bone tired, and she angry, he might have kissed her.

He'd never seen her like this before, and it made his cock harden.

"She hasn't killed me yet," Haakon pointed out, his voice rasping from the pain. There'd been no more blood, but his chest still ached, and breathing was hard.

The wrong thing to say.

She spun on him, her amber eyes alight with fury. "That is not the point! She could! She could steal you away in the night, before I even knew she was there. She could burn your spirit to cold ash, and there would be nothing I could do about it. I would wake to a cold empty body beside me, and—"

The sound she made almost choked him.

"Árja!" He managed to stand and grabbed her wrists, and she pulled against him, as though she needed to lash out at something. Blankets fell away from him, except for the one he held around his waist with one hand. Anguish stole away some of her fierceness, and he realized how frightened she was. Crushing her against his chest, he cupped his hand over the base of her skull, and forced her into his arms. "Árja, just breathe. Listen to my heart. Calm yourself. She's not going to kill me." He didn't know why, but he was certain of the fact. "Or she would have done so already."

If the queen had managed to curl her hand around his heart from such a distance, then she could have done it at any stage of the dream. No, this hadn't been intended to kill him. Not truly. This had been a warning.

A flex of power.

An, *I can kill him whenever I want to, if you don't obey me.*

If she killed him, then Árdís had no reason to return.

"You nearly threw yourself overboard," Árdís sobbed. "I almost slept through it."

"You always were a sound sleeper." Haakon pressed a kiss to the top of her head.

This fear of hers was overwhelming. But he finally understood it.

Words couldn't offer the full extent of the danger. Neither Árdís's, nor Marek's. He'd held hope after his visit with Marek—the queen wasn't physically strong enough to stand against any challenges, and relied on her brother, Stellan, to protect her thusly, so it had seemed simple.

Remove Stellan, and the queen suddenly had a weakness.

But whatever she'd done to him in that dream, from hundreds of miles away, proved she was in no way weak. He breathed in the scent of Árdís's hair, a mixture of his fragrant soap and her, and suddenly he realized he had no way to counteract the queen's power. Her magic.

Magic was something he didn't understand.

But Árdís did.

"I don't want to lose you," she choked out, her fingers splaying over his chest. "I can't lose you. I can't."

"You won't lose me," he promised. "You will never lose me, or what we share. No matter what your mother can throw at us. I refuse to let her tear us apart."

"I hate this," she moaned, her fingernails leaving little white half-moons in his forearms. "I hate feeling so powerless."

"You're not powerless." He stroked her spine. "You're a survivor. And you have me at your side, always and forever. I promise you this: I will be there at your side, until you have no more need of me. I will guard your back, and protect you from anything your mother can throw at you. I will fight at your side, if you will it. And if you're too frightened to fight *for* me, then I shall fight for *you*. I will love you—"

A scalded sound broke from her mouth.

"—no matter whether you dare love me back. We were written in the stars. I knew it the first moment I laid eyes upon you. Fight for that, Árja. Fight for *us*."

She buried her face in his chest again, breathing hard.

These were the moments he cherished.

To be in her bed was glorious, but to hold her in his arms.... He squeezed his eyes shut and felt the warmth of her body steal through his aching muscles. The pressure in his chest eased, and he almost fancied he could feel something fluttering against his mind, gentle fingers trying to push their way in. *Árdís*. Her magic trying to meld with him.

"I love you," he whispered again. "I will always love you. And I know now you love me. Nothing is more powerful than that. Nothing."

Her fingers gave a little twitch against his chest, but she didn't say the words and he didn't push for them.

He didn't need to.

Not anymore.

Árdís looked up, her eyes glittering strangely. "You're right," she whispered, and suddenly it was the fierce *dreki* princess before him, and not merely his wife. "I'm not powerless. I'm not defenseless. Not anymore. And I am done with running from her and letting her take away the things I hold dear."

Yes.

Slowly, she drew back from him, her shoulders squaring. "If my mother wants to fight, then she has underestimated me. You are mine, Haakon Haraldsson, and I will fight anyone who dares try to take you from me."

Outside a spear of lightning slashed through the skies, but he barely noticed. All he could feel was the surge of her mouth crashing over his, and her fists curling in the blanket around his waist as she nudged him toward the bed.

His cock surged into her hands, and then his back hit the mattress as Árdís climbed onto his lap. Her amber eyes flared, and he found himself staring directly at the *dreki* within her.

His *dreki*.

"Mine," she hissed, not entirely human in that moment. And then she captured his mouth, her tongue pressing insistently against his, and Haakon decided not to argue.

Dreki or not, she didn't scare him.

He'd have preferred to stay in bed with his sated wife curled in his arms, but Árdís had other ideas. Slipping into her gown, she paced out onto the deck and he had no choice but to follow.

The skies had stilled into darkness, the wind and clouds long gone as if they'd never been. Unusual. The weather here in the Arctic was always unpredictable, but changes didn't happen this swiftly.

You are *traveling with a dreki.*

One whose command of the elements was leashed.

Haakon frowned. Manacled or not, her *dreki* rode just below the surface of her mortal skin. He could still feel the bite of her nails in his shoulders and back, and she'd been somewhat territorial in her affections. Not that he was complaining, but her *dreki* seemed to be chafing at the manacle's hold tonight.

A landscape of color caught his eye. A flicker of green on the horizon.

Haakon leaned on the rail as soft green light fused with the horizon. Hints of pink streaked through the colors, and he half imagined he could see the spirits of Árdís's ancestors. His breath caught, and though holding Árdís had seemed to heal him, the muscles surrounding his lungs clenched a little. He barely felt it. Wonder filled him. "The Bifrost Bridge," Haakon murmured, tilting his face back to stare up at the sky.

Or so his mother had always told him.

But tonight was different. He'd seen the lights many a time, but never like this. This was no Valhalla, but soaring shapes flickering on the horizon, as if something lured *dreki* spirits back into the mortal world.

"Árdís," he whispered, "what are you doing?"

Árdís stared up at the *aurora borealis*, her shawl draped over her shoulders and a faint green light shining in her pupils. The weight of portent chilled his skin. The very air felt thick and heavy to breathe, and he felt, for a moment, as though she was so very far away.

And that he should not interrupt her.

Lifting her palms up, Árdís let the shawl fall, her hands shaking minutely. Wisps of green light began to illuminate her pale skin, and writhe over her limbs.

Chaos magic.

Haakon swallowed hard, forcing his hand not to reach for her. The last time she'd manipulated the dangerous magic, she'd been comatose for hours.

But what would happen if he interrupted her?

"Haakon?" Tormund breathed, but he held a hand up and shook his head.

All along the rail, men lifted their faces to the sky, eyes widening.

He saw wings gliding through the *aurora*, as if a flight of *dreki* rode the horizon, calling to her. Ethereal. Unearthly. The sort of thing a man would remember for the rest of his life.

Árdís began to glow.

Her magic fused into a monstrous shape, wings spanning out of her back, and then forming distinctly in the air above her. A *dreki* of pure spirit form, similar to what she'd conjured last time, but not as furious, or *weighted*. This was far more insubstantial, like a ghost.

"Árja?"

The shimmering *dreki* spirit hissed at him, but subsided when he glared at it.

Haakon's hands closed over her shoulders. "Árja, be careful. Don't overstretch yourself."

Her lashes fluttered open, and the unearthly green depths of her eyes blinked up at him, as if slowly coming into focus. He'd never before seen that look upon her face; a mixture of violence, barely suppressed; a fierceness he'd only ever encountered the day his little sister, Margit, stumbled across a bear, and his mother, still frail from the birth of little Arne, picked up a stick and faced it down. That expression said: *I will die before I let you take what is mine,* but it wasn't aimed at him.

"You were right," she whispered. "She uses my fear as a trap. It's time I was free of it."

She was glorious, and wild, and fierce.

A creature he could barely fit within the framework of his reference to the wife he'd once loved.

She was both utterly fascinating and terrifying, for this was not the woman he held before him in this moment, but the *dreki* princess in all her glory.

His *dreki* princess.

"Begone," she whispered, and the ethereal *dreki* soared above her head, and then swept into the night sky, racing counterpoint to the aurora. It fled south, ethereal wings trailing streamers of light.

Árdís shuddered, as if the effort had cost her.

"What are you doing?" he whispered, taking her chin and checking to see if her nose was bleeding again.

"Sending my mother a message. And I'm fine. It was easier this time. It seems I need a strong enough motive to be able to wield my Chaos magic, and my mother provided it." Árdís tucked a strand of hair behind her ear, her shaking hand belying the words. "You were right. I cannot run. I cannot hide you, not now, when she knows who you are and what you mean to me."

The blood in his veins ran cold. "What message?"

Árdís's head turned unerringly toward the south and the soaring *dreki* wraith that fled across the velvet skies, and this time, her expression was like nothing he'd ever seen, nothing human, anyway. "I told her if she comes for you, if she tries to harm you in any way, then she will face me. And I will do my best to kill her."

This was what he'd wanted, but those damned protective urges rose. Haakon forced them down. "Are you sure you're ready for this?"

"I have challenged my mother for your life." Árdís's smile was chilling. "I have decided it's time I stopped letting her—and fear—rule my choices. This time, I am the one who makes the decisions. And I choose you."

He pressed a kiss to the tip of her nose. Words he'd longed to hear. "I'm glad. But next time, is there any chance we could discuss our moves before making them? I'm trying to let you do this, but it would be easier on my nerves if you forewarned me."

Árdís's smile softened. "Poor mortal man," she purred. "Have you only just learned what you're in for?"

Haakon's eyes narrowed. He'd wanted the *dreki* princess, after all. "I am more than well equipped to handle you if you prove unruly."

"Oh?" Árdís trailed her fingertips down his hip, her eyes promising a thousand pleasures.

"Don't make me throw you over my shoulder again," he whispered, and slid his hand into hers, to drag her back to their cabin.

CHAPTER TWENTY

AMADEA CAME AWAKE with a hiss, her heart racing in her *dreki* chest. For a second she thought she saw a ghost, but it was only a fragment of the dream lingering; a promise of doom unfolding with sweet, whispered malice. As she lifted her enormous head, surveying the Chaos bubble that held her innermost realm, she could see nothing, and yet the echoes of pure Chaos magic lingered like a sulfurous stink.

She'd heard Árdís's voice, ringing in her dream like a bell.

And she'd felt the girl's raw, unrestrained magic slam through her, burning a warning into her skin.

Chaos magic.

Her daughter had somehow learned to master the art of Chaos.

Forcing magic through her veins, Amadea transformed into her mortal shape, and stared at the white burn mark on her arm. A small print shaped like *dreki* claws.

A violent quiver went through her.

"Be careful what you wrought, my child," her grandmother, the mighty seer of the *Zilittu* clan that had birthed her, had once said. *"You dabble with Fate and she is capricious. For your downfall will be a gift you spawn yourself. Your own blood will be the blade that ends your immortal life."*

She'd thought all along it would be Rurik, the golden prince who looked far too much like his father.

Conjuring clothes out of Chaos, Amadea gowned herself in bloodred leather and strode toward the portal that led from her Chaos bubble to the court. Fear churned within her, but she did not dare show it.

The corridors were dark with fire flickering in the torches that lined them, though there was no sign of any of her *dreki*. They didn't stroll the court as they used to when her husband was alive.

Amadea finally arrived at the golden doors that led into the Hall of Mirrors. She could feel her brother within, his soul bonded to hers in the womb in a way few understood. He was the only one she could trust, and she needed him now to quell her fears. Amadea slammed her hands against the double doors, forcing them wide, and startling two of the three *dreki* within.

Stellan was already looking toward the doors when she entered, as if he'd felt her coming.

"What is it?" he asked sharply.

Mirrors lined the walls, images of the world outside flickering in them. Stellan pushed away from one of the mirrors, his eyes narrowing when he saw her warrior garb.

Amadea hissed at the pair of *dreki* warriors who guarded her brother. "Out."

The pair of them bolted, but she waited until the doors closed.

"What is it?" Stellan asked again.

"You've found nothing?"

The mirrors weren't foolproof, but her brother's elemental weavings of Fire were powerful enough to manipulate the images they showed. "No sign of her," he replied. "I swear I've scoured every blasted volcano on this rotten island."

Amadea bared her teeth, her heart rabbiting in her chest as she paced. "She's got to be out there somewhere."

"Of course. We'll find her, Dea. She cannot simply vanish, and my sons are searching for her as we speak." His tone softened. "I told you it's not something to worry about. It wouldn't be the first time Árdís has disappeared, but she will be brought back again, and this time we can remind her of her place in the world. Word has been contained. None of the court knows what has happened, outside of those loyal to us. They still believe she's pouting within her Chaos bubble. We just need to manage the situation a few more days, and when she's back, she will mate with one of my sons and we can stabilize the power structure here at court. There's nothing to worry about."

Amadea rolled up her sleeve, revealing the stark burn scar on her arm. "Isn't there?"

His dark eyes sharpened, and he captured her hand, turning her wrist to view the burn. Their eyes met.

"It seems my daughter has been keeping secrets," she snapped, tugging her sleeve back down. Nobody else could know. "If she learns to master Chaos magic then she's no longer a pawn, Stellan. She's a threat."

"She's never revealed a hint of it before."

Amadea turned away, wrapping her arms around her as she sought a soothing view in one of the mirrors. Each mirror had been spelled to reflect the skies outside, for there were no windows in Hekla, and this one showed the smoking caldera that surrounded Krafla, the volcano that housed her exiled son.

"I shouldn't be surprised," she admitted. "Our grandmother had the gift, and so do I. It runs in the matriarchal line."

His hands came to rest upon her shoulders, and he squeezed. "Chaos magic or not, the girl's untrained."

"So was I." A whisper, torn from her throat. She rested her fingers upon his, clinging to that small touch. "And I can still see the look on Grandmother's face when I killed her."

"You were protecting me. You had more to fight for than she did. And now you have both skill *and* cause."

"*Your own blood will be the blade that ends your immortal life.*" Amadea pushed away from him. "Grandmother laughed at me before I took her life, because she could see my future. *This* future. Why should I not be worried?"

Stellan's eyes hooded, and he moved to pour them both wine. "We of the *Zillittu* make our own fate."

"Do we?" She pitched her voice lower again. "*Three children you will bear. The blood of their father will stain your hands.*" She paced recklessly. "We thought we would make our own fate and take our own court, but *everything* Grandmother ever predicted came true."

"Not exactly. There were four children."

She pressed her hands to her womb, the image of that Chaos-blighted abomination forever etched into her memory. "That thing was a monster. An abomination. And you took care of it, didn't you?" His expression shifted minutely. "*Didn't you?*"

Stellan came to her, capturing her arms and rubbing his palms down them. "I took care of it. I will always take care of you. We are one, Dea. First and foremost."

Twin souls, who could never be torn apart by their loyalties to mere mates... or children.

A psychic thought caught their attention; one of the *dreki* guards requesting entrance. Amadea snarled, but Stellan shook his head.

"He wouldn't dare interrupt," he pointed out. "Not unless it was important."

True. Amadea snatched her wineglass up and curled into her golden throne, glaring at the door. "Enter."

The second she saw who knocked, she almost found her feet again.

Balder staggered in with Roar draped over his shoulder. They wore the signs of failure all over them, and her nostrils flared as the stink of charred flesh hit her.

"What happened?" Amadea demanded, but she felt that twist of unease unfurl within her again.

Roar collapsed to one knee, his face a smoking ruin.

"We found the princess," he said, wincing as his lips pulled against the burn scars marking his cheek. "She was with a mortal man, and she refused to come with us."

Árdís. Again.

Amadea's fingers curled over the ends of her throne. "I don't believe I suggested you should *request* her return."

Roar looked up, revealing the full horror of his face. "We didn't. We were forced to the ground. The man had some sort of weapon that nearly tore me from the sky." He swiftly filled in the details. "And then your daughter unleashed some kind of green fire upon me." His breath caught. "It won't heal, even with the shift. I've tried everything. I can still feel it eating away at my flesh—"

"Do you mean to tell me *Árdís* killed Ylve in single combat, and then forced you and Balder to flee?" Amadea found her feet, her voice trembling with rage. "Three of my finest *dreki* warriors couldn't handle a spoiled princess just past her first cycle and a *human?*"

"She had some sort of magic!" Roar snarled. "We couldn't fight it. And it burned right through my shields. We had no choice but to flee."

Amadea gave a twist of her hand and a ball of Chaos fire sprang to life in the air above her hand. "Did it look a little something like this?"

Roar fell back on his hands, his face paling. "Yes! Sweet goddess, what is it?"

Amadea advanced upon him, the ball of fire burning a sickly green that lit his face. "Chaos magic. Tell me, how did my daughter wield it? Was it a pale green? Or hot and burning like this? Did she have full control over it?"

He flinched, shielding the ruined side of his face with one hand. "It was bright green, like yours. But it wasn't fire, it was a flaming *dreki* that soared above her. It attacked me, and I could feel its fangs and claws rip through me as if they were solid, but there was nothing to fight. Nothing but air, when I lashed out. It wasn't real."

Amadea froze.

"A spirit form," she whispered, half to herself.

Stellan caught her eye and she knew they shared the exact same thought.

The spirit form had eluded her for years, no matter how many times she'd tried to master the art of it.

But her grandmother had known how to create one.

"How long did she hold it for?"

Roar shook his head. "I don't know. It felt like forever. She was tearing me apart."

"Seconds at most, my queen," Balder said from the side.

She looked at him, feeling cold to her bones. How long had her daughter been meddling with Chaos magic right beneath her nose? How much did Árdís know? What could she do with it?

Did she have the instinct for it, or had she been keeping secrets all along? Was there a reason Árdís had chosen Norway for her exile? Did she know that was where the roots of her *Zillittu* ancestry came from? Or had she been looking for something else? A mentor? Someone to train her?

None of the *Zilittu* clan would have helped her.

Their loyalty belonged to Amadea and her brother, but there were other *dreki* out there. Outcasts. Loners. Some mystics who could no longer survive at the *Zilittu* court.

How had Árdís learned to cast a spirit form?

"How much of a threat is she?" Stellan murmured in her mind, linking with her as if he sensed her unease.

"I don't know."

And the unknown scared her.

"Where was the girl going?" Stellan asked. "Do you think she means to join with her brother Rurik?"

"She was heading for the north coast," Balder said. "They were on foot for some reason, and she never took wing."

Interesting. Amadea mapped Árdís's path in her mind. "She's trying to hide on land," she murmured, straightening to her full height. "She could have been at Rurik's side within a day if she'd taken wing, and we'd never have been able to stop her."

"It's the human," Roar spat. "It wasn't until I threatened his life that she formed her wretched attack."

"The human." Stellan's lips pressed firmly together. "How dare she slight her bloodlines like this."

She'd not truly considered him a threat until now. Merely a bedmate her daughter despoiled herself with, and a means to toy with Árdís.

It's the human.

Haakon Dragonsbane. She should have killed him when she'd had the chance.

Now Árdís would be on her guard, and she didn't dare.

Amadea turned, her leather skirts sweeping behind her with a faint serpentine *swish.* "Tell me," she whispered, "about the human. Tell me about the fight. Every little detail."

Roar complied, and a thought began to form.

"What are you thinking?" Stellan asked, his eyes heavy-lidded as he surveyed his bastard.

"She only resorted to her magic when the human's life was threatened." Amadea's eyes narrowed. *"I don't think she's trained at all. I think she was desperate, the same way I was when I tore grandmother's soul to shreds. You were my catalyst to push me over the edge into Chaos. Just as the human is hers."*

"It's been mere days," he scoffed. *"She couldn't have formed an attachment to him in such a short time."*

"Has it been mere days?" Amadea turned to confront him, and the room fell silent, as if they all sensed their words were no longer being heeded. *"She was unaccounted for during three entire years. Seeing the world, she said. Spreading her wings. I didn't pay enough attention to her. I've never paid enough attention to her."*

She'd never expected Árdís to be the threat.

"My queen?" Roar dared to ask.

"Find them," Amadea said, turning back to the mirrors. "I want the human dead."

It would shatter Árdís's newfound confidence. Make her weaker.

"But what of her magic?" Roar asked. "We can't fight that."

"You won't have to," Amadea said coldly. "When you find her, you will contact me."

"And we will handle it," Stellan murmured, his gaze meeting hers once more. *"Don't do something foolish, Dea. She might be your match."*

Never.

"I'll bring her back," Roar promised. "She will be my mate. And then I shall repay her for this." He gingerly touched his raw cheek.

The queen merely smiled.

Poor boy. He thought she was going to allow Árdís to live.

CHAPTER TWENTY

HAAKON TOOK A slow breath of relief as the enormous volcanic peak of Krafla came into view.

Árdís peered around him, her arms squeezing him tight. "We're here. We're finally safe."

The breath eased out of him. The ride had been fraught, with all of them watching the skies closely.

"I cannot wait to see Rurik," she breathed, giddy with happiness. "Do you think his mate will like me?"

Freyja was as different from the princess as the sun from the moon. "She'll like you," he said, unable to avoid a smile. "I should warn you though. She'll probably put you to work cleaning the barn."

"Barn?" Árdís's chin rested on his shoulder as she tried to see his face.

"She made your brother clean her barn for her, while he was courting her."

"The *dreki* prince heir cleaned a barn?" Árdís sounded both a little horrified and in awe. "What sort of powers does this Freyja wield?"

Haakon laughed. "He did it of his own volition, I believe. Freyja could give the tide lessons in wearing away a rock." His laughter faded. And she'd forgiven him for trying to use her to lure out the *dreki* who had a fascination with her. That didn't mean she'd welcome him back into her life. His voice roughened. "But she'll adore you, Árdís. Who could not?"

Árdís made a strange purring sound in her throat. "The only one whose adoration I seek is a certain thickheaded dragon hunter."

"Well, you've already won him over, despite the fact you like to call him unruly names."

"Have I?"

Haakon captured her hand, and brought it up to his lips to kiss. "You had him from the very first moment he saw you. You had his heart. His soul. It was fate, and he knew it. He'd found the one woman he intended to marry. His adoration was never in any doubt. He just wonders if this capricious *dreki* princess could ever love a lowly dragon hunter."

Árdís squeezed her arms around him. "He might think himself merely a dragon hunter, but he's proven remarkably skilled. He captured the heart of a *dreki* princess," she whispered, "before she even knew it herself."

Relief. Sweet relief.

"It was never about capturing her heart. But about keeping it."

She hesitated, and Haakon held his breath. "Haakon," she said in a confessional tone, and he twisted in the saddle to see her face. "There's something you need to know—"

"Ho!" Tormund bellowed, showing inordinately terrible timing. "There he is!"

An enormous golden *dreki* swooped in lazy circles in the air above them.

"Rurik," Árdís breathed, staring up in delight.

"The prince," Marek whispered, his voice rough with awe.

Whatever she wanted to tell him, the moment was gone.

Later, he promised himself.

He watched the light break over her expression. She was the most beautiful thing he'd ever seen. And she deserved to be there in the skies, soaring like the wild creature she was.

Gliding on wings of gold beside her brother.

The *dreki* landed, a wash of golden light breaking across him. It was so bright, Haakon was forced to throw up a hand in front of his face.

And then the light vanished, and a man stood there, tall and nude and completely unperturbed by the fact. Blond hair raked back from his brow, and his eyes were the same color as Árdís's. Someone had broken Rurik's nose long ago, but it only made him look slightly more dangerous. The first time Haakon had met the prince, he'd thought the man strange, but there'd been something about Rurik that unsettled him. The man had been vaguely amused by Haakon's determination to kill the local "dragon", and completely unthreatened. It was only when Freyja had been imperiled, that darkness rippled through Rurik's eyes, and a monster stared back.

Don't turn your back on him, he'd thought, even though Rurik had never so much as made a threat against him.

Rurik's gaze raked the company, locking on Árdís and softening. But Haakon had seen those amber eyes harden when Rurik had gone to fight Magnus, and knew if one crossed the prince, then the lazy, insouciant smile would vanish, and you would be facing a whirlwind trapped into human flesh.

The carnage he'd seen as the pair of *dreki* fought had been furious and devastating. Two enormous beasts grappling in the air before him, tearing at each other with teeth and claws, and slamming shoulder-to-shoulder in an effort to cripple each other's wings.

He couldn't face that. Not as a man. Not on foot.

"Sweet Jesus," Tormund breathed. "Remind me never to piss beside that bastard."

Clearly he was not the only one sizing Rurik up, albeit in different areas.

"Here we are." Haakon offered his arm, and Árdís swung down, barely giving him a second glance. "You're safe."

There was a bag at the *dreki's* feet. Rurik tugged a pair of trousers out of it, putting them on. "Welcome."

"Rurik!" Árdís ran toward her brother, and he swept her up into his arms, twirling her in a tight circle.

Haakon slowly dismounted. Time to pay his dues.

Rurik's arms tightened around her, and Árdís drank in the sensation. Thirty long years without her family.

"I missed you," she told him, burying her face against his chest. *"So much."*

"I missed you."

Her feet left the ground as he squeezed her so tightly she thought her ribs were going to break. This strong brother of hers, the light of the *dreki* court. She was so proud of him. So hungry to see him again, and talk of old times.

So furious.

The second he let her go, Árdís stepped back and punched him in the arm. "You barely ever contacted me."

Rurik captured her fist before she could hit him again. "It was too dangerous. You were too young, and I didn't wish to drag you into the mess."

"You're my brother! Do you have any idea what it was like to be left behind, barely daring to mourn you or father?" She wasn't going to cry. She wasn't. But there was a storm of fury within her, one she hadn't even known she'd held.

"Do you have any idea what it was like to leave?" Rurik snapped.

Someone cleared their throat behind them.

"Before we launch into a reminiscence of old times— or war, as it might be—do you think we ought to find shelter?" Haakon asked. "We don't know what else is in the skies."

Rurik's eyes sharpened. "What does that mean?"

Árdís took the opportunity of her brother's distraction to punch him in the arm again. "You told him all my secrets."

"That's not fair," Haakon said, running a hand down her spine. "It's the best thing that ever happened to you, and you know it."

"Still," she sniffed. "He's supposed to be on my side."

Rurik tilted a lazy brow up. "I *am* on your side. Sometimes brothers need to do what is best for their little sister, not necessarily what she thinks she wants. Where have you been? What are you doing here? Why are we supposed to be taking shelter?"

Both she and Haakon took a deep breath and looked at each other.

"It's your story," her husband said.

So Árdís told him.

Most of it.

"And you didn't think to fly here?" Rurik demanded, when she was done.

"It's complicated," Árdís said. "I—"

"I bartered with a *svartálfar* for a manacle that would trap her in her human form so I could talk to her," Haakon said brusquely. "The problem is, the manacle is will-based. I can't remove it, because a part of me doesn't want to lose her again."

"I see." The *dreki's* golden eyes narrowed, and tension slid through his shoulders. "I gave you the truth about my sister because I thought she owed you a debt."

"Rurik," Árdís growled. "Don't you dare."

The prince blinked down at her.

"I haven't seen you for half a cycle," she said, advancing upon him and digging a finger into his chest. "You do *not* get to play the overprotective *dreki* male with me. It is a matter between Haakon and me."

Rurik held his hands up and backed off. "Fine. Haakon's correct. We should probably get you back home."

Home. "You don't mind?" she whispered.

He rubbed his arm. "I had initial doubts, but if you promise not to hit me again, then I'm sure we can come to some sort of arrangement."

Árdís burst into a nervous laugh. "Thank you."

Rurik kissed her forehead. "Of course I'll protect you. You can always come to me."

She'd been so long without an ally that there'd been a part of her that had wondered. "And Marek? He's a *drekling* from the court who swore his loyalty to you."

Rurik's gaze sharpened as he made out the angry 'T' on Marek's forehead. He would know what it meant, and looked troubled. "You seek asylum?"

"If you would have me, my prince."

Rurik hauled the *drekling* upright when he made as if to bow. "If you are loyal and true, then I shall shield you. But you shall not grovel before me. Not with this mark upon you."

Clasping both hands around Marek's face, power spilled over his hands in a heated shimmer. The scab flared with gold light, and then vanished, revealing smooth, unblemished skin. Marek gasped, and pressed his fingers there.

"My healing abilities are limited," Rurik said, stepping back from the *drekling*. "You're lucky the scab hadn't begun to scar."

"My prince," poor Marek whispered, as if he'd seen a god land upon the earth.

Rurik chuckled, a deep rumble in his chest. "A prince in exile, Marek. Nothing more."

And nothing less.

"He's going to worship you forever," Árdís said, as she connected with her brother. *"You'll be insufferable."*

"Not with Freyja to keep my feet firmly upon the ground." Rurik held out his hand to her. "Come. You can fly on my back. I want you to meet my mate."

"What about Haakon and the others?" She looked back.

"They can follow," Rurik said curtly. His eyes met Haakon's. "I might have to warn Freyja he's coming."

"Why would you have to warn her?"

Rurik's grin widened. "Didn't he tell you? Haakon was trying to lure me out of my volcano. So he tied Freyja to a stake and offered her as my monthly tithe. As you can imagine, she wasn't very happy with him."

Árdís gasped.

"I apologized," Haakon said.

"And then you saved her life," Rurik said, his eyes glittering. "Which is the only reason you're still alive today."

"You're not the one I was scared of," Haakon replied coolly. "And I am trying to make amends."

"Freyja is dangerous?" Árdís asked.

"She shoots lightning bolts from the sky, and rips the earth apart with a thought," Haakon muttered. "She broke my ballista twice."

"Fierce," Rurik said, with some satisfaction.

Árdís stepped inside the small farmhouse, feeling a little nervous. It was one thing to meet her brother after so long—quite another to meet his mate. His fierce, dangerous mate, who had a powerful magic.

She ran a hand over the wooden paneling on the walls. The house was small, with grass on the roof, and goats in the yard. It seemed incongruous that her brother—a *dreki* prince—could find his happiness living here, but Rurik had already told her this house belonged to Freyja's father, and Freyja insisted on spending several nights of the week here, rather than in Rurik's Chaos bubble.

It reminded her a little of Viksholm.

Perhaps the pair of them were not so different, after all.

"Freyja," Rurik called, dragging his shirt over his broad shoulders. "We have a guest."

"Coming!"

The woman who stepped through the kitchen door wore a blonde braid tucked over her shoulder. One of her eyes was green, and the other brown. Árdís blinked, but then the other woman was smiling.

"Welcome," Freyja said, crossing to take her by the forearms. "Rurik said you've had a long journey. I've put a lamb on to roast, and dinner should be ready within the hour. I'm sure you're famished."

"Starving," she admitted, her head turning between the pair of them. "How did you—?"

"Freyja is my twin flame," Rurik said, his eyes warm as he looked at his mate. "She knows everything I know."

His twin flame.

"Oh, I'm so happy for you." She sounded anything but. "No, truly, I am."

Freyja exchanged a glance with him. "Perhaps you'd care for a bath? I have fresh soap."

A bath. Her eyes glazed over. She and Haakon had been making do with streams and cold water, but she was desperate to soak herself in hot water. She missed the thermal springs near her volcano. "Please. That would be lovely." She shot her brother a look. "I though you said she was horribly fierce?"

Rurik's grin turned wolflike. "She tried to stick me with a sword."

"That was one time," Freyja protested, her cheeks flushing. "And *you'd* stolen my ram. You ate him."

"I bought you another," he replied. "I didn't want to see you starve."

"Rurik said you can manipulate storms, and the earth itself." Árdís couldn't stop looking between the two of them. There was a camaraderie there that warmed her. "Is she part *drekling*, Rurik?"

Her brother's lips thinned. "She is something. We're not entirely certain what. There might be *dreki* blood in her bloodlines somewhere, though I suspect there's something else as well."

"The queen won't like that," she whispered, mind-to-mind with him.

"Well, the queen is not here," Freyja said, proving just how closely linked they were. "Come, I'll show you to the bathing chambers. Rurik found an enormous copper tub somewhere in Europe and brought it back for me. I've filled it already, so I merely need to heat the water."

"Heat the water?"

Freyja captured her hand with a bland smile. Heat radiated through her palms. "Oh." She followed Freyja up the staircase. "You don't have to wait upon me. If you just show me where it is, I can...."

Sit in cold water.

It wasn't as though she could heat the damned thing herself, curse this wretched manacle.

Haakon ground his teeth as he waded into the shallows of the river, the biting cold coming directly from some distant glacier. Not for him the hot bath, or scented soap. He sighed, and made do with his own. It was good to feel clean, and the water ate away at the numbness inside him.

Árdís was safely arrived in her brother's territory, where her mother could not get to her.

He'd done what he'd set out to achieve.

Just one more thing....

Ducking under the surface of the river, he shot back up with a startled gasp, flipping his hair back. The shock of it stirred him. Little pinpricks of sensation prickled all over his skin. Along with the sensation he was being watched.

He knew, even before he turned.

Árdís rested on the bank, her knees tucked up in front of her and her chin resting upon them. She'd given up even pretending to be human at this point, her eyes flaring gold with the *dreki* within. She wore a skautbúningur of black wool, with golden embroidery down the center, and the color of the gown suited her. Freyja's, he suspected. Damp strands of hair tumbled down her back.

Haakon waded to shore, scraping water off his face.

Her eyes ravished him, caressing every muscle of his body as it was revealed. Hungry eyes. They met his, and despite the cold, he felt a flush of blood below.

"Are you trying to tempt me again?" she called.

He snatched the dry cloth from her side and briskly rubbed himself down. "Yes. That's definitely why I'm out here freezing my balls off. It has absolutely nothing to do with Freyja taking revenge upon me."

He probably deserved it. A little cold water never killed anyone.

Árdís laughed, reclining on her elbow like a lady of repose. If not for the mess of her tangled curls, she might have been able to sustain the illusion. He liked her hair down like this. It made him want to drag his fingers through it. In the past he'd bought her a silver-backed hairbrush—which had cost him a small fortune—when it became clear she didn't own one. She'd let him brush her hair each night, which often made her almost purr with quiet content, and Haakon had liked those moments the best.

Dragging on his last clean pair of trousers, Haakon did the buttons up, as she watched. The look in those heated eyes made it hard to stuff his dawning erection in. Haakon cursed. "Behave."

"You don't have to put it away," she murmured, shooting him a sly smile.

"I'm fairly certain your brother could see us from the house, if he chose."

"Are you worried he's going to take affront at you seducing his sister?"

"No." Haakon lay down beside her, clasping his hands behind his head. The grassy slope protected them from view, if they both lay down. "But I've only just gotten back into his good graces. I don't wish to push my luck."

"I thought you were allies," she said curiously. "He gave you a necklace to tempt me with, and then sent you in my direction."

"He said you owed me a debt."

"He always *had* to meddle," she said with a snort.

Árdís rolled onto her hip, one finger stirring through the trail of blond hair that led from his navel into the top of his trousers.

"You're insatiable," he accused.

"I have seven years to make up for." Her gaze grew distant.

"Árdís?"

Nothing. Only glazed eyes.

Then she blinked and leaned closer, biting her lower lip. "I just told Rurik not to look out the window for a while."

Jesus. "I'm not certain whether I like him knowing what we're about."

Árdís rolled her eyes. "We're not 'about' anything yet. My husband is being frustratingly stubborn. And I was vague. He thinks we're having a discussion that shouldn't be disturbed. I hinted we might even kiss."

Husband. He liked that. "I'll claim that kiss."

Their lips met.

A slow and heated kiss. He felt like he could take all the time in the world. Dragging her into his arms, he ran his hands all over her body, caressing the soft wool. Árdís, however, had other ideas.

She straddled him with a wicked gleam in her eye.

"I intend to claim something else." Kissing her way down his chest, she began to unbutton his trousers. "I do feel as though I owe you some sweet torture. Remember the hut?"

"How could I forget?"

Whisper soft lips skated over his abdominals. His cock might as well be a battering ram. Árdís laughed, a smoky sound as she looked up at him, and then she was licking her way lower, her eyes smoldering with their cat-slit *dreki* pupils. Clever hands slid his erection free, and her mouth swallowed the weeping head of him, surrounding his cock with wet heat.

Mother of kraken. He watched her through slitted eyes, all of his attention locked on the rosy curve of her mouth. Haakon slid both hands through her silken hair, his fingers curling into fists. This was her turn to torture him, but he couldn't help trying to control the encounter. Coaxing her to bob lower, until the head of his cock hit the back of her throat.

Bliss. Pure, fucking bliss. He arched his spine, biting his lip as he threw his head back and surrendered to Árdís's expert manipulation.

"I'm not sure... if this is torture," he gasped, hips thrusting helplessly in a quickening rhythm.

Árdís broke the pressure with a wet popping sound, her hand fisting around him.

"Wait for it. You denied me for days," she whispered, her lips wet with her own saliva, and the glistening trace of his seed.

Swirling a tongue over the crown, she taunted him with lazy, lightening strokes, until he was on the verge of begging.

Those wicked eyes mocked him, as if she knew exactly what she was doing to him.

"You're playing a dangerous game," he whispered, flexing up to slide a hand through her hair. Cupping the back of her head, he insisted she rise.

"I'm not done yet."

"And I'm not started." Dragging her into his lap, he captured her mouth, stroking her clever tongue with his own.

Haakon's hands slid under the curve of her ass, grinding her against him. *Yes.* Árdís slid her palms up the lean flanks of his hips, clearly reveling in the sensation of his heated skin. Her tongue twined with his, even as the backs of her knuckles skated over his quivering abdomen. Darting her hand back down between them, as if she could turn the tables on him once more.

"Enough," he growled, biting her lip.

"I have barely begun."

"A pity you're not the one in charge, then." Capturing her behind the thighs, he picked her up, her skirts bunching between them, and shoved himself to his feet somewhat precariously. "Grab my trousers."

Árdís's breath caught as she clung to his broad shoulders. She did as told, her eyes twinkling merrily as he strode toward the stand of birch trees for some more privacy, with half his ass hanging out.

"I think you enjoy playing the marauding Viking," she said. "You've turned positively heathen in some ways."

He spilled her onto her back on the grass beneath the birches, pinning her to the ground, as his weight settled between her parted thighs. "Have I?"

An intriguing gleam darkened her eyes. Haakon nipped at her lips, sliding her skirts up between them.

He stoked his hand up her thigh, questing fingers finding her wet and swollen. "I think you like wreaking havoc upon me."

"Maybe." Árdís laughed.

He would treasure the sight of her joy for the rest of his life.

Gentle hands threaded through his hair as he kissed her again. It wasn't enough. He didn't want gentle. He wanted her to pull his hair as he drove into her, the heavy weight of his body pressing her into the ground. He wanted skin beneath his hands, and his mouth on her throat and breasts. He wanted inside her.

Now.

Árdís bit his lower lip, and Haakon responded with a low groan. The flex of his hips drove the burgeoning press of his erection against her belly. *Yes.* A sweet twist of feeling knotted inside him, and their mouths parted with a faint gasp on both their behalf.

"Sweet lord." Haakon exhaled, drawing back just a fraction to catch his breath. The dark need burning in her eyes made his cock clench. "Are you ready?"

He didn't think he'd last long.

"For you? Always."

Haakon drove up into her, and she cried out as joy turned to pleasure.

Hard fingers curled in his shoulders as he rode her, working into her in slow, hard pumps as he sought to find that particular spot she liked. Capturing her knee, he drove it up against his chest, and there.... There it was. He felt her shiver as the head of him brushed against that responsive little pad of sensation within her. When she threw her head back, he kept himself there, grinding his hips in slow circles. A lick of pure pleasure swept up his spine, and his balls tightened as she clenched around him. Couldn't hold it... much longer.

"Come for me," he breathed, cupping her breast and pushing her nipple free of the confines of her groan. Hot lips clamped down over it, and he suckled hard as Árdís screamed, her body pulsing with pleasure.

She raked her nails down his back, no longer hiding what she was. A hiss escaped her. "Mine," she whispered, tangling her fingers in his hair.

Mine. The word echoed in his ears. Threw him over the edge. He bucked into her, flooding her with his semen. Hard little thrusts that wrung every last ounce of pleasure from him.

And then he collapsed, her knee still locked up between them.

Haakon held himself lightly on his fingertips as she wilted beneath him. Somehow her knee slipped loose, and then those long legs cradled his hips, her heart pounding against his. He rested his elbows on either side of his head, and pressed his face into the crook of her throat.

It took long minutes to catch his breath.

He wanted her so desperately.

Forever.

But he could not keep her caged like a pet bird, its wings fluttering madly as it looked to the skies. He could not ask her to make this choice, while she *was* trapped.

Love was not a prison. It should never be a cage. Her happiness was all he'd ever desired in this life.

He'd fought dragons, trying to find her. He'd risked it all, just for the chance she was out there somewhere, and he could rescue her.

But he was the one keeping her locked up now.

Haakon's fingers caressed her face as he drew back, and his body slipped from hers. He'd made so many mistakes. Let the raging emotions within him push him into foolish decisions.

But this was not one of them.

"I love you," he said, rearing back onto his knees.

A happy but slightly confused smile dawned on her lips as she swiftly collected the cloth he'd used to dry himself and cleaned herself up.

"I love you too," she whispered, squeezing his hand.

He looked down, taking a deep breath as he reached for the golden manacle around her wrist. He hadn't dared attempt to remove it since the last failure. Just in case he ruined her hopes. "*Er þér sjálfrátt fararleyfi.*"

And this time he meant it.

Golden light flashed and the manacle fell apart, the golden links tumbling into his cupped hands.

Árdís's entire face lit up with wonder, and she curled her thumb and forefinger around her empty wrist. "How did you—?"

"Simple." His hand closed over the cursed thing. "Dúrnir was right. I didn't want to take the manacle off, because deep in my heart I feared I'd lose you again."

"And now?"

He pressed his head to her shoulder, breathing in the scent of her. "I want you to fly. I want you to be free, Árdís." *More than I'm afraid to lose you.*

"Thank you."

She staggered to her feet, and moved away from him, clouds whipping through the skies above her as she laughed and stripped her gown off.

His breath caught. His stubborn *dreki* princess.

Utterly glorious.

Wild and free.

Turning in the center of the grass, she held her hands up. Sparkles of light began to dance over her skin and hair, leaving her radiant. Light flared, heat and power spilling over him in a hot wash.

And then a golden *dreki* stood there, snapping her wings out with a sharp flap.

Haakon's breath caught in wonder. Árdís's scales gleamed the same newly minted gold as her brother's. But she was much smaller, her lithe limbs sleek and elegant, and her head sharply defined.

"You're beautiful," he breathed, and she preened. He hastily dragged his trousers back up, and then reached out to stroke the supple skin, and those smooth scales.

"Go," he said, tipping his head to the sky. "Fly."

She turned and looked at him, pure joy filling her expression, and then with a sharp flap of her wings, she launched herself into the sky.

Haakon stared after her, his head tilted back.

Árdís roared her happiness into the world, swooping around the roof of the small cottage. Haakon followed, his bare feet crushing the grass, and his heart strangely lifted. He laughed as she soared over the barn, sending the herd of sheep bleating in a mad panic.

A door banged open, and then Rurik joined him, his face tilted up. "You let her go."

A soft ache in his chest made him smile, a little sadly. "She was never mine to keep." She belonged there, in the skies, and if she chose to stay with him, then so be it.

A sideways glance. "Perhaps. Now what?"

Rurik's steady gaze held weight.

"Now we kill a *dreki* queen," Haakon replied, releasing a slow breath. He met the other *dreki's* eyes. "She thinks she's safe here. That your presence will drive off any who seek to take her. But I don't think your mother's going to just brush off her hands and claim defeat."

"No." Rurik's gaze shuttered. "Árdís doesn't realize, but her coming here is a slap in my mother's face. She's effectively thrown down a gauntlet. They'll come for her. It's just a matter of time."

"I have a plan." He'd spent the entire journey from Akureyri to Rurik's territory thinking of ways to defeat the seemingly invincible *dreki* queen. For he would not see Árdís's newfound freedom and happiness so compromised.

"I have a feeling Árdís isn't going to like it, is she?"

"No." He smiled grimly. "Because, for it to succeed, I have to get close to your mother. Close enough for her to be able to kill me."

CHAPTER
TWENTY-ONE

RURIK FOUND HER on the edge of his volcano. She'd erupted into flight, unable to bear her mortal skin for another second longer. Haakon had merely waved her off, and then Árdís had soared into the skies, pure delight streaming through her as she spread her wings.

Her brother had followed, and though she knew it was because he feared intruders, it was so nice to fly with him again.

He'd been the one who'd first pushed her into the skies as a kit.

"I'm faster than you are," she laughed, linking with him.

"I didn't know it was a race."

Arrogant *dreki* male. Árdís took a half-hearted swipe at his ribs. Then she summoned her power and let it flow over her, melding back into human shape. Wind caressed her skin, and her hair whipped around her as she found herself on bare feet. Árdís stared at her hands. The shift came so easily now. She'd never take it for granted again. Tugging her dress from her travel bag, she slipped it on. "No sign of them. Not yet."

Rurik dressed swiftly. "They're coming."

She sighed.

"Something you want to talk about?" he asked, towering over her.

Her sense of connection to the world had muted with the shift, but the exchange was the depth of her emotions. Árdís stared sightlessly over the landscape. "I don't know."

"Not the queen," he pointed out. "Or you would have spoken about it in front of the others."

No. This was personal. Árdís stared out over the landscape. His volcano was beautiful. Smoking fumaroles dotted the landscape and she'd seen a crystalline lake tucked within the caldera.

Her hand pressed to her chest. "I miss my ring."

"Your wedding ring?" His eyes sharpened.

She'd told him everything that morning, after her bath.

"Yes." Árdís bit her lip. "I feel incomplete somehow. I could be lying there in Haakon's arms, and it feels like my *dreki* wants to push beyond my skin. I'm so... angry. And I have these violent urges whenever I think of mother." She looked up into his eyes. "It's all I can do not to storm back home and challenge her. She threatened him. She *threatened* him."

Curling her hands into her hair, she pulled hard, to try and contain it.

"Árdís, it's not the ring."

Árdís sunk to her knees. "I know."

Rurik stretched out beside her, slinging his legs over the edge of the ledge. "It sounds like you're trying to bond with your husband. Your *dreki*, your soul, has chosen him as a mate. If you were a male, I would be certain of it."

"It's not possible," she blurted, heart pounding swiftly. It was the same argument she'd told herself. "I'm a female *dreki*. And he's human."

"As is Freyja," Rurik countered, and then frowned again. "At least, I'm fairly certain she's mostly human."

The wind whipped her hair behind her, but it was her thoughts that felt scattered.

How could this be?

She'd been so uncertain, but all of the puzzle pieces seemed to lock together until she could no longer see them separately, but only as a whole. Her heart swelled at the thought.

But while she might have finally discovered what her strange behavioral patterns meant, it only complicated matters further.

"He's my twin flame," she whispered, daring to say the words out loud for the first time. If she bonded with him, then Haakon's life would extend to match hers. He'd be harder to kill, but she'd become more vulnerable. They could have forever. If she could bond with him.... "I'm a female *dreki*, Rurik. And the males initiate the bond. Not the females."

How ironic that she could find what she'd been looking for all her life, only to be unable to take this last crucial step.

It all made too much sense for her to dispute. A shudder ran through her, the *dreki* sliding beneath her skin as if to reassure her, that yes, this was what it had been trying to tell her all along.

What Fáfnir had sensed.

It had never been about the ring at all.

"Do they?" Rurik rested a hand on her shoulder. "Árdís, perhaps it's not that females cannot initiate a bond, but that the males always do first, as they know before the females do."

"I was married to him, Rurik. Surely there would have been some signs during those three years. Perhaps we're simply grasping at straws." She couldn't help feeling doubt. Wanting reassurance.

"You were young, barely past your first cycle of life."

And she'd been frightened of the future, of committing herself to Haakon. Her heart skipped a beat. A part of her had always held back from him.

"How many mated couples have you known where one of the pair is human?" he asked.

She paused.

"I know none myself. To take a human lover can be overlooked, but to take one as a mate? The court would gasp in horror."

"You are not helping this situation."

He smiled and bumped his shoulder against hers, and it reminded her of how long it had been since she'd been able to enjoy the company of those she called family, let alone trusted them. "Don't give up hope. You're *dreki*. There's nothing a male *dreki* can do—in my experience— that a female cannot, so I doubt you couldn't choose to bond with your husband if you truly wished to do so. And if he accepted the bond."

"Mother will kill him if she hears word of this."

Rurik made a low, growling sound in his throat. "She will try. Just as she will try to harm Freyja if she comes to know of her existence. But first she has to get through either of us."

"I daresay Freyja has her own opinions on that."

"I daresay." His lips kicked up. "She usually does."

"I like her."

"So do I."

Árdís curled against her brother's side, and he squeezed her shoulders.

"I've missed you," she said. "So much."

He rested his chin on her head, and breathed in her scent. "I noticed. I can still feel how much you missed me. Right in the ribs."

"You deserved that."

Rurik laughed.

Slowly it faded, and Árdís rubbed a hand to her chest again.

"How do you initiate the bond?" she asked softly.

Rurik reared away, hand held up. "This is something older brothers don't talk about with their sisters."

"Rurik, please," she begged. "I've lain with him many times before. It cannot simply be bedding him, or it would have already happened."

He appeared to give it great thought, a hint of red creeping up his throat. "That's partly to do with it. I don't.... I don't precisely know. I wanted to claim Freyja, and she returned the sentiment, but it was mostly instinct. You said you're feeling territorial. Perhaps that's all you need? To run with those feelings and...." He coughed. "Where is Marduk when you need him?"

"I don't know," she whispered sadly. "He's been gone for over ten years."

Rurik's eyes locked on her face, and then he dragged her into another hug. "I've felt him out there in the world."

"So have I."

"He'll come back, Árdís. One day."

She pressed her cheek against his chest and listened to his heart. "Perhaps he'd come back if you staked a claim upon the throne and fought for it?"

A grumble echoed in his chest. "That wasn't even subtle."

She smiled a little sadly. "You don't know what the court is like, Rurik. They need you. We need you. You only have to look at what they did to Marek to know that."

"First Andri. Now you." A sigh escaped him. "I cannot fight her and win," he whispered. "I've been thinking of what to do all month as I healed from my fight with Magnus. I can't fight all of them. And Freyja...."

Árdís looked up. The confession was torn from him, and she knew he was fighting his mighty *dreki* pride in admitting such a thing.

"It's not a weakness to ask for help," she said. "The reason they've ruled the court for so long is because they're together. Mother provides the magic, and Stellan the muscle. They're seemingly invincible. No one *dreki* could ever face the pair of them and survive. But perhaps you need to stop thinking you need to face them alone." She bit her lip. "There's one thing I haven't told you.... One thing that might be able to sway the tides of battle."

His eyes sharpened intently.

Árdís climbed to her feet, taking several steps before she closed her eyes and reached for that swirling energy deep within her. Once unlocked, the door in her mind seemed to open swifter every time she reached for it. Power slammed through her, completely unlike the elemental magic every *dreki* could manipulate. It was like riding a bucking horse, or a ship through a fierce storm. The power fought her at every turn, twisting and sliding through her metaphorical hands.

She felt invincible.

Wild.

Destructive.

And unstoppable.

When she opened her eyes, she saw her brother gaping at her, as her spirit *dreki* formed above her, spreading its ethereal wings.

"Mother's not the only one who can wield Chaos," she whispered, feeling the very earth beneath her feet tremble.

I'll think about it, Rurik had said, looking troubled.

Frustration surged within her. She knew she'd surprised him, and he wasn't saying no, but some part of her still yearned to bring the battle to her mother.

They were almost back to Freyja's farm when a bugle of challenge suddenly echoed from the air.

Rurik turned with a screech, soaring toward the west. Árdís banked, hovering in midair as she turned to watch him go.

"Rurik! No!"

"They're here," he snapped back.

In the distance, a lone *dreki* soared mockingly along the line that marked the edge of his territory. The size of it was enormous, its black wings vanishing the sun as it soared between it and them.

Árdís's heart pounded. *"It's Sirius."*

The Blackfrost was here.

Árdís pushed herself into the skies, darting after her brother. It was probably a trap, but no male *dreki* could deny a challenge. She might as soon try and stop the tide, as drag her brother back.

"Is he coming?" Malin asked.

Sirius stared at the volcano ahead of him. He'd changed back into mortal form, knowing the prince would take it as a challenge if he were in the skies. And while he might win that challenge, and the *dreki* within him stirred to take the chance to thwart his old enemy, he had Malin to think about.

And his protective urges overrode his territorial ones.
Barely.

He didn't dare walk any further. This was Rurik's
territory, and to cross the line meant a declaration of war.

Not the best sort of way to beg for a favor.

"He will. He won't be able to resist."

He could still taste the angry lash as Rurik's mind
connected with his.

Two flapping specks appeared in the skies over the
volcano. Sirius's eyes narrowed. He'd expected to see only
one, which meant Rurik had an ally.

He'd be outnumbered.

But the prince played by the rules. It was one of the
reasons he'd been exiled from court. If a challenge came, it
would be one against one, the way it should be.

"Here," he said, reaching for Malin's arm. "They're
coming. Stay behind me at all times."

"I doubt they'll hurt *me*," she said, and refused to go
where he directed.

He couldn't focus on the battle ahead with her
potentially at risk.

"Malin—"

She tipped her chin up.

Everything within him burned to answer her defiance
with a kiss, but he knew that would get him nowhere. It
went against all of his proud nature to do this but.... The
words crawled up his throat. "*Please*. Please do as I say."

Her eyes widened.

"I.... Very well."

That was it? "That's all it takes to make you stop
arguing with me?"

He should have tried this days ago.

She scowled. "Be careful or you'll undo all your good
work."

A surge of dark laughter went through him. Drawing the sword he wore at his belt, he stabbed it into the earth to make it clear he came in peace, before striding forward to the top of the hill.

"Wait!"

She caught his arm, and Sirius paused.

Wind blew strands of her brown hair across her forehead. Those rosy lips parted, her eyes wide, as she fought to say something and failed.

There were a thousand unspoken words left between them.

"Thank you," she whispered, her thumb stroking over the vambrace on his arm. Malin's dark lashes fluttered as she slowly looked up at him. "I will tell the prince everything you've done for me."

He felt the hot stroke of her hand as if it were on his naked skin, and every single muscle in his stomach locked up tight.

"Don't make me out to be a hero. Rurik knows who I am."

"Maybe," she whispered, her brown eyes so very large. "I thought I knew too. But now I'm not so sure."

Pressing her hand to his chest, she lifted up onto her toes, and Sirius's breath caught in his chest. He turned his face sharply, just as she went to press her lips to his cheek. Their mouths met instead, a spark of lightning jolting through him at the unexpected contact. Malin's hand trembled against his chest, and while she didn't draw back, she didn't press forward either.

Instead she hovered there, her eyes very wide as their breath mingled.

It was all he could do not to capture her face and kiss her properly. The *dreki* beat its wings inside him, demanding one last taste.

He might never see her again.

He hoped he'd never have cause to see her again.

But then she slowly lowered herself onto her heels, her palm sliding down the center of his chest, and her cheeks flushed with warm desire.

The moment to press forward was over.

His lips still tingled.

"Don't get yourself killed. *Please*," she said.

"You'll be safe here," he told her roughly. "Whatever else might fall between Rurik and me, he has my respect. He's an honorable *dreki*."

Silence.

Her hand slowly withdrew from his chest.

Malin's eyes narrowed. "You wouldn't say that if you believed he'd had anything to do with his father's death."

Sirius's teeth snapped together. The moment was definitely gone, but his head was still in the clouds, to be so careless with his words.

"Your father said he did. Your aunt said he did. But you *know* he didn't kill his father." The words held a question behind them. "Why would you be so certain?"

"Malin—"

"Why would you be so certain he was honorable?" she repeated.

He glanced up, at the visibly larger *dreki* flying toward him. The storm was coming. A whirlwind of secrets threatening to tear his world apart. "Because I know who did."

Malin gasped, capturing his hand in hers. "Sirius! One word from you, and the entire court would know their prince was innocent of the charges. You have to tell them." She caught her breath, spots of red blooming in her cheeks. "They would overthrow the queen and your father if they knew. Rurik could return. We could be—" She broke off. "The *court* would be a place of light and laughter again."

But not for him.

The truth choked him. "Malin." He stroked his thumb over her knuckles. "I cannot. I am bound by an oath I swore my father."

"Burn your oath," she snapped, her eyes flashing with heat. "You say you're not a hero? You could be. You could break this entire vicious cycle. You could be the key to your father's destruction. I know you have no love of him. You could free Andri, and return the court to the hands of its rightful heir—"

"Damn it, Malin. Now is not the time."

He could hear wings beating through the air now.

"But you won't." She tore her hand free from his. "You won't do the right thing, will you?"

Curse her. Looking at him as though he had all of the answers in the world. As though he *was* a bloody hero. "It's not that simple."

He made to grab Malin's hand, but a sudden screech of fury battered at him. Sirius leapt out of the way as a golden *dreki* swooped. The raking claws missed, and he slowly lowered his arms from over his head, his heart hammering in his chest. Being in this mortal body left him feeling remarkably vulnerable, but he'd known Rurik would be curious, and see it as less of a threat.

However, Rurik wasn't alone.

"I wasn't going to hurt her, Árdís!" he bellowed as the *dreki* princess swooped in a tight circle, as if she were coming back around to take another swipe at him. So much for being trapped in human form.

The other *dreki* landed behind him, and Sirius turned to face the prince. Hot breath snorted over him, and he could see the hard amber glare as Rurik bared his teeth.

333

Holding his arms wide, he stared back, channeling every ounce of arrogance he owned.

"Surprise," he mocked, sending the thought to the prince.

Rurik's lungs expanded, and Sirius's eyes widened. The prince could breathe pure fire if he willed it.

And so it ended, not in battle, but in a gesture of good faith....

"No!" Malin darted in front of him, before he could stop her, arms spread wide as if to protect him.

His heart jacked into his throat.

Sirius grabbed her around the waist, staggering her out of the way, before he could even think, using his body to shield her from—

—a blast of fire that never came.

Sirius released the breath he'd been holding.

A flare of golden light washed over Rurik, and then he shrank dramatically, until he was kneeling before them with his arms spread.

If Stellan were here, he'd take the chance presented, to attack Rurik while he was disorientated with the shift.

But I am not my father.

Sirius held his hands up in surrender, backing away from Malin as the prince straightened

Thirty years flashed past in the blink of an eye. They'd been raised as cousins, and though they'd never been close, he knew this man. This prince.

"You dare walk these lands?" Rurik said, his eyes still cat-slit, as if the *dreki* rested uneasily beneath his skin.

Sirius tipped his head toward the standing stones that marked the borders. "I'm not in your lands."

Rurik picked up the bag he'd dropped and dragged out a pair of leather trousers. He was an inch taller than Sirius, though not quite as broad through the shoulders. And his eyes never shifted from Sirius as he dressed.

"Semantics," he snapped. "You had better have a damned good reason for being here."

"Couldn't I have simply missed my cousin?"

A sharp elbow dug into his gut, and Sirius's breath exploded out of him.

Malin shot him a sharp glare, then made a clumsy curtsy to the prince. *Her* prince, Sirius realized, for her features softened when she looked at Rurik and her eyes grew very big again. She would never have seen Rurik before. She'd barely been at court for ten years, but she'd have heard all about the golden prince from her friends and the other servants.

She'd never bloody looked at *him* like that.

"My prince." Malin's voice came out soft and breathy, as she rose from her curtsy. "Please don't burn Sirius alive. He's not quite as stupid as his loose mouth would suggest, and I owe him my life."

"If you bat your eyelashes at him, I swear I shall throw you over my shoulder and dump you in the nearest pool of stagnant water," Sirius growled at her, mind-to-mind. *"And I don't care whether Rurik challenges me for it or not."*

Malin wasn't strong enough to return the psychic connection, but her teeth ground together and she turned a positively evil glare upon him.

"Go ahead," he dared her, with an arch of his brow.

Rurik gave them both a perplexed look.

"Árdís," Rurik warned, and Sirius realized he'd left a potential threat at his back.

"I'm fairly certain Malin was saying 'no' from what I could see of her body language from the air," Árdís snapped, pulling her hair out of the neckline of the loose green dress she wore. She strode directly toward him, her fingers curled into claws. "You had better not have laid hands upon her if she was unwilling. Malin, are you all right?" Árdís went to her, and the pair of them clasped forearms. "He hasn't hurt you, has he?"

Color stained Malin's cheeks. "No. And he wasn't hurting me then. We were arguing. It's good to see you."

The two women threw their arms around each other.

"What are you doing here?" Árdís demanded.

"She's no longer safe at court," Sirius called.

Árdís turned hot eyes upon him and he held up his hands in surrender again. He might as bloody well stay in this pose.

Which went against all his natural instincts.

The things a dreki did for his mate....

"Blame yourself, if you want to blame anyone," he shot back. "Your little ruse in tying her up didn't work. My father wanted her dead."

"Then why is she with *you*?"

Malin caught the enraged princess by the wrist, and their eyes met briefly. "He... he rescued me and promised to bring me here, where I might be safe." She turned to the prince and curtsied again. "If you would have me."

Rurik glanced at Árdís.

"Of course you can stay," Árdís promised.

"Not just yet," Sirius broke in coldly, meeting the exiled prince's amber eyes. "I'm here to offer Malin in exchange for Árdís. If I take her back, then no fight shall come of this."

"What?" The word exploded out of Árdís, and she shoved forward, her golden hair tangled in loose curls around her face. "We *had* an agreement."

"I don't want this," he sent, on psychic threads between the three of them. *"But I have no choice. After Andri's betrayal, father's been treating Roar as an heir. If he thinks to replace my brother with Roar.... And Malin, I couldn't leave her there, I couldn't...."*

Soft understanding dawned on her face. *"She's the one, isn't she?"*

A faint nod.

Árdís's jaw dropped open. "Oh."

"You could stay here," she sent back. *"With us. You could fight with us. And you could have her as your own."*

"Árdís," Rurik scolded sharply. It wasn't a bargain she could offer, as these were the prince's lands.

"Even if I were welcome," he said mockingly. "*I cannot.*"

"You would choose your father over your mate?"

"It's not—" He sucked in a sharp breath. *"You forget the second creed my father's line stands for: Family before all else. It's what I've believed all my life."* And he'd done things—horrible things—for that cause, for if he couldn't believe in family, then what else could he believe in?

"Do you think they would give a damn? Do you think they would choose you?" she said.

"I know they wouldn't."

Árdís's eyes flared gold. *"Then how can you choose to fight at their side, knowing what they're like?"*

"Because if I don't go back," he hissed, *"then he will kill my brother. I was the only thing stopping him."*

Family before all else. And in Sirius's eyes, there was one *dreki* left to him in this world that belonged in that category.

"Andri." Rurik broke in sharply. *"He's threatened Andri?"*

"Andri betrayed Magnus when he saved you from my brother's wrath. And Magnus was father's favorite. Stellan doesn't believe in disloyalty." Unless it came from him. He turned to her. *"I made a deal, Árdís. I would serve my father's every whim if he allowed my brother to live. I would... I would mate with you, and secure the family's hold on the throne."*

"You let me go."

"A foolish plan made on the spur of the moment." He glanced toward Malin, who was watching the three of them as if aware they communicated privately. *"I hoped if you weren't there, then I could not be forced to mate with you, and could sidestep my part of the bargain. But my father will not accept such a loss. He demands your return at my side, and I fear if I don't, then he will renege upon his end of the bargain."*

"You cannot win."

"No." He gave a bitter smile. *"I cannot win. If you choose to stay, then you shall face me on the field as an enemy. I have no choice."*

Árdís pressed a hand to her temples. *"Damn it."*

"You're not going," Rurik told her.

"There is one other thing you should know," he told her. *"They are coming for you right now, and they are coming in force. Your mother rides with them. To confront your brother means she must accept his claim as a potential rival for her throne, but she's been in a lather all night. They'll be here within hours. If I hand you over, it's done."*

"I can't," she said out loud. She turned to Rurik. "I can't."

"I don't expect you to," Rurik replied. His eyes glittered queerly as he turned to glare at Sirius. "My sister is mated already. She cannot undo what is already done, and even if she weren't, I would not trade her freedom for another's life. And there is one last choice left to us.... Let your father and my mother come for Árdís. If Stellan dies on the field of war, then he can't lift a hand against Andri."

"You don't understand—"

Rurik hissed at him. "They're not invincible. We have weapons you cannot even dream of. When your father comes, I will challenge him. There's a reason he's afraid to face me."

Sirius stared at him. "It won't be my father they send to battle with you."

Lightning crackled in distant skies.

"Sirius?" Malin whispered, her hands clenched in her skirts.

He looked at her, his heart freezing in her chest. "I'll have no choice."

"That's not true," Rurik murmured. "If you defy your father then *he'll* have no choice but to face me. You want Malin to be safe? I'm the only one who can keep her out of his hands. Your choice, Sirius. Stay off the field of battle. Defy your father. And both your brother and your... Malin might survive."

"You don't know what you're asking," Sirius called as they both stepped away from him. *Damn them.*

Árdís held out her hand to Malin.

"Your choice," Rurik said softly as power blurred around him, leaving only a powerful *dreki* behind.

CHAPTER TWENTY-TWO

BATTLE ARRIVED ON the wings of a storm, just as the sun began its steady decline toward the horizon.

Árdís landed on the grassy plain that marked the edge of Rurik's territory, and Haakon slipped down from her back, looking faintly queasy. Thick brewing clouds darkened the west, and she could see lashes of lightning flickering there and a hint of wings. A brief shimmer of her power, and she stood next to Haakon in her mortal flesh. He handed her the bag with her clothes.

"Magnus fought in his *dreki* form," he murmured, his hard gaze raking the *dreki* in the air opposite them. "You truly think they'll change to mortal shape?"

"There's too many of us," she replied, dressing swiftly. Lightning crackled above them as Rurik landed with Freyja and Malin astride him. "*Dreki* don't fight in numbers. There would be simply too much damage, and more than ten *dreki* clashing would tear the earth apart, and fuel a set of storms that could change the weather patterns of the entire world. We'd send a sudden winter hammering down through

Europe. It's a pact between the different courts that even my mother dares not break.

"It will be a challenge, one-on-one," Árdís added. "Mostly physical, to keep magic out of the fray as much as possible. One of them will challenge Rurik. He's the strongest male here. Another will possibly challenge me. Or your claim upon me."

"Your customs make no sense," he muttered.

"You're talking about an entire race of arrogant creatures driven by conceit," she pointed out. "Honor is everything. To defeat another in battle is a source of pride, but how can one be proud if you destroyed a puny mortal? It's an uneven battle. It means nothing. It is shameful."

"Watch your back today," he said, helping her into her lightweight leather body armor.

He wore a shirt of chainmail, with a ruff of fur on his shoulders. He looked dangerous, and vicious, and all hers.

Árdís kissed him quickly. "I will. You watch yours. I've managed to shield you psychically, so they cannot overcome you the way they did last time. You're difficult to kill, but not impossible."

He grinned at her suddenly. "Nothing's impossible to kill. I plan to add to my tally today."

She rolled her eyes and sniffed. "Dragons don't count. They're practically wyrms."

"Tormund thinks he's going to cut down more *dreki* than I." Haakon drew his sword with a steely rasp. "I have a point to prove. But I *will* watch my back—and yours—and tonight we'll celebrate."

Men.

She wished she had half his confidence. Her eyes lifted to the skies. *One, two, three, four, five....*

"She's not here," Árdís whispered, searching the group for the distinct emerald green scales of her mother. Her

341

heart lifted as hope began to tease through her. "My mother didn't come."

A single *dreki* soared in slow circles in the air above them. Keeping track of the forthcoming battle for Amadea, no doubt.

"Why would they not bring their greatest weapon?" Haakon murmured, his eyes narrowing.

"They're *dreki*," she said, as if that explained everything. "And she can wield her powers from a distance."

"Her powers are stronger if she's closer. Isn't that what you said?"

Árdís shrugged. "Maybe she's afraid of me?"

No. That didn't feel quite right. Árdís frowned. Her mother would be wary, but there was more than one way to handle a threat. *I will definitely be watching my back.*

They joined the others, watching as Tormund, Gunnar, and Bjorn rode up behind them. The enormous ballista lumbered along on a wagon driven by Marek, just in case the tides of battle turned, but the three men were here to fight by hand.

It evened out the numbers somewhat.

A lone *dreki* stood on the hill overlooking the grassy plain. She didn't need to look closer to know who it was.

"Go to him," she told Malin, who'd braided her hair in a crown around her head and was wearing an old dress of Freyja's.

Her handmaid shot her an uneasy look, and then started up the hill. It was dangerous to bring her to the battle, but they had to find a way to keep Sirius out of the fight.

And Árdís was playing dirty.

If they fell here today, then there'd be no place her handmaid was safe anyway. At least here, Malin could perhaps turn the tide of battle.

The ground started quivering beneath their feet. Lightning lashed through the skies, and one of the *dreki* screamed as a bolt of it seared the air dangerously close to him. Freyja held her hands into the air, her eyes turning electric blue as power speared through her.

She was controlling the storm.

"*Rurik?*" Árdís turned to her brother.

"*I told you,*" he replied on a psychic thread of gold. "*She's not human. We don't know what she is, but she's been growing in power for the last month, ever since we mated.*"

The enemy *dreki* landed on the smoking ground, and light flashed as they shifted shapes to their mortal forms and dressed.

"It's time," Árdís whispered, drawing her sword.

Stellan was the first to stride forward, his legs eating up the ground. Lightning flickered and danced behind him.

"Uncle," Rurik called, forcing the other *dreki* to come and meet him.

Stellan ignored him, turning his head to stare at her. "You've caused a great deal of trouble, Árdís."

"I am *not* returning to court," Árdís said. "I have chosen my mate, and I will not submit to the will of either of your sons."

"We no longer wish for your return." Stellan's lips thinned. "You are not worthy of the right to bear the *Zilittu* name, nor to mate with any of my sons. You have despoiled your blood with this human. Your mother has made the proclamation before the court, exiling you from the clan. You bear no *dreki* title, nor can you lay claim to your previous place. You are nothing. No one. Rut with whoever you want."

It took her aback. All along she'd been fighting to free herself, and yet the sudden loss sheared through her.

No longer a princess. No longer a part of her father's court. She might have held no ties to her mother's family, but her father's.... It was her inheritance. Her *place* in this world.

A hand slid into hers, fingers lacing between them. Haakon. She squeezed back, grateful for the silent support.

"You're my wife. That is your place," he muttered, and she looked at him sharply, surprised he'd heard her thoughts, though she shouldn't have been.

They were one now.

Almost.

"You do not have the right to strip Árdís of her name," Rurik growled, stepping forward. "And the court belonged to my father. My mother's claim upon it is spurious, if nothing else."

"I hear the words of a ghost," Stellan mocked, his eyes glittering. "Your words have no weight here."

"I hear the words of a coward," Rurik shot back, and every *dreki* within the area sucked in an audible gasp. "One who likes to hide behind lies, and the lives of his sons." He gestured to the barren lands around him. "Well, I have helped take one of your sons from this world. Perhaps you would like to step out from behind the others? Face me as the *dreki* warrior you claim to be."

Stellan's eyes narrowed.

"Enough."

The word echoed through all their minds, like a lash of lightning.

The *dreki* parted, and behind them, Árdís saw a woman skirting the bubbling pools of mud, stagnant ponds, and the hissing steam vents that marked the caldera. The heat drained from Árdís's face. Her mother walked

344

with stately grace, wearing a gown of emerald green velvet, her unbound hair tumbling in loose golden waves down her back.

She hadn't been hiding after all. She'd been waiting to make an entrance.

"You sent me a challenge," Amadea hissed, her golden hair streaming behind her in the winds. "Are you ready to face me, daughter?"

Árdís stared at her mother, swallowing her fear.

"A challenge?" Rurik called. "I haven't heard anyone here offer challenge."

"Oh, but that's not true, is it, Árdís?" Her mother's smile widened. "Go ahead and tell them the truth. How many nights ago was it when you sent your spirit *dreki* to me? And now I am here to fight for my crown."

The blood drained out of her face. "But I didn't mean...."

A green glow began to ignite in the queen's eyes. "You stupid kit. Did you think I would merely hide in Hekla and wait for you to grow in strength?"

She'd barely begun to master her magic.

But she'd told her mother she'd kill her if she ever touched Haakon again. A wince went through her as she remembered what else she'd said. *You are not the only one with power*, she'd hissed. *I'm waiting for you, Mother. Come and get me.*

Technically a challenge. She slid her sword back into its sheath. Her breath hitched. This wasn't the fight she'd expected, but she could do this.

She *had* to do this.

"Árdís," Haakon said, his face grim.

"This is my battle," she whispered to Haakon. "If I fall, then remember the plan."

"You're not going to fall."

She pressed a gentle hand to his arm. "I love you."

"I love you too." He bent and kissed her cheek. "And I don't think she'd be here if she wasn't a little afraid of you, Árja. I also think she's going to cheat."

"She can't. If she breaks her word, then the entire court will turn on her."

All her life she'd been too afraid to take what she wanted. She was no longer that young woman, sheltered and alone, looking for someone to fight her battles for her.

This was *her* fight.

And she was no longer afraid.

"Árdís?" Rurik called.

"I challenged her," she said, striding to the middle of the ground between both groups. "She has the right of it."

Amadea stood before her, weaving wisps of electric green light to life. A net of shimmering, incandescent green.

Excellent. Who knew *what* that could do?

Árdís planted her feet, and reached down deep within her.

Just as she drew her breath to delve into her new power, a sudden shocking slam of another *dreki's* mind lashed against hers. A blow of psychic proportions, that she narrowly turned away with a psychic shield. Stellan.

"Árdís!" someone bellowed.

She was on the ground, on her knees, and her magic evaporated through her fingers. The net flared wide as her mother cast it at her, filling her vision.

Move! Árdís threw herself aside, still trying to blink through the shock of the assault. She splashed through hot mud, and the net sizzled as it hit the ground where she'd been standing, and vanished into the earth, leaving behind a carved grid.

Behind her, swords clashed as Stellan leapt forward to drive her brother back. Árdís staggered to her feet as her mother's *dreki* charged forward, cutting her off from the others. Amadea had vanished behind them, taking her dangerous magic with her.

What was happening? This wasn't how *dreki* fought. The challenge had been accepted by her mother, which meant the fight ought to remain between the pair of them. Árdís drew her sword as two of the *dreki* advanced. Behind them, she could just make out Haakon, advancing upon Roar with his sword drawn.

He was cut off from her by the two *dreki* circling her. She recognized Lor, one of her mother's pets, and Florian, who generally preferred to keep to the shadows.

"This is a challenge," she snapped. "Between my mother and me. Get out of my way."

Lor's smile sent a shiver down her spine. He towered over her, and his reputation was brutal enough to make her very wary. "Your mother changed the rules. It *was* a challenge. But who's going to tell the court?"

And they were the only ones who mattered.

Árdís took a step backward. This had been the plan all along. Lure her out and cut her off from the others, who were battling behind her to break through. Keep her distracted by fighting for her life, unable to take a second to bring her magic to bear. "You think there won't be any witnesses to this fight? This is breaking *all the rules*."

"I know," Lor said, and lunged forward, bringing his sword down upon hers.

"We have to do something," Malin cried as the melee beneath them suddenly shifted, revealing how outnumbered Rurik and Árdís were.

Every muscle in Sirius's body locked tight.

"Get down here," Stellan snarled in his head. *"It should have been you attacking the prince."*

Rurik and Stellan fought like a pair of titans, their entire focus locked upon each other as they bashed and hammered at each other's swords. Mud churned up beneath their feet, but Sirius's father was keeping the prince busy. Behind him, Rurik's woman paced nervously, not daring to intervene with her magic.

Amadea laughed as she withdrew to a grassy knoll, leaving Árdís facing Lor and Florian. Árdís was holding her own. Barely. But Lor was letting her wear herself down, waiting for an opportunity to strike.

And beyond them, Árdís's mortal husband kept trying to reach her side, but Roar danced between them, grinning as he lunged forward with his sword. Behind Haakon, Rolf shot the queen a sidelong glance, then withdrew the dagger at his belt and took a stealthy step toward the Norseman.

It would be death from behind, with Roar deliberately distracting Árdís's husband.

Sirius could see the tides of the battle turning. The man would fall, and then both Rolf and Roar could take on Rurik. The humans who were trying to wade into battle to save their friend would be obliterated with a thought.

This had never been intended to be a fair fight. Both Amadea and Stellan had accepted challenges, but they weren't going to finish them. Árdís would be worn down, and the only one remaining who could fight would be Rurik.

The prince's odds narrowed the second the others fell.

They should have known the queen would never fight honorably. Not after she'd arranged to have their father murdered.

Rurik's strength—and weakness—was his sense of honor.

"Please," Malin whispered, turning to him. "Please don't let this happen. You could stop this. You're the only one here who can."

Sirius closed his eyes. "This is how it was always going to end."

"It doesn't have to. I said I despised you, but it wasn't true. There is something good within you. I don't know how your father didn't crush it out of you, but it's there. I've seen it."

To take a side meant he could never go back. He could cost Andri his life.

But if Rurik lost today, if Stellan and Amadea were victorious, then there was nowhere Malin would be safe. They would kill her. Or they would try. And then he would be taking a side anyway, for he could not let that happen.

"Please be a hero," she begged.

The words cut right to the core of him.

"I'm not a hero," he snapped.

"Then be *my* hero," she whispered.

Of all the things that could have changed his mind.... He was trapped, no matter which choice he made. He knew if he entered the field of battle below, he would not return. Stellan would never allow him to survive such a betrayal.

But the decision was made. For Malin's sake

His life for hers. The price would be worth it.

Here it ends.

It almost felt like there was finally something to fight for.

"Stay here," Sirius told her softly, pressing his dagger into her hands. "And don't let anyone near you."

She watched him go, relief filling those beautiful eyes, and he knew she did not realize this was goodbye.

Mud kicked up, and Haakon whirled, deflecting the blow from the bastard prince. Shock echoed through his arms as their swords met. Roar was stronger than he was, and slightly taller. For a man used to hunting dragons, Haakon was suddenly in the fight of his life. The edge of Roar's sword shuddered down his, and glanced off the leather vambrace he wore on his arm as they fell apart.

No time to breathe.

The fight was chaos. A fist slammed into his face, and he responded with a boot to Roar's knee. He caught flashes of the others as his cheek throbbed, especially Árdís. She'd been right. They weren't trying to kill her, but if they disarmed her....

His cheek stung as the very tip of Roar's sword kissed it. *Right. Pay attention.* Because while Árdís wasn't in any immediate danger, he was.

"First blood," Roar grinned at him, as if that made any damned difference. "You can fight. For a mortal. But I'm going to win."

Haakon twisted and slammed his shoulder into the bastard. Roar staggered, and he followed through with his fist, his knuckles driving into Roar's scarred cheek.

There was a pistol at his waist. A grappling hook. And no time to grab any of it.

Roar lunged forward, beating him back, the intensity of the fight suddenly increasing. Haakon barely had time to wonder why. Moves that flowed like water down a hill were suddenly sloppy and careless. They battered at each other, hammering with fist and sword, until all he could see was the *dreki*. His sword arm was getting heavier. But he was meeting every strike, and he could see the bastard prince's frustration growing.

The *dreki* had expected an easy fight.

"I think I'm going to fuck her right here in the mud for the first time." Roar laughed as they broke apart. "Right next to your dead body."

Like hell. Árdís was his. Haakon slammed into him in a violent crunch of steel and leather, and drove the bastard back. He couldn't get his sword up in time. Simply slammed the pommel of it into Roar's teeth, and heard a satisfying crunch. Blood sprayed across his face, and then they were locked together, the steel inserts on his chainmail tangled with Roar's. Metal shrieked. Clapping a hand over Roar's to pin his sword low, he drove a knee into the other man's thigh.

They finally broke apart, and Haakon sucked in a much-needed breath, his lungs burning. Roar hopped out of the way, favoring his leg and spitting blood and bits of tongue. His eyes flashed *dreki*-gold. Murderous.

"Guess I'm not the only one who can bleed," Haakon mocked, though every inch of him was starting to ache. There was a sharp ache of exertion deep in his side and groin. The world seemed far too bright and chaotic, and he knew he needed to finish this quickly, before the tide of energy racing through his veins suddenly broke and came crashing down upon him.

There was something about the other man's vicious bloodied smile that made the hairs on the back of his neck rise. "We'll see."

"Behind you!" A man yelled.

Instincts honed by years of battle, Haakon turned, catching a glimpse of a dark shadow rushing toward him. His elbow was moving, up, up, into the newcomer's face, but silver flashed beneath his arm, into the gaping vulnerability of his chainmail.

A knife.

Haakon's breath exploded out of him as it rammed into his side. He felt the punch of it as the hilt hit skin, and slammed his elbow into the would-be assassins face. The *dreki* went down, taking the knife with him, and it was only then that Haakon felt the rest of it.

Burning agony exploded through him. There was a tight pulling up under his arm. Pain searing along his nerves.

His legs weren't working properly, his right knee threatening to go out from under him. Blood. All over his side. He clapped his other hand there, and felt it weeping warmly over his fingers. *Sweet gods.*

How bad?

White began sucking at his vision. Between one second and the next, he found himself on his knees, his sword in the mud. He couldn't remember dropping it. Couldn't remember hitting the ground.

"*No!*" Even from across the field, he heard Árdís's scream cut through the air as if the very sound vibrated.

Everyone clapped their hands over their ears.

Haakon blinked, and then the *dreki* who'd stabbed him was on his feet. Moving toward him with the knife held low against his thigh.

"He's mine. I get to do the honors," Roar said, spitting blood into the mud as he stalked forward with an unhurried step, bringing his sword up. "I want her to see it."

Haakon's fingers groped for his sword. His vision was narrowing. Fingers slippery with blood as he tried to pick it up. His right side throbbed just under the ribs.

"Haakon!" He couldn't see her, but he knew Árdís was fighting her way toward him.

Árdís, his sunlit princess.

His heart.

His everything.

No. He didn't want her to see this.

Roar lifted the sword, and sunlight flashed off it as it began its descent—

Steel whined as it shaved the air next to his ear, and then a shower of sparks rained over him as another sword met Roar's.

The bastard prince's eyes widened, and then he was staggering back, a boot in his chest, as someone stepped between them.

Not just anyone.

But the *dreki* who'd once sworn to kill him.

"Hello, brother," Sirius almost purred.

CHAPTER TWENTY-THREE

"YOU," SAID A sharp voice loaded with hate.

Haakon gasped, trying to kick his way back across the ground as the queen appeared, a knife held low against her skirts. Blood bubbled over his lips, and he coughed. A lung. The bastard had hit his lung. The pressure in his chest was back, and he felt like he could barely breathe.

"You dared to touch a *dreki* princess?" the queen hissed. "You dared defile her blood?"

Swords clashed nearby. Sirius taking on both Roar and the *dreki* who'd stabbed him. They sounded a world away.

"Wife," he managed to gasp, trying to reach inside his chainmail. "She's... my wife."

The queen's vicious green eyes narrowed. "Then let me make her a widow."

Striding forward, she brought the knife up sharply.

"Mother!" Árdís screamed, sliding to her knees between them and crouching over him. "No!"

"So be it, Árdís," the queen snarled, and moved to stab her.

It was now or never.

"Árdís," he wheezed, fumbling with what he held in his hand.

She captured her mother's hand, halting the downward strike. But the queen was stronger than she looked. Árdís's hands shook as she fought to hold the blade at bay. The queen leaned all her weight onto it, a lash of green light beginning to smoke from her eyes.

Árdís couldn't fight both knife and magic.

Hauling together every last bit of strength, Haakon lunged forward and locked the manacle around the queen's wrist, then slumped at her feet.

Golden light flared as the metallic links fused together. Amadea staggered back, looking down in shock and shaking her hand as if to remove it. "What have you done?"

"Trapped you," he rasped. "No magic. No *dreki*. Only your weak, pathetic human... form."

The strength was draining out of him. Somehow he ended up in Árdís's lap.

"You rotten cur," the queen snarled, taking a step toward them with the knife.

"Only he can remove it from your wrist. If he dies, then you'll wear that manacle for the rest of your immortal life." Árdís snapped. "Or perhaps it will only be a mortal lifespan, as the manacle warps both your ability to utilize magic *and* to shift forms. Perhaps it will drain the years from your future, as well."

The queen's face paled, and she tore at the manacle. "Get it off me! Stellan!"

A roar sounded. An enormous *dreki* lashed into the skies, abandoning his duel with Rurik.

"You should never underestimate me, mother," Árdís snapped. "I knew you'd cheat somehow. So we evened the odds. Enjoy your mortal life. I'd suggest you retreat, before I unleash my *dreki* upon you."

Stellan swooped down and plucked the queen into the air with his claws. A ragged slash of red ran down his flank as he lifted into the air, carrying her away.

Haakon blinked. He felt light-headed, but he knew the battle had broken. The surge of energy that had allowed him to manacle the queen vanished. All he could feel now was pain. Árdís knees cushioned his head. A tear splashed into his face. He reached up to her, his fingers numb as he brushed her cheek. "Worth it," he whispered.

Or thought he did.

His lips felt like they weren't moving.

"No!" Árdís screamed, and it was the last thing he heard as darkness rushed up to take him.

"Haakon?"

She shook him, but his head lolled to the side, a rasp coming from his chest.

Árdís scrambled out from beneath him, pressing her fingers to the pulse in his neck. His heart still beat, but it was very weak, and blood covered the mud. Tearing his chainmail open, she tried to find the cause of it. There. Under his arm.

"Somebody help me!" she cried, her fingers coming away wet and slick. She didn't know what to do. Some *dreki* could heal others, but it was not one of her gifts. *"Rurik!"*

His mind touched hers, and then he was by her side.

"He's been stabbed," she whispered, cradling Haakon's face. "He's barely breathing."

A hesitation. "I'm not a very good healer."

"Please. Just try." She reached for Haakon with her psychic gifts, her mind brushing against his, even as her hand curled around his cheek.

"Árdís." Haakon twitched.

"I love you," she sent back, her mind tangling with his. *"Please don't leave me. You promised you'd protect me forever. I will follow you through the gates of death itself,"* she whispered, feeling the clouds swirl over them.

Her vision blurred. She stood on a grassed slope with the skies racing above her, a meld of furious clouds one second, and the next sunlight. Haakon walked ahead of her, his enormous cloak swirling around his boots. Sunlight turned the world into a glorious green haven. One she recognized. A goat bleated. The thatched roof of a house peaked over the horizon.

Home.

He was going home.

"Haakon!" She sprinted along the path behind him, snatching for his arm.

Her hand locked around his, and he turned, his skin pale and bloodless. *"Árdís?"*

"You're mine, Haakon Dragonsbane, and I will not let you go. Not now. Not ever."

Thunder crashed, and her head jerked up.

Then a pair of hands captured her face, tilting her mouth up. *"Mine,"* Haakon agreed, just before his lips took hers.

The kiss fused the pair of them together, and a whirlwind of power swept up through her. It sparked all across her skin. Suddenly she didn't know where he began, and she ended. She felt like Haakon's mind brushed back against her. A sickening whirl began to pull her down, toward him. Árdís swayed.

"Hold him there," Rurik snapped.

She stood on the edge of life and death, energy draining through her as she gritted her teeth. If she let go, even for second, then she'd lose him, she knew.

Heat flushed through the pair of them all of a sudden, and Árdís sensed her brother trying to direct weaves of pure Fire. Haakon suddenly screamed, his spine arching as they wove through him. Árdís wrapped her arms around him, standing in two worlds as she fought to hold him.

"I will never let you go," she promised.

Thunder clapped, and the skies spit lightning. Haakon collapsed beneath her, and then Árdís was blinking back into the natural world. Exhausted.

"The Great Goddess has heard your vow," Rurik murmured, sitting back on his knees. A relieved smile graced his face as she blinked at him. "You've claimed him as yours."

"What happened?" she whispered.

"Instinct, Árdís. That's all you ever truly needed."

She could feel the whisper of her husband's thoughts against hers. His life tied to hers. A surge of pure happiness shot through her. "I bound him."

"Árja?" Haakon rasped, reaching up to touch her skin.

She captured his hand, consumed by the strange feelings inside her. "Haakon!" Leaning down, she threw her arms around him, careless of the mud or the blood, or anything but the feel of him against her. "You're alive. And mine. Forever."

CHAPTER
TWENTY-FOUR

"MY LORD?" MALIN whispered, her hands curled into tight little fists as she interrupted Prince Rurik before he could open the door to his mate's little farmhouse.

The golden prince stirred, looking weary. "Malin."

She tried to curtsy, but he caught her hand and shook his head. "I understand the court is different these days to the one I matured within. But you owe me no obeisance." His smile lit up the night. "Technically, I'm not even a prince anymore."

"Yes, you are," she breathed, swallowing the tight lump in her throat. "The entire court whispers your name. You're the rightful ruler, the rightful heir. They all want to see you overthrow your mother."

Rurik turned, but he didn't look happy by the news. "Were you troubled, Malin? Did Freyja not find you someplace to sleep?"

"Yes, she did, but...." Malin drew on all of her courage, and blurted. "Sirius flew after his father and the rest of them."

The prince's eyes narrowed. "He made his choice."

"No, he didn't!" she cried, catching at his sleeve. "He entered the fray, and he fought Roar. If he hadn't, then...."

Silence. She found herself the focus of those intense eyes.

"He was afraid for his brother," she said. "He touched minds with me when he left. He flew after them because he feared they might kill Andri in response for his betrayal. They'll hurt him, I know they will. Or worse. We have to rescue them."

He paused. "I cannot attack the court. Its defenses are too strong, and my mother and Stellan have proven they won't play fair. I can't challenge them and lure them out. I can't get inside the court, Malin. They'll feel me coming."

"He fought for you," she snapped, and then swallowed hard. Oh, sweet heavens.... But the prince didn't look as though he was going to strike her. "*Please*, my prince. If Sirius hadn't joined the battle when he did, Haakon would be dead and you overthrown. He betrayed his father for you."

Rurik's lips pressed tightly together. "He *killed* my father."

She looked up in shock. "*What?*"

"I felt his magic in my father's chambers that night. Sirius was there the night my father died."

"That doesn't mean he murdered the king," she said brokenly. *No.*

"It doesn't mean he didn't. But he knows who did, either way. He was one of the *dreki* who told the court I'd done it."

The Blackfrost.... It didn't sound like him. She'd come to learn he respected honor and *dreki* laws. There had to be more to this story than she imagined. "So you'll just leave him there?" she whispered. "And Andri? Is this how you repay two *dreki* who saved your life?"

360

Rurik pinched the bridge of his nose. "I'll handle it, Malin. I promise. I'll... work out some way to free the both of them, and then... then Sirius and I can have a reckoning."

Her shoulders fell. "But it will be too late."

"Nothing's too late," Rurik murmured. "I have something Stellan and my mother want—or Haakon does anyway—and they have something I want. I'll offer a trade. We'll remove mother's bracelet in exchange for my cousins lives."

He touched her chin. "It will be all right, Malin. I promise."

She tried to swallow her doubt. There was only one bracelet, after all, and two *dreki* brothers to rescue.

"Thank you," she whispered.

Rurik nodded shortly, and then entered the farmhouse, leaving her out there in the night.

He would save them. She was certain of it. He had to.

He was the prince.

But what if he was forced to make a choice between Andri, the good brother everyone loved, and the Blackfrost, who he suspected had a hand in his father's death?

A shiver ran through her.

EPILOGUE

Six months later....

THE WIND BLEW a pair of strangers through her door, and Árdís glared as they tracked mud all over her floors. It felt strange to have a home, especially one that lurked in the shadow of her brother's volcano. Haakon had built it for her with his bare hands, and though his heart belonged elsewhere, they would stay here until the threat of her mother was subdued once and for all.

"What do you think you're doing?" she demanded, pointing to the muddy floor even as a surge of joy made her dizzy. "And what is that on your face?"

The stranger scrubbed a hand through his fine blond bristles. "It's called a beard. I haven't been able to shave. Someone broke my mirror," he said with a pointed look toward his companion, who laughed.

"You see," she said, setting her hands on her hips. "You look like my husband. You smell like him. But he was supposed to be home weeks ago, and he doesn't wear a beard. How do I know you're really him?"

Haakon eyed her. "You have a little mole, right here," he said, stabbing a finger into the right side of his chest.

"You adore emeralds, and you are a terrible cook, and you are very ticklish right between—"

"That's enough!" she said breathlessly. "I believe you."

"Right between where?" Tormund asked, looking mildly interested.

"You don't like it?" Haakon drew his hand through his beard, his eyes twinkling. *"And you know it's me. Haven't you felt me coming closer every day?"*

"I didn't say I didn't like it." Her heart throbbed in her chest, and she took a step toward him. "I could grow used to it, perhaps. Where have you been? You were supposed to go see your mother and then come straight back home to me. If I couldn't feel you out there, then I'd have been terrified you'd met your end."

Haakon grinned at her, "And this is the way you greet me after I've been gone for nearly two months?"

She couldn't hold herself back anymore. She threw herself into his arms, pressing her hungry mouth to his. The taste of him exploded through her, and his hands cupped her under the bottom, driving her against a certain sign he was more than happy to see her. It was a sloppy kiss, and his beard tickled her mouth, but she couldn't draw away. It left her breathless, and suddenly she couldn't remember why she was so angry anymore.

Haakon slowly set her down, a certain look in his eyes. *"It's been a long time."*

"It has," she returned.

He smiled. "But I need a bath first."

Haakon stepped aside, swinging his cloak from his shoulders. Tormund held his arms wide with a suggestive waggle of his eyebrows. "My turn?"

She rolled her eyes, but she hugged him too.

"Just keep your hands and lips to yourself," Haakon warned, from where he was settling his saddlebags over the back of her kitchen chair. "I'd hate to have to break your fingers."

She could barely control herself. She felt giddy. "You still haven't told me where you've been. What happened? Is your mother well? The children? Your sisters?"

"All well. I have more nephews and nieces. They're breeding like rabbits."

Her smile softened, and she didn't quite press her hand to her lower abdomen. That was a secret between them, and she didn't wish to share it with Tormund yet.

Haakon stripped out of his coat, the white of his shirt blinding. He tugged something from the collar of his shirt, but she couldn't see what it was. Something on the end of a chain. "We made a slight detour on the way home."

It took the wind right out of her sails. "Is that—?"

Haakon's palm unfolded, revealing a very familiar ring. The ring twinkled on her finger. Árdís clapped her hands to her mouth, and tears filled her eyes, as they were prone to do these days.

"Your ring," Haakon said gruffly, taking her hand and sliding it slowly onto her finger.

Árdís could barely breathe. She had her ring back. Her *ring*.

"We are legends now. You are looking at Tormund Kraken-slayer." Tormund grinned at her. "Your husband said he could spear the bastard first, but I was the one who took him down. And then we dragged it ashore, and cut out its heart—"

"That was the easy part," Haakon muttered. "Its heart was the size of a cow, so we had to find a wagon to haul it. You cannot *imagine* the stink of it after a week overland. I daresay Lord Fáfnir was not as pleased with his end of the bargain as he thought he might be."

She stared at him, her mouth open.

"Aye," Tormund added. "It was almost a relief to hit those sulfurous mud pools. Something to cleanse the nostrils."

"You *slew* a kraken?"

"Not a simple endeavor," Haakon drawled, "but it was easier than the other options Fáfnir would trade for, and I was pressed for time."

Árdís slammed a fist against his chest. "You idiot! You could have been killed. You know my mother and her *dreki* are watching us. And a kraken! They've been known to tear ships to pieces."

"Damned near did," Tormund admitted, and then shut his mouth abruptly when Haakon's head turned sharply toward him. "Not," he added. "It did *not* come close to tearing the ship apart."

"What were you thinking?" she cried.

"I told you not to trade the ring to him."

"I had no choice! It was either it—or you. Now I'm starting to regret that decision."

"Ah, ah, ah." A growl curled out of his throat, and he hauled her into his arms. "Mind your temper, Árdís. I just battled a kraken for you, and then tricked an enormous *dreki* into handing over your ring in exchange for its heart. I'm not scared of you anymore."

She grabbed a fistful of his collar.

He smiled.

God, that beard. A lick of heat wet her thighs. If she didn't kiss him again, and soon, then she was going to erupt.

"Tormund." Haakon gave his cousin a telling look.

Tormund sighed, and slapped a pile of coins on the table. "Fine. You do know her better. And on that note, I think I have a sudden urge to go see to my horse."

"Do that."

"And stay in the barn tonight," she called.

Tormund backed away with both hands in the air.

Árdís growled as soon as the enormous man vanished through the doorway, shutting it quickly behind him. "You *bet* on me?"

Haakon let her go, and crossed his arms over his chest. "He seemed to think he knew you better than I did. He said you'd be overwhelmed with gratitude when I brought your ring home. I said you'd be furious. At first."

Árdís stabbed a finger into his chest. "Fáfnir is not someone to toy with, damn you. He hates my father. He made me trade the ring because he knew it would cause me the most pain. Or he thought it would. Do you know why I gave it to him? Because if he had any clue how much *you meant to me*, he would have bartered for you instead."

"It's your wedding ring," he growled back, trying to fight a smile. "It belongs on your finger, so all the world knows you're mine."

Her voice rose. "Stop smiling at me. You're ruining this."

"Ruining what?" He took a step toward her, and her back hit the wall. "Are you trying to work up to a good fight, sweetheart?"

"Trying."

Haakon pressed his forearms against the wall, and leaned closer. "Mmm." He bit his lip, a twinkle in his eyes. "Maybe we could just skip the argument for once? Get right to the good stuff."

She sucked in a sharp breath. "I swear—"

"To all the gods." The back of his fingertips brushed her cheek. "Are you happy to have it back, Árdís?" he murmured, pressing her to the door and brushing his lips along her jaw.

"Don't think...." A soft gasp escaped her as his erection ground right where she wanted it. "Don't think you're going to kiss your way out of this one."

"No?" His mouth whispered across her lips.

A surge of pure heat sheared through her. Somehow her unruly hands were in his hair.

"Damn you, I *love* you. My mother could have captured you. Any of the court could have made a play for you, and I wouldn't have known until it was too late." She held his face to hers, staring deep into his eyes. "You knew I couldn't follow you."

"Not without risking the child, no."

The precious child she'd discovered she was carrying. She'd gone into heat the second she bound his soul to hers, as if the bond had flicked some switch in her brain. It had been an overwhelming couple of weeks where everyone, even Rurik, had barely dared knock on their door. All Árdís could remember was naked skin beneath her lips, her hands, and her husband pinning her to the bed, driving himself into her. She'd been insatiable, and Haakon had more than made up for lost time, until they could barely move.

Heat incinerated her. Haakon licked at her lips. "Perhaps I can kiss it all better?"

Oh, gods. She gave up, and wrapped her arms around him. "I will let you kiss it better," she growled, "as long as you promise not to go hunting any more dragons or kraken, or wyrms or trolls.... Or anything else that might take you from my side."

Haakon caught her up under the thighs, and locked her legs around his hips as he strode toward the bedroom. "It's a deal, my love. No more dragons for me. Just this one little temperamental *dreki* to master."

"I'll give you 'master.'"

He laughed, even as he captured her mouth in a kiss.

COMING 2018

CLASH OF STORMS

BOOK THREE: LEGENDS OF THE STORM

The old eddas speak of *dreki*—fabled creatures who haunt the depths of Iceland's volcanoes and steal away fair maidens.

The Blackfrost is a name both feared and reviled within the *dreki* clan that rules Iceland. When Malin joins forces with Sirius to help rescue the princess she loves, she has no idea of the journey ahead of her. This dark prince watches her every move, and protects her from those who might harm her—but is there something more to the look in Sirius's eyes?

A dark prince. An unsuitable mate. Can this villain become her hero?

Malin is a nobody in the *dreki* world. A servant far beneath him. And though Sirius's kiss burns through her like lightning, he's keeping far too many secrets for her to trust him….

But when Sirius sacrifices himself at her bequest, does Malin have the strength to save him from a fate worse than death? And can she ever give this wicked prince her heart?

Want to know more about Clash of Storms? Make sure you sign up to my newsletter at www.becmcmaster.com to be the first to know its release date, read exclusive excerpts, and see cover reveals.

Dear Readers,

Thank you so much for reading Storm of Desire! If you enjoyed it, please consider leaving a review online.

Iceland. And dragons (or dreki, because I wouldn't want to offend them). Two of my all-time greatest loves combined in one book: travel and fantasy. You can probably tell I simply adore writing in this world.

But its one thing to write the darned book, and another thing to create something worth reading. I couldn't have done it without a lot of help from these amazing people:

I owe huge thanks to my editor Olivia from Hot Tree Editing for her work in making sure everything is in its right place; to the wonderful readers in my Facebook Fan Page, Joylyn, Candance, Steph and Tami for help with the beta reader feedback; to my cover artists from Damonza.com who consistently hit it out of the park; and Marisa Shor and Allyson Gottlieb from Cover Me Darling for the print formatting. To Kylie Griffin and Jennie Kew, as always, who are the best support team any writer could dream of, and for digging into the nitty-gritty during the beta read; and the Central Victorian Writers group for keeping me sane and celebrating the small goals with all those chocolates! And special thanks to my family, and to my other half—my very own beta hero, Byron—who has always been unabashedly proud of this dream of mine, even when I didn't know if I could do it.

Last, not least, to all of my readers who support me on this journey, and have been crazy vocal about their love for the London Steampunk series, and anything else I write! I hope you enjoy this crazy little detour into a fantasy world!

Cheers,

Bec McMaster

ABOUT THE AUTHOR

BEC MCMASTER is a writer, a dreamer, and a travel addict. If she's not sitting in front of the computer, she's probably plotting her next overseas trip, and plans to see the whole world, whether it's by paper, plane, or imagination. She grew up on a steady diet of '80s fantasy movies like *Ladyhawke*, *Labyrinth*, and *The Princess Bride*, and loves creating epic, fantasy-based romances with heroes and heroines who must defeat all the odds to have their HEA. She lives in Australia with her very own hero, where she can be found creating the dark and dangerous worlds of the London Steampunk, Dark Arts, Legends of The Storm, or Burned Lands series, where even the darkest hero can find love.

For news on new releases, cover reveals, contests, and special promotions, join her mailing list at www.becmcmaster.com

Printed in Poland
by Amazon Fulfillment
Poland Sp. z o.o., Wrocław

58487920R00221